Rock Chick

ISBN: 0-6157-7041-X
ISBN-13: 9780615770413

Rock Chick

Kristen Ashley

Discover other titles by Kristen Ashley at:

www.kristenashley.net

Chapter 1

The Great Liam Chase

Until now, I've never been in trouble with the law.

It's cosmically impossible. I'm a cop's daughter.

Cop's Daughter Karma protects me, and seeing as I'm not a drug addict, drug dealer, thief, prostitute, gangster or murderer (all traits that would negate Cop's Daughter Karma), I'm protected.

This isn't to say I haven't done stupid things that are not exactly law abiding. In fact, I've done a lot of stupid things that are not exactly law abiding.

⌘

Let's see...

I've had a number of parking tickets, but they don't really count.

I've been stopped for speeding on occasion, though I never got a ticket.

I've been known to jaywalk when I'm in a hurry (which is a lot).

Further possibly-non-law-abiding exploits include the fact that I conned my way backstage at an Aerosmith concert. I went so far as to touch Joe Perry's chest with the very tips of my index and middle fingers, and after making contact I felt an electric spasm of sheer delight fly through my body (especially certain parts of my body) that has gone unequaled before or since. Unfortunately, I only got the touch in before the bodyguard hauled me out.

I'm not certain it's against the law to lie your way backstage and touch Joe Perry's chest, but considering the experience had to be far better than many illegal activities, it should be.

⌘

But, twenty minutes ago, my employee, Rosie, told me something I didn't want to hear.

Rosie could be difficult, but this was ridiculous.

And he'd involved another employee (and one of my most favorite people in the world), Duke.

Five minutes ago, Rosie and I locked up and stood at the front of my bookstore, Fortnum's, wondering what to do about that something.

Then two guys came up to us. We had a chat that did not go well (and if I'm honest, the reason it didn't go well is because of me) and then they shot at us.

Shot.

At.

Us.

With guns.

Guns filled with bullets.

We made a hasty getaway, which, luckily, didn't leave a trail of blood.

Now, we're in my car, hyperventilating, sitting in a dark corner of a dark alley in the bowels of Baker Historical District that hadn't yet been re-gentrified. I'm staring at my cell phone, wondering what in the fucking hell to do.

Let's rewind.

I'm India Savage, known by all as Indy. I'm Tom Savage's daughter, and practically every cop knows me, even the rookies. That's because when I was young, I spent a lot of time at the station waiting for Dad or hanging out with Dad's friends.

Oh, and Dad and I still go together to the Fraternal Order of Police (or F.O.P.) hog roasts.

There is also the fact that I look the way I look. I'm not bragging or anything, it's just that being a cop means you have to have an overabundance of testosterone, and, well, I'm a girl.

Most of Dad's colleagues noticed me from the age of about sixteen. Unfortunately, if any one of them touched me (even after I came of age), the others would have shot him.

Such is the life of a cop's daughter. You take the ups with the downs.

In my not-so-clean-and-tidy past, I was caught one night by Dad's friends, Jimmy Marker and Danny Rose. My best friend, Ally Nightingale, and I were underage drinking and were taken to the station.

My Dad had not been angry at this youthful stunt. Dad had one kid and a dead wife. He'd been hoping for a boy to come along, but my Mom died when I was five. Seeing as they had their hands full with me, they'd never got around to a second child, and Dad had never got over Mom enough to find another wife.

Dad always said Katherine Savage was the kind of woman you didn't get over.

He also said I looked a lot like her and the pictures prove it (except, of course, my blue eyes, which come from my Dad).

And everyone says I act *exactly* like her.

Anyway, Dad thought my drinking binge was kind of cute, and if I had been a boy, my getting picked up by his cronies would be a rite of passage. His best friend and longtime partner, Malcolm Nightingale, agreed.

Malcolm's wife, Kitty Sue, was my Mom's best friend and the woman who swore to my mother on her death bed that she would help Dad raise me right, so she did not find my short lived incarceration amusing.

Kitty Sue didn't find any of my youthful foibles amusing, not in any way, shape, or form. Kitty Sue worried over my immortal soul.

Kitty Sue had her hands full. Not only did she make a death bed promise to my Mom, she also had three kids of her own to look after. And two of those kids were Lee and Ally, and that right there is enough said.

Kitty Sue talked to preachers, teachers and high school counselors, little league softball, baseball and football coaches, neighborhood busybodies—anyone she could to set up her network of Nightingale/Savage Child Watch. Even with all this effort it didn't work so well.

Allyson Nightingale is my best friend and has been since birth. Ally is Kitty Sue and Malcolm's youngest child and she's far crazier than me, mainly because she isn't scared of anything.

Lee's another story altogether. Lee's a Bad Boy with capital Bs.

After getting caught on the side of the road puking our inebriated guts out by Jimmy and Danny, Ally and I smartened up. After that, when Ally and I were underage, out partying and were done over-imbibing, we called Lee and he came to get us.

No matter what, no matter where, Lee would show up in his vintage Mustang, hold open the passenger side door and grin as we stumbled out of someone's house and into his car. Lee knew the exact sounds a person would make before they were going to hurl and thus knew when to stop and haul a body out so they could do it on the side of the road and not in his car. Lee also had *lots* of experience with holding a girl's hair back when she threw up.

In our partying days, we tried calling Ally's other brother, Hank, a couple of times, but he would always give us a lecture. Hank's the oldest of the three Nightingale children and therefore felt the need to behave responsibly. He may have lectured, but he didn't snitch. Snitching was a shade too far.

Not surprisingly, Hank became a cop.

No one knows what Lee is.

Henry "Hank" Nightingale was captain of the football team, prom king. He was voted Best Athlete, Most Popular, one half of Best Couple and Best Smile. He's six foot one, has thighs that could crack walnuts and just the right assets to fill both the seat and crotch of his jeans, a killer smile, thick, dark brown hair with just enough wave and whisky-colored eyes. In high school, Hank was good-natured, chivalrous and had a steady girl. Not much has changed (except there was no longer a girl).

Liam "Lee" Nightingale could hotwire any car going. He had both a Mustang and a motorcycle, started smoking when he was thirteen, was rumored to be able to get a girl pregnant by just looking at her and was also voted Best Smile. He's six foot two and gives the impression that faded jeans had been divinely created just for him. Lee also has thick, dark brown hair with just enough wave and chocolate-colored eyes with a heavy rim of long lashes. Lee was good-natured as well, but in an entirely different way. Without any effort at all, (mostly by crooking his finger, casting a glance, or if a girl was playing hard to get, he'd pull out The Smile), Lee nailed everything that was female, had long hair, big boobs, a fine ass and was breathing.

Every female, that is, but me, no matter how hard I tried. And let's just say I tried real hard.

I, too, have big boobs, a helluvan ass, long, russet hair (with just enough wave) and was, as far as I could tell, not the walking dead.

I'd been throwing myself at Lee since I could remember.

I should have picked Hank. If I'd have picked Hank, I would now be married with children, probably very happy and definitely getting it regularly.

But I like them bad.

I'm a rock 'n' roll chick. That's just the way it is.

Ally and I decided when we were eight that I was going to marry Lee so I could be her "real" sister. She was going to be my maid of honor, we were going to live across the street from each other in houses with white picket fences and Lee and I were going to name our first daughter after her.

We even made a blood pact on it by sticking our thumbs with safety pins and mashing them together. We spent the next twelve years attempting to make that fantasy a reality in every way our somewhat devious and definitely outrageous minds could dream up.

It was my bad luck, considering Lee's moral code was a bit sketchy, that I fell into Liam Nightingale's Ethical Rule Book at Rule Number Two (with Rule Number One being "Thou shalt not nail your brother's girlfriend"). I was "Thou shalt not nail your little sister's best friend".

I also grew up like a member of the family, which made me practically his little sister by default. In my last effort to throw myself at him, when I was twenty and he was twenty-three, he'd told me exactly that. It was pretty fucking embarrassing, but then again, so were all of my other attempts and that never stopped me.

Still, for some reason, that last one really hurt. Lee wasn't cruel or anything he was just… final.

The Great Liam Chase ended right then and there, at least for me. Ally still has (very) high hopes. Not to mention Kitty Sue, who I think has always wanted me to fall for one of her sons, and it's been pretty clear that her druthers would put me with Lee. Probably because she thinks we deserve each other.

I resigned myself to seeing Lee at Christmas, Thanksgiving, Fourth of July, every birthday celebration, most family parties and barbeques and over at Hank's when we're watching a game and the like. Unfortunately, this means I see Lee a lot. Usually, there are always enough other people around to run interference.

If, on the odd occasion that he's at his parents' house for dinner (these days it's less odd—more like Kitty Sue is getting a bit desperate and becoming far more obvious at playing matchmaker) and I'm also invited, I make my excuses (mostly lies) and leave as fast as my boots will take me. This usually pisses off Ally and Kitty Sue, but *they* hadn't thrown themselves at the guy for over a decade and been rebuffed repeatedly, and then had to live the rest of their lives seeing that guy at dinner and on holidays. It's mortifying, let me tell you.

Not to mention, Lee went from Bad Boy to Badass in half a decade. By the end of that decade he was Badass Extraordinaire. You didn't mess with Lee. I may have been a bit of a wild child, but I knew enough about playing with fire and getting burned, and Lee Nightingale had gone from a bonfire to a towering fucking inferno in ten years.

Don't get me wrong, Liam Nightingale still has killer good looks, only slightly marred by a small, crescent moon scar under his left eye. He also still has a killer bod that looks great in jeans, great in sweats, great in suits, great in anything. He also still has a killer smile on the odd occasions he flashes it. And, finally, he also still likes women with lots of T&A and lots of hair (and I was still a woman just like that).

But he's also dangerous.

I don't know how to explain this. He just is. Trust me.

⚒

These days, I still go to rock concerts. I still listen to music way too loud. I still wear my red hair long and wild in a tangle of waves that fall in a deep V down my back. I still have some serious T&A. Let's just say my body is my gift and my curse. A body like mine isn't difficult to maintain—just feed it loads of crap to keep the curves, but keep in shape because you've got to lug it around everywhere.

These days, though, my parties have real, home cooked hors d'oeuvres and bowls of cashews, and nobody passes out in my bed or pukes in the backyard anymore.

These days I'm also the owner of a used bookstore located on Broadway. Not *the* Broadway in NYC. The other Broadway, in Denver, Colorado, US of A.

My grandmother left me the store when she died. It would seem a rather staid profession, owning a bookstore. You'd think I wore tortoiseshell glasses and had my hair back in a bun. This isn't true about my bookstore or me, by any stretch of the imagination.

You see, my grandmother was a hellion, she'd raised a hellion in my Mom, Katherine, and she and Dad carefully oversaw raising the third generation hellion that was me.

My bookstore is on the southeast corner of Broadway and Bayaud. Not the greatest neighborhood, not the worst. In the times of my grandmother, the 'hood had been in decline. Now it's on an upswing.

My inheritance came with half a duplex one block down on Bayaud in the Baker Historical District. I live in the east side of the duplex, a gay couple live in a west side, another gay couple live east of me and another behind me. This is why Baker is safe. It's populated mainly by gay couples, DINKS, hippies and Mexicans. When I, a single white female who looks like (and is) a rock 'n' roll groupie of the highest order, moved in, they all called each other and said "there goes the neighborhood".

My bookstore is named Fortnum's. There was no reason for this, except Gram had gone to Fortnum and Mason's in London the year before she opened it and she thought it sounded high brow.

There's nothing high brow about Fortnum's.

In the day (that was Gram's day), it was a hippie hang out and still is, in a way. Harley boys often came there, too, don't ask me why. Now it's also filled with preppies, yuppies and DINKS trying to be trendy, and boarders and goths because it is trendy.

It has a bunch of mismatched shelves stuffed full of all sorts of used books and tables piled high with vinyl records. It's a rabbits warren of organized disorganization, every once in a while punctuated by a fluffy, overstuffed chair. Most people come in, find a book, read in a chair and leave without buying the book, maybe coming back the next day to pick it up again and read some more.

With the shop, I also inherited Gram's two employees, which, shall we say diplomatically, are just as eccentric as she was.

Jane's my romance (our biggest seller) expert. She's six foot and weighs in at about one-twenty, painfully thin, painfully shy. She keeps her nose in a novel nearly every minute of the day, when she isn't buying them off people hawking their books for our shelves or selling them to people with mumbled recommendations. She's told me she'd written over forty novels herself but never had the gumption to try to get them published. She didn't even have the courage to allow me to read them, and I ask all the time.

There's also Duke. Duke's a Harley man, all leather and denim with a big ole gray beard and loads of long, steel gray hair with a bandana tied around his forehead. He talks rough, lives rough and is tough as nails, but can be soft as a marshmallow if he likes you (luckily, he likes me). He used to be an English Lit professor at Stanford before he dropped out and moved to the mountains. He's married to Dolores, who works part-time at The Little Bear up in Evergreen, where Duke and Dolores own a tiny cabin.

Gram loved Fortnum's. She looked at it kinda like her own personal community center. She was not an especially good business woman, but she was happy to make do and play hostess to her eclectic group of pals. Gramps brought in an okay salary, and when he died left her with a decent pension so she didn't have much to worry about.

Fortnum's smells musty and old, and just like Gram, I love every inch of it.

When I wasn't at the police station, with the Nightingales or out with Ally, I was at Fortnum's with Gram, Duke, and then came Jane. It was always one of my homes away from home, and those come with being a motherless child, believe you me.

But the way I'd inherited it, it sure as hell wasn't going to keep me in my cowboy boots, Levi's, and huge, silver belt buckles attached to tooled-leather belts, my signature outerwear. My signature underwear was strictly sexy-girlie lace and silk. Gram said that looking like a cowboy-inspired groupie on the outside was one thing, but every girl had to have a secret, and sexy underwear was the best secret a girl could have.

Now the front of the store is where I do my business. There are a bunch of comfortable couches and arm chairs and a few tables. I invested in an espresso machine and coaxed my favorite barista, Ambrose "Rosie" Coltrane, from the chain coffee store down the road.

Rosie's a coffee god. Rosie could make a skinny vanilla latte that could give you an orgasm if you just sniffed it. Rosie's a bit of a pain in the ass, a kind of semi-coffee recluse (he comes in, he makes coffee, he goes home), but his talent is undeniable.

My addition of coffee was a hit. When the espresso started flowing, the books also started going, and now I have new furniture in my living room and a fast growing collection of kickass belts and cowboy boots.

I see all this flashing before my eyes

I learned quickly that lots of stuff flashes before your eyes when you get shot at.

⌲

As I stared at my cell, trying not to have a heart attack, I tried to figure out who to call.

I could, and probably should, call Dad, Malcolm or Hank.

Considering those choices and this situation, in the cop stakes Hank would be my best bet. He'd go ballistic when he heard I'd been shot at and would probably arrest Rosie on the spot, but he was least likely to kill Rosie for putting me in danger.

Hank had control. That was why Hank was such a good athlete, why he was a good student and why he's a good cop.

Dad was my father, and Malcolm considered himself like a father, so they'd just lose it and make a scene, which would freak Rosie out.

Rosie was a coffee artiste.

As an artiste, Rosie had a delicate disposition. He freaks out easily. You could only give him two coffee orders at a time or he'd have a mini-mental-breakdown. That chain coffee shop hadn't been right for him. Fortnum's was his nirvana. He could create his drinks, and even when it got busy and the pressure got heavy someone else—Jane, Duke or me—took the burden and just let Rosie perform.

But right now, Rosie said no cops.

And I understand why.

So even though I *really, really* wanted to call Hank, I didn't.

⌲

I could call Lee. Lee isn't a cop. I had his numbers in my cell. Ally put them there.

Lee would be a good bet. Lee had gone into the Army after high school. Lee had gone on to be Special Operations Force. Lee had done some serious shit while in the armed services. Shit that took the good ole boy look right out of his dark brown eyes and put in something else, something colder, more serious and far scarier, Lee had come out and gotten himself a private investigator's license and opened an office in LoDo (or Lower Downtown Denver). Lee was supposed to be a PI, but no one really knows what Lee does. I'm not even certain anyone has even been to Lee's offices.

I could call Lee and tell him someone shot at me. That would take care of things pretty quickly. I mean, I hadn't really had much of a relationship with Lee for ten years, but it would be a kind of family responsibility, considering he thought of me as his little sister (huh).

Lee might track them down (whoever they were) and shoot them, though. Torture them first and shoot them. Lee had skills I could not comprehend. At least that's what I heard Malcolm and Dad muttering about, more than once.

It wasn't like when I was sixteen and Brian Archer was telling everyone he'd gotten to third base with me (when he'd *barely* slid into second) and Lee had found Brian and broken his nose.

This would be serious.

Maybe Lee wasn't a good idea.

⋈

This left me with Ally.

Allyson Nightingale is always up for an adventure.

Allyson Nightingale can keep her mouth shut.

And Ally is not a cop.

Chapter 2
I Should Turn You over My Knee

Twenty minutes later, I found myself standing in the living room of Lee's condo.

I'd been there before, only a few times, but my visits had been brief. Mainly dropping something off or picking something up, and always I was with Kitty Sue or Ally.

And always, Lee was there.

Now, Lee was not.

"This is *not* a good idea," I said to Ally.

Ally and I were the same height, both at five foot nine. Ally weighed twenty pounds less than me, was a jeans size smaller because she had much less ass and one cup-size smaller because she had much less boobage. She had whisky-brown eyes like Hank, and thick, dark brown hair like all the Nightingales, hair that she kept rock 'n' roll crazy long, just like me.

Right now she was wearing a denim miniskirt with a ragged, cutoff hem, a bright yellow tank top with "Sugar" written across the chest in glitter, and flip-flops.

We're both thirty years old, with Ally two weeks younger than me. We'd be eighty and wearing denim miniskirts and I'm-with-the-band t-shirts. I foresaw this for our future, and even though I thought it was cool, it also kinda scared me.

Ally was talking. "Lee's out of town. He's not due back for ages. Definitely not tonight. And anyway, no one's crazy enough to break into Lee's condo."

I considered her words as I looked at Rosie.

Rosie was having a "talented artist in a crisis" moment. His eyes were wild and he looked about to bolt.

Rosie wasn't my favorite person at that particular time. Rosie nearly got me shot, but it wasn't entirely his fault. *He* didn't shoot at me and *he* didn't mouth off to the bad guys.

I'd always had trouble with my mouth.

Anyway, he was my friend and I had to keep him safe. That's what friends do. They don't drink so they can drive you home when you're drunk. They like your boyfriends when you're with them and then trash them after you've broken up. And they find you a safe house when people are shooting at you.

And Ally was right, only someone with a death wish would break into Lee's condo. Even I was having heart palpitations at daring to enter Lee's lair, worried he'd go all commando if he found us there.

Not only that, it was a secure building and Lee lived on the fourteenth floor (with an unobstructed view of the Front Range, by the way).

Ally looked between Rosie and me. "What's this about?"

"Don't tell her!" Rosie shouted.

"I'm not gonna tell her!" I shouted back, beginning to lose patience with Rosie. I forgave myself for losing patience. I figured that happened when you got shot at. I'd never been shot at, but I was always a quick learner.

Ally lifted her brows at me and I gave her my "later" look.

"I need caffeine," Rosie whined and walked to Lee's couch. It was soft, rich leather and faced an enormous LCD TV. Rosie threw himself on it and rubbed his temples with his fingers, trying to find his Zen nirvana without a stainless steel pitcher filled with frothing milk in his hand

"You don't need caffeine, you need Valium," I said.

"I've got Valium," Ally put in.

Ally could generally find all different kinds of pharmaceuticals, either in her personal medicine cabinet or through her network of contacts.

"I don't want Valium. I want to get the bag back from Duke as soon as possible and go to San Salvador," Rosie said, grabbing the remote and being a bit dramatic.

"He's an artist with an artistic temperament," I explained as I walked Ally to the door.

"He makes coffee," Ally replied.

I ignored that. Ally didn't understand the beauty of coffee. She preferred tequila.

"You sure Lee isn't gonna come back?"

I didn't want to be caught in Lee's condo when Lee didn't know I was here. I hadn't been somewhat successfully avoiding him for ten years only to be found in his condo in the middle of the night, harboring a possible felon who had bad people after him. There was a good possibility Lee would frown on that.

"He's in DC," Ally replied. "I think you should take his bed." Her eyes got big and happy when she said this, and I sighed and rested my shoulder against the wall.

"Maybe you should call him," I suggested.

"He doesn't like to be disturbed when he's out-of-town on business. Only in emergencies."

"This might be considered an emergency," I explained unnecessarily, as I'd called her only twenty minutes ago, hyperventilating, and telling her some-one had shot at me and Rosie and we needed a safe house. Such things didn't happen every day. In fact, they *never* happened, at least not to me.

Ally looked through the open plan kitchen to Rosie, who'd turned on the TV and was watching the Food Network.

"What bag is he talking about?" Ally whispered.

"I'll explain it later. Just call Lee and warn him that we're here, just in case."

Ally swung her eyes back to me. "Was a time when you'd live for that kind of 'just in case'."

"I've told you, that time's long gone."

Ally studied me. She'd heard this for ten years and still didn't believe it, the silly, stubborn bimbo.

"Right. I'll call him. Still, I think if he was gonna come home, he'd rather come home to find you in his bed than Rosie."

"I'll sleep in the guest room."

"Girl," Ally smiled, "Lee doesn't have a guest room. That second bed-room is locked up tight and no one gets into that room. Hank and I call it the Command Center, but no one knows what's in there."

I turned to look at the three closed doors that opened off the hall and when I turned back Ally had the front door open.

"Later." Then she was gone.

I grabbed the door and watched her sashay down the hall.

"Call him!" I shouted.

She gave me the peace sign and got on the elevator.

"She's not gonna call him," I said to the empty hallway.

Ally was right.

I did a wee bit of snooping (as you do). Two doors in Lee's hall opened, one to the bathroom and one to Lee's bedroom. The other one was locked up tight. I even walked along the wraparound balcony to check if I could see in, but the French doors to the second bedroom had curtains and those curtains were firmly closed.

After what seemed like a lifetime of Food Network, I found Rosie a pillow and blanket and crawled, bleary-eyed and still a little scared (not only at the night's events but at our accommodation), into Lee's big bed.

I considered sleeping on the floor, but I was too tired, and anyway, Lee was busy these days and never in Denver unless it was someone's birthday, a holiday or a weekend the Broncos were playing at home. I'd heard Kitty Sue lamenting that fact so often, if I had a dime for every time she said it, I'd be rich.

I'd taken off my jeans, boots, socks, and bra and found a wife beater t-shirt of Lee's, luckily in the first drawer I opened. I didn't want to be rifling through Lee's drawers. He might not like it.

I had to borrow Lee's tee because I was wearing my Guns 'n' Roses shirt that had rhinestones stitched in and they would snag at the sheets. Not to mention it was one of my favorites and I didn't want it to get misshapen while I slept.

I was not a light sleeper. I slept deep and I moved around a lot, as in *a lot*. I moved around so much that most of my boyfriends eventually opted for the couch, usually right before they opted for the door. I tried to sleep in attire that would not get me into trouble during my nocturnal twisting and turning, which usually meant I slept in underpants and nothing else. However, the thought of sleeping in Lee's bed nearly naked was simply not to be entertained.

I tried not to think of crawling into Lee's bed at all. It was just a bed. So it was Liam Nightingale's bed. So it kinda smelled like him, like leather and tobacco and spice. So what?

The smell and the bed made me feel a little bit like I felt when I touched Joe Perry's chest and I had this niggling inclination to do a little naughty activity, but thankfully I fell asleep before I could do anything about it.

The next thing I knew, something was wrapped around my ankle and dragging me down the length of the bed, just like the heroine in a horror movie.

When my knees slammed into the footboard, I whipped around to my back and gave a small yelp. I saw a big shadow looming over me in the dark and I opened my mouth to scream, knowing that whoever had shot at us had found us and this was the end.

My life was over, finished, and I'd never seen Pearl Jam play live.

Before I could scream, the hand left my ankle, two hands grabbed at my hips and yanked me out of bed in a way that my back arched painfully. My head snapped back and I swallowed my scream on a surprised gulp.

I was set down on my feet. Both of my wrists were seized and pulled behind my back, making me give a whimper of pain, and I was slammed against a hard body.

"Talk," a deep voice demanded, and I could smell tobacco, leather and spice.

It was Lee.

Shit, shit, shit.

Either I had really bad luck or Ally set me up.

Maybe Ally *and* Rosie set me up. Ally was really into the sister-in-law shit and maybe she was getting impatient enough to hire someone to shoot at me.

"Two seconds," Lee warned.

"Lee, it's me. Indy."

The hands on my wrists loosened but didn't let go.

"What the fuck?"

I took in a deep breath, which pressed my breasts further into his chest.

This was the closest I'd ever been to him. We were full-frontal. Even in the days when I was throwing myself at him I hadn't made it this close.

I explained (hastily), "I'm in a bit of a bind and needed someplace safe to stay for a night. Ally let me in."

Lee took a moment to let this sink in.

"Who's the guy on the couch?"

"Rosie, my barista."

"Your what?"

"He makes the coffee at my bookstore."

"Shit."

He hadn't let me go until that point, but he released me, turned on his heel and walked out of the room.

Something about the way he did it made me follow him.

When I made it to the living room, Lee snapped on a light and Rosie was lying face down in the middle of the floor. His hands and feet were taped together behind his back with duct tape and there was tape on his mouth.

"Lee! Jesus! What'd you do to him?" I asked, running forward and going down on my knees by Rosie. Rosie eyes were rabid and shifting everywhere as he struggled against the tape.

I couldn't believe it. I hadn't heard a thing.

Man, Lee was *good*.

Lee already had his pocketknife out and was cutting through the tape.

"I came home and he was on my couch, you were in my bed. What'd you think I'd do?" Lee answered as he ripped the tape off Rosie's mouth.

"Yeow!" Rosie cried.

I sat back, resting my behind on my calves and stared at Lee.

This was exactly what I thought he'd do.

"Ally didn't call you," I surmised.

"No, Ally didn't call me," Lee stated.

"I'm gonna kill her," I snapped.

"Jesus, fuck, shit," Rosie said.

Lee had gone down to a crouch when he'd released Rosie, and now he stood, arms crossed on his chest.

"You okay?" I asked Rosie, and Rosie gave me an "are you nuts, that lunatic just tied me up with duct tape" look.

You would think you couldn't read all that in a look, but trust me, you could.

"What's goin' on?" Lee asked, surveying us.

It was then I realized I was in a pair of peach, lace, hipster briefs that showed a good deal of cheek, and Lee's wife beater. Not exactly the attire I wanted to be wearing during this conversation.

Not exactly the attire I wanted to be wearing *ever* in the presence of Lee.

"I'll go get dressed," I said, standing.

Lee shook his head.

"You'll talk."

"I need to put on some clothes!"

"What you need to do is tell me what the fuck's goin' on," Lee countered, and let's just say his tone brooked no argument and his face registered pretty severe unhappiness.

Regardless, I glared at him, just for good measure.

"Jesus, shit, fuck," Rosie said, tearing the remnants of tape from his wrists.

I took another deep breath and let go of the glare. It was time to expedite this situation so I could get to my Levi's. Generally, I felt naked without my jeans, but at that moment I practically *was* naked without my jeans.

"Okay, we have a situation here. Rosie and I need somewhere to crash for the night and we'll be gone tomorrow."

"Why?" Lee asked.

"Don't tell him!" Rosie cried, looking panicked.

"You talk or you walk," Lee said.

I looked at Lee then I looked at Rosie.

I'd known Rosie for five years. He'd come to parties at my house. We'd gone to concerts together. He was a cool guy. A bit flighty and secretive, and not as mellow as one would expect, considering he was a screaming stoner.

I had no idea he had a business on the side. I knew he made great coffee, I knew he thought Jim Morrison was an earthbound god and I knew he was a stoner.

I looked back at Lee.

"You have to promise to keep quiet."

"No!" Rosie shouted, getting to his feet.

"I don't have to promise anything," Lee replied.

I did another glance at both of them.

Lee was being difficult. He was entitled. We were in his domain without his permission.

Rosie was also being difficult, but Rosie was always difficult.

All I could think was I really needed my jeans.

"You can trust him," I told Rosie.

Rosie was staring at Lee. Rosie was definitely far beyond mellow at this point. Rosie had been shot at tonight and then trussed up like a Christmas goose, and I'd slept through it

However, Rosie had a lot to worry about. Rosie needed to start making good decisions about who to trust.

Rosie made a decision, a decision I hoped would take me closer to my Levi's.

"He has to promise not to say anything to anyone. This'll all be over tomorrow," Rosie announced.

Lee hadn't uncrossed his arms. Lee still wasn't happy. This wasn't hard to read. Everything about him screamed it.

"Can I talk to you a minute?" I asked and then did a wave with my arm and Lee followed me to the entry hall.

First things first. Since the situation was still not stable, and taking the time to dress (thus leaving Lee and Rosie alone) did not seem a smart option, I tried a different tactic in the hopes of covering my ass cheeks.

"Do you have a robe I could borrow?" I asked.

"No," Lee answered.

"Does that mean you don't have a robe I could borrow or I can't borrow your robe?"

Lee stared at me some more.

Then he said, "Indy, start talking."

His patience, it seemed, was running out. I'd have to leave my ass cheeks bared. I told myself this was Lee. He'd seen me in bikinis in his backyard (and mine, and on a family holiday to Mexico, and the one to San Diego). I was far more dressed than a bikini.

I soldiered on. "Okay, the thing is, Rosie has a little side business. Someone paid him in something and that something is kinda valuable, as in kinda *really* valuable. It's also kinda stolen from someone else, and that someone else wants it back. Rosie gave it to Duke for safekeeping and Rosie doesn't have it. Duke's away for a few days, back tomorrow morning. So until he can get it from Duke, we have to lay low."

"Why is this a 'we' situation?" Lee asked.

"Well, I was kinda with Rosie when they came after it," I answered.

"And?" he prompted.

"And like I said, he didn't have it."

"And?"

"And I had a few words with them, in, er... Rosie's defense," I told him.

Loaded and pissed-off hesitation, complete with narrowing of eyes, then, "And?"

"And that's when they shot at us and we took off and called Ally."

No verbal comment, but a muscle jerked in Lee's cheek.

I didn't take this as a good sign.

Probably, he wasn't so happy I involved his sister in this mess.

Probably, he was equally unhappy that I'd involved him in this mess.

"What is it?" Lee asked.

"I can't say."

"If you don't say, I'll let him loose."

I shook my head. "He's pretty adamant that no one knows."

"I'll escort him out of the building myself."

I looked back in the living room. Rosie was peering around the corner, eavesdropping.

I let out another heavy sigh. "Maybe we should go, get a hotel room."

Rosie looked pleased at this announcement.

We only had a few hours to wait. Denver was a big city. It'd take longer than a few hours to find us.

"I didn't say I'd let *you* loose. I said I'd let *him* loose."

This announcement gave me a start and I turned to Lee.

"What?"

No answer.

"What do you mean?" I asked.

Still no answer.

"What are you gonna do with me?" I kept trying.

"You tell me what this is about, nothing."

"And if I don't tell you?"

"I haven't decided."

"Lee!"

Lee's patience ran out. He grabbed my arm, pointed at Rosie and said, "You move, you'll regret it," in a way that I figured Rosie would do a statue impersonation until he saw Lee again.

Then Lee yanked me into the bedroom, hit the light switch and closed the door behind us.

"Ow! You're hurting me!" I pulled my arm free.

"I should turn you over my knee," he snapped.

My mouth dropped open for a moment, then my eyes narrowed. "What did you just say?"

"He has a bag of diamonds and I cannot believe you're caught up in this disaster."

I gasped. "How did you know?"

He didn't answer.

"How did you know?" I said it a lot louder this time.

"You get into bed. I'll go talk to your friend. Tomorrow, I'll take care of the diamonds."

"You can't tell me what to do." Now my voice was *a lot* louder.

I mean, who did he think he was?

He took a step forward and dipped his face to mine so we were nose-to-nose. "You've ignored me for years and now you lay this shit on my doorstep. This is *not* a good situation, Indy. This is a total fuck up. You'd do well to do exactly what I tell you, keep your mouth shut and pray that the man who wants those diamonds back is patient enough to wait through the night."

"I haven't been ignoring you for years!" Now I was shouting (and lying).

Lee decided nose-to-nose wasn't good enough and took the last step forward so I could feel his body heat.

Which, by the way, was immense.

"Bullshit," he whispered.

Okay, so I'd been trying to ignore him for years, but I didn't actually succeed. I mean, didn't he remember all those Christmases and Thanksgivings?

"I bought you Christmas presents!"

"That doesn't count."

I made a choked sound. "So you're saying you didn't like the Billie Holiday boxed set?"

"I'm sayin' it doesn't count."

"I thought you liked blues!"

He edged in closer, predatory and angry. "Indy, this isn't something you can cute your way out of."

Okay, so, maybe in the past I'd used my girlie status to cute my way out of things. Numerous things. Most especially using it with Lee, Hank and Malcolm. Dad always saw through it.

"Fine!" I stalked to the bed, giving in mainly to get away from him. He was too overpowering at close range. Then I whipped around when I reached the foot of the bed. "What are you gonna do?"

"I'm gonna calm down your friend, make a call that should set some minds at ease, and tomorrow, I'll take him to get the diamonds and make the delivery."

"Well then," I said snottily, the wind out of my sails, "thank you."

Lee started to turn. He stopped, dropped his head back and looked at the ceiling and then turned around and came back to me. Again, he was so close I could feel his heat.

"Normally I charge five hundred dollars an hour for this."

I sucked in breath.

"For what?" I asked.

"This go-between shit," Lee answered.

My eyes rounded in shock.

Wow.

No wonder he could afford this condo with a view and an office in LoDo. Not to mention his car. He had a great car. And he still had a bike.

"You do? Why?"

He came closer. So close he was all I could see.

"Because I make the call tonight, that puts me in the middle of this mess, and, if tomorrow I don't have the diamonds, then it'll be *me* they shoot at. I don't like getting shot at."

I shook my head, bit my lip and agreed wholeheartedly, "Me either, it's not very fun."

He didn't move and I realized he expected a different response.

"I don't think Rosie has that kind of money," I noted. "You wouldn't consider doing this on, say, a family discount?"

He shook his head. "We're not family."

"I meant you and me," I explained.

"We're not family either."

"Yes we are. Ten years ago you told me I was like your little sister," I reminded him.

He waited a beat.

Something dawned on him. I could see the flicker in his eyes as it registered. I didn't understand it, but he did, and whatever it was made his face soften a little from the seriously pissed-off angry look he'd been wearing all night. In fact, he looked almost... *pleased*.

"That was then, this is now." Even his voice was quieter and less hacked off.

Kristen Ashley

"Well, how many hours will this take? It could be thousands of dollars. Rosie doesn't have that kind of money, even with his side business."

"It's not Rosie who's gonna pay."

My head did an involuntary little jerk when I understood what he meant.

"*I* don't have that kind of money."

"You aren't gonna pay me in cash."

My stomach clenched and my heart stopped for a couple of beats.

"How am I gonna pay you?" I asked.

"We'll talk about it tomorrow," he didn't exactly answer.

"We'll talk about it now!" I snapped.

"Get in bed, go to sleep," he ordered.

"Quit bossing me around!"

He came closer and I let out a little peep. I couldn't help it. He was pressed up against me, I had nowhere to go and the backs of my knees were up against the footboard. And I've already told you Lee's a seriously scary, badass individual.

"You get in that bed yourself or I tie you to it," he threatened.

His face had gone back to the seriously pissed-off angry look, and I decided from the hard glittering in his eyes that he was not making an idle threat.

"Okay," I whispered.

Shit, I was *such* a wuss.

Chapter 3
I'll Choose Door Number Two

I tried to stay awake and listen to what was happening between Lee and Rosie, but it was hard because I was tired. Getting shot at takes a lot out of you. Anyway, whatever was happening took a really long time and I'm a girl who likes her sleep.

When I did wake up, it was still dark and my back was pressed up to something hard and warm. Something heavy and warm was wrapped around my waist.

Lee.

Liam Nightingale was in bed with me.

Holy fucking shit.

You see, there were women in Denver who would pay a lot of money to be in this situation. Hell, there were likely women across the country who would do it.

Not me.

No way.

That boat had sailed.

There was a time when we were kids that Lee, Ally, Hank and I slept together all the time. Our parents would have dinner parties and we'd be tucked into Kitty Sue and Malcolm's big bed, all four in a row, according to age. This put me between Lee and Ally. Of course, once we got older, we were separated.

Then there were the times when we were in the tent when Dad and Malcolm would take us camping in the mountains. Always, I was stuck between Lee and Ally in my sleeping bag. As I tumbled headlong into my teens, and thus more and more desperate for Lee to declare his undying love for me, this was a form of torture. I couldn't exactly throw myself at him when Hank, Dad and Malcolm were around (Ally would have slept through it).

And then there was that brief time when Ally and I were nineteen and had gone off rock 'n' roll and discovered cowboys. Lee took us to Cheyenne for the rodeo and we got a motel room that just had a big king-sized bed. Out of necessity, we all slept in it together and I slept in the middle. Or at least I slept in the middle until Lee moved to the floor, likely to give me room to move. I never woke Ally up with my restless sleeping. Ally could sleep through an earthquake.

So it wasn't as if I hadn't already slept with Lee.

But not alone. Not just the two of us. Not when we were full-fledged, consenting adults. Not ever in *his* bed.

I moved forward, thinking the floor sounded quite comfy.

The heavy warm thing around my waist tightened.

"Don't move," Lee mumbled, his voice kinda husky.

My stomach fluttered, and as Lee's hand was splayed and pressed against it I was pretty certain he could feel it.

Shit.

"What're you doing?" I asked.

"I *was* sleeping." His voice was still husky.

"I mean in this bed," I clarified, what I thought was unnecessarily.

"It's my bed."

True enough.

Time for a different tact.

"I'm gonna sleep on the floor," I said.

"No you're not."

I hesitated for a moment, confused, and then tried Plan C.

"Then I'm gonna sleep on the other side of the bed."

"No you're not."

What in *the* hell?

I didn't get it.

"Why?"

"Because you were sleepin' over there and you hit me in the chest twice and kicked me in the shin three times."

Oopsie.

I'd heard that before.

"I'm kind of an active sleeper," I informed him.

"No kidding."

I thought about my options.

There was the floor, which apparently was not an option for me.

There was the Command Center, which I probably couldn't breach and likely didn't have a couch or bed, considering in my imagination it was filled with supercomputers that had a direct link to the Pentagon.

My cobwebby mind chugged along for minute, registering somewhere deep down how warm and cozy I currently was.

Rosie was a little guy, at least three inches shorter than me and wiry. Rosie was also kind of asexual and never had a girlfriend. His life was coffee, pot and rock 'n' roll.

Lee, on the other hand, was not asexual. He might think of me as his little sister and could calmly sleep next to me without his nipples getting hard (or anything else getting hard for that matter), but I was pretty certain I could not do the same.

Lee had one of those big, deep-seated couches, the better to sit on and watch *Monday Night Football*.

Maybe both Rosie and I would fit on the couch.

"I'll go sleep with Rosie."

The reply was instantaneous.

"The hell you will."

Hmm, all sleepy-husky gone from his voice. Lee was now all business and using that "brook no argument" tone.

I was stuck.

See, I was too afraid to go against Badass Lee Nightingale and I was too tired to try to get comfortable with Rosie.

Actually, bottom line, I was just too comfortable even to contemplate moving.

So I went back to sleep.

It wasn't as hard as I thought it would be.

❧

I woke up again hours later in an entirely different position. Lee was on his back and I was sprawled half on him, half off him.

Yikes.

I blinked at the clock on the bedside table. It was seven after six.

I might be a party girl, but I'd never been able to sleep late. Even when I fell into bed at four a.m., I woke up before seven.

This caused me, over the years, to perfect the art of the mid-day Disco Nap.

Today was going to be a Disco Nap Day, I could feel it.

There was no way I was getting back to sleep and no way I was gonna remain sprawled all over Lee.

I moved to get up and the arm he had wrapped around my lower back tightened and his fingers dug into my hip.

"Jesus, what is it with you?" he grumbled.

"It's morning."

He opened an eye and glanced at the clock.

Then he closed it.

"Barely," he muttered.

"I'm gonna make coffee," I announced.

This was apparently an acceptable reason to move as his arm fell away.

"Do you have an extra toothbrush?" I asked.

"Probably."

That was a stupid question. Lee may not still be the dawg he was in high school, but that didn't mean he didn't nail his fair share of anatomically impossible babes. He probably had a box full of extra toothbrushes.

"Do you have two?" I went on.

The eye opened again and focused on me.

Yikes part deux.

I jumped out of bed, grabbed my clothes and ran to the bathroom. I located one extra toothbrush still in its packaging and went to town on my teeth.

I took care of my teeth. I made a promise to myself that I'd die with my original set and that's what I intended to do.

I opened the door to the bedroom. "Do you have floss?" I called.

"For Christ's sake."

Obviously, Lee didn't care that much about his teeth.

That's okay. Lee seemed to be doing a *very* good job at taking care of other parts of his body.

I pulled on my jeans and struggled into my bra under the wife beater because I'd decided to steal the wife beater if I could get away with it, to keep as a little memento. Then I padded into the kitchen trying to be quiet for Rosie.

Rosie had a big day today and he needed his beauty rest.

The living room, dining room and kitchen were open plan in an L shape. The condo was on a corner and the entirety of it had a balcony wrapped around it. There were French doors from the dining room, which was across from the kitchen. There were also French doors from the living room, which was an extension of the dining room, and French doors in the bedrooms. Big money for this kind of location, the huge, airy rooms and the view afforded.

The kitchen was state-of-the-art and mostly hidden from the living room behind the wall that made up the bathroom and extra bedroom.

Still, I had to be quiet.

Normally, I'd have the coffee ready to roll the night before so I could just flip a switch after I'd stumbled out of bed and down the stairs.

Normally, my coffeemaker had a cup under the spout, rather than a pot, so I could just stand there and wait until it was done filling the cup, and then switch it over to the pot so I didn't have to wait until the pot was full.

Normally, I didn't function properly until cup number two.

Caffeine was my drug of choice.

It took me a while to find all the coffee paraphernalia. I lucked out because obviously Lee liked his coffee and he had a high quality bag of java.

I made it strong and did the cup thing. It was pretty clear from his Mr. Grouch impersonation that Lee wasn't getting up anytime soon, and there was not a sound from the couch so I could be greedy and selfish with the coffee.

I was concentrating on the stream of life-affirming joe filling the cup, so I was a little surprised when hands settled on the counter on either side of me and I felt the warmth of a body against my back.

They weren't Rosie's hands.

I looked over my shoulder.

Lee had fenced me in.

His dark hair was wild in a very sexy way, and his eyes were soft, as were his features. His chest was bare. I knew this because I could see his shoulders.

I didn't dare look down.

After ten years of practice, I was able (barely) to put the wild, sexy hair out of my mind and to ignore (barely) the fact he was bare-chested. However, it was kind of hard to ignore his proximity.

"What are you doing?" I asked.

He glanced over my shoulder. "You makin' coffee for everyone, or just you?"

There were certain times when honesty was the best policy. In my life those times didn't come very often, but if there was the possibility that you might not get the first cup of coffee, and brutal honesty would get it for you, you had to be brutally honest.

"Just me, for now."

I turned back to the coffee, deciding I didn't want an answer to my question about what he was doing. Something was going on and I was three quarts low on caffeine, not to mention sleep. I could hardly think past the next second, much less figure out what game Lee was playing. Likely he was still pissed at me for bringing trouble to his doorstep and decided to make my life miserable as repayment. I could understand that. I'd probably do the same.

I went back to ignoring him as the coffee cup was full. I expertly switched out the cup for the pot, intent on my first sip, all the while wondering why Lee still hadn't moved.

Then he did. A hand disappeared and a second later I felt my hair being swept off my left shoulder, around my neck and over my right.

I jumped at this intimate gesture and so did other parts of my anatomy. I didn't even try to ignore it. Any effort would have been futile.

Lee's chin went to where my hair used to be just as his hand slid across my abdomen and pulled me to him.

My entire body went still.

"We need to talk," he said into my ear.

I stood there, frozen, coffee cup aloft, nowhere near awake enough to process his extraordinary actions, and also in kind of *total* shock.

I said the only thing I could think to say.

"I need milk."

Without moving his body or head his hand left my middle. I heard the fridge open and the glug of milk against plastic and then the fridge closed again. Lee set the milk in front of me and his hand went back to the counter, keeping me where I was.

Real slick.

My stomach fluttered.

"Thank you," I said politely, blinking a lot and wondering if I was still asleep and dreaming.

I poured some milk in my joe, concentrating on not letting my body tremble. I was trying to be cool, but I was confused. This kind of behavior from Lee had never happened before.

As in ever.

I took a sip of coffee and tried to get my mind in gear.

"Do you want to explain to me why you have me pressed up against the counter?" I asked, using what I hoped was a questioning yet diplomatic tone rather than a freaked out 'ohmigod, hell has just frozen over' tone.

This was hard for me. I needed to be alert and aware in any situation involving Lee in order not to snap and declare my undying love for him, but I'd only had one sip of coffee.

And somehow, this was definitely a situation involving Lee. In fact, it was more like a *dangerous* situation involving Lee.

I took another sip, going for the gusto, and burned my tongue.

"Yeow!"

While I was recovering, Lee turned me around and moved further into me.

He did this well, considering there wasn't a lot of space to move and even less space to move into. Not to mention I had the coffee cup between us. He settled his hands on the counter on either side of me again.

"Why have you been avoiding me?" he asked.

Yikes.

Direct shot.

He didn't even lead into it.

Although his eyes and features were still gentle, it wasn't from just waking up. I could tell Lee was as alert and aware as you could get. The gentleness was from something else.

Shit, shit, *shit*.

What in holy hell was going on?

I decided to play stupid.

"What?" I asked.

"You heard me," he answered.

Then there are those times when honesty was *not* the best policy.

"I haven't been avoiding you." I took another sip, thinking I should have put another scoop or two of coffee in the filter.

"You're lying. The last time we were both at dinner, you got up in the middle of Mom's fajita presentation and said you forgot to feed your cat."

Uh-oh.

"So?"

"You don't have a cat."

"I was cat sitting," I lied.

He smiled.

He smiled The Smile.

Fuck, fuck, *fuck*.

Man, Lee could smile.

Then he said, "All right, I'm all out of patience with this one. You have two choices. Either you talk to me about what's been botherin' you for the last decade, or I tell you how you're gonna pay me back for this Rosie debacle."

"Is there a choice number three?" I asked.

He shook his head.

I slid my eyes to the right, chewed the inside of my bottom lip and thought about my choices. I did my best to forget about the glimpse of hard, muscled chest and six-pack I'd seen in the weak moment I allowed myself to look down.

And he was wearing faded jeans with the top button not done up.

Yikes.

Okay.

Focus.

Choices.

Firstly, I was never, never, never in a million years going to tell Lee Nightingale that I'd been in love with him since I was five and he sat next to me during my Mom's memorial service and held my hand. I was never going to tell him it was a Bon Jovi-style shot-through-the-heart when he told me he wasn't interested in me because I was his little sister's best friend. And I was never, never, never, *ever* going to tell him that something had changed in him and he scared the pants off me.

Secondly, no matter what he said, he was Lee and he was right all those years ago. In a way, we were family. We did all our holidays together as family and went to Broncos games with our Dads when we were kids. We had barbeques at each other's houses nearly every Saturday during the summer, even now. Hell, it was mid-June and I'd just had the barbeque at my house two weeks ago, and Lee had been there. Even though he'd changed, he would always be Lee. He probably wanted cheap maid service or something. Someone to do his laundry. Take his car to have the oil changed.

I could do that.

All this business with sleeping together and swiping at my hair and talking in my ear was just him trying to intimidate me. He probably wouldn't let Ally sleep with Rosie or on the floor either.

"I'll choose door number two," I decided.

The smile widened and something happened to his eyes that made my nether regions quiver.

Uh-oh.

Clearly, I made the wrong choice.

"I was hopin' you'd say that."

I scrambled. "Maybe I'll rethink my choice."

"Too late."

I scrunched my nose and narrowed my eyes at him. "Why can't you just be a nice guy?"

"I've never been a nice guy."

This was true, mostly.

"Yes you have," I returned. "You used to come pick Ally and me up from parties so we wouldn't get in trouble."

"I hate to burst your bubble, but that was for entertainment value. You and Ally were hilarious drunks. Once, you sang 'My Favorite Things' all the way home and got all the words wrong."

I made a frustrated noise then stated, "There was that time when I was grounded and I was climbing out of my window so I could go to Darren Pilcher's party and I got stuck between the tree and the house and you came over to get me down."

"I could see up your skirt."

I gasped.

Then I sighed.

Only I would try to climb out of a window in a skirt.

I knew better than to argue. The only time Lee could say for certain he was a good guy was when he was in the Army, and during some of that time I was ignoring him, and most of his missions were top secret so I had no examples to give.

I took another sip of coffee before I gave in. "All right, what do I have to do to pay you back for Rosie? And I'll warn you, I won't clean your bathroom."

"You sure that's the only stipulation you wanna make?" I thought about it for a second, wondering what else I should throw in when he said, "Time's up."

He was playing with me and I was losing my temper.

"Oh for goodness sake, just tell me!" I snapped.

No sooner had I got out the word "me", he moved.

31

And he moved fast, faster than I think I've ever seen anyone move, especially at that hour of the morning.

My coffee cup was gone. He had his hands at my ass and then I was going up, my behind settled on the counter and Lee moved in. Both his arms went around my back. I had no choice but to spread my legs or I'd gouge his abs with my knees. His arms pulled me to him, my nether regions pressed to his crotch, and he bent his head and kissed me.

The first time in my life that *Lee* kissed *me*.

Holy shit.

Holy, holy, shit, shit, *shit*.

He was a fine kisser.

In fact, just that one kiss blew the entire Joe Perry experience out of the water, and that's saying something.

When he lifted his head, I said (or kinda shouted, at this point I'd totally forgotten Rosie), "What the hell was that?"

I was covering and *recovering*. My mouth was the only thing that worked. Every other part of my body had been reduced to Jell-o.

"Advance payment on services rendered," he answered.

I stared at him, thrown.

He looked down, likely to further assess my reaction.

"Is this my shirt?" His hand came from around my back and lifted to touch the wife beater, very close to my breast. I slapped it away, feeling my nipple harden and thanking the Lord above for lightly padded bras that hid hard nipples.

"Yes, it's your shirt, and what do you mean, advance payment on services rendered?"

His hand went to the side of my breast, rather than to the actual breast, which was only a relief for about five seconds as it then slid around my back, pulling me to him again.

This was not brother-sister behavior.

What was he playing at?

He told me.

And he told me bluntly.

"I do this thing for Rosie, you sleep with me."

I stared at him, open-mouthed and in stunned silence.

I did, of course, understand what he meant, but he explained further.

"Not like last night. We'll both be naked and sexual acts will be performed."

My expression didn't change, except maybe my mouth opened wider.

"I'll expect your participation," he went on.

Holy shit.

He kept going. "Your avid participation."

Dear Lord in Heaven.

Eventually, I whispered, "You must be joking."

He shook his head and watched me.

I dropped my eyes, unable to hold his stare.

"I think I need more coffee," I told his throat.

His hand went into my hair and with a gentle pull he tilted my head back again.

A light bulb clicked on.

A way out.

"You're already involved. You made the calls last night, you said you would."

Lee verbally waved it away because his hand was twisting in my hair.

"I know the principles. I can back out this morning. Rosie will be on his own."

This, I thought, was not a bad thing, considering the expected payment.

"Okay then, Rosie will be fine. I'll go with him," I declared.

"Rosie will do this alone. You're not going anywhere near these guys. You don't exist to them and I'm gonna keep it that way."

"There's a flaw in your plan, Lee. They saw me last night," I pointed out.

"Minor blip. During the call I told them you were mine and that's why I'm getting involved. They'll keep a distance."

Holy shit! He was already telling other people! And I hadn't even agreed!

"I'm not yours!" I snapped.

"You will be tonight," he returned smoothly.

Holy shit, shit, *shit*.

What was happening here?

Was I in an alternate universe?

"You can't do this! We can't do this!" I stated hotly.

"Why not?"

He was calm and blasé. One of his hands was tangled in my hair and the other arm was wrapped around my back, the hand resting at my waist like we did this every morning of our lives.

Both my hands were pressed on the counter and I was about ready to shoot through the ceiling.

Lee was not just a Bad Boy, a Badass or a Badass Extraordinaire. He was a fucking crazy man.

I thought hard about it for a second, partially hysterically, and then came up with something. It wasn't original but it was something.

"You're like my older brother," I told him.

"Is that why you tried to stick your tongue down my throat when you were fifteen?" he asked.

Yikes.

"And sixteen?" he continued.

Crap.

"And seventeen?" he carried on.

"Okay, okay, I get it. Jeez," I broke into his trip down memory lane. "You said you thought of me like your younger sister."

"I lied."

My eyes bugged out at this piece of news.

"*What?*"

"I was into some serious shit back then," he replied. "Depending on the assignment, I didn't know if I'd come home breathing and in one piece. You were twenty years old and hung up on me."

Oh for fuck's sake.

"I was *not* hung up on you."

He grinned. "Yes you were."

I was but I wasn't going to admit it.

I narrowed my eyes and he kept talking.

"I didn't need any entanglements. I didn't need anything on my mind but what I was doing. I didn't need to worry if I'd leave a girl at home brokenhearted because something happened to me."

I had to admit, that made sense and it was kind of thoughtful.

I wasn't going to acknowledge that to him either.

He kept going.

"By the time I got out, you backed off. You had a man then and I thought you were over me."

He shrugged, nonchalant, like he didn't care, and that kinda pissed me off.

No wait, that *really* pissed me off.

He wasn't done.

"Then that guy was gone and you kept avoiding me. Guys came, guys went. I figured you had no trouble approaching me before. When you were ready, you'd come to me."

I was no longer avoiding his eyes or him. I was staring daggers at him.

What an arrogant jerk!

He calmly returned my gaze. "I'm a bit tired of waiting and I'm *definitely* tired of your man parade." His voice was slightly edgy and a little scary. "Fortunately, you've presented me with this golden opportunity."

He could damn well wait until hell froze over. He wasn't going to keep me at arm's length for ages and then just reel me in when he felt like it.

"Well, I'm not done avoiding you!" I said.

As he was talking, he'd moved slightly back.

He came in close again.

"Nope." He shook his head. "No more waiting, no more games, no more avoiding and no more other guys. You want this and I want this and it's going to happen."

"I don't want this," I lied. Self-protection and all that. He was an arrogant jerk. He was scary as hell. He was trying to force me to sleep with him and using my friend to do it. He was bad news. I wanted no part in Lee Nightingale.

And that was that.

He laughed softly. "Bullshit."

He thought I was funny.

I saw red.

"Of all the—"

He kissed me again, and this time Joe Perry was a fleeting memory.

I gave into the kiss immediately.

What could I say? It was Lee.

It was getting good. His mouth was open and so was mine, his tongue was in my mouth and then mine was in his. My legs opened further and he got closer. His arms tightened and my breasts flattened against his chest. My arms went around his neck and I pressed against him.

Then his lips tore away from mine as his head shot up and twisted around, his entire body tensed, coiled, waiting.

Then Kitty Sue and Ally turned the corner from the entryway into the kitchen.

Kitty Sue's hand went to her throat. Her eyes widened and then, I swear, they filled with tears.

Ally started laughing.

I looked to the ceiling.

Shit.

Chapter 4
Do I Need to Kiss You Again?

My reaction was immediate.

"I'm gonna kill you," I told Ally.

She walked in and dropped an overnight bag on the floor, chuckling.

She set me up. She knew Lee was coming home last night. Crazy bitch.

"What's going on here?" Kitty Sue asked hopefully, rooted to the spot and staring at us, not with disapproval at our carnal clinch, but with eyes filled with hopeful bliss.

Lee got his eyes from Kitty Sue, and all the kids got their long, lean body from her. Kitty Sue was always a bundle of energy, the kind of Mom who held down a full-time job, made dinner every night, had home-baked cookies in the cookie jar and, every year, sewed all her kids' Halloween costumes from scratch.

Lee moved to the side then jumped up and sat on the counter beside me. I hastily closed my legs.

"Anyone want coffee?" Lee asked courteously.

I jumped down and took a step forward, escape on my mind. It was pretty clear to me that I'd slid through a tear between the worlds and I had to find my way back to my home world pretty damn quick.

Further, now that the Lee of this world was no longer kissing me, I had to get away from him or I was going to wrap my hands around his neck and squeeze.

Lee leaned forward, caught me by the waistband of my jeans and hauled me back between his legs.

"What's going on here?" Kitty Sue repeated, her eyes taking in the cozy scene.

Far too cozy. Far too fast. Far too weird.

Shit.

I opened my mouth to speak but Lee beat me to it.

"Indy and I are together now."

My entire body froze in disbelief, my mouth still open.

"Oh my God. Oh my God," Kitty Sue chanted.

"Righteous!" Ally exclaimed.

I twisted around and glared at Lee. "You said one night of sex!"

Lee's eyes held mine. "I didn't say one night. We've been waitin' a long time. One night won't do it." Then he paused and said, "But, if you want, we can try."

My breasts swelled at the idea of trying to fit years of sex into one night with Lee.

I ignored my breasts and paid attention to my temper.

I figured it would be bad form to smack Lee in front of his mother.

And definitely strangulation was out.

Kitty Sue was in her little slice of heaven, so much so that she missed my "one night of sex" comment and Lee's response.

"I can't wait to tell your father," she told me. "And *your* father," she told Lee.

"I wouldn't do that," I said, beginning to panic.

"Of course, we all shouldn't get too excited. This is happening fast, though not *that* fast, if you know what I mean," Kitty Sue went on.

Fast? This wasn't fast. This was warp speed

Kitty Sue was staring dreamily ahead, not focused on a thing, and we'd all melted into the atmosphere. She was picking wedding colors. She was deciding china patterns. She was mentally knitting baby booties. She was planning her visit to my mother's grave to impart the blissful news.

Shit.

I twisted back to Lee.

"Asshole," I mouthed.

He was unfazed at my word, though he seemed somewhat fascinated with watching my mouth form it.

"I brought you a change of clothes and some of your stuff," Ally said, reaching behind us and grabbing the coffeepot. "Looks like I should have brought more."

I moved my glare to her.

She was just as good at ignoring it as Lee. Better, she'd had more practice.

"I'll take some of that. Indy already has a cup," Lee murmured.

"Not surprising," Ally said, pouring coffee into three mugs.

They were acting like it was business as usual at Lee's condo, just like it was any other day, and I decided I was most definitely in an alternate universe because this was all just plain old nuts.

"Listen people!" I cried, trying to get everyone's attention. "This is not what it seems."

Ally looked at me.

Kitty Sue's happily dazed eyes focused on me.

Lee's hard thighs tightened on my sides and his forearm wrapped around my chest and neck. His chin dipped to the curve of my shoulder, his lips at my ear.

"Don't spoil Mom's moment," he murmured there.

"What is it, then?" Kitty Sue asked.

Lee's fingers dug into my shoulder and I could feel the muscles flexing in his forearm at my neck. I took one look in Kitty Sue's eyes.

Damn it all to hell.

"We're taking it slow," I said for lack of anything else to say, like the truth.

Wouldn't sound so good to say, *Your son is trying to extort sex from me. News at eleven.*

Kitty Sue breathed a sigh of relief, sent us a dazzling smile and put sugar in her coffee.

Ally wandered into the living room.

Lee brushed my hair aside with his chin and softly kissed the spot where my shoulder met my neck.

I guessed that was his way of saying thank you.

It was a good way.

"Hey, where's Rosie?" Ally asked.

I froze.

So did Lee.

We'd completely forgotten about Rosie.

"Fuck," Lee said.

He moved me forward and jumped off the counter, prowling into the living room. I caught a good look, both of his muscled back and his ass in his jeans, and went a little weak in the knees.

"Liam Nightingale, that mouth!" Kitty Sue admonished.

I followed Lee, but he was already moving out of the living room and through the kitchen.

I looked at the quilt and pillow on the couch.

No Rosie.

"Fuck!" Lee clipped from somewhere else in the condo.

I ran to him.

The second bedroom door was closed. The bathroom door was open with the bathroom empty. I walked into Lee's room and he stalked out of his bathroom.

"That fucking twat," Lee muttered.

"Mouth!" Superpower-Mom-eared Kitty Sue called from the kitchen.

Lee could always swear really, really well. He'd been doing it since I could remember.

Lee walked to the dresser and slid a drawer open. He pulled on a navy, long-sleeved t-shirt that fit super-snug to his chest and arms and grabbed a pair of socks. I watched as he sat on the bed to pull on the socks and a pair of black motorcycle boots with square toes and silver hoops at the sides.

Seriously kickass boots.

I shook my head to clear thoughts of Lee's boots and started to worry about Rosie and why he would leave, what he was doing, where he was going and what was in that pot-addled brain of his.

Then something occurred to me as Lee got off the bed.

And for the first time that morning, I smiled.

If I found Rosie first, and got the diamonds back to their owner, then I wouldn't owe Lee a thing.

Hee hee.

I was so happy with my thought, I had to share it.

"I guess this puts a crimp in your sex extortion plans."

I'd timed my "nanny nanny foo foo" very poorly. Lee was close enough to hook me around the back of the neck with enough force to send me slamming into him. He gave my hair an erotically rough yank, tilting my head back.

Then he kissed me.

It was a hard, deep and serious kiss with a liberal dose of tongue.

My toes curled into the thick carpet.

When he lifted his head, he announced, "I have plans for you. Don't leave this apartment."

I nodded.

I had every intention of leaving his apartment.

He watched me.

"Indy, you leave this apartment, I'll come lookin' for you."

"Jeez, we haven't even slept together and already you don't trust me."

"I've known you all your life, not to mention the fact that my idiot sister is in the next room and when you two get together it's like Laurel and Hardy do Denver."

"It is not!" I cried.

"What about that time you bought scalped tickets to a Garth Brooks concert from Carmine Alfonzo?"

Carmine Alfonzo, better known as Uncle Carmine. We'd known him since we were seven. He used to ride the squad car with Dad.

"He was in disguise!" I defended myself.

"He was wearing a baseball hat," Lee returned.

"Yes, but he's a *Cubs* fan, he was wearing a *Sox* hat. His head should have been on fire."

The sides of Lee's eyes crinkled in a grin that didn't involve his mouth, but was nevertheless ultra-effective, and he let go of my hair.

"We aren't finished yet," he told me.

"Yes we are," I retorted.

Lee's crinkles disappeared and his face got serious.

"This is happening between you and me," he threatened.

I wasn't entirely sure what "this" meant since he announced to his mother and sister that we were "together". Considering what I *did* know was that a goodly part of it involved us being naked, in his bed, participating in activities which required my avid participation, I wasn't going to have any part of it.

"No, it isn't," I snapped back.

"We'll talk about it later."

"No, we won't."

His eyes narrowed. "Do I need to kiss you again?"

I took a hasty step back and watched my toe draw a pattern in the carpet.

"No," I muttered.

"Christ, I need to get my head examined."

My head snapped up.

"What does that mean?" I asked angrily.

"Nothin'. Be here when I get back."

"Sure."

Kristen Ashley

Not on his life.

☙❧

Ally Nightingale had yet to decide on a career. Currently, she was on her one hundred and eleventh bartending job. She already had a Bachelor's degree (majored in political science and squeaked by), was a certified radiology technician (a tough gig, but she saw it through and worked the MRI machine at Swedish Medical Center for two months before quitting; Malcolm's head nearly exploded after that one) as well as a certified nail technician.

Of all those things, Ally gave good nails, but she found sitting in a chair all day filing, polishing and forming plastic glop into nail shapes was not compatible with her energetic personality.

Luckily, bartending left most of her days free, and whenever she needed a bit of cash (which was often), she worked part-time for me at Fortnum's.

Before coming over with Kitty Sue, Ally had gone to my house and chosen an Ally Outfit for me. If I was to choose a search-for-Rosie outfit or a night-after-Liam outfit it would have included Levi's. But then most of my outfits included Levi's unless I had a backstage pass.

Ally had chosen a denim skirt that was mini in the sense that it hit five inches above my knees, not mini in the way Ally wore them, which was five centimeters below her ass. She also brought my vintage Rolling Stones t-shirt (I wasn't a Stones fan but the shirt was way cool), a wide, red belt with a big silver buckle with a delicate filigree-and-braided design and my red cowboy boots.

After Lee and Kitty Sue left, I filled Ally in on the whole Rosie Debacle and my plan to find him. She (not surprisingly) immediately volunteered her assistance and I (equally not surprisingly) took her up on it.

I showered and dressed while Ally tried, and failed, to call Duke.

Then we went to the bookstore to help Jane. With Duke and Rosie out, Jane was alone at the store and was in a tizzy because she was handling the espresso machine by herself and thus, actually had to speak to people. Jane was not good at speaking to people. She could shelve a mean book and was really good at tidying, vacuuming and updating our computer book inventory, but customer relations was not her strong suit.

Ally and I worked alongside Jane until the morning crush was over. The regulars weren't happy that Rosie wasn't there, but we'd all been working alongside Rosie enough to be able to do a fair imitation. Still, it wasn't the same.

Then Ally swung by Rosie's house on the off chance he was there. This was off-limits for me because Lee might have found out Rosie's address using one of his mysterious "ways" and might be there, and I didn't want to bump into Lee just yet, especially not searching for Rosie or the diamonds. He didn't know my plan and I wasn't about to let on.

And anyway, business on a weekday didn't really die down until after the lunch hour and I couldn't leave Jane on her own.

While Ally was doing the stop off at Rosie's place, my cell rang.

It was Dad.

"Hey Daddy-o," I said.

"What's this about you hookin' up with Lee?"

Shit.

Kitty Sue.

"We're taking it slow."

"Take it *real* slow," Dad said. "That boy's a tomcat. Jesus, why couldn't you choose Hank? Hank's a good guy, a solid cop, has a job where both of his feet are planted on the *right* side of the law."

Yikes.

Dad went on, "Don't get me wrong. Lee's his own man, doesn't take shit from anyone, gotta respect that, but hell. My daughter?"

I was silent and Dad was on a roll. You couldn't really get much in when Dad was on a roll.

"Kitty Sue is beside herself," he told me. "Your mother and her had some sort of blood pact where they stuck their thumbs with pins and put them together, silly girl crap, and they promised their kids would get married, have babies, and that way they'd be related."

That sounded familiar.

Dad's voice changed from frustrated to coaxing. "Hank'll have a good pension."

"Dad, I'd make Hank's head explode. We'd last, like, a day."

"Shee-it."

Dad knew this was true.

He didn't say much more before he hung up.

Guess Lee didn't have the Dad Vote.

I shook off the call and mentally assigned Lee the duty of letting his mother down easy. He'd gotten us into this, he'd have to get us out.

I decided to call a couple of Rosie's friends that he'd put down in his file as emergency contacts to see if Rosie was with them or if they'd seen him. I got no response from one. The other was home, sleeping it off, unhappy to be disturbed, and had not heard from Rosie in a few days.

I called Duke again. Twice. No answer. No answering machine, either. Duke really needed to get into the twenty-first century, and I mentally added items onto my Christmas present buying list.

Then the door opened and Marianne Meyer walked in.

Marianne Meyer lived next door to the Nightingales in Washington Park all the while we were growing up. She was between Lee and Ally and me in age and she was a good friend. She had been fettered by a scoliosis brace in junior high and orthodontics in high school. She married a jerk, got a divorce and moved back in with her parents a year ago. Marianne was taking her divorce hard, and living with her parents at age thirty-one harder. She was five foot five and used to be cute as a button, but the divorce was taking its toll and she was drowning her sorrows in Oreos. She was a nurse at Pres-St. Luke's. She took the evening shifts so she'd have her days free and had made house hunting a full-time hobby.

She rushed up to me at the espresso counter, her cheeks flushed.

"I heard you finally hooked up with Lee Nightingale," she said.

Shit, shit, *shit*.

Marianne was intimately acquainted with my lifelong crush and had been recruited for some of my Lee Maneuvers in the past. She probably thought I was in seventh heaven and needed a friend to take me wedding dress shopping.

"We're taking it slow," I said.

"Have you… you know… *done it* yet?" Her eyes were beginning to glaze over at the very thought of *doing it* with the legendary Liam Nightingale.

"Nope."

"What are you waiting for?" she nearly shouted, and if she'd reached across the counter and grabbed me by my shirt and shook me, I wouldn't have been surprised.

I took Marianne's mind off Lee with a mocha, heavy on the chocolate syrup and whipped cream.

After Marianne left, making me promise to phone her the minute I *did it* with Lee and give her all the details (not gonna happen), I called Hank.

I did this because I thought maybe Rosie might do something stupid, like hock the diamonds and go to San Salvador. According to him, he was owed fifty dollars for some of the "primo" grass I never knew that he grew in his basement, and the guy gave him a gazillion dollars worth of diamonds.

That was seriously fishy, and Rosie was seriously stupid for taking the damn things.

Though, what did one do when presented with a fortune of diamonds? Say no?

I didn't actually blame Rosie for wanting to cash in his windfall and skip town. Personally, I wouldn't have picked San Salvador though.

If Rosie successfully skipped, and Lee was right in what he said last night, this meant that Rosie would be in San Salvador, and there was a good possibility that either Lee or I or both of us would be target practice. I really shouldn't have mouthed off to those guys, and I was in wholehearted agreement with Lee. I'm sure he'd been shot at tons of times, and if he didn't like it, I'd *never* like it.

This would also mean I owed Lee big time for putting his life in danger. Not to mention *my* life would be in danger and I'd have a hard time talking myself out of having sex with Lee (at least once) before I died.

Further, I'd never replace Rosie at the espresso machine. He had a God given talent, no joke. He was the Picasso of Coffee.

The first thing Hank said, "I hear you've finally hooked up with Lee."

Shit.

Kitty Sue, the fastest dialing fingers in the West.

Something had to be done.

"Not exactly," I responded.

"Yeah, takin' it slow."

"Something like that." Really slow. Snail with a hernia slow. "Listen, can I talk to you about something?"

"Anything."

"Can you step out of your cop shoes for five minutes?"

Silence.

Hank wasn't very fond of me asking that question, which I did over the years a lot.

"Shit. You and Ally haven't stolen candy from Walgreens again, have you?" he asked.

"We didn't steal it! We were just buying a bunch and didn't know what we could carry, so we started putting it in our pockets early to see how much we could pack in."

"They have bags at Walgreens, you know," Hank pointed out.

"Those plastic bags clog the landfills and choke the environment."

Or something.

"Jesus, a politically-correct Indy. God save us," he muttered.

"Smartass," I said on a smile.

"What did you wanna talk about?"

Big breath.

"How would I go about finding a missing person?"

Hank became all business. I couldn't see him but I heard it, for sure. "Who is it?"

"You don't know him." Well, Hank did know Rosie, but only to buy coffee from when he came to Fortnum's.

"How long have they been missing?"

I tried to calculate it. "About ten hours."

"Sorry, Indy. Not missing yet."

"What if they actually are?"

"Who is it?" he repeated.

"An employee of mine. He's a steady guy." That was a lie. Rosie was anything but steady. But Rosie never missed a chance to make coffee. He worked seven days a week and never complained. "He didn't show up for work today," I went on. "His name is Ambrose Coltrane." Best not use his alias, just in case Lee called in a favor.

"The same Ambrose Coltrane that Lee's lookin' for?"

Say what?

"Lee only knows him as Rosie," I snapped.

Hesitation then, "Lee has ways."

Grr.

Everybody was always saying this. Lee had ways of getting into girls' panties. Lee had ways of getting parts for his car when he didn't have a job. Lee had ways of finding choice parking spots wherever he went. Lee had ways of getting out of being grounded an average of one hour after the grounding, when

Ally and I would usually have to do the whole week, or month, or whatever our transgression had bought.

Hank didn't read my frustration. He just kept talking.

"Starting with his PI databases. He can tap into a lot of things. Lee called in a couple hours ago. Asked me to let him know if Coltrane surfaces. He doin' this favor for you?"

Pause for answer.

I kept my mouth shut.

"What's goin' on?" Hank was losing his good-natured, business-like voice and was lapsing into his stern older brother voice. "Why are you and Lee looking for the same guy?"

Rule Number One in the India Savage Life Code: When in doubt or possible trouble, lie.

"Don't know. Listen, Hank, can you call *me* first if you hear anything about Rosie? And then forget about it for about an hour or two or twenty before calling Lee?"

"Not if you don't tell me what this is about."

Like brother, like brother. Stubborn to the last.

"Forget it. See you Saturday at Dad's barbeque."

"You comin' with Lee?'

"No, I'm not coming with Lee. I'm pretty sure we'll be broken up by then. Later."

I hung up and opened the phonebook on my cell. I scrolled down to Lee, took a big breath and punched the button that would call Lee, a button I'd never punched before in my life.

He answered after one ring. "Yeah?"

"Lee? It's Indy."

A customer walked up and asked for a double espresso and I gave him a one minute finger and Jane started banging the portafilter against the sink to loosen the last pot of grounds.

"Where are you?" he asked.

"Fortnum's."

"I thought I told you to stay at the condo."

As if I ever did what I was told.

"I have a business and I'm down two employees. I had to come to work."

"Less than twenty-four hours ago, people were shootin' at you."

Hmm, he sounded pissed-off.

"Jane can't handle the store in the morning all alone. She'll go meltdown."

Why was I explaining myself to him?

"Listen, you have to stop Kitty Sue, she's telling everyone we're together."

"We are together."

"We're not together."

"Who has she told?"

"Dad, Marianne Meyer, Hank, God knows who else. This is getting out of hand. It has to stop."

"Mom didn't tell Hank. I told Hank."

"Why would you tell Hank?" This was said in a near shout, and the customer took a step back.

Lee was silent for a second, thinking thoughts I could not fathom, then he changed the subject. "When do you close?"

"Six."

"Don't leave the store. I'll come by tonight at six to pick you up."

"Lee—"

"See you at six."

Then he hung up.

Rat bastard.

Ally came back to get me with news of no Rosie at his house.

I asked if there was any Lee at Rosie's house and that was a negatory too.

We took off to go see Rosie's friend, emergency contact numero uno. He had a house in the Highlands area. Great old houses and bungalows, though Rosie's friend didn't live in one that had been renovated. For that matter, he didn't live in a block that had a single house that had been renovated. Or in a block that had a single house with more than a dozen blades of genuine grass growing in their yards or decent curtains in their windows. It was semi-wasteland.

We knocked to no answer.

We sat in my car and called the house number on my cell phone, no answer.

We scanned the neighborhood and Ally pointed to the end of the block.

We got out of the car and walked to the corner Stop & Stab, which had surprisingly not been crushed by the overabundance of Denver's convenience stores. A guy of Arab descent stood behind the counter.

We walked up to him and he smiled.

"You want gum?" he asked.

"No, we're——" I started to say.

"Cigarettes? They're bad for you but I have to sell them or I'll go bust. Everyone in this neighborhood smokes cigarettes."

I shook my head and then wondered briefly why Lee smelled like tobacco. I hadn't seen him smoke since he enlisted.

I noticed Ally staring at me like, *Hello?* and I shook out of my Lee Reverie.

"You know Rosie Coltrane?" I asked.

"You're not buying goods?" the counter man asked back, looking both disappointed and defeated.

I couldn't help myself. He immediately made me sad.

"Yes, mints," I grabbed a pack of mints and put it on the counter.

He stared at the mints.

I stared at the mints.

Ally stared at the mints.

The mints seemed lonely and the purchase of the mints was not going to do anything to help feed this man's family.

I put another pack of mints on the counter, followed it with two candy bars and then walked over to the fridge and grabbed two bottles of water and two diet pops.

On the way back to the counter, I grabbed a box of cream-filled, prepackaged cupcakes. I hadn't had a cupcake in ages.

He happily started ringing up my purchases. "Who are you looking for again?"

"Rosie Coltrane. He works for me and didn't come into work today and I'm worried," I lied.

I was a good liar. I'd been doing it since Lee, Ally and I were caught behind the garage trying to smoke leaves when Ally and I were eight and Lee was eleven. I came up with the imaginative excuse that we were thinking about roasting marshmallows but didn't know how. Malcolm bought it. Kids, marshmallows, my cute, angelic smile. It all seemed benign and plausible.

After we got off with just a lecture about fire safety and the danger of matches, Lee tousled my hair.

Happy memories.

"I do not know a man named Rosie. What kind of man has a name like Rosie?" the counter man stated.

"Rosey Grier?" Ally tried.

"I don't know a Rosey Grier either," the counter man said.

"Football player? Helped catch Sirhan Sirhan?" Ally prompted.

"I don't follow American football. I know no Sirhan Sirhan. Is he a football player too?"

"No, he assassinated Bobby Kennedy," Ally explained.

"Oh my gracious! I certainly don't know of him!" the counter man exclaimed, horrified.

I decided to cut into the history lesson. "Our Rosie doesn't live around here, but his friend does, down and across the street about four houses. His name is Tim Shubert."

"I know Tim. He buys lots of cheese puffs and frozen pizzas."

If Tim was a stoner the caliber of Rosie, I had no doubt he bought a lot of cheese puffs and pizzas.

"Rosie's thin, about five foot six, dirty blond hair. Looks a bit like Kurt Cobain but his face isn't as pointy," Ally put in.

"I know no Kurt Cobain, but I have seen a man of this description with Tim. Is his name really Rosie?"

"Nickname," I said. "His name is Ambrose."

"Ambrose is a perfectly fine name. Why does he not call himself Ambrose?"

Ally looked at me.

I decided to ignore that one. Any answer would have to span a generation *and* a culture gap. I didn't have it in me today. In less than twenty-four hours, I'd been shot at, physically dragged out of bed and kissed by Lee Nightingale three and a half times (yes, I was counting, and the half was the kiss he planted on my neck). I was a woman on a mission and I didn't have time to explain a dud name like Ambrose.

"Have you seen him lately, like say, today?" I asked as I paid for my purchase.

"No, not today."

"Tim?" Ally asked.

"Not Tim either."

He handed me the bag and I took it at a loss for what to do next.

"Jeez, Indy. Don't you read detective novels? You own a bookstore for God's sake," Ally hissed and then turned to the store owner.

The counter man smiled huge. "You own a bookstore? I love books. What bookstore do you own?"

"Fortnum's, on the corner of Bayaud and Broadway," I answered.

"I know that. My wife goes there. Books are cheap there and then you can sell them back and get cash money."

"Yep, that's it." I nodded and smiled, happy to meet a customer by proxy.

Ally was busy scribbling my name and numbers on a piece a paper she found in her purse, and when she was done she handed him the paper. "Maybe you could give us a call if you see Rosie or Tim. Would you do that?"

"Of course. I'm an employer. Only my wife works for me, but I understand how important it is to trust your hired help. I will call you."

"Thanks."

We went out and sat in my car and stared at Tim's house while we thought about what to do next. We both were new at this. Neither of us had tracked down a stoner on the run before. We'd stalked plenty of guys, but we'd known where to find them.

We both ate a cupcake to get the brain juices flowing.

"That was a nice guy," I said through yellow cake and cream.

"Yep," Ally replied, her mouth equally full.

Someone tapped on Ally's window and we both jumped and swiveled our heads to the side.

I nearly spewed better-living-through-chemistry cream on my windshield at what I saw.

It was Grizzly Adams, but the serial killer version. He was enormous, had lots of wild, blond hair, a thick, seriously overlong (we're talking ZZ Top here) russet beard and was wearing a flannel shirt even though it had to be nearly ninety degrees.

He was also carrying a shotgun and had some kind of freaky-ass goggle apparatus on the top of his head.

"You want somethin'?" he growled.

"We're looking for Tim Shubert," Ally replied calmly.

"He's not here," Grizzly said. "Move along."

"Yep, yep. Going!" I shouted and started the car, put it into gear and took off.

"Where are we going?" Ally asked.

"Hell if I know," I answered.

"We should have asked him some questions," Ally said, completely at ease

"Right. No. We're trying to *avoid* me getting dead. Definitely *you* getting dead. I don't talk to people who carry shotguns around in broad daylight."

"He looked interesting," Ally replied contemplatively.

Shit.

⊰⊱

It was just after four.

After our introduction to Grizzly, we'd swung back by Fortnum's to help out Jane for a while and ask if she'd heard from Duke (answer: no).

Now Ally and I were in my dark blue VW Beetle, windows down, sunroof back, sitting outside Rosie's house sipping leftover water and waiting.

My Beetle wasn't exactly a rock 'n' roll-mobile, but it was cute. It had cream leather seats that were great in the winter because they heated up. Now that it was summer, the seats stuck to your legs, and every time you got out it felt like three layers of skin tore off (another reason to wear jeans).

Denver had killer weather, as in nearly perfect. Summers were hot, but usually at night it cooled off enough to sleep under a cover. Spring and fall were volatile and allowed for variety in wardrobe. Winter was never too cold because there was no moisture in the air. The occasional blizzard was a bummer, and sometimes there were snowstorms in July, but nearly every day was sunny and the blue skies of Denver could not be beat.

We'd already called Duke, like, a gazillion times. Duke and Dolores were visiting Dolores's parents in Pagosa Springs. They were supposed to be home in the morning but had still not arrived. I didn't know Dolores's parents' number or her maiden name. We were stuck on that score.

I found Duke's disappearance curious and a little scary, although Duke had been known to go walkabout, except it was walkabout on a Harley.

Duke didn't do cell phones and I was loath to go to Evergreen. Although Rosie would likely be there or go there, at least eventually as that was where the diamonds were, so might Lee, and I had decided I was definitely back to avoiding Lee.

I had not come to terms with this abrupt about-face and needed time to process it.

Who was I kidding?

There was no processing going on.

Lee and I were not gonna happen.

I hated to break Ally and Kitty Sue's hearts, but I'd seen Lee tear through a variety of women's lives and I wasn't going to be one of them.

These days he was never home.

I had no idea what he did for a living, but I was pretty sure it was dangerous.

And he was way too damn cocky.

Ally and I were both staring at Rosie's house and I was trying to pluck up the courage to drive to Evergreen, and maybe have a scary faceoff with Lee that I had to have the cojones to win, when someone tapped on the back passenger window.

"Shit!" I jumped and shouted.

"Sorry. Didn't mean to scare you."

In Ally's window was a nice-looking man. A wee bit steroid ridden and overdeveloped in the chest area, but he had a good haircut, shirt, tie and slacks.

"We're a bit jumpy. We've had kind of a rough day," Ally explained, smiling her flirty smile.

Conversely, although Ally could head bang with the best, she was a White Hat type of gal. She liked the good boys. She liked preppies and corporate types and definitely men in uniform. She understood a good guitar riff, but she liked her men clean-cut, and ties and uniforms drove her wild.

"You lookin' for Rosie?" the man asked.

I blinked.

Were we that obvious?

"Uh, yeah," I replied.

He nodded. "I live over there."

He pointed in the vague direction of "over there" and both Ally and I followed his finger, not sure precisely which house "over there" was his, then looked back to him.

"Is Rosie in trouble?" the guy asked.

"Does Rosie get in trouble, do you know?" I asked in return.

The guy shook his head. "Not that I know of. Quiet guy. Killer coffee."

We all nodded.

"I'm Gary," he said.

Ally extended her hand. "Ally," she said and then she pointed to me. "And this is India."

Upon hearing my name, he turned, looked over his shoulder and gave a nod.

Ally and I turned and looked over our shoulders too.

Too late.

Before I could react to the two men running toward our car, my door was wrenched open. I was dragged out and I let out a howl when the backs of my legs were ripped from the hot leather seats.

I stopped my howl midway with an "oof" because I hadn't taken my seatbelt off, and when the guy yanked me out my belt jerked me back.

"Jesus, Teddy. Release the belt," another man said.

I took this opportunity to scream.

Teddy dropped me. I hit the side of the seat and I used the steering wheel to pull myself back into it.

Ally had already been hauled out the other side. She wasn't screaming and that scared the shit out of me.

I had no time to look for Ally as Teddy's hands came around to undo the belt and I bent forward and bit his arm.

"Fuck!" He reared back and punched me in the cheekbone.

Hard.

I have never, in my life, been hit by a man.

I got in a bitch slapping catfight at a Public Image Limited/Big Audio Dynamite double bill, but we were in a mosh pit gone bad. It was punk, it was expected.

Getting hit by a man hurt.

A fucking lot.

So much, I quit screaming and concentrated on the burning hurt that was radiating out of my cheekbone into my entire face.

"Teddy, for Christ sake. Are you nuts? She's Nightingale's. He's gonna rip your dick off. This is supposed to go smooth."

I opened my mouth to scream again and started back with the struggling.

Then Teddy was pulled away, someone touched me with something, and after that I didn't remember a thing.

Chapter 5

Cupcakes

I came to feeling very funky and unable to move my limbs.

I focused on what appeared to be the ceiling of a car and heard voices from what sounded like really far away.

By the time the car stopped, I was able to move a little, bit but not much. I was feeling tingly all over and my head was fuzzy.

The door to the car was opened and I was hauled out with hands under my armpits. Whoever hauled me out put me on my feet. My legs buckled and I nearly went down before I was caught. It was time again to lament the miniskirt, as a girl doesn't want to be tossed around by bad guys while wearing a short skirt.

"Shit, hold her up, you moron."

Two guys, one of them I noted was Goon Gary (not The Moron), dragged me by my upper arms through a tidy garage and into a house. I was shaking my head, trying to clear it and thinking not much of anything except that I wished I was wearing jeans.

I was taken into a room and heard a man say, "Jesus, what the fuck?"

The answer came hesitantly. "We had to stun her."

"What happened to her face?"

This answer was more hesitant. "She bit Teddy so he hit her."

"Christ! Which part of 'I want this to go smooth' did you not understand? Nightingale's going to have a shit hemorrhage. Get her some ice then call Teddy, get him out of town."

I was planted on a couch and not processing much of their conversation. I was focused on getting my fingers to move. I was together only enough to notice Goon Gary and The Moron making a hasty exit and that the couch I was on was a really nice couch, fluffy and covered in cream silk damask. I'd only just bought my couch a couple of months ago and I was still in couch assessment mode, the kind of mode that unconsciously comes whenever you make a major purchase.

I succeeded in lifting my head to look at the guy who'd been talking. He was wearing gray slacks and a maroon shirt with a monochromatic tie. He was short, had to be in his fifties and had jet black hair with white at each temple. He looked like what I would guess a younger Grandpa Munster would look like, except a lot more creepy and definitely scary, but not in a comic way.

"You okay?" he asked me.

No, I wasn't okay. I'd just been punched in the face and then kidnapped.

I just stared at him.

"I'm really sorry about his," he said. "I'm having troubles with some of my employees."

No shit.

I thought it but didn't say it. I hadn't recovered enough to form words.

Gary came back with an ice bag wrapped in a kitchen towel and handed it to me. I was happy I had enough limb coordination to put it on my face. My cheekbone hurt like hell.

"This didn't go as I'd planned. I just wanted to have a chat. I heard Nightingale had a woman and I was curious," the man said to me, his tone surprisingly conciliatory.

"Where's Ally?" I asked.

First things first. I wanted to know Ally was okay and then I wanted to have a nervous breakdown.

Young Grandpa Munster looked at Goon Gary.

"She was with another woman. We stunned her too," Goon Gary explained. "We left her in the car with the keys. Teddy's behind watching the car to make sure she's okay."

"Ally?" Young Grandpa Munster asked.

Gary shrugged.

Mr. Munster's face tightened. "As in Allyson Nightingale, Lee Nightingale's little sister?"

Gary began to look a wee bit uncomfortable.

It would appear this was an oopsie moment for Goon Gary.

"I'm at a loss for words. You do know that this isn't only Lee's woman, she's Tom Savage's daughter? And her friend is *a Nightingale,*" Munster stated.

Gary shifted on his feet while the color rose in his face.

Young Grandpa Munster sat down, shaking his head. "This whole thing is a complete fuck up."

He looked at me and his face had an expression that was somewhere between resigned and depressed. In normal circumstances, I'd probably feel sorry for him. Since I didn't know if I'd live to see the end of this scene in the film that was my life, I was too busy feeling sorry for myself.

"The simple life is holding some appeal," he said, and I nodded because I could see where he was coming from.

My life had been simple a day ago. Work, coffee, rock 'n' roll. Now I was being shot at, dragged around by bad guys and propositioned by the love of my life, who I had decided I didn't want anymore.

The simple life seemed far superior to all of that.

"I'm Terry Wilcox," he went on.

I nodded again. I was beginning to feel enough of myself to be scared, but not enough to be polite.

"You're India Savage, Lee's woman," he noted.

It was on the tip of my tongue to say I was *not* Lee's *anything* but these people seemed scared enough of Lee for me to decide that I should keep my mouth shut on that score.

It was then Wilcox really looked at me, from head to toe, and he sat back, getting comfortable, his face changing from depressed to assessing.

"Lee's always had good taste in women," he said quietly, and something in his eyes made my skin crawl.

Serious euw.

Then he said, "I'm looking for Rosie Coltrane, do you know where he is?"

Great.

Rosie.

The bane of my existence.

I was pissed-off enough with Rosie, who had got me into this mess *and* the one with Lee, to be a little snippy.

"If I knew where he was, why would I be sitting in my car outside his house?"

Something dangerous changed in Wilcox's eyes and I realized I'd just let my mouth run away with me and that being a little snippy might not go over too well. Like with the guys who shot at me. Evidence was clearly suggesting that bad guys did not like snippy women. I should maybe have been more polite, maybe more meek. Then again, I didn't have a lot of experience with conversing with creepy, scary, bad guys.

"He has something of mine," Wilcox continued.

"I know," I felt it safe to admit.

"I was supposed to get it back this morning. Do you know what happened?"

Hmm, I'd never taken the "how much information to divulge during interview with bad guys who kidnap you" course at the local community college. I'd barely squeaked by with computers and business accounting. I was feeling a little bit out of my depth.

"He was staying with Lee, but this morning me and Lee got kinda... er..." I stopped and searched for a word to describe that morning's trauma, "busy... and we didn't notice he took off."

"Busy." His eyes dropped to my chest, the Euw Look still in them. I felt my stomach lurch uncomfortably and tried really hard not to let my lip curl in disgust. "I bet. Do you know where he might be?"

I shook my head. "I wish I knew. He's my coffee guy. He didn't come to work. If I lose him, it'll affect my profit margin."

"He's a good coffee guy," Goon Gary offered. "Sheer talent."

Wilcox was throwing a "shut the fuck up, you idiot" look at Gary. Gary's mouth snapped shut.

Wilcox turned back to me. "Do you know where the diamonds are?"

This I knew, but I shook my head again. I wasn't going to drag Duke into this mess.

Since I was such an accomplished liar, I think he bought it.

He then informed me, "It's a million dollars worth of diamonds."

My mouth dropped open.

Holy crap.

"It is?" I asked.

"Yes, and I think you can understand that I want them back."

I nodded, this time fervently.

If I had a million dollars worth of diamonds, I'd definitely want them back. Rosie must grow seriously primo grass to get paid a million dollars in diamonds for it.

Gary moved slightly, looking out the window, then he murmured, "Nightingale's here."

This news sent a surge of hope through me as I immediately decided that, just for the next thirty minutes or so, I wasn't avoiding Lee.

Wilcox didn't say anything at first. He just watched me.

Then he asked, "Are you sure you don't know where Rosie is?"

"San Salvador?" I tried, and I wasn't joking.

He smiled. He thought I was amusing. It was an oily smile and my skin started crawling again.

Lee walked in. I turned my head to him, the ice still held to my face.

One look and I could understand why these guys were scared of him.

This was a Lee I'd never seen.

He was still wearing his jeans, skintight, navy tee and biker boots, and his hands hung loose and casual at his sides. However, the minute he entered, any other presence was forced from the room as his invaded. His eyes were hyper-alert and sharp. He was emanating pure, brutal energy and he was seriously and obviously pissed-off.

He stopped and glanced at the ice on my face.

A muscle in his cheek jumped.

Uh-oh.

He cut his eyes to Wilcox.

"I thought we had an understanding," Lee said.

Wilcox had come to his feet and he put his hands up in a placating gesture.

"Lee, it was a mistake. I just wanted to have a talk with your girl here and things got out of hand."

"Coxy, things are gettin' out of hand a lot these days. Who hit her?" Lee's pissed-off glance slid to Goon Gary.

Wilcox looked to Gary and I looked to Gary.

Gary looked a little pale.

"Let me take care of it," Wilcox said.

"You don't tell me, I'll go through every one of your men," Lee replied. "That way I'll be sure to get the fuck."

Holy shit.

I nearly wet myself.

The way Lee said that made me shiver, and *not* in the usual way Lee made me shiver.

Wilcox sighed, obviously overwhelmed by the stupidity of his workforce. Clearly, sometimes it's tough being the leader of the bad guys.

"It was Teddy," Wilcox answered.

Lee nodded, walked toward me and pulled me off the couch.

"It was nice to meet you," Wilcox said calmly as Lee escorted me out of the room, his hand curled around my upper arm.

I looked over my shoulder and said (perhaps feeling a bit tougher now that Scary Lee was with me). "The pleasure was all yours."

I heard him laugh as we left.

Lee did not laugh. Lee ignored the whole exchange.

Lee put me into the passenger seat of his silver Crossfire and got in the driver's side. He started the car and we shot from the curb. Before I could say a word he grabbed his cell and punched a number.

"Pick up Teddy and take him to the office," he paused, "Coxy's boy."

Then he hit a button and tossed the cell on the console.

Yep, angry.

"Ally—" I started to say.

"She's fine."

I took in a breath.

"How did you know where I was?"

"I've got a man at Rosie's. He saw the whole thing."

Uh, say what?

"Why didn't he do something?" I asked, somewhat loudly.

"He didn't know who you were," Lee paused. "*Now* he knows."

Yikes.

I decided not to talk loudly anymore.

"You have a man?"

His eyes moved to me. His face was blank. He was still angry.

He turned back to the road. "I have a lot of men."

"Oh."

I found that surprising, but I decided that maybe it was not the time to give Lee the third degree about his secret life, such as how many men he had and how he knew lowlife kidnapping scum like "Coxy". I wasn't even certain I wanted to know about his secret life. In fact, I think I was more certain I *didn't* want to know.

Maybe it was the time to begin planning how to avoid Lee again. However, I didn't know how to accomplish that when I was actually *with* Lee.

The house I was taken to was in the Denver Country Club area, very ritzy, very wealthy. Lee hit Speer Boulevard and drove faster than was allowed or safe, changing lanes on the three lane road deftly and often. I decided it was probably best not to say anything about this as Lee's energy wasn't exactly inviting conversation, and definitely not admonishments, about driving safety.

He passed the turn to Broadway.

"I need to go back to the store," I informed him.

He ignored me.

"Lee, I need to get back to the store," I repeated.

He continued to ignore me and headed downtown, toward his condo.

Damn.

I sat back and crossed one arm on my stomach, still holding the ice to my cheek and I evaluated my situation.

First, I clearly was not in any position of power here. Lee was driving, Lee was angry and Lee was, as usual, going to do whatever he damn well wanted to do.

Second, I'd been kidnapped. I tried to ignore that.

Third, I'd been kidnapped. I couldn't ignore that.

Big, bad, steroid-fueled guys dragged me out of my car, made me go unconscious somehow and took me someplace I didn't want to go.

Post-traumatic stress settled in and my hands started shaking.

Lee drove into the underground garage, parked and came around to open my door. We walked to the elevator, Lee's hand at the small of my back.

We stood together in the elevator. Curiosity and a desire to end the frightening silence made me say, "They did something to make me black out."

"Stun gun," Lee replied shortly, his features showing his thoughts were grim.

I started shaking some more. Someone had stun-gunned me.

Holy crap.

I'd never even *seen* a stun gun before. Now one had been used on me.

He let us into his apartment and I followed him into the kitchen. I was mildly surprised when he took a gun out of the back waistband of his jeans and set it on the kitchen counter.

Being the daughter of a cop, guns didn't scare me. Dad taught me years ago how to respect a firearm. He did this by showing me how to use them, taking me to the shooting range a couple of times a year and lecturing a lot. He was always careful with his guns in the house, what with me, Ally and all of our friends running around. Nevertheless, Lee casually setting a gun on the kitchen counter like it was a pizza cutter was a trifle frightening.

Then he turned and opened his mouth to speak.

Or, by the look on his face, perhaps roar.

Before he could get a word in, I threw up both of my hands, waving around the ice bag.

"Don't start!" I yelled and let the trembling take over my body just as I felt tears sting the backs of my eyes.

Definitely delayed reaction.

To keep from crying, or collapsing, I started shouting.

"Oh. My. *God!* I've just been stun-gunned and kidnapped and hit in the face by a guy! And it *hurt!*" Lee closed his mouth and started toward me, but I threw out my arm to ward him off. "No, no, no! Don't come near me!" He stopped and crossed his arms on his chest.

I paced to the sink, and then back, then to the sink, and so on, holding the ice to my cheek with one hand and waving the other one around in the air, the whole time babbling.

"I mean, this is unreal! Rosie's disappeared and he's half idiot so who knows where he is. I've been shot at, stun-gunned, pulled out of bed in the middle of the night by my *ankle!* There's a million dollars worth of diamonds out there and that dude wanted to have a chat with *me* about them. I don't know anything about them. I haven't even *seen* them! What's worse, I think Grandpa Munster has the hots for me and I think you've just done something that makes me owe you another favor, which does *not* make me happy." I took a breath and continued, "Not to mention, I'm dog tired. I've not been able to have my nap yet today, and last, but definitely *not* least, I'm starving because I had cupcakes for lunch! Cupcakes!"

I'd stopped my tirade standing in the middle of his kitchen, my arms straight down, my hands clenched into fists, the ice bag dripping and I was trying not to cry. I'd been brought up by a man without a wife who loved me to death, but also wanted a boy. Crying wasn't something that was tolerated. Crying was sissy.

I took a shaky breath to control my emotions, and I think my bottom lip may have trembled. Lee assessed that the shouting was over and took a step toward me, grabbed the bag of ice, threw it in the sink and slid his hands around my waist.

"Cupcakes?" he asked.

I hauled in another shaky breath.

"Yes, cupcakes."

The wrinkles next to his eyes creased. "We need to get you some food."

I nodded in agreement.

His grim thoughts were gone and so was his anger. His face had changed. The tightness relaxed, and there was something entirely different there.

One of his hands went to my temple by where Terrible Teddy socked me in the face and Lee tucked my hair behind my ear. Then he let his hand rest against my hair with his thumb splayed and gentle on the underside of my cheekbone. His gaze rested on my cheek for a couple of beats then he looked in my eyes.

"First, maybe we should do the nap," he said quietly.

I ignored his soft touch and his words, which held a little promise of what might happen before or after the nap (or both).

I'd had enough.

I needed a bottle of red wine, a darkened room and the Disco Nap to beat all Disco Naps. And not one that happened with Lee next to me. Preferably one that happened with Lee not even in the same state as me.

"I'd like to go home, please," I requested, trying to sound calm and rational, over my tirade and unaffected by his intimate gesture.

He changed the subject.

"I told you this morning to stay in the condo," he said this with just a hint of soft menace, but more accepting-yet-frustrated annoyance (yes, I could read all this in his tone, I'd known Lee a long time).

"I don't often do what I'm told," I noted.

He shook his head, likely a gesture to indicate he thought of my stupidity as irritating but cute (at least I hoped so).

Then he brushed his lips against mine. That counted as a half a kiss too, which put me at four kisses from Lee in one, single day.

"These are really bad guys. They may seem like imbeciles, but they're not nice guys," he said. "You don't mess with these guys."

"They're scared of you," I told him.

"I can probably protect you from them. I likely can't protect you from yourself. What did you think you were you doing?"

"I was looking for Rosie," I said out loud.

"I thought *I* was looking for Rosie."

"If I find him first then I don't owe you anything."

"You owe me for this afternoon."

"That wasn't that hard. You just walked in and took me out. That's only worth, say, me making you a batch of cookies." His lips twitched. I decided to change the subject. "Please take me home."

He shook his head and watched me for a beat.

Then he demanded, "Leave Rosie to me."

I didn't respond. I may have been shot at, stun-gunned and kidnapped, which would make any logical-minded person back off. Not me. Now I was on a mission. I was going to find Rosie, beat the crap out of him, turn the diamonds over to Terry Wilcox and then move to Bangladesh to avoid Lee and, possibly, Terry Wilcox.

"I don't like what I'm seeing," Lee said. "You look like you looked when your Dad told you that you couldn't go to Vegas to see Whitesnake in concert."

Hmm. That was a good concert and very worth the month's grounding I got when I returned.

Lee's arm around my waist brought me closer, in direct, full-frontal contact.

"You better be worth the trouble you're undoubtedly gonna cause," he said softly, his lips very close to mine.

Somewhere along the line I got mesmerized by his dark brown eyes.

"Of course I'm worth it," I whispered.

Damn it all! I was losing control and beginning to flirt.

I tipped my head back and licked my lips, my tongue touching his lips as I did so.

"Jesus," Lee muttered.

The door buzzer went.

He ignored it. His hand at my face moved back to tangle in my hair, his other arm tightened further at my waist.

I went up on tiptoe to get closer.

The door buzzer went again. This time whoever was pushing it didn't let up.

"Maybe it's Rosie," I said.

"Shit." Lee let me go and walked to the door.

Two minutes later, the entirety of both our families walked through the door.

"We've decided we're going to have a celebratory dinner," Kitty Sue announced as she came in.

"*You* decided. The rest of us were all just hungry," Malcolm said, starting to smile at me, then the smile froze on his face.

Indeed, everyone stopped dead when they saw me.

"What happened to you?" Dad shouted.

Hmm. I hadn't seen my face, but clearly it looked as bad as it felt.

Malcolm Nightingale's sons looked like him. Even now that he was getting older he looked fit and lean, and his face was still handsome and interesting. He kept in shape by running, a lot, sometimes traveling around the country to do marathons.

Tom Savage was tall, with a still-handsome face, sky blue eyes, and most of the time he could be very charming. He had salt and pepper hair and had been built like a defensive lineman when he was young. Over the years, that had given way to just a bit of a potbelly fueled by beer and his obsession for Mexican food.

He turned to Lee. "You hit her?"

I took in a sharp breath at this insulting question and so did everyone else.

Lee stared at Dad for a beat and then I watched as his face closed down. He leaned his hips against the kitchen counter and crossed his arms on his chest and didn't deign to answer.

Dad loved Lee. Dad thought about Hank, Lee and Ally like Malcolm and Kitty Sue thought about me. I knew Dad even admired Lee.

But Dad was a cop and he knew things about Lee and his past that I didn't know, things of which he didn't approve. Things that made Lee being involved with his daughter not a happy circumstance to celebrate.

Regardless, I had the weird and irrational desire to kick Dad in the shin.

"No, he didn't hit me. Jeez, Dad," I said.

"Of course he didn't hit her, Tommy. How could you think such a thing? What happened?" Kitty Sue, ever the diplomat, brushed off Dad's idiotic remark and came toward me.

I looked at Ally, who had dropped another bag on the floor. This one was not an overnighter. This one was bigger and stuffed full. Undoubtedly packed with enough of my clothes to get me through a week of staying at Lee's, by the end of which I would likely be pregnant or Lee's love slave, or both.

If I wasn't so worried about her and didn't love her with every fiber of my being, I would have strangled her.

"You okay?" I asked.

Ally nodded.

Kitty Sue stopped and looked between the pair of us. "Oh no, what are you two up to?"

I answered quickly, "Nothing. As for my cheek, *Dad*, I got hit in the face with some books falling off a shelf. Lee came over and got me so he could take a look at it and put ice on it." I walked to the sink and showed Dad the ice bag, then, for some reason, I leaned my shoulder into Lee.

Don't ask me why I did this. I just didn't like the way my Dad spoke to him, and I didn't like to see Lee's face close down like that.

"You have ice at Fortnum's," Dad said.

Oopsie.

This was true.

"Lee's ice is better," I replied.

Lame. I was losing my touch.

"I bet Lee's ice is better," Ally muttered, and both Kitty Sue and I gave her a killing look.

Hank and Lee were exchanging glances. Hank sighed and rocked back on his heels. Lee uncrossed his arms and draped one around my shoulders. I didn't even try to decipher what the Lee/Hank glance was all about. It had been a scary enough day.

And anyway, all I could think was that their coming over meant I was off the hook with the Lee Nap. It had been getting pretty flirty there and I needed to restore control.

"Where are we going to dinner?" I asked happily, and Lee's eyes slid sideways and his look made a definite promise of "later", shattering any illusions of my being off the hook.

"Sushi Den," Ally answered.

At those two words, Ally and I both immediately threw up our hands, index finger and pinkie extended in the famous devil's horns "Rock On!" gesture and squealed, "Sushi!"

"We're not having sushi," Malcolm declared.

"We decided this. We're having sushi," Kitty Sue said.

"Sushi's shit," Malcolm stated.

"Sushi's good for you," Kitty Sue returned.

"Mexican is good for you," Dad said.

Kitty Sue rolled her eyes.

I went to the bag excitedly.

I loved sushi, but I loved Sushi Den even more. It was one of my favorite restaurants in Denver. It was on Pearl Street, next to Pearl Street Grill and across from Stella's Coffee Haus.

Sushi Den was made out of cement and glass. They had hostesses filled with attitude who, with a look, could make lesser mortals feel small and even suicidal, and they had the best sushi I'd ever tasted. They never took reservations because they were always wall-to-wall people. Ally and I went to Sushi Den at least twice a month and had an ongoing battle to out-attitude the hostesses (with hostesses winning).

"Did you bring me a Sushi Den outfit?" I asked Ally.

You didn't go to Sushi Den in jeans and cowboy boots. Sushi Den demanded something else entirely. Clothing... black. Shoes... stiletto. I had a full section of my closet devoted to Sushi Den clothes.

"You bet your ass," Ally replied.

⌁

I woke up in Lee's bed again and my first thought was sake.

I didn't even *like* sake, but I drank it with Ally at Sushi Den because that's what you had to do.

When in Rome, do as the Romans do.

When at Sushi Den, drink hot sake.

I was on my belly, left leg crooked, right one straight. My left arm was bent with my hand resting on the pillow, and my right arm was crushed between me and what I knew had to be the weight of Lee's warm, hard body.

In one night, Lee had perfected a strategy of keeping me in one place while I was sleeping. He was pressed against my back, a good deal of his body resting on mine, his arm around me. His left leg was bent into the crook of mine and his thigh pressed against my nether regions. This was surprisingly not uncomfortable. It was cozy and warm, and made me feel, somehow, safe.

Fucking hell, how did I get myself into these situations?

I thought back to our sake-soaked family "celebration" dinner and was thankful to discover that I remembered everything.

Eat, drink sake, eat more, drink more sake, get drunk.

Let Lee put me in his Crossfire while I blew kisses to Ally, Hank, Dad, Kitty Sue, Malcolm and the parking valet

Come back to Lee's condo, stagger into his bedroom, take off clothes, confiscate another wife beater, fall face first in Lee's big bed because of drunkenness and lack of Disco Nap, and fall asleep.

With my left hand, I checked the status of my clothing.

Panties, check.

Wife beater t-shirt, check.

Either Lee didn't ravish my drunken self or he dressed me when he was done. I figured it was the former.

My left cheekbone felt tight and there was a dull ache that, without sake working its way through my system, I could now actually feel.

I quickly strategized my next twenty minutes as best as I could without the aid of caffeine.

I needed to get away from Lee without waking him, call a taxi and go home.

Fine, good, sounded like a plan.

I inched forward, trying to be sneaky.

And failing.

"Un-unh," Lee mumbled behind me, his arm tightening.

Foiled at the first hurdle.

I tried again using yesterday's successful excuse for escape.

"I need to make coffee."

Lee's arm went away, but the weight of his body was enough to keep me where I was. He slid further onto me. He bent, and I felt his lips touch my shoulder at the same time I felt his hand travel up the side of the thigh of my crooked leg, stopping at my hip.

"You can have coffee after," he said in my ear.

Every muscle in my body tensed even as my stomach melted.

"After what?"

His hand moved forward from my hip and his fingers traced the waistband of my underwear just below my navel.

"This is gonna happen," he said, and I didn't need him to explain what "this" meant. Then he said, "Now."

Holy shit.

Belatedly, I felt the evidence of his determination against my behind and my heart started racing.

Ever since I knew that such a thing as sex existed, I had wanted to do it with Lee.

Now, faced with the imminent act, I was terrified.

"I have a hangover," I tried.

Lee's lips were at my neck. Either he didn't hear me or he didn't believe me and thought my lie unworthy of a response.

He pressed his hips into my ass as his hand slid up my belly, and I felt tingles shoot down my legs.

Holy, holy, shit, shit, shit.

I sank my teeth into my lip to stop from groaning as pure electricity raced from everywhere in my body, with pinpoint accuracy, straight between my legs.

I tried again.

"I have a headache."

His hand went up my shirt and stopped just under my breast, his knuckles brushing along the swell of the underside.

"Probably tension. Don't worry, I know how to ease tension."

I bet he did.

I gave it one last shot.

"My face hurts."

I felt his tongue right behind my ear before he said, "I can take your mind off that."

"Lee—"

His hand splayed on my midriff and his weight and thigh went away. He pushed me on my back and leaned over me.

"Give me one good reason not to do this," he demanded, looking me straight in the eye.

His hair was sexy wild again. His face was both soft and hard. Soft with whatever it was I'd seen the last couple of days whenever he looked at me, hard with determination and desire.

In the face of that, without my morning coffee, I had difficulty answering.

"That's what I thought." His head started to come down when the phone rang.

"Are you gonna answer that?" I asked against his lips. His arms were going around me, pulling me to him.

"Fuck no."

He kissed me and I melted into him, immediately, happily, the fight simply just went out of me. He was that fine of a kisser.

So be it. I was finally going to make love with Liam Nightingale.

My whole body rejoiced.

He fell to his back and pulled me over him, his arms wrapped around me, holding me tight.

The phone rang again and then something clattered on the night table, but he ignored them as he dragged his lips along my jaw to my ear.

I shivered.

One of his hands slid over my ass while the other one held tight at my waist.

"I love your ass," he murmured in my ear. "I've always loved your ass."

His words shivered through me. I had no idea he loved my ass. The very thought thrilled me to the core. So much so, I kissed him for all I was worth.

I heard him groan under my kiss and that thrilled me too.

The phone was ringing again and the thing on the night table vibrated and clattered. Lee's hand was in my underwear and my hand was at his belly, exploring his washboard abs on a downward descent.

Then the door buzzer went, three quick buzzes and then a longer one.

Lee's hand stilled.

"*Fuck!*" he clipped from behind clenched teeth.

"What?"

He flipped me on my back as if I weighed no more than a sack of feathers and gave me a quick kiss.

"Don't fucking move," he warned and angled out of bed.

He grabbed a pair of jeans before he walked to the door, and I watched him go, frozen solid and fascinated by my first, unadulterated view of his perfect, naked body, including the particularly generous gift with which God had chosen fit to endow him.

At the sight and the realization that I was sleeping next to a naked Liam Nightingale, I'm not embarrassed to admit, I think I had a mini-orgasm.

I heard voices. I tried to get my body back under my control (and failed), but then in mere moments Lee came back into the room.

He walked straight to the bed and hauled me out. I slammed against him and he kissed me, hard and deep, but unfortunately not long.

"I have to go," he told me.

I wanted to scream, "*No!*" I was beginning to get *seriously* hot and bothered. He'd just admitted he loved my ass and always had. And I wanted to explore his God-given talents.

Instead, I just kept holding onto his shoulders because that was all I was capable of doing after his kiss.

He smiled.

Damn the man.

"I'll pick you up at Fortnum's as soon as I can. Promise me in the meantime you won't get into trouble."

I nodded my head.

He stared at me a second, then sighed. "You're lying."

"No I'm not," I replied.

"Just don't do anything too stupid."

As if!

He brushed his lips against mine. He let me go, headed straight to the bathroom, took a shower, dressed and left.

I called and asked Ally to come pick me up.

We had a long, busy day ahead of us if we were going to find Rosie.

Chapter 6
Kinky Friedman Zone

I decided to drag Jane into the search. In fact, I decided to drag *everyone* into the search.

We spent the morning waiting on coffee customers, the one person who actually wanted to buy a book, and making phone calls to everyone we knew, putting an APB out on both Rosie and Duke.

Regardless of her first shock at seeing the state of my face (I had a mini-shiner, not a full-blown black eye but a killer bruise on my cheekbone and yellow discoloring under the eye), Jane was excited. Jane thought this was fun. Jane had not been shot at or stunned-gunned (yet). She read romances, but she also read mysteries and detective novels. She was in the Kinky Friedman zone.

Jane headed off to Evergreen after the morning rush to put a note under Duke's door, telling him to call me the minute he got home, with a little PS to Dolores, inviting her to Girl's Night Out next Wednesday.

I had decided that the morning's weakness with Lee was temporary insanity and the aftereffects of sake. I was back to my decision that Lee and I weren't a good idea. Most especially if he could (and would) leave me hot and bothered for whatever scary shit he did for a living. I knew my control was slipping, but I had a new plan. All I had to do was not end up in his car, his company, his condo and especially his bed. That was the extent of my new plan.

The minute Jane left, I called Rosie's parents in North Dakota. He had them as next of kin on his employment records. In order not to freak them out, I pretended I was an old friend from high school, calling to catch up.

"Isn't that a funny coincidence?" Rosie's Mom said. "Two nice gentlemen came around yesterday saying the same thing!"

I glanced at Ally with my "uh-oh" face and she returned an eyebrow raise.

Either it was Lee or it was Terry Wilcox. One spelled disaster for me and the other spelled disaster for Rosie.

I gave my name and number, disconnected and told Ally.

"Probably Lee, he has ways," she decided.

Great.

"Tell me again why we're doing this?" she asked.

"Lee and I have a bet, the kind of bet I don't wanna lose." It wasn't a total lie. If Lee found Rosie, I would lose a lot: peace of mind, my grip on reality, things like that.

"So you bet Lee you'd find Rosie before he did and return a bag of diamonds to a bad guy?" Ally stared at me like I'd just had half my brain sucked out by brain-eaters.

"Yep."

"Girl," she drawled, "you're so gonna lose."

Lucky for me, Ally was into the underdog.

The door to Fortnum's burst open and Andrea Cocetti stormed in.

Andrea was at school with Ally and me and she was in our pack. Rumor had it that Andrea made out with Richie Sambora backstage after a Bon Jovi concert, but this had never been publicly confirmed or denied. Privately, though, she admitted to both Ally and I that it didn't happen, and thus, in secret, I reigned supreme with my Joe Perry encounter.

We'd stayed friends over the years but didn't see each other often. Andrea got married about twelve minutes after we graduated and now had four kids. Four kids, especially hellions like Andrea's, were a good reason not to see each other that often.

Now Andrea was Andrea Moran. She was pushing a stroller and dragging a child alongside her, while an older one followed, carrying a purse the size of an overnight bag and a diaper bag stuffed full to bursting. All this done with such practiced ease it was as if they were all merely accessories, including the children.

"You hooked up with Lee Nightingale!" she shrieked, causing the four customers who were calmly sitting around reading and enjoying their coffees in quiet surroundings to jump and stare. "Why didn't you tell me?"

Over the years, Andrea, too, had been drafted in some of my Lee Maneuvers. Andrea, too, was on Kitty Sue Nightingale's Christmas Card List and therefore in her address book, and therefore, no doubt, received a call. Perhaps, considering a day had passed, during the second wave.

"It only happened yesterday," Ally said.

Andrea ignored Ally. "Have you and Lee *done it* yet?" Her voice was still, really, really loud and the four customers stopped staring at Andrea and swiveled their heads to look at me.

I sighed then said, "We're taking it slow."

"*Slow!*" Her eyes moved from me to Ally and back to me. They looked like they were going to pop out of her head. "I... you..." She made a strangled sound, and I was starting to get concerned. "That isn't possible. Slow isn't possible. Lee Nightingale doesn't move slow. One second he's looking at you, the next second he's walking away and he has the little satin bow from your panties as a souvenir."

God, I hoped it wasn't *that* fast. That would be disappointing.

What was I thinking? It wasn't going to happen at all.

"That isn't true," Ally replied. "He'd take the little satin bow from your bra. Not all panties have them but most bras do. Sometimes they're rosettes. He'd take those as well."

I stared at her.

"You're joking," I breathed, really not wanting to be a little satin rosette bouncing around with hundreds of other little rosettes and bows in Lee's sock drawer.

Ally shrugged. "That's the rumor."

"Have you seen them? How many of them are there?" Andrea asked.

"I haven't seen them. It's just the rumor. I'm just keeping rumors straight. Maybe when Indy stops *taking it slow*, we'll find out."

I calmed Andrea down with an iced hazelnut decaf latte and promised her I'd call her the minute I *did it* with Lee. At this rate, post-coital, I'd be on the phone for a week.

Once Andrea was settled, I noticed a guy who'd arrived practically the minute the door opened. He'd already bought three espressos, which he sucked down in one swallow, and he'd been reading a sports magazine now for three and a half hours. He had dark blond hair a week or two past needing a cut, a killer bod, compact with muscles and not an ounce of fat. He was wearing a white t-shirt, jeans and running shoes.

If he wasn't my height, I didn't have an ugly bruise on my face and I didn't already have enough man problems, I would have been flirting with him ages ago. I didn't do men my height or shorter. They had to be taller than me if I was wearing heels. That was a rule.

I watched him for a few minutes, thinking that had to be a helluva magazine to require more than three hours of study.

Kristen Ashley

Lee told me he had a lot of men. Maybe men enough to go to North Dakota and sit in surveillance at Rosie's. Maybe men enough to hang out at Fortnum's and keep an eye on me.

Fucking Lee.

I sauntered over to the guy and stood in front of him until he looked up.

"Hey," I said.

"Hey," he replied and smiled. Definitely cute, and definitely not one of Terry Wilcox's steroid-ridden bad guys. The look of this dude said he would never hit a woman. Or at least I hoped so.

"You need another espresso?" I asked, giving my head a flirty tilt.

"Nah, thanks, I'm juiced up enough." He went back to reading.

Hmm. What did I do now? Never really had someone gone back to reading after I gave them the flirty tilt. Even if they weren't entirely interested, they gave more reaction to the flirty tilt. Maybe it was the mini-shiner.

"Good magazine?" I asked, and he looked up again.

"Yeah, the best."

I nodded and wished I'd worn a tank top or camisole that day so I could have leaned over and given him some of my power cleavage. My cleavage would have negated the effects of the shiner.

Instead, I was in jeans, a brown, hand-tooled belt with a big, silver buckle that had a design made out of what looked like miniature rope, brown cowboy boots and a chocolate-brown fitted tee that said "I do all my own stunts" across my boobs in yellow and red lettering.

"I'm not into sports," I told him and then sat on the arm of his chair, peering over the magazine to look at it. His entire body tensed. He turned his head to stare at me and I gave him a mega-watt smile. "Though I like going to games and stuff. Do you go to games?"

I pressed the side of my breast against his arm, still pretending to try and get a look at his magazine.

"What are you doing?" he asked.

I gave him an innocent look.

"Who, me?" Then I winked.

His face went pale and his cell phone rang. He stood up to get it out of his jeans, and he stood so fast he nearly knocked me off the arm of the chair.

I righted myself as he said, "Talk to me."

Then his eyes cut to me and he handed me the phone. I stared at it, astonished, then took it and put it to my ear.

"Leave Matt alone. He's just doin' his job," Lee said in my ear.

I was a little shocked at the call. I just wanted to fluster Matt a bit.

How did he…?

Fucking, *fucking* Lee.

"What's his job?" I asked, my blood pressure ratcheting up a notch.

"Making sure you don't get kidnapped or shot at."

"Or do anything stupid?"

"That too."

"How did you know I was screwing with him?"

"Trade secret."

"Tell me or I'm moving to Venezuela, losing myself in the jungle and shacking up with a local."

Silence, then a sigh.

"Fortnum's is wired and there are cameras. We did it last night."

"What? Why?"

"Remember the conversation we had in the kitchen yesterday?"

I remembered every encounter I'd had with Lee since I was five. I most vividly remembered those that occurred in the last twenty-four hours, and not just because they were the most recent.

"Yeah."

"You're on Terry Wilcox's radar. That's not good. I'm trying to keep you safe."

"By bugging my store?"

"That and anything else I can think of."

I stood staring at Matt, who was beginning to look amused.

"Do *you* remember the part of the conversation this morning where you said you'd be at Fortnum's whenever you were done?" I asked.

I got silence, but I didn't wait for a response. "Well, don't bother."

⌐⌐

Ally and I walked up to Rosie's house.

Matt followed us there and was now sitting in his SUV watching us, but we were ignoring him.

Jane had returned, no sign of Duke or Dolores, but she'd taken the opportunity to, what she called, "canvass the neighborhood". As Duke lived in log cabin surrounded by four acres of evergreen trees, I wondered what neighborhood she was talking about. Nevertheless, she scored some points by learning that the dirt lane to Duke's cabin had been a hive of activity in the last day or so, including a sighting yesterday morning that could have been Rosie. No sign of Duke's return before or after Rosie.

This meant that Rosie was looking for Duke, too, or had been yesterday morning. Whether he found him or not was anyone's guess.

We stood on Rosie's porch and knocked. Rosie lived alone, in a bungalow that needed serious renovation. I used to wonder how he could afford the bungalow. I didn't exactly pay him a fortune. It was on the out-out-outskirts of Platte Park, but close enough to the park and to Pearl Street to be a prime piece of real estate.

Now I knew how he could afford it.

No answer on the knock so we looked in the windows. I'd been to Rosie's dozens of times and it didn't look any different than normal.

"Be a shame to lose those primo pot plants. Do you think someone's taking care of those plants?" I asked.

Ally gave a shrug and then turned brightly to me. "I bet I know who'd know!"

"Who?"

"Lee."

I shoved her shoulder. "Smartass."

Deciding to take a page out of Jane's book, we "canvassed the neighborhood", knocking on doors and asking people if they knew or had seen Rosie.

No luck. Most people were away at work. The ones that were in barely knew him and no one had seen him. He didn't seem incredibly popular, nor did Ally and I for knocking on their doors.

Somewhere between getting stun-gunned and our current adventure, Ally had business cards made up with her and my names and numbers on them.

When she gave the first one out, I nearly choked.

"Where'd you get those?" I asked her as we walked away from the house.

"I called Brody. He made them up last night. Put them in my mailbox. Aren't they righteous?"

Dear Lord.

Brody was a friend of ours, had been since high school. He was a computer dweeb, worked at home programming PC games, barely ever left the house and he made a shed load of money. He also barely ever slept. He lived on energy drinks and cheese puffs and shopped for groceries exclusively at open-all-night convenience stores.

We headed to the emergency contact of Rosie's we hadn't yet gone after, the one whose beauty sleep I'd disturbed the day before. Rosie had recorded his name in the employee file as Kevin "The Kevster" James.

The Kevster answered the door wearing a pair of filthy jeans, a black Hendrix tee so faded it was now gray over a thermal long-john shirt (even though it was firmly eighty-six degrees). He had scraggly hair of an indescribable color and it was pretty clear we'd found out who was looking after Rosie's pot plants, with liberal sampling.

"Hey dudettes," was his greeting.

We introduced ourselves and he smiled. "Dig it! I heard about you guys." He turned to me. "Rosie talks about you all the time, thinks you are *the shit*. Best job he's ever had, man, workin' for a rock chick."

I felt the first rush of warmth toward Rosie I'd had in two days.

"Hey!" Kevin asked. "What happened to your eye?"

"Got hit in the face by a bad guy," I told him.

"Hope you kneed him in the nuts," The Kevster said, leaning forward to look at my eye.

"I bit him."

"That's good, too," he replied, though it was clear a knee to the nuts would have been the preferred form of retaliation. Unfortunately, by that time I was stun-gunned.

"We're looking for Rosie," I explained.

"Step in line, dudette. Everybody's looking for Rosie. Ehv-ree-bud-ee. Had dudes here all day yesterday asking about him."

"Who are these dudes? Do you know them?" Ally asked.

"Most of 'em, yeah. They want some product, if-you-know-what-I-mean." We nodded. We knew what he meant.

"Anyone else?" I said.

"Sure. First up a couple of guys I'm pretty certain were vice. You know, cool as shit, but still smelled like cop. Scared the bee-jee-zus out of me that they'd want to come in, but they weren't interested in me. Then two sets of dudes who need to switch pharmaceuticals or their muscles will explode, like The Hulk. Ka-pow!" He clapped and then jiggled his hands in front of his chest.

I looked at Ally then back to The Kevster. The first ones were likely Lee's men. The last ones were Wilcox's boys.

"Two sets?" I asked.

"Yeah, one set two guys came to the door, two sat in the car. Second set was only two."

I had a gut feeling, so I described the shooters who started this whole fiasco, and he nodded.

"Yeah, man, that's them. The set of four were steady, but the twosome were nervous-as-shit, looked like they needed sleep. Hey, I'm sorry I haven't been to any of your parties. Rosie says your parties *rock*. He says you have cashews and everything. I've never been to a party with cashews."

Ally handed him a card. "If you see him or hear anything, let one of us know."

"Wow! A Rock Chick Card. That's the shit, man. Does, like, Axl Rose have one of these?"

"Not yet," Ally said.

"Cool." The Kevster nodded. "You wanna come in? I'm just about to slip in *The Big Lebowski* and light up a spliff. Would be cool to watch The Dude with a couple of Rock Chicks."

I declined, though I wouldn't mind watching *The Big Lebowski*. It was one of my favorite movies. So much so, it was a friend test. If you didn't like The Dude and *Lebowski* you could be a friend, but would never be a good friend. Ever.

"No, thanks, gotta find Rosie."

"That's cool, come back whenever. Later."

We sat in the car and stared at The Kevster's house. Matt was on his cell in his SUV parked directly behind us.

"The second set are the shooters and it doesn't appear they're working together with Terry's goons."

"So you have a four-way competition with Lee," Ally said.

"Yeah, except I know what'll happen to Rosie if Lee or I find him. I don't know what'll happen if those guys find him."

Ally kept staring at the house. "You sure we should be doing this?"

I answered truthfully, "Hell no."

"We still gonna do this?"

"Doesn't have to be a we," I told her.

She turned to me. "Girl, the cards have both of our names on 'em. Let's motor."

Best friends like Ally don't grow on trees, let me tell you. She liked *The Big Lebowski* as much as I did, that's all I'm saying.

We went back to Tim's with Lee's man Matt following us. We parked two houses down and noticed crazy Grizzly sitting on his porch, the goggles still on top his head. Grizzly's house was directly across the street from Tim's and Grizzly looked like he spent a lot of time on the porch.

"We should talk to him. He looks like he keeps an eye on the neighborhood," Ally noted.

She was right. I knew she was right. I still didn't want to talk to him.

My cell phone rang and I looked at the display. It said, "Lee Calling". Shit.

I flipped it open.

"Hey."

"What are you doing?" he asked.

"Looking for Rosie," I answered.

"Jesus, Indy."

"He's *my* friend and he's *my* employee and *you* haven't been shot at and kidnapped."

"Leave it to me." He sounded kind of bossy.

"Not at the current price, no." I sounded kind of huffy.

"All right, then this is no cost."

I felt a wave of relief sweep through me, followed closely by a wave of despair.

I pushed down the despair.

"Good, so I don't have to sleep with you?"

Ally's eyebrows went up.

"No, you're gonna sleep with me, just not as payment for finding Rosie."

"Lee—"

"Go back to Fortnum's. I'll be at your house at seven to take you to dinner."

I harrumphed.

Then I asked, mainly out of curiosity, because there was *no way* I was going to dinner with Lee. That might mean inebriation, or kissing, or something else that would take my mind off my plan and that couldn't happen, "Where're we going?"

"Barolo Grill."

For a second, I forgot about my vow to avoid all things Lee.

"Oh. My. God! How did you know? I love it there!"

"Honey, you demand your family birthday dinners are there every year. It's not hard to figure out you love it."

Then he disconnected.

Something about his calling me "honey" and processing my desired birthday destination made my stomach flip over in a happy way.

"What's this about not sleeping with Lee?" Ally asked.

I stared at Grizzly then looked in my rearview mirror. Matt was taking a call and shaking his head.

"You know how I'm saying Lee and I are taking it slow?"

"Yeah."

"Well, I'm taking it slow. Lee wants things to go a little faster."

"I see." Ally was grinning.

"What's with the grin?" I demanded.

"Girl, you are so *not* gonna go slow."

Great.

We got out of the car and walked up to Grizzly's house. Ally forged ahead without a care in the world. I drug my heels and looked back at Matt. He'd gotten out of his SUV, pulled a handgun out of the back waistband of his jeans and tucked it in full view at the hipbone in the front. He leaned against his SUV and crossed his arms.

"They come back, sportin' a bodyguard," Grizzly said by way of greeting, not looking at us, but looking at Matt. "So now, I suppose you want me to think you're serious. Especially now with you and a shiner. Jeez. You knee him in the nuts?"

"How do you know it was a him?" I asked.

"Girls don't go for the cheekbones," he answered.

"Oh." I didn't know that.

"Did you?" Grizzly persisted.

"What?"

"Knee him in the nuts?"

"I bit him."

"Bit him!" He threw his head back and laughed. "Next time, go for the gonads."

"Good advice," I said.

He looked at Matt. "Let me guess, trainee PIs."

"No," I said.

Grizzly swung his big head to me. "Bounty hunters?"

"Nope."

"Not cops," he said with derision.

"Un-unh."

"Feds?" This was said with incredulity.

"I own a bookstore."

Grizzly didn't answer. Grizzly was staring at me as if a second head decided to sprout out of my neck at that moment.

"I'm a bartender and back up barista," Ally put in.

Grizzly still didn't answer. I noticed he had a cat in his lap and was stroking it. Two more cats sat on the cement railings of his porch and another one was curled up on his welcome mat, a welcome mat that had kitty-cat footprints printed on it.

"You like cats?" I asked.

"Who doesn't like cats?" Grizzly returned.

"I like cats," I assured him, and it was no lie, but I would have said it anyway because he also had a shotgun sitting across his lap.

"Me too," Ally said.

Grizzly looked at Matt then back to us. "Who's the guy?"

"Just ignore him, we are," I told him.

Grizzly shrugged as if it was all the same to him, then said, "Good thing you did for Mr. Kumar. He has it rough. Told me you were the biggest score he had all day with your cupcakes."

I looked down the street to the corner store. Mr. Kumar was standing outside it waving at us.

We waved back.

"We gotta take care of the little guy, you know? Franchises are takin' over the fuckin' world. In ten years this great nation is gonna be wall-to-wall franchise and every mom and pop shop is gonna be out of business. The franchise was the beginnin' of the fuckin' end for America. That, and being able to turn on red. It's red, man, don't turn on red. Fuckin' Nixon."

I wasn't sure what Nixon had to do with franchises and traffic lights, but I wasn't going to disagree with a guy who had a shotgun on his lap and weird goggles on his head.

"We're looking for a friend of Tim Shubert's. Tim lives across the road."

"I know Tim. I know who you're lookin' for too. Mr. Kumar told me. Tim's had lots of visitors the last couple of days. Seen him before," he nodded at Matt then looked to us, "seen you before, too."

"His friend's name is Rosie, little wiry guy, dirty blond hair?" Ally put in.

"The Coffee Man?" he asked then didn't wait for an answer. "Yeah, Tim brings back coffees for me. That guy is a genius."

"Well, Rosie is *my* coffee man, he works at my bookstore." I told him.

"No shit?"

"No shit," I confirmed.

"That's a great bookstore. Used to be you could read all day and not be disturbed. The old lady was cool," he noted. "It still like that?"

"That old lady was my Gram. She left me the store when she died, I just added coffee," I replied.

"You thinkin' of franchisin'?"

"No way." I threw up my hands for emphasis, just in case he had any doubts to my sincerity.

He nodded. "Then you're the little guy too. I'd come to support you, 'cause I read a lot, but I don't leave this block. Need to keep my eye on things."

"Sure," I agreed.

This guy was nuts, but I liked him anyway.

Ally gave him our card and he put his hand in his shirt pocket and gave Ally one in return.

All it said was, "Tex, Cat Sitter", and had his number.

"You have a cat and go on vacation, you know who to call. Though, I warn you, I do both dry and wet food. I'm not into doin' just wet or just dry. They need a treat, but they need to keep their teeth clean. It's important."

We nodded our agreement and then jogged down to see Mr. Kumar.

"Me and Tex have been looking for your Rosie, but we haven't found him," he assured us when we got to the door.

"Thanks Mr. Kumar," I said.

"No Tim, either. Now I'm worried and I think Tex is getting worried, too. Lots of people coming to knock on Tim's door. He's never been this popular."

"Rosie had a following. He makes good coffee and people miss him," I told him.

"I can see this," Mr. Kumar said.

I bought milk, corn chips, two diet pops and all the ingredients for the macaroni salad and brownies I needed to make for Dad's barbeque. This cost me twice as much as it would if I'd just gone to King Soopers, but Tex was right, we had to watch out for the little guy, especially me, as I, too, was a little guy.

Mr. Kumar's eyes filled up with tears as I brought all my stuff the counter.

"You are an angel from heaven," he breathed.

Chapter 7
B and E Darlin'

Ally and I went to my house and unloaded the groceries, then back to Fortnum's, where we sent Jane home and worked the last couple of hours before shutting down at six.

Ally took her car and I walked the two blocks home, Matt following me at a crawl.

On the walk home, I formed a plan. Rosie couldn't go up in a puff of smoke and he wasn't smart enough to hide so well. If Lee hadn't found him, then something was up. If he got the diamonds and went to San Salvador, then where was Duke?

Unless something had happened to Rosie *and* Duke (which I hoped it had not), or Rosie had gone off looking for Duke (which would be stupid therefore not unheard of), then Rosie had to be hanging out, waiting for Duke. If he was camping out near Duke's house, waiting, then there would have been a forest fire by now. I didn't imagine Rosie paid a lot of attention to fire safety.

Rosie was a bit of a loner. He came to parties and went to concerts only when asked and without an entourage. I was certain Tim and The Kevster were his only friends.

Except me.

I boiled all these things down as best I could, considering I was not a spy, a detective or a criminal mastermind.

What I came up with was that Rosie had to be somewhere close. He had to be taking advantage of a friend's kindness. And, to my mind, since he wasn't with The Kevster and Tim had also disappeared, then Rosie and Tim were holed up somewhere. Maybe at Tim's house, in the basement, with copious amounts of cheese puffs, coming out only when the coast was clear or to bake a frozen pizza.

Or even if they'd stayed there for a while and then cleared out, there may be evidence or a clue to where they went.

I needed to establish a pattern of Rosie's movements. His car wasn't at his house and he'd been to Duke's yesterday morning. These were the only things I knew.

I decided I needed to search Tim's house for clues. We were coming up with a big fat zero everywhere we went and I might as well.

Since it was illegal, first, I didn't want Ally involved, and second, I didn't want to do it in broad daylight.

I sent Matt a jaunty wave, then I blew him a kiss for good measure before I went in the front of my house and closed the door behind me.

I stood there in happy oblivion at being home for the first time in two days.

I loved my duplex. Gram had died six years ago and it had taken me that long to make the place, which had been stuffed full of all her and Gramps' crap (and there was a lot of it), my own.

The living room and dining room were one huge room, though it looked like at one time it had been two. The kitchen was in the back, obviously added on sometime after the house was originally built.

I'd painted everything a soft peach. I had chartreuse arm chairs and an electric blue sofa with clean lines, and a kickass dining room table that could fold out to seat twelve people, though in a little bit of a crush. All of this gave off a feel of light, airy, modern and uncluttered. The floors were new hardwood and gleaming and I wanted to throw myself on them and kiss them.

Instead, I ran to the phone and grabbed it. Lee would be at my place soon and I didn't have a lot of time. I was sacrificing Barolo Grill for this, not to mention what was to be my first-ever "date" with Lee. If I didn't hurry, I'd lose control and give in, give up and go with Lee.

Then something occurred to me and I put the phone down and stared at it.

If Lee and his boys could disable the alarm, get into my store, wire it, install cameras and re-enable the alarm, then they could bug my phones too.

Crap.

I looked out the window and saw Matt sitting in his SUV. He wasn't leaving.

Crap again.

Maybe I was being paranoid, but I wasn't going to take any chances.

I ran upstairs. Two bedrooms separated by a bath, my bedroom in back had a door to a balcony that was half the roof of my kitchen, half overhanging my brick paved backyard. The front room was the TV room and where I kept my desk.

I wrote a note for Lee and ran downstairs and put it on the ottoman that sat between my sofa and chairs and served as a coffee table.

The note said, "Something came up. Rain check?"

I had no idea if he'd come into my house, but if he did, he'd see it. If he didn't, I wasn't going to put the note on the door for Matt to see it now. Lee would just have to think he was stood up. I'd explain later or find a believable lie.

I ran back upstairs, went out to the balcony and jumped the small railing to my neighbor's balcony and then banged on their outside bedroom door.

Tod and Stevie lived next door. They were both flight attendants. They had a Chow dog named Chowleena who gave more attitude than either Tod or Stevie, and as Tod was the top drag queen in Denver, this meant Chowleena threw a lot of 'tude. I watched Chowleena when they were both on flights and I loved that dog. I understood attitude, admired it, respected it and encouraged it. Her two Dads were of her ilk. Stevie made Eggs Benedict from scratch and always smiled and kissed your cheek when he saw you. Tod could lip sync to "Time and Tide" like nobody's business, could make me laugh so hard tears rolled down my cheeks and we shared the same dress size. They kept the yard tidy and were quiet. They were the best neighbors ever.

Tod opened the door and stared at me.

"Girlie, what in *the* hell are you doing? And what happened to your face?"

I pushed into their bedroom, shut the door behind me and ran it down for him.

I told him about the shooting, diamonds, coffee guy, stun-gunning, kidnapping, Lee's sex extortion plans, the love of my life business, and even Tex with the goggles. I explained I needed to hang out at their house until Lee came and went or I'd likely be charmed out of my panties and have my heart broken by seven o'clock Monday morning.

Tod blinked.

Then he said, as he linked arms with me and walked me out of his room, "Stevie's barbequing chops. I'm sure we have extra."

They always had extra and not much fazed Tod. We'd been living next to each other for years. He was used to my escapades, not to mention he was a drag queen. I'd have to add murder and perhaps an international incident involving royalty to faze Tod.

⌇⌇

At eleven o'clock, I jumped the railing back to my house.

Stevie had interrupted our Yahtzee marathon, played nosy neighbor and saw Lee come and go. Somehow, Lee had gone into my house, opened the door with what Stevie said appeared to be a key and left with the note in his hand.

"Uh-oh, gorgeous hunk is *un*happy," Stevie said.

My stomach lurched.

I decided I'd worry about that later.

While Stevie was still looking out the window, he asked, "Tell me again *why* you don't want him in your panties?"

Jeez.

For my evening's activities, I pulled my hair back at my nape in a ponytail and put on a black turtleneck, black jeans, black cowboy boots and my black belt with the tiny rhinestones in the buckle because if I was gonna get arrested, I was gonna go in looking good, regardless of my shiner.

I grabbed my bag and keys and jumped the railing again. In an effort to avoid a tail, I made a deal to trade car keys with Stevie and Tod for the night, so I took off in their CR-V.

The whole way I checked for a tail, spending more time looking in my mirrors than at the road. I was looking for any car that might be following me, but looking especially for Lee's Crossfire, a motorcycle that looked like it was being driven by an unhappy hunk or an SUV. Since nearly every car in Denver was an SUV, I was panicked throughout the drive to Tim's, but I couldn't see anyone following me.

By the time I turned down Tim's block, no one was behind me, not for blocks.

I didn't waste any time. I wanted to be in and out of there as fast as I could. I had no idea what I'd find, but I hoped it would be Rosie hiding in the basement and this whole mess would be over.

I got out of the car and walked right up to the house.

No lights on at Tim's, no lights on at the neighbors. It was nearing midnight, and even though the next day was a Saturday it seemed like no one was keeping a late night.

I knocked on the door and waited for an answer. I listened for any sound at all to come from the house.

Nothing.

"It's Indy Savage. If Rosie's in there, I'm just here to help. I swear," I whispered as loud as I dared.

Still nothing.

I tried the door and it was locked.

I did the same with the backdoor and then I went around the house, trying to look in the windows and checking to see if they'd slide up. I couldn't see much, and every single window was either painted shut or locked.

"*Fuck!*" I hissed under my breath, standing next to a window at the east side of the house.

Then something settled on my shoulder.

I gave a little screech and whirled, not knowing who I'd see. It could be Lee, Wilcox's goons, the shooters, a police officer or Dracula.

Instead, it was Tex standing there with the goggles no longer on the top of his head, but over his eyes.

He put his finger to his lips then, a scant second later, put his fist through the window.

I stared at the window then back at Tex then back at the window.

"What are you doing?" I whispered.

"B and E, darlin'," he answered casually. He was wearing a flannel shirt and work gloves and pushing all the glass away from the window pane.

"You can't break someone's window! We should have tried to jimmy one open."

"Quit your squawkin' and get in there." Then he grabbed me by the waist, picked me up and threw me through the window like I weighed no more than a bag of flour.

"Careful of the glass," he called.

Too late. I'd landed on the glass and rolled away, hoping nothing cut me, but I was too wired to feel a thing. I got to my feet and looked around in the darkness a little hysterically. Something smelled seriously funky and not in a good way.

Tex heaved himself in behind me and I spun around to glare at his hulking shadow.

"Are you crazy?" I asked a crazy man. "You just threw me through a window."

"You looked like you were gettin' second thoughts."

"It's dark, you can't *see* me."

He tapped his goggles. "Night vision."

Shit.

Shit, shit, *shit*.

"Don't like that smell," Tex remarked, and I could hear him sniffing the air because I couldn't see a thing. "That's not a good smell."

He was right, it was a terrible smell.

"You stay here. I'll have a look around." Then I saw his shadow move off.

"Don't leave me here!"

"Don't be such a girl," he returned, already somewhere else in the house, and I found it odd such a big man could walk on such quiet feet. He barely made a sound.

I stood in the dark, thinking we'd probably made an awful lot of noise breaking the window, and I listened for the sirens that would mean my doom. Dad would be seriously hacked off and Malcolm would make sure Kitty Sue didn't invite me to the Fourth of July barbeque. I didn't even want to think what Hank would say.

Then I wondered if one of the other teams in the Rosie Hunt would have the same idea and come, say tonight, say at that exact time. Say that team was the shooters, say it was the shooters with guns drawn.

"Tex, where are you?" I whispered. Loudly.

I started to make my way through the shadowy rooms, and the further I got into the house the funkier the smell was.

"You don't wanna come in here." I heard Tex say when it seemed I'd hit ground zero on the smell.

I put my hand over my nose and mouth. "What is it?"

His shadow was still as a statue and the way he was holding himself scared me.

"Is it Rosie?" I asked, looking around the dark room, which I could tell was a kitchen but not much else.

Tex moved. He took off the goggles and then settled them on my face. My hand fell away from my mouth and everything went green. I could see much better, but unfortunately this included the body of a man, his butt on the floor, back to the cupboards, legs splayed out in front. He had dark stains on his face, the origin of which came from what appeared to be a hole in his forehead.

"Oh. My. God," I breathed and then everything went bright. So bright it blinded me and I cried out in surprise.

A hand came over my mouth and the goggles were torn from my head.

"Keep quiet, for fuck's sake."

It was Lee. He'd turned on the kitchen light, and when he was certain I wouldn't yell again he took his hand from my mouth.

I turned and looked at him and he was staring down at the body, his face tight.

"What are you doing here?" I asked.

"Yeah? What're we? Havin' a party?" Tex asked.

Lee turned cold eyes to Tex and Tex said no more.

Then Lee turned to me.

"I followed you."

"No one followed me. I kept checking."

He gave me a look.

Fucking Lee.

"You with her?" Tex ventured.

"Yeah," Lee answered.

I wanted to scream I was not *with* Lee and he was not *with* me, but the situation kept my mouth shut. Instead, I turned back to the body and there he was, not in the eerie green night vision, but lit up and easy to see. And I could see not only him, but all the blood and gunk that had come out of the back of his head to splatter all over the kitchen wall.

Not Rosie.

It was disgusting. I'd never seen anything so foul. It was a nasty, awful, horrible, smelly, sad death.

I gulped, almost sure I was going to hurl. Lee heard it, grabbed my arm and pulled me through the house and out the backdoor.

"Lean over. Deep breaths," he ordered.

We were standing in the backyard and he pressed his hand to the back of my neck to force me over. I put my hands on my knees and gulped deep breaths of fresh air, leaving the Death Air behind. With some effort, I fought back the nausea and stood up straight.

Tex had followed us out.

"Was that Tim?" I asked Tex.

"Yep."

"Ohmigod."

"Please tell me you didn't touch anything in there," Lee said to me.

I shook my head.

"Please tell me you didn't break that window," Lee went on.

"I did the breakin' *and* the enterin' for both of us. After I did the breakin', I threw her through the window," Tex offered this information and Lee's eyes cut to Tex.

"I'm sorry?" Lee asked and his voice was scary.

Tex seemed not to notice it. "She was gettin' second thoughts."

Lee stared at Tex for a beat.

"Jesus," he muttered then he pointed at me. "Stay here. Don't move." His finger moved to Tex. "You come with me."

Lee tossed the goggles to Tex and they re-entered the house. I was a little surprised that Tex followed Lee's command, but then again, Lee was using that brook no argument tone again.

I sat down on the grass, too freaked out to stand any longer, and I put my forehead on my knees.

I feared this did *not* bode well for Rosie, and I feared more that this did not bode well for Duke.

They came back out. Lee closed the door, fiddled with the handle and then walked toward me, removing surgical gloves.

"No Rosie," he told me.

"Thank God," I said on a whoosh and didn't realize I was holding my breath.

He put a hand on my upper arm and hauled me up.

"I'm callin' Hank in on this one," he announced.

My eyes nearly popped out of my head. "You can't! He's gonna freak that I'm here!"

"You weren't here. Tex was here. Tex, the concerned neighbor," Lee replied.

"That's me. Everyone around here knows I'm a concerned neighbor. Gotta go make a call." Tex put his big hand on top of my head. "You did good, for a girl. Didn't puke or nothin'."

"Thanks Tex," I said on a shaky smile, not quite sure that was a compliment, but willing to accept it as one all the same.

Tex ambled off and Lee dragged me to a Mercedes sedan. He'd hit a button on his cell phone and was waiting for it to ring through.

"Lee…" I said.

He pulled me to a stop at the passenger side, opened the door and pushed me in. He stood in the opening of the door while his call was picked up. I sat in the car, too freaked out by the dead body to fume at him pushing me around.

"Hank, a call's gonna come into 911 soon. I need to talk to you about it." Pause. "Yeah." Then he disconnected.

Lee slammed my door and got in on the driver's side of the car.

I turned to him. "I have a car here. It's my neighbor's. My bag's in there. I have to—"

Lee held up a hand and I stopped talking.

"What you have to do is keep your mouth shut until we get back to the condo so I can take that time to talk myself out of strangling you."

Yikes.

I felt it prudent to do as he requested. I'd had a rough couple of days. I didn't want it to end in strangulation. And anyway, Lee was such a badass, even if it didn't end in strangulation he might come up with some more creative punishment.

Lee didn't say word one until we were in his condo. He dragged me by the arm into the bedroom, pulled out a drawer and threw me a t-shirt.

"Get ready for bed," he said to me.

I immediately saw red.

It was not surprising. I wasn't one of his boys. I wasn't one of the troops. I wasn't a child. He couldn't tell me what to do. I'd had a tough night. I'd seen a dead body, for goodness sake!

I was willing to give him some leeway with his being pushy when I was in the vicinity of said dead body, but this was too much.

"No!" I snapped. "Stop telling me what to do. I want to go home. I want to sleep in my own bed. I want—"

I didn't say any more because Lee came at me. I backed up and slammed against the wall. Lee's body came up against mine and he bent his face so he was nose-to-nose with me.

"You want your Dad to see crime scene photos of you, dead, sitting on that sweet ass of yours with your brains splattered against the wall?"

Yikes.

My stomach lurched and my legs went weak.

"No."

"Then this ends tonight."

I stared at him.

"Indy, by God, if you don't promise me—"

"Of course it ends tonight! I just saw a dead body! You can't think I'm that stupid."

His face said he thought I was that stupid.

"Lee! Rosie's my friend. He's out there, somewhere. And they're not only looking for him, they're looking for Duke. And now they're killing people."

"I'll find him and I'll find Duke."

We looked at each other for what seemed like days. His brown eyes were hard and angry. I tried to tell myself that all his anger wasn't directed at me, but I was having trouble believing it.

My gaze slid away. "I couldn't have known I was going to find that to-night," I whispered.

"I told you these were bad guys."

My gaze slid back.

"What kind of job do you do that you know about this shit?"

He shook his head. He'd moved back an inch so we weren't nose-to-nose anymore, but he was still close.

"Un-unh, you aren't gonna make this about me."

I moved out from between him and the wall and I stomped to the bathroom on my favorite parting line.

"Whatever."

I brushed my teeth with what now seemed like my toothbrush, which was cozily resting next to Lee's.

I tried not to think of my day's plan of not ending up in Lee's car, company, condo or bed, all of which I'd failed to do. I tried not to think of Tim Shubert, dead and smelly and left to rot in his house while his neighbors worried about him. I tried not to think of Rosie or Duke in a similar position, either now or later. I tried not to think of Tod and Stevie's car, which I had left outside a crime scene. I tried not to think of what a fuck up I was, or how Lee could move around in these situations so casually without blinking an eye.

I got undressed and put his t-shirt on. It was huge on me and had a Night Stalkers insignia emblazoned across the chest. Too big. I was going to get tangled up in it the way I slept but I wasn't going to tell Lee that.

Plus, it was a fucking cool shirt.

I walked into the bedroom, about to dump my clothes on my bag I'd left on the floor, when I saw my bag was missing.

"Where's my bag?" I asked Lee as he walked into the room, coming toward me. I dumped my clothes on an armchair.

"Judy unpacked you," Lee replied, still coming toward me. He grabbed my wrist and walked me toward the bed.

"Judy?" I asked, not paying much attention because I was thinking of being unpacked, my clothes hanging next to Lee's. My undies in a drawer. My toothbrush next to his. My body in his bed. How did this happen so fast? It had only been two days, for God's sake! Whatever happened to taking it slow?

"My housekeeper," he answered.

"You have a housekeeper?" I was shocked he had a housekeeper. I was shocked that I was kind of living with a man who I didn't know had a housekeeper. I was shocked that I was kind of living with a man, period, dot, the end, much less that man being Lee.

He pushed me gently and I fell back on the bed and finally realized where I was and what he was doing.

"Lee—"

Then he moved fast. He pulled my wrist over my head, leaned into me, I heard a snap and ratchet, then I heard another snap and ratchet.

Then I was handcuffed to his bed.

"What the hell!" I yelled.

I was on my back, my left arm over my head and cuffed to one of the slats in the headboard of Lee's mission style bed. Lee was leaning over me.

"I'm goin' out and I'm makin' sure you don't do anything stupid."

"You can't leave me handcuffed to your bed! What if there's a fire, a break in?"

He shook his head, pushed away from me and got off the bed.

"I won't do anything stupid," I told him, my voice just this side of seriously pissed-off, saying clearly that the first stupid thing I'd do when he let me go was kill him.

He came back, leaned in and kissed my forehead. "I know."

Then he walked across the room, turned off the light and was gone.

Fucking, *fucking* Lee.

Normally, I could sleep just about anywhere. Crash on someone's couch, in a double bed with four other people (mainly because my activity cleared the bed), in the back of a van.

I was learning I had a great many life skills I had not known I possessed, such as running away when people were shooting at me, holding my own when I'd been kidnapped and not throwing up when I found a dead body.

Unfortunately, those new life skills did not include being able to sleep while I was cuffed to Liam Nightingale's bed.

I found a somewhat comfortable position and tried to sleep, but I was spitting mad, and every time I closed my eyes all I could see was Tim and his brains that were no longer contained in his body.

What seemed like hours later, I heard the door open and my body tensed. I kept myself perfectly still and listened as someone walked through the house. They didn't turn on any lights and they were quiet as a cat, the only noise a barely distinct rustling. Then that someone walked into the bedroom. I heard something fall on the chair. The whisper of movement of the sheets, then hands at my wrist. The smell of leather, spice and tobacco, and when I was released from the headboard, I knew it was Lee.

No sooner was I released than I rolled toward the other side of the bed and freedom.

I got a roll and a half in before an arm hooked around my waist and I was stopped.

"Where are you going?"

"I'm getting a taxi home," I said between clenched teeth.

"No."

"Then, I'm sleeping on the couch."

"No."

Great. We were going to go through this rigmarole again.

"I'm sleeping on the other side of the bed."

"No."

"You're an asshole."

"Maybe."

Shit.

Lee settled in and tucked my back to his front, his arm wrapped around my waist.

I laid there wondering if I should flip over, knee him in the 'nads and take off.

Then, for some reason, the vision of Tim floated into my head and my body started trembling, like, a lot. Full-on human earthquake.

"Shit," I whispered, and Lee turned me to facing him and wrapped both his arms around me, tight.

I pressed into his warmth and tried not to cry.

"Did you know him?" Lee asked softly.

"No." My voice sounded shaky, even on that one word. I took in a big, broken breath. "Though I think he'd come into the store every once in a while." I took another breath to control the threatening tears. "It's an ugly way to go. What are his parents gonna think?"

Lee started stroking my back and he didn't answer, likely because he had no idea what Tim's parents would think and didn't want to dwell on it.

Lee started to play with my hair and I pressed my face into his neck. His body was hard and warm and I could hear his steady breathing. His hand at my hair relaxed me and his arm around my waist made me feel safe.

After a while, I fell asleep.

Chapter 8

He Doesn't Like Nixon Much

I woke up in Lee's bed, but this time, no Lee.

I didn't have enough mental capacity to wonder where he was and certainly not enough to process my sense of disappointment. I told myself there should be no disappointment at the absence of a man who would handcuff me to his bed against my will, so I shoved it aside.

It was twenty past six, and I had decided, when I had all that time to think when I was handcuffed to the bed, that Fortnum's was going to close for the weekend.

Sometimes it was good being the boss.

Truth was, working there wasn't tough. There were four of us, five when Ally was around, which was most of the time. We were open seven thirty to six on weekdays, eight thirty to six on Saturdays and ten to four on Sundays. Outside of the morning rush, most of that time was spent hanging around. We all came and went when we pleased.

With two staff down, it was beginning to seem like work. With me and Ally gallivanting across town looking for Rosie, Jane was taking the burden.

I didn't make shifts or assign hours. Everyone worked whenever they wanted, which was pretty much seven days a week, give or take a couple hours here or there to run errands, go to lunch with a friend, go shopping at Cherry Creek Mall, come in late if you were sleeping it off, leave early whenever or to tie one on at Lincoln's Road House, the local biker bar. People took days off whenever they wanted and no one did more than the others. Gram had set the precedent. We all pitched in, and somehow it worked.

I needed a break after the last couple of days, and I was sure Ally and Jane needed one, too. Hopefully, by Monday, now that the police were involved, this would be sorted and all would be back to normal. That was to say, normal with Duke back, and normal as it would ever be.

Rosie, I knew after last night, was likely never coming back.

I just hoped whatever he did in not coming back, he did it breathing.

This made me sad, but I pushed that thought aside too.

I got up, staggered to the bathroom and brushed my teeth. I was running on empty, not just my morning caffeine jolt, but also the fact that I'd had a lot less sleep than I usually required. I stared in the mirror noting the bruising on my face was subsiding, but not by much, or perhaps the scary dark circles under my eyes were running interference for the bruising.

I walked out of the bedroom to make coffee and stopped dead, staring at the Command Center door, which was open.

I expected that Lee was gone. Off for a run, off to command mercenary troops in a drug war in Peru, off to put tracking devices on my car.

Instead, I heard him talking on the phone like it was an everyday room and not the nerve center for an international commando cartel.

Normally, curiosity would have forced me to walk right in or at least eavesdrop on his conversation.

Instead, I went straight to the coffeepot.

Priorities.

The pot was almost full.

I emitted a sigh of delight.

I filled a cup, splashed in the milk and walked it to the balcony off the living room, sipping my coffee and staring at the beauty of the Front Range.

Lee had a killer view.

As the caffeine permeated, I allowed my foggy brain to plan my day.

I was going to call Jane and Ally and go put a note up at Fortnum's. I was going to go get Tod and Stevie's car, go home and make macaroni salad so it had time to ferment before the barbeque. Then I was going to go to bed until I had to wake up to make the brownies and get ready for the barbeque.

If I felt like it, I might lay out in the sun rather than sleeping in my bed.

That was going to be my day.

It sounded like a good day.

Two hands, undoubtedly connected to arms which connected to Lee's body, settled on the balcony railing on either side of me. I felt his warmth at my back.

I had a moment where I felt I should turn around, screaming like a banshee and scratching his eyes out for having the audacity to handcuff me to his bed.

Then I thought about how he held me while I trembled and played with my hair until I fell asleep and decided against it.

"Hey," I said as he moved my hair with his chin and kissed my neck.

"How're you feelin' this morning?" His voice sounded in my ear and tingles slid across my skin.

"Okay."

I realized I forgot to factor Lee in my plans for the day.

I didn't have time to perform any mental recalculations as he turned me around, took the coffee cup and put it on the teak table that was just within reach. Then his arms slid around me, I opened my mouth to say something, anything, and then he kissed me.

The tingles intensified by about one hundred percent and started to target specific zones.

After the kiss, his lips trailed along my cheek to my ear. I had my hands pressed against his chest and I said, perhaps stupidly and definitely shakily, "What are you doing?"

He answered, "Saying good morning."

He said, "good morning" really, really well. Far better than he said, "thank you".

Okay, I decided something had to give here.

All this playing around was all well and good (some of it *really* good). The thing was, I'd made a decision about keeping my distance from Lee a decade ago and I wasn't so sure I wanted to go back on that decision.

Well, if I was honest, I had to admit I wanted to, no doubt about it. It was Lee and I'd spent a lifetime wanting exactly this.

But there was a lot at stake here. What happened if it didn't work out? What happened if he got bored and moved on? It would change everything. I'd be devastated, but also there were relationships to consider, family and people that meant a great deal to both of us.

"Lee, we need to talk."

"Mm?" This was mumbled before his tongue ran from the skin at the hinge of my jaw, down the line of my neck.

"Lee!" My toes were curling, my nipples were hard.

This was getting serious.

"Talk," he said. "I'm listening."

He was *not* listening. His hands had gone up under my shirt and were sliding up my sides.

"We need to talk about what's happening between us."

His mouth came to mine again. "Okay, shoot."

Then he kissed me, this time serious tongue action, and I was forced to put my arms around his neck to remain standing.

When his mouth went away, one of his hands went to cup my ass and pull me closer and I could feel his God given talent pressing against my belly. Tingles shot down the insides of my thighs.

"I'm not sure about this," I told him, even though I was kind of sure and my body was definitely sure, and getting surer by the second.

"No?" he asked, his head coming up and he was looking at me. His brown eyes were melty-chocolate, and one look at them made me catch my breath.

The hand at my ass came up and in and then cupped my breast, the rough pad of his thumb sliding across my hardened nipple. I bit my lip as electricity shot straight from my nipple to my nether regions.

"That feels pretty sure," he said.

"That's not what I mean," I whispered.

"I see. You mean something else. I'll check there too." He grinned, his hand moving from my breast down my belly straight to...

"Lee!" My body jerked, half to get away from him and half in surprise, but I had nowhere to go except over the railing and to an icky death on the sidewalk fourteen stories below.

He smiled, full-fledged, causing my stomach to do a quick dip, and his hand detoured back to my ass. "Let's have this talk *after* I make love to you."

My stomach had lurched at the smile, my legs went even weaker at his hand at my ass and I knew I couldn't take much more. And somehow, don't ask me why, that made my eyes sting with tears.

Both his hands went to my ass and he lifted me up. I gave a small cry of surprise and my arms tightened around his neck as I threw my legs around his hips.

Holding me by the bottom, he turned and strode back into the condo. One hand left my ass and went into my hair and he tilted my head back with a soft yank, kissing me as he walked me to the couch. He put me down and came down right on top of me, his mouth still on mine.

I moved my head, and using the last shreds of my ragged control, tried one last time to talk. "We fuck this up, Lee, we fuck everything up. Ally, Hank, your folks, my Dad. Are you prepared for that?"

His body became still.

After a moment he slid a hand in the hair at either side of my head and held my face to look at him.

And when I did, it felt like a lead weight settled in my chest at what I saw.

Something significant had changed. Something significant *and* scary. He wasn't happy, the melty-chocolate look was gone and something hard had come into his face.

"You think I want a quick fuck?"

I shook my head and bit my lip. Honestly, I didn't know what he wanted, but at that precise moment, I wasn't going to say that.

"You think I'd touch you unless it meant something?"

Holy crap.

I held my breath thinking about what that might mean. My eyes widened and the tears stinging them began to threaten to fill them.

His hands moved from my face to my hips.

"Christ, Indy, there's more to me than this." He yanked my hips, putting them in brutal, intimate contact with his and the hardness between them.

He held me there for a minute and stared into my eyes.

Then he bit out, "Forget it."

He put his hands on the couch, pushed himself up and got off me.

"What?" I asked, dumbfounded, my body in temporary shock at the loss of the weight of his, my brain not caffeinated enough to think clearly.

He stared down at me, his face hard and blank. Just like it was when it closed down when Dad asked him if he hit me.

"Get dressed, I'll take you home."

I blinked.

"What?" I asked again.

He hauled me off the couch and set me on my jellied legs.

"I said, get dressed, pack your shit. I'll take you home."

I blinked again. Then I did it again.

Say what?

"Hang on a second..." I started.

He was walking away, muttering to himself. "I knew I shouldn't have started this. You're more trouble than you're worth."

Um, *say what?*

I narrowed my eyes at his back. "Excuse me?"

He was gone.

The tears were no longer threatening in my eyes. They'd filled them and they were flowing over. But instead of them being full of the confused emotions of a woman who was close to getting everything she ever wanted and was scared to death of it, they were tears of a pissed-off woman-on-the-edge who was close to murdering someone.

Emotional tears were unacceptable.

Pissed-off tears were perfectly fine, so I let them flow.

I stomped into the bedroom and started to tear through it. I pulled on a pair of jeans, my bra and my Def Leppard T-shirt, my black belt and boots from the night before. I found my handbag sitting on my clothes in the armchair, which Lee must have recovered for me last night.

He'd get no thanks from me for that act of thoughtfulness.

I shoved anything I found that was mine in my bag, rifling through drawers and the closet, making an utter mess along the way. I didn't care. I was way beyond caring about tidiness.

I went into the bathroom and got my face soap. He could keep the goddamn toothbrush. Lee was leaning against the doorjamb when I walked back into the room.

"Ready?" he asked, his face stony.

"Damn straight," I answered, stalking to my bag and pushing stuff into it, zipping it with a vicious tug. "You're a crazy man. You're nuts. You and Tex should form a club. After years and years, you think you can crook your finger and I'd come running, no questions asked. I just wanted to talk! I wasn't asking for an act of devotion akin to wrestling a tiger." Some of my stuff poked out of the bag and I jammed it in and carried on with my rant. "Getting me all hot and bothered, *twice*..." I stopped and held up two fingers at him as he stood in the doorway, then I went back to my bag, lugged it up and looped the strap over my shoulder. "Then walking off leaving me that way. *I'm* more trouble than *I'm* worth? Ha!"

I grabbed my handbag and stomped toward him with the intention of going right by him.

"Don't bother taking me home. I'll call a taxi. I'll call Ally. I'll call my Dad. No more favors from *you!*"

I had made it to him and said (maybe yelled) the last bit up on my toes and leaning into his face.

When I was done ranting, he stood in the doorway and I stood in front of him, too close for comfort. I was still crying and I was sure my face was red and wet with angry tears.

"Get out of my way," I demanded.

He didn't move.

"I said, *get out of my way!*" I shouted.

"Why are you crying?" he asked conversationally.

"Because you piss me off."

"You're crying because you're angry?"

"Seems like it. Now get out of my way."

Quick as a flash, he grabbed my purse and threw it across the room.

I watched it sail and land in the armchair again, then I turned back to him, eyes wide.

"What the—" I started.

He pulled the bag off my arm and also threw that across the room. It landed on the floor with a soft "phunf" a foot away from the armchair.

I watched it go and then turned back to him. Words escaped me so I just stared.

His hands came up to my face, his thumbs running along the tears on my cheeks.

"Stop crying," he demanded.

My mouth dropped open.

"You can't just tell me to stop crying," I informed him.

"How hot and bothered were you?" he asked.

That was the time to try my knee him in the balls maneuver, I was pretty much sure of it.

"Get out of my way." I jerked my face out of his hands and started to walk back to my bags.

He stopped me with a hand on my arm and swung me around.

"Quit it!" I yelled as he pulled me to him. His face was no longer blank and stony, it was soft again and I was pretty certain he was a raving lunatic.

"No. Now I'm gonna take you to bed and make love to you. Later, we're gonna go to your Dad's barbeque. After that, we'll talk."

I shook my head and tried to pull free. "Sorry, I have different plans for the day."

His arms slid around me. "Honey, it occurs to me from what you asked me earlier that you have the wrong impression about me. Today, I'm gonna show you who I am. Tonight, I'm gonna tell you what I want. Tomorrow, you can make up your mind."

I blinked at him.

"I've known you all my life," I reminded him.

"You have no fucking clue."

I stared for a beat, and fear, curiosity and elation shivered through me at the promise I saw in his face.

I shook my head. "I have to go to the bookstore, get Tod and Stevie's car, make macaroni salad."

"Matt returned your neighbor's car last night. Ally can go to the Fortnum's. King Soopers has macaroni salad."

"No."

One of his hands slid into my hair and pulled my head back and to the side, exposing my neck. His mouth, all of sudden, was there.

"Yes," he said against my neck while walking me back to the bed.

"Stop it, you're crazy! One second you tell me to pack my bags, the next second you're on me like white on rice."

The backs of my knees hit the bed and we both went down, him on top of me, his lips on mine. "Gorgeous, give me ten minutes and I'll be *in* you."

At that promise, and him calling me "gorgeous", an electric spasm went straight through my lower belly. He kissed me and that was it.

I'm a slut. I don't know what to say. Even with the emotional scene, I gave in.

To tell you the whole truth, I wanted him to show me who he was and tell me what he wanted, and I didn't want to wait another second to find out.

And then the buzzer went. Three quick blasts and then one long one.

Lee stopped kissing me and put his forehead on mine. "You have got to be *fucking* kidding me."

"What is it?" I asked.

"It's code, urgent, God damn it." He put his hands on either side of me, pushed up and started to walk away then turned back. "How hot and bothered are you now?"

"On a scale of one to ten?"

His eyes crinkled at the corners and he walked out of the room.

Fucking Lee.

⌐×⌐

I lay on the bed and stared at the ceiling thinking to myself, *what was that?*

My cell phone was ringing, so I rolled off the bed, grabbed my bag, sat in the chair and saw it was Andrea. Probably calling for a Lee and Indy Sex Update. Boy, was she going to be disappointed.

I answered the phone with, "No, we haven't done it yet."

"Uh-oh, I feel bad vibes," Andrea replied.

"We're on the phone, how can you feel bad vibes?" I asked.

"I've known you since you were twelve. I can *sense* bad vibes."

So I told her. About Lee, about his getting pissed-off and essentially kicking me out then changing his mind again and the whole, "who I am, what I want, you decide" speech.

Andrea was silent for a moment then she said, "Well, he's fighting his reputation. And that man has a *reputation*. Only boy worse than him was his best friend Eddie. It was like they were in a competition to see who was the worst rutting dawg out there. Can't be fun to be practically famous for fucking anything that breathes and being able to do so by expending the immense effort of just sending a smile their way. Then, later, you find yourself in a position where you're serious about a woman who's known you all your life and knows this fact *real* well and have to convince her you're serious."

Man, Andrea was a mother and she still had a mouth on her.

Still, it was true.

I sat down on the chair and I tried to ignore the fact that my stomach was clenched.

"Do you think he's serious?"

Andrea was silent for a second. "Are you being funny?"

"Funny 'ha ha' or the other kind of funny?" I asked.

"I can't believe…" Andrea started. "Girl, at Kitty Sue and Malcolm's New Year's Bash you were there with what's his name…"

Oh Lord, I didn't remember his name. "Um," I muttered. "Brad? Brett?"

"Whatever," Andrea cut in. "Anyway, when Lee wasn't looking at you with a look in his eyes that, let's face it, made every woman in the room breathe heavy, he was looking at Brad-Brett like he wanted to rip his head off."

"No way!"

"Way."

Holy shit.

"So yeah, I think he's serious," she went on. "And I can't imagine that Liam Nightingale is the kind of guy who appreciates the woman he's serious about questioning his seriousness when he's right in the middle of… you know."

Holy shit.

Holy, holy, shit, shit, shit.

"Anyway, call me when you actually get around to doing it. I want details."

Great.

Andrea disconnected and I flipped the phone shut. It rang again immediately.

It was Ally.

I took a deep breath, pretending everything was all right (which *it wasn't*) and answered, "What's up, chickie?"

"Girl, I've had half a dozen calls. Everyone's seen Rosie *and* Duke. We got leads coming out of our ears. We gotta roll."

I immediately got excited. I had to admit, I was kind of digging this super-sleuth stuff.

Then I remembered last night.

I let out a sigh.

"No can do. Tex, the cat sitter and me kinda broke into Tim's last night. Found him dead in his kitchen, and it wasn't pretty."

Ally was silent for a beat and then she said, "You went without me? You went with the *crazy cat sitter?*"

"I was breaking and entering! Tex showed up in the middle of it. We found Tim dead, Ally. Trust me, be glad you weren't there. This is over. Lee's turned it over to Hank."

"What about your bet?" Ally asked.

I thought about Lee's plans for the day. I thought about what Andrea said.

"I think I lost."

Truthfully, I wasn't too broken up about it.

"Well, at least *that's* a piece of good news," she mumbled.

I told her about Fortnum's and she told me she'd call Jane if I put up the sign. Then I flipped the phone shut and walked into the kitchen.

Matt was there and so was another guy. The other guy was at least six foot six and looked like Tex's son, except without the beard and with a little bit more of his mental health intact.

Matt said, "Hey."

I tilted my head and smiled.

"Hey yourself."

Lee was standing in the kitchen with his fists at his hips and he watched this exchange, his mouth set.

I noticed, belatedly, that Lee had already showered that morning. His dark hair was still slightly damp, curling a bit along his neck and behind his ear. I also noted he needed a haircut, but it looked good on him. Very good. Too good. He wore supremely faded jeans and a red t-shirt that was tight in all the right places. His feet were bare.

When I got within reaching distance, his arm shot out and pulled me to him with a hand hooked around my neck. My front pretty much slammed against his side and his arm curled further around my shoulders. From the blood draining out of Matt's face, I'd say that the Lee's point had been made. If he banged on his chest and grunted, "Indy, my woman," he wouldn't have made the point any better.

Men.

Lee introduced the other guy as Bobby and then said, "We've found Duke."

My stomach clenched and my body tensed. At that point I simply could not handle bad news, especially about Duke.

I tilted my head to look up at Lee and before I could control my reaction and not look like a total girl in front of the guys, I breathed, "Please."

Lee's eyes went that melty-chocolate again as he looked at me and his hand went from my shoulder to stroke my jaw.

"He's fine, took a bender detour to Sturgis. He's been briefed and he's on his way home now."

That sounded like Duke. Only Duke would detour from the Western Slope of Colorado to South Dakota for a bender.

The door buzzer rang and I disengaged from Lee to answer it. It was Hank.

Hank smiled his greeting at the door and we walked in, his arm slung around my shoulders.

"I guess you were wrong about being broken up with Lee by your Dad's barbeque," he teased.

My eyes shot to Lee and his eyebrows went up.

Oopsie.

"Yeah, guess I was wrong," I muttered.

Hank dropped his arm and looked at Lee, no more teasing, all business.

"We gotta talk about last night."

"Yeah?" Lee said.

"Anyone want coffee?" I asked.

Hank's eyes slid to me then back to Lee.

"Maybe we should go into the Command Center," Hank said.

Lee's lips twitched at Hank's reference to the Command Center, but he said, "You can talk in front of Indy."

Hank quickly sucked some breath into his nose, and then on an exhalation said, "I was afraid of that."

I passed coffee all around. Everyone took it black except me. Once I accomplished this, I jumped up on the counter to listen.

Hank started in after I settled.

"They think they caught a break. Shubert had been dead more than a day. Looks professional, but they found fresh blood at scene. Whoever broke in cut themselves at the window. They're hoping that the killer went back in search of something."

Without thinking, I looked to my shoulder, where I'd landed on the glass, pulling back my tee to see if I'd been cut. I hadn't noticed any cuts or felt any, but the time since the break-in had been pretty filled up with emotional mayhem. A cut could go unnoticed.

Then it hit me how very, *very* stupid I was and I turned, slowly, back to the men.

Lee had a hand at his waist, the other one holding the mug and he was looking at his feet. I was pretty sure he was trying not to smile (at least I hoped so). Matt and Bobby, who were undoubtedly recruited for clean up last night and knew the whole story, were both watching me and smiling, flat out.

Hank was staring at me like I was a particularly gruesome roadside accident.

Hank's eyes swung to Lee. "I was worried it was *yours*."

Both Matt and Bobby pulled in breath at this shocking statement.

Even Lee was incredulous. "I wouldn't leave blood at a scene. Hell, I wouldn't even break a fucking window."

I stared at Lee, wondering uncomfortably how often he had the opportunity to "leave blood at a scene".

Hank's eyes swung back to me.

Uh-oh.

"Please tell me you didn't have anything to do with this."

I tried to look innocent. Since I was not, it was hard. Especially with Hank. Hank was a smart guy and he knew me too well.

"With what?" I asked.

"Indy, I swear to God——" Hank started.

Lee's coffee cup hit the counter. He grabbed mine and set it down, pulled me off the counter and into the bedroom where he closed the door.

"Shirt off," he demanded.

"What? Now?" I stared at him, confused.

Lightning quick, he had the shirt pulled over my head. At this point, I was pretty glad I put on my bra.

"Where'd you land?" he asked and I stared at him. "When Tex threw you through the window, where'd you land?"

Oh. That's what he was talking about.

"Back right shoulder," I told him.

He whipped me around and his hands roamed my skin, then before I knew what he was doing, they came around to the front and undid my jeans and the jeans were down to my ankles.

"For goodness sake, Lee!" I cried.

He'd disrobed me in nary a second. I would have thought it was impossible if he hadn't just done it.

I tried to bend over and grab my jeans but his hands were all business and running down the backs of my hips, thighs and calves.

He pulled up my jeans and turned me again. Pulling my hands away from doing up my fly, he checked the palms.

"You're clean," he announced.

"Thank you," I said it snippy, as I should. As *anyone* should.

His hands ran up my sides, forcing my arms over my head, and he put my shirt back on me. I finished my zip, buttoned my jeans and hooked my belt buckle.

"Was that really necessary?" I snapped.

He smiled The Smile, pleased with himself.

"Nope, but it was fun."

He kissed my nose and then strode out of the room.

I was on his heels, staring daggers at his back and plotting his murder when we made it to the kitchen.

"She doesn't have anything to do with this," Lee told Hank, and I could swear I heard Bobby do a mini-snort laugh.

Hank's eyes were narrowed. "Do we need to send someone over to check Ally?"

I shook my head, all innocence and light, a halo could be shining over my head. "Can't imagine why you'd need to do that."

"Would you like me to give you half an hour to answer that question so you can call Ally?" Hank offered.

I looked Hank in the eye. "Why would I need that?"

"Thank God," Hank breathed, rolling his eyes to the ceiling to make sure God knew he was taking his gratitude seriously. Then his eyes focused on me. "Anything else you want to say?"

I thought about it and then said, "Just when you find out whose blood it is, remember there are all kinds of breaking and entering. There's the naughty kind and the nice kind."

Lee's arm shot out again, this time his hand hooked around my mouth and he pulled me head first into his side, hand still covering my mouth.

"Hey!" I said, but it came out, "Hrr."

Bobby had walked into the living room and I could hear his quiet laughter. Matt was staring at the ceiling as if it was fascinating.

Hank looked from me to Lee, then back to me.

"I've been lookin' into Tex MacMillan and he has a record. He's a Vietnam Vet who didn't deal when he got home and he got into some deep shit with drugs. Not takin' them. Vigilante justice against the ones who sold them. He didn't handle prison well. That kind of confinement was not his gig. Fucked with his head. He got out and has barely left his porch in twenty years. Every once in a while, he'll aim some buckshot at someone who tries to steal a car radio on his block, but won't go so far as nailing them. It won't go so good for him if he's involved in a homicide and he'll never make it through another jail sentence, and as an ex-offender, even with a *nice* B and E, he might be facing one."

Lee kept me where I was with his hand over my mouth. Hank kept watching me.

"You got something for me that might help Tex out?"

I pulled Lee's hand off my face and said, "I know Tex. I do my shopping at Mr. Kumar's corner store down the street from him. Tex wouldn't hurt a fly, unless you're Nixon. He doesn't like Nixon much. Since Nixon's dead then the rest of the human population is pretty safe. If he's messed up in this some way, I'll be happy to stand as a character witness."

I could hear Bobby's laughing in the living room. Matt was leaned over on his elbows on the counter that separated the kitchen from the dining room, his head hanging down and his shoulders shaking. Lee pulled me deeper into his side with his arm around my neck.

"This isn't funny," Hank said quietly to me. "This is a homicide. A man is dead, his brains splattered against a wall."

Just as quietly, I said, "I know."

Hank cut his eyes to Lee. "Tell me she's done."

Lee's face was serious. "She's done."

Hank nodded. "Now, do *you* have anything for me?"

Lee's hand moved to my shoulder.

"Duke's been found. He's knows what's happening and he's coming home. His house has been tossed."

I froze and asked Lee, "Someone was in his house?"

"Yeah," Lee answered.

"A good someone or a bad someone?" I pressed.

Lee looked down at me. "Both, but only the bad someone tossed the house."

"Do they have the diamonds?" I went on.

Lee exchanged another glance with Hank that I did not understand and then shrugged.

"Duke wouldn't say where he stashed them. We won't know until he comes home to check."

I looked between the two brothers and I got the distinct feeling that something was going on.

Hank glanced at Matt, who'd straightened and was quietly watching and listening.

"I hope you and your boys are being careful," he told Lee, and I had this weird feeling we were on a different subject.

"We're workin' this for a client," Lee answered.

There were more looks passed around, then Hank sighed the sigh of a man beleaguered, kissed me on the top of my head and left. Matt and Bobby waited around expectantly. Lee turned me into his arms.

"Don't let Hank scare you about Tex. He's trying to mess with your head enough to keep you out of this. Tex'll be all right."

I nodded.

"We're gonna have to postpone our plans for the day," Lee continued. "I'll take you to the store, then I have to go check a lead on Rosie. I also need to have a chat with Tex. I'll be at your house no later than three. Earlier if I can make it."

I nodded. "Do you think Rosie went into Duke's house?"

His hand went to my chin and tilted it up.

"You have to prepare for the worst. Rosie may no longer be of this world, and if he is, he may no longer be able to walk free amongst its citizens."

I nodded again.

Then, right in front of his boys, he kissed me, full-on, full tongue, full throttle. His arms wrapped around my back and mine went around his neck.

He lifted his head and I breathed, "That shot me straight to a six."

Good ole boy Lee used to laugh all the time, but when he went into the Army that changed. The grins were few, the smiles were rare, and a laugh from Lee felt like a gift.

After I said that, for the first time in a long time, I watched as Lee threw his head back and laughed.

Chapter 9

The New Definition of Fine

Lee dropped me by Fortnum's, kissing me quickly before he took off in his Crossfire. I watched him go and tried to shut down my mind.

I failed.

I was trying not to think of the night before or that morning. I had a feeling of definitive joy mixed with complete and total fear. It was sinking into my brain that Lee told Kitty Sue we were together, not because it was what she wanted to hear or because it got us out of a tight jam being caught in a clinch, but instead, because we were.

Together, that was.

Liam Nightingale and India Savage, an item.

There was evidence that Andrea was right, he *was* serious.

Oh. My. God.

I put out a sign, closing Fortnum's for the weekend, then walked home.

It was cool and comfortable in my house, but it felt like it had been a week since I'd been home, rather than just a night.

In an effort not to think about Lee, I put the water on to boil for the macaroni, opened the backdoor to let in the non-existent breeze and checked my voicemail.

Seventeen messages.

Of course, it had been several days since I checked my mail, but seventeen messages was an all time high. I listened to the messages as I got out the ingredients for my salad, thinking most of the messages would be Duke and Rosie sightings.

I was wrong.

The news had spread that Lee and I were together and every girlfriend I'd ever had, even some who had moved out of town and one who lived in England, felt it necessary to phone and get the lowdown first hand. Both Marianne and Andrea had called (Marianne twice), demanding updates.

For women far and wide who knew him, hooking up with Lee was a hot news item. Lee was the Holy Grail of boyfriend-dom. Especially since it was me, who had been on the sacred quest for many long, fruitless years. They all wanted the facts, *all* the facts.

If I but breathed a word of what it actually was like to kiss Lee, be held by Lee, or, dear Lord, what Lee looked like naked, I might cause a riot, even a war. I might have to arm myself and fight them all back lest Lee be torn limb from limb.

It was for the better health of the female population and peace in the land that I kept my mouth shut.

Of course, I had kinda told Andrea, but I'd kept Andrea's Richie Sambora secret. She'd keep my Lee secret, no sweat.

I made a pot of strong coffee and started cutting up pickles and onions and I let my mind wander.

Lee had made it pretty clear that I meant something to him and this was the cause of the joy that I couldn't quite tamp down. He didn't like me thinking I was a quick fuck. He didn't like me crying. He didn't like me trembling. And he *really* didn't like it when Terrible Teddy punched me in the face.

I shivered a little bit at what might have happened to Teddy if Lee's boys had picked him up as Lee ordered.

Which brought me to the subject of just who Lee was. He said I didn't have a fucking clue, and at the rate he'd surprised me the last couple of days, I was thinking he was right.

I ran down the facts.

I thought Lee thought of me as his little sister. That obviously was not the case.

Lee had a workforce, people he employed. At least two of them, three if you counted Judy, the housekeeper. There were likely more. This meant responsibility and dependability. This meant people counted on him to keep them paid so they could put food on their table and roofs over their heads. This meant that somewhere along the line, Lee had become disturbingly grown up.

I, on the other hand, was avoiding growing up. My grandmother never grew up. I remembered many a time when my grandfather said to my grandmother, "Ellen, some day you're gonna have to grow up." And Gram would always say, "Why would I do a fool thing like that?"

I agreed with my grandmother. Growing up didn't sound like much fun. Growing up meant diaper bags, ironing your clothes and balancing your checkbook. That seemed really boring and I was avoiding it.

Then there was the fact that Lee seemed to be a little bit better at this relationship stuff than I was. It had only been a couple of days, but he talked casually about going out to dinner or when he'd pick me up from the store. He seemed pretty comfortable with me in his bed, in his house, my clothes in his drawers, my toothbrush next to his.

How this could be when Lee went through women like water was beyond me.

Granted, the longest relationship I'd had lasted eight months, but there was a reason for that. None of the guys were Lee.

Now that it seemed like I had Lee, would I drive him away with my thrashing around in bed (although he seemed to have conquered that obstacle pretty quickly)? Then there were my crazy escapades with Ally, although he'd had a lifetime of that and always seemed to find it amusing. Of course, there was also my somewhat crazy and uncontrollable bent towards doing stupid shit all the time, although he was showing alarming dexterity at cleaning up the messes I made. And, of course, my hell bent independence and need for space, although he'd also managed to get by that by forcing me out of my space and into his. And his space was rather nice, with a great view and a housekeeper.

Yikes.

Finally, there was the scary part of Lee.

My Dad was a cop. The danger level to that job was a lot higher than most and I'd lived with it my whole life. I knew it and understood it. I didn't like it but I was proud of him. He was one of the good guys that made the world safe. The world needed guys like Dad, Malcolm and Hank, and the people in their lives had to give them space to do their jobs or we'd all be up shit creek.

Lee was... I didn't know.

Death didn't freak him out. He seemed to wander around comfortably both in the sunny real world that I inhabited and the slimy underworld that I hoped was temporary for me.

For Lee, bad guys had nicknames.

For Lee, driving twenty miles per hour over the speed limit, weaving in and out of crowded mid-day traffic on Speer Boulevard was like a Sunday drive.

Lee was offended at the thought that he'd botch a B and E. Lee oozed so much authority that crazy guys like Tex did what he ordered without comment. Lee was so dangerous that even Goon Gary and Creepy Terry Wilcox barely could hide their fear of him.

I dumped the cooked macaroni in the colander, rinsed it and left it to cool.

Then I went upstairs and slathered my body in factor 8 suntan oil that smelled deliciously coconutty. I dressed in my turquoise bikini that had the silver hoop between my boobs and the ones holding the material together at my hips and wrapped a sarong around my hips, tying it in a big knot at the front.

After doing this, I decided that I'd just have to wait and see what Lee had to say.

He told me he'd show me who he was, what he wanted and then I could make my decision. This did nothing to shift the joy or the fear, but it definitely mingled it with not a small amount of excitement.

It felt like Christmas Eve.

I was assembling my macaroni salad extravaganza when the back security door was thrown open and Rosie stepped into the kitchen.

He was carrying a gun.

And the gun was pointed at me.

I stared at him, wooden spoon in hand, dripping mayonnaise.

He looked like hell. Rosie had never been one to worry about personal hygiene overly-much. He groomed enough to make it not gross that he was serving coffee and that was it.

It was clear he'd slept a helluva lot less than I had and hadn't had a shower since I last saw him.

"Rosie!" I cried. "Where have you been? I've been looking all over and worried sick."

"Where are the diamonds?"

Uh, excuse me but this was beginning to piss me off. Why did everyone think I had the diamonds or knew where they were? I hadn't even seen the fucking things.

He moved the gun jerkily and I quit thinking about the diamonds.

"Where are the diamonds?" he repeated in a shout.

I stopped staring at Rosie and started staring at the gun. "I don't know where they are."

"Duke's gone. They aren't at his house."

My eyes moved back to Rosie. He was definitely freaked out, panicked, and not in an artist-on-the-verge kind of way. It was far worse than that.

"You didn't toss Duke's house did you?" I asked.

"No! It was like that when I got there. I thought it was you and that crazy guy who taped me up."

"I haven't been to Duke's, but he's coming back and I'm sure he knows where the diamonds are." I tried to be calm and calm him. "Rosie, put down the gun. You need to stay someplace safe. I can call Lee—"

Rosie started waving the gun around and I stopped talking and stepped back.

"Don't call that maniac. He taped me up!" he shouted. "It took him, like, two seconds. I didn't even get the chance to yell. I didn't even hear him come in. He's nuts."

"Okay, I won't call Lee. But Rosie, you have to be smart. Your friend—"

"He's dead. They shot him. They fucking shot him!" He was shouting really loud now, waving the gun around and seriously freaked out.

"Rosie—" I started.

"Yoo hoo!"

I heard the call from out the backdoor complete with the clickety-clack of high heeled shoes and Chowleena's nails on the bricks.

My neighbor, Tod.

"Tod, go back!" I yelled, but Rosie had turned and pulled the trigger, shooting wild out the backdoor. Three shots were squeezed off in as many seconds. I saw Tod's arms flung out before him as he hit the deck and Chowleena started barking, each bark sending her upper body straight in the air. I knew this because I could hear the click of her nails hit the bricks every time she landed.

Rosie stared at the gun as if he forgot he was holding it and then ran out the door.

I ran after him.

"Rosie! Come back here! Don't be stupid!" I yelled.

But Rosie wasn't listening to me. Rosie threw himself in a dark gray, old-model Nissan Sentra that was parked blocking my back alley and took off. I managed to read half the license plate before he turned left on Bannock and disappeared.

I ran back to the house. Tod was standing at my backdoor wearing a pair of white to-the-knee jeans shorts, a wife beater and a killer pair of high-heeled, strappy black sandals with sweet little bows on the peek-a-boo toes with rhinestones in the bows. He had his hand at his chest, his face was pale, and considering the bloody areas, he'd scraped his knees and palms.

"Great shoes," I said, trying to stay calm.

"I was coming over to show them to you, bought them yesterday," Tod replied.

"Can I borrow them sometime?"

"Sure."

Chowleena walked forward and shoved her face against my shins, completely unfazed by the gunplay. She was beige, small for a chow, fluffy in the extreme around her ruff with her butt shaved. The shin-butt was her way of giving a hug and saying, "hi" and, "give me a dog biscuit". Her Dads were pretty strict about her diet, but Auntie Indy was a pushover. One Chowleena hug and I had the dog biscuit box out.

We walked into the kitchen and I grabbed my cell, scrolled down to Lee's number and hit the green button.

"Yeah?" Lee said after one ring.

"Rosie was just here. Took off north out of the alley onto Bannock in a dark gray Nissan Sentra." I gave him the part of the license I could remember and he related the info to someone he was with then he came back to me.

"How's he look?"

"Not good, and he had a gun."

"How do you know he had a gun?"

"He was waving it at me and then he shot off three rounds when Tod came over for a surprise visit."

Silence for a beat and then, "Tod?"

"My neighbor."

Another silent beat, then, "Everyone okay?"

"Yeah."

"Why'd Rosie come to you?"

"He thinks I know where the diamonds are."

Lee sighed.

"Be there in ten."

I flipped the phone shut, threw Chowleena a dog biscuit and deposited a still stunned Tod in a chartreuse chair. I ran up the stairs to my bathroom to get my medical supplies.

I was sitting on the ottoman, dabbing at Tod's palm with alcohol soaked cotton balls then blowing on it to take the pain away when Tod said, "I thought you were making up a story when you said you'd been shot at. I thought it was another one of your stories."

"I don't have any stories. All that shit I tell you actually happens."

Tod stared at me while he processed this.

This was a new dimension in our relationship.

I always thought Tod and Stevie accepted who I was and were so world-weary that nothing fazed them. I mean, they were flight attendants. They'd seen it all.

I did not expect that they thought I was making up things to make my life sound more interesting.

For Tod, this meant I really *was* crazy and he lived next to a woman who gets herself into a situation where she gets shot at and kidnapped.

"Stevie wants to sell the duplex, buy a condo. Says it will mean no yard work and we can have underground parking so we don't have to scrape our windshields in the winter," Tod told me.

I was not happy about this news. They were the best neighbors ever and they were my friends, and when I needed someone with a steady hand to put on my liquid eyeliner, where was I going to turn?

Tod went on, "We both didn't want to leave you. You're incapable of yard work and Stevie spent a lot of time on that yard. It's his legacy."

"So now you're getting shot at, you're gonna leave me?"

"Girlie, I'm from Texas. We shoot at each other to say good morning. Now *you're* getting shot at, we *can't* go."

I didn't have time to feel relief or gratitude at this news as the front door opened and Lee and Matt walked in.

I was on the ottoman doing my Florence Nightingale impersonation. Tod was still wearing the high-heeled sandals. Blood was dripping from his knees down his hairy shins and he had not yet shaved his face. Chowleena barked three times, her nails clicking on the hardwood floor each time her upper body landed after a bark. Then she sat down, looking excitedly between the four of us, obviously wondering which one would toss her a dog biscuit.

I introduced everyone then Lee said, "Can I talk to you alone?"

He didn't wait for an answer, and neither he nor Matt reacted to me administering to a from-the-ankles-down drag queen. Lee calmly walked up the stairs.

Kristen Ashley

"There're cold drinks in the fridge," I told Matt and Tod, and followed Lee, finding him in my bedroom.

He was looking around with curiosity. The walls were pale pink and the floors were covered in cream wool, thick weave carpet. There was a dressing table with a big mirror and padded bench with tubs, brushes and bottles scattered across the top. The bed was big and had a pink Pottery Barn comforter cover with little hot-pink flowers and lots of fluffy pillows at the head.

It was a girlie room, not the room of a Rock Chick, and thus was kind of a naughty little secret, just like my underwear.

When I entered, Lee turned melty-chocolate eyes to me.

"Nice room."

My toes curled into the carpet. I read a magazine article once about how guys actually liked feminine rooms because it made them feel like a conqueror when they invaded such a room.

Lee's face showed he was in the conquering mood.

This didn't last long. His eyes cleared and he became all business.

"Tell me about it."

I ran down the story of Rosie and Lee showed no reaction.

When I was done, he asked, "How did he know Shubert had been killed?"

I shook my head. "He didn't say."

"Was he there?"

"He didn't say, but he seemed pretty freaked about it."

"Why are you the focal point of all this?"

I shrugged.

He watched me for a second then noted, "You smell like a beach."

"Suntan oil," I replied.

His eyes dropped to my body and they became melty again, and his intentions were clear before he made a move. He snagged the knot in my sarong and brought me closer.

"You'll get oil all over you." I told him.

"Then I'll take my clothes off."

Holy shit.

My heart skipped a beat.

"Have you heard from Duke?" I asked, changing the subject.

Lee obviously didn't want the subject to change. He was yanking his t-shirt out of his jeans.

"Duke'll be home in a couple of hours. Tex is cool. He knows the drill. We abandoned the lead on Rosie when he showed up here."

Lee had unknotted my sarong and it dropped to the floor. His melty eyes started glittering.

"Matt and Tod are downstairs," I informed him.

He reached beyond me and shut the door.

"Lee! I'm in the middle of making macaroni salad and there are bullet holes in my fence! This has got to stop and you're supposed to be the one stopping it."

He pulled me into him, close enough for my breasts to brush his chest. A rush of electricity shot through my body as his arms slid around me.

"I don't get a taste of you soon, I'm givin' up the search and takin' you to my cabin in Grand Lake. No phones, no cell coverage, no buzzer. Anyone knocks on the door and I'm shooting them."

Lee had a cabin in Grand Lake.

I didn't know that.

I *loved* Grand Lake.

I shook off thoughts of Grand Lake.

"We're supposed to be having a talk," I reminded him.

"Oh, we'll talk," he promised and I had that Christmas Eve feeling again, except it was Christmas Eve with the devil.

He was watching me. "I can't read your face."

"Some thoughts are secret."

He seemed happy with that, which was surprising.

In my experience, there were two types of guys. One type asked you every five minutes what was on your mind and then got pissy when you didn't feel like sharing. The other type never asked and you got pissy when they didn't seem to care.

Lee, apparently, was a third type, a mutant type, knowing something was on my mind but happy to leave me to it. I didn't know what to make of that. I did know it made me feel less pressured, but more confused, because one of us was supposed to be feeling pissy and neither of us were.

"I'll tell you one thing," I said to him. "I don't know what to make of you. I can't get my head wrapped around any of this."

His arms tightened and his face came closer, then deviated from its course at the last minute. He whispered in my ear a couple of things I could make of him and another couple of things I could wrap around him. My nether regions quivered and I couldn't help myself. I put my lips to his neck then touched my tongue there. It seemed I couldn't wait to taste him either.

Then the door bell rang.

Lee stopped whispering in my ear and started cursing.

I pulled out of his arms, grabbed the sarong and knotted it at my hips. Lee tucked his shirt back in.

Maybe Grand Lake was the way to go.

By the time we made it downstairs, Tod and Matt were both staring at a huge, glossy white box with a red ribbon tied around it that was sitting on the ottoman. Matt was holding a can of diet pop. Tod was holding a pop in one hand with his other arm wrapped around the biggest display of long stemmed red roses I'd ever seen, at least two dozen of them.

I'd had flowers delivered before, but never on this scale, and never accompanied by glossy boxes. I looked to Lee, but he was staring at the flowers, his face tight. Clearly, whatever this was, it was not from Lee.

"There's a card on the box," Tod said. He was staring at Lee too.

I grabbed the card and it read, *Dinner Wednesday night. Wear the dress. Terry*

I'd just finished reading it and experiencing the sick clutch in my stomach when Lee snagged the card out of my fingers.

I stared at the box as if it was ticking.

"Aren't you gonna open it?" Tod asked.

"You open it," I said.

Tod needed no further encouragement. He plopped the huge array of flowers in my arms, set aside his pop and dug into the box. He squealed in delight as he pulled out a fabulous little black dress.

"I saw this at Saks when I was looking for shoes. It cost one thousand seven hundred and fifty dollars!" he announced.

That sick clutch in my stomach lurched and became full blown nausea.

Tod was happily looking at Lee, thinking it was from him and that I'd hit the mother lode of hunky boyfriends with platinum credit cards.

The muscle in Lee's cheek was working and his eyes cut to Tod.

"Put the dress back in the box," Lee ordered, and Tod quickly did as he was told, his face turning confused. Then to Matt, "Coxy."

Matt's jaw went rigid and his eyes turned to me.

"I didn't do anything!" I cried. "He kidnapped me! I didn't encourage him at all! He's creepy."

"Who's creepy?" Tod asked.

"The guy who sent these to me. He looks like Grandpa Munster except genuinely scary."

"You didn't send them?" Tod turned to Lee.

Lee didn't answer. He just grabbed the box and tucked it under his arm. "I'm returning this," he announced, and he was using his scary voice.

I nodded.

"Don't leave the house. Don't open the door to anyone. Bobby's following up on Rosie, and after we visit Wilcox, Matt and I will run down that lead. I'll be back as soon as I can."

I nodded again.

"I'll do my best to convince Coxy that you aren't interested," Lee continued.

"I'd appreciate that." I told him the truth.

Lee's face was totally blank and he watched me for several seconds. Once he started speaking, I realized that he'd been in a struggle with how much information to share and he'd decided he'd trust me not to freak out.

"You've captured his attention. Coxy's a man who's used to getting what he wants. He knows I consider you mine. This is a declaration of war."

I gasped. Tod gasped. Chowleena barked.

"But I don't want him! He's icky," I replied.

"A lot of women get past icky when they get seventeen hundred dollar dresses delivered to their door," Lee answered.

"I might get past icky for that dress. It'd go with my shoes," Tod put in.

Lee was looking at me. "What about you?"

I felt my blood begin to boil and my eyes narrow. I put my free hand on my hip and assumed a posture that screamed *attitude*.

"Seriously?" I asked, and I couldn't believe he actually expected an answer.

Lee kept watching me so I kept talking.

"Icky is icky. There's no getting past icky. He's not only icky, he's creepy. Even if you could get past icky, you can't get past creepy. Jeez."

Lee showed no reaction to my response. "Don't leave the house."

Then he was gone, leaving me with the roses.

Once the door closed, Tod turned to me.

"Girlie, he is *fine*. He's fine times twelve. He's the new definition of fine."

"I've been in love with him since I was five," I told Tod.

"I'm in love with him now. I want to have his children," Tod told me.

We were both still staring at the door and I was still holding the roses.

Then I shared, "He scares me now. He's an adult. He has a head on his shoulders. He's good at this relationship stuff. I think he's serious about me. And he runs in some pretty frightening circles."

"Girlie, you fuck this up and I'm calling the boys in the white jackets. You let something that fine slip through your fingers, you deserve a padded room. Especially if he's good at relationship stuff. Most especially if he's serious about you. No one who looks like that and fills out a pair of jeans like that is good at relationship stuff. I don't care if he runs through the seven circles of hell."

Tod had a point.

I put the roses down on a side table. I needed to do something normal. If I didn't do something normal, I was gonna get a first class ticket on the first plane to San Salvador. I was beginning to realize the allure of San Salvador.

"I need to finish my macaroni salad and make brownies. Wanna help?"

Tod shrugged.

"Sure. You watch Chowleena. I'm going next door to get my gun."

"Your gun?"

"Hunk of Burning Love is out there fighting a war for you so someone has to protect you. I'll be right back."

Tod left to get his gun and I threw a doggie biscuit to Chowleena.

This new turn with Terry Wilcox meant my life was officially fucked up.

I could have a meltdown, but instead I made macaroni salad.

I'd save the meltdown for later...

Hopefully when I was in Grand Lake.

Chapter 10

We're in Together Limbo

Tod and I finished the macaroni salad and made the brownies, and because we were both pumped up on adrenalin by being held at gunpoint and shot at, we made chocolate pecan pie. The whole time we did this, I fielded phone calls. Some of them were (obviously bogus) Rosie or Duke sightings. Most of them were from girlfriends, and the conversations with my girlfriends were all the same.

Question: Was it true, had I hooked up with Liam Nightingale?

Answer: (a hesitant) Yes.

Option: (pick one or multiple choice) Squeal / Shout / Curse / Scream / Shriek (usually the word: Ohmigod!)

Question: Had we *done it* yet?

Answer: We're taking it slow.

Then a lot of yelling about what was taking me so long, questions about how Lee kissed ("you *have* kissed him, haven't you?"), more resurfacing of the nasty bra bow rumor, etc. I thanked God that I had such a long apprenticeship at being cagey and a master liar because it sure came in handy.

After all of our grueling activity, Tod and I headed up to my balcony with the phone and an egg timer and collapsed into lounge chairs.

I didn't trust myself not to fall asleep and get burned to a crisp so we set the timer and every fifteen minutes we turned.

Unfortunately, we eventually forgot to set the timer. The phone finally went silent and I fell into an unscheduled Disco Nap. Fortunately, I was not the kind of redhead with freckles all over that burned within seconds of the sun touching my skin. Not to mention I'd re-dosed with factor 8 before hitting the lounge and was already nursing a pretty deep base tan.

I was lying on my stomach and I felt something on my shoulder. I whirled around on my lounge chair and brought my hands up in the karate position that all of Charlie's Angels used.

Lee was crouched beside me.

"I thought I told you to stay in the house," he said, his voice low but not angry. His eyes were on my hands and I could see the corners crinkled in a semi-smile at the sides of his cool sunglasses.

Since I didn't need to karate chop him, I dropped my stance.

"I did stay in the house. Then the house got boring and we couldn't get a tan in the house. Anyway, Tod's protecting me."

We both looked to Tod, who was on his stomach on the lounge. His gun was unattended on the balcony floor and Chowleena was lying on her side in the shade under Tod's lounge. They both were fast asleep.

Oopsie.

"He's from Texas and he's a drag queen. He has quick reflexes," I assured Lee.

Tod opened an eye and looked between me and Lee.

"Am I off-duty?" he asked Lee.

Lee nodded.

Tod got up, taking his gun with him. He patted his leg to call Chowleena and said to me, "Got a fund raiser tomorrow night. You on Drag Duty?"

Tod and the rest of the drag community of Denver often did fund raisers where they lip-synched their hearts out and gave their tips to charity. Stevie and I were Tod's alter-ego, Burgundy Rose's official drag hags. It was the only true workout I got—lugging around Burgundy's sequined dresses. They weighed a ton. As Tod said, "They don't call it drag for nothing, girlie."

I nodded to him. "If I'm alive, wild horses couldn't keep me away."

Tod's eyes moved to Lee. "It's a drag show for charity. You bringing Indy?"

Lee stood, and since Tod was no longer wearing his high heels, he went from looking down on Lee to looking up. Tod's gaze didn't waver.

"If I'm not workin', I'll be there."

Tod looked again to me. "Swear to God, you fuck this up, I'm calling the white jackets."

Then he and Chowleena left.

"You find Rosie?" I asked Lee, coming out of the lounge.

"No."

"The diamonds?"

"No."

"Is Duke back?"

"Yes."

"Is he safe?"

"Yes."

"No diamonds?"

"They're gone."

"Fuck!" I stomped my foot. "Who has them?"

"That's a good question."

"Fuck, fuck, fuck!" I snapped again. "Did you talk to Terry Wilcox?"

"Yes."

"How'd that go?"

I had lifted my hand up to shield my eyes from the sun so I could look at him. During my questioning, Lee was looking beyond me to the alley and into the backyards of my neighbors. When he answered, his eyes shifted to me.

"I gave him your excuses for missing dinner on Wednesday."

"What were those?"

"You'd be with me and I'd be fucking your brains out."

My vagina went into spasm and my knees went week.

"How'd he take that?" I asked, trying to pretend I wasn't about to collapse.

"He wasn't pleased."

"Erm, can you explain what you meant earlier by 'declaration of war'?"

"Only if we do it inside. We're exposed up here."

I grabbed the phone, the timer and my sarong and walked into the bedroom. I threw everything on the bed and tied the sarong around my hips. Lee closed the door behind him and pulled off his shades.

He walked up to me, tossed his sunglasses on the bed and untied the sarong from around my hips.

"I just tied that," I told him, grabbing for it.

He ignored me and threw it on the bed, out of my reach, and put his hands on my hips, drawing me to him.

"I thought you were gonna tell me about this war thing," I reminded him.

"Simple," Lee replied. "He wants something. That something belongs to me. He begins his campaign to get what he wants and I begin mine to keep it."

I was trying not to be pissed-off, but it was hard.

"I don't belong to you."

"I know that and you know that, but men like Coxy don't know that. He acquires things, even humans. Especially women. His men don't work for him because they respect and trust him. They do it because he pays them a lot."

Okay, that made sense.

My hips were against his hips and his hands were going up my back, pulling the rest of my body into contact with his.

I ignored it.

"Have you dissuaded him from this war?" I asked.

"Not likely," he answered.

"What happens now?"

"I deal with it. You hear from him, see him, you tell me."

I could do that. That sounded easy.

Lee's hands made it to my shoulders and my entire torso was pressed against his.

"What time is it?" I asked.

Lee's head came down and his lips were on my neck.

"Quarter to two," he said against my skin.

"Ohmigod!" I shouted and tried to pull away, but Lee's arms tightened and brought me back. "I have to take a shower. We have to get to Dad's. I'm supposed to be making the hamburger patties."

"Your father can make the hamburgers. We're gonna be latè."

I stared at him in horror. "Late? We can't be late! Dad loves you, Lee, but he's not exactly jumping for joy that we're together. We can't be late the first time we go home for a barbeque!"

Lee's face changed and his eyes became warm.

"Are we together?"

Oh crap.

I started thinking fast.

"We're not *not* together."

"I'm not entirely certain what to do with that."

I explained, "We're not exactly together and were not *not* together. We're in together limbo. We're test driving together to see if we want to buy it."

"We go to your Dad's late, I could convince you to buy it."

I was pretty certain he was right, so in self-defense I put my hands against his chest and pushed.

He didn't budge.

I changed tactics. "How are *you* so sure you want to buy it?"

"I'm sure."

"How are you sure?" I pressed.

"Trust me, I'm sure."

"How?"

"I have an idea. Why don't we shower together?" he suggested.

"That isn't telling me how," I pointed out.

"No, but it would be showing you."

"So 'how' is a showing thing, not a telling thing?"

"'How' is show and tell. I just feel in the mood to show."

Grr.

On to Plan C.

"When you show me the how, do you want me to have my mind on hamburger patties?"

He smiled his killer smile. "Your mind wouldn't be on hamburger patties."

I was pretty certain he was right about that, too.

This took me to Plan D.

"Lee, give me a break. It's my Dad and I promised him I'd be there early to help."

He watched me for a second then he relented, sort of.

"Okay, but you have to give me something to go on."

I was starting to get panicked and a little desperate.

"Something? What something?"

Lee's arms dropped away. "You pick."

I was running late. Dad was going to be hacked off. Terry Wilcox had thrown down the gauntlet to Lee over me. There was still the whole Rosie Fiasco going on, someone had the diamonds and yet everyone was still looking for them. And lastly, Lee and I were in together limbo, and until we had three sane seconds that was where we were going to stay. I didn't have a lot of time to do anything creative.

So I kissed him.

Or, at least, I started out kissing him, my mouth open under his, my arms around his neck, my tongue sliding against his.

When it ended, he was definitely kissing me. One arm around my back, the other hand twisted in my hair, his tongue sliding against mine.

"Christ, you're good at that," he said when he lifted his head.

I blinked.

"I am?"

His eyes were hot on me when I looked into them. "Yeah, you are, and I like it that you have to ask."

At his answer, I pressed deeper into him, but his hands were at my waist, pushing me away.

"If you don't get in the shower now, the family will do without macaroni salad and brownies."

I pushed against his hands. "Maybe we can be a little late."

His hands tensed but he kept me away. "I'm not talkin' late, I'm talkin' no show."

I stared at him.

"Indy, get in the shower," he ordered.

I got in the shower.

⌖

I was sitting in my Dad's backyard with Kitty Sue.

It was my backyard, too, since I grew up there, but I'd been away from home long enough for Dad to have reclaimed it. That was, he had enough time with me out of the house and not worrying him every second of the day that he was able to make the yard look nice, rather than just something he mowed every two weeks in the summer.

Dad's house was in Bonnie Brae, about eight blocks from Kitty Sue and Malcolm's. When I was really young, it seemed it took forever to get to Ally. As I grew older, that distance lessened until one or the other of us walked it several times a day.

"How's it going?" Kitty Sue asked, her eyes on me and her mind on Lee and me.

Lee and I had made it to Dad's fifteen minutes before everyone else was due. This was fifteen minutes after I promised Dad I'd be there. Dad blamed Lee, even though I told him it was my fault for falling asleep in the sun.

I'd caught a second to talk to Lee when Dad put the hamburgers on the grill.

"Don't take it personally. He never liked any of the guys I brought home."

Even though this was true, it was not what Lee wanted to hear. After I said it, his eyes cut to me and I realized my mistake at bringing up the subject of the other guys I brought home.

Then, trying to smooth things over for myself, I made matters worse.

"Even if I'd chosen Hank, Dad would find something to be crotchety about. That's his job, he's a dad."

When Lee had cut his eyes to me, he hadn't moved his body. After I said my last, he turned full body to me and cut me off from view of everyone else.

"Was Hank an option?" he asked.

Uh-oh.

"I'm just saying," I responded.

"You're just saying… what? Exactly."

"I'm trying to make you feel better."

"I wasn't feeling badly. I know your father has an issue with you and me. He'll come around. I don't need thoughts of you and Hank in my head. Jesus, Indy."

Hank walked up. "You should know, you have an audience."

I peeked around Lee and saw everyone quickly turning their heads away. Great.

Hank threw his arm casually around my shoulders like he'd done a million times before. Except this time Lee's eyes narrowed. *At me.*

"I need a beer," I said kind of desperately, and I left.

By the time I settled in beside Kitty Sue, I was into my third Fat Tire beer and had eaten a burger, a goodly amount of macaroni salad and Kitty Sue's oriental slaw. I'd worn a pair of cutoffs made from a pair of old army-green pants and a black tank top with a thin design of red roses laced with gray and white barbed wire that snaked up my waist, across my torso, over my shoulder and down my back. It was too hot for cowboy boots, and anyway, boots looked ridiculous with shorts (and I'd tried that look on numerous occasions), so I'd worn a pair of black thick-soled flip-flops. My cutoffs were already feeling tight at the waistband and I hadn't even had brownies or pecan pie yet.

I'd successfully avoided Lee since our little discussion. This was not hard. I'd had a decade of successfully avoiding Lee at family gatherings.

I turned to Kitty Sue and surprised myself by answering honestly, "I'm fine. Lee's fine. Lee's more fine than me. I'm having troubles adjusting. Lee seems pretty sure of himself. Lee seems pretty sure of everything."

This, I realized, was true about Lee always. I'd never met someone as confident in my life. Well, maybe Hank, but Hank's confidence was quiet and assured. And there was Lee's best friend, Eddie, of course. But Eddie was like Lee's twin, separated at birth, cut from the same cloth. Lee's confidence, and Eddie's, wasn't like Hank's. It was cocky and assertive.

"And you aren't sure?" Kitty Sue asked.

I looked at her and thought maybe I should have lied. It was too late now.

"Nope. He scares me," I admitted.

She nodded. "Yep, he's pretty dang scary."

I stared. My God, the woman was talking about her son.

"You agree?"

She looked at Lee then back at me. "Honey, that boy drives me to distraction. It's like he's not of my loins. I don't even know where he came from. If Ally hadn't been the exact replica of Lee, personality-wise, except female, I would have wondered if there was a mix up at the hospital."

I kept staring. Kitty Sue kept talking.

"Hank's just like his Dad. Smart, cautious, controlled, taking only calculated risks. I'm sure Lee calculates his risks, but I think he allows for a much larger margin for error and counts on... I don't know what he counts on to get him out of whatever scrapes he gets into."

I couldn't stop staring. She kept talking, and everything that came out of her mouth was like a verbal car accident. If she was trying to convince me to stick with her son, she should have tried a different tact.

"He does... you know?" Kitty Sue said.

I realized she was asking me a question, so I shook my head that no, I didn't know.

She explained, "He gets out of every scrape. Always did and always did it on his own. Though it'll take some kind of woman to live a life like that, knowing what he's like, knowing the risks he takes."

Her hand went to my knee and she squeezed it before she went on.

"Not anyone here would think less of you if you aren't that woman. I'm telling you because it's true. We all love you both and we'll always love you both, no matter what happens between you." She stopped, sighed and continued, "Anyway, I don't even know if that kind of woman exists. I'm his mother. I've lived with him surviving scrapes that would make your hair stand on end and I worry about him every day. He scares the hell out of me."

I didn't want my hair standing on end, that was true. It didn't sound like a good look.

I also didn't want to think of any other woman being the kind of woman who blithely accepted Lee's 'Death Cheating Margin of Error', and therefore being the one he came home to every night. And lastly, I didn't want the family not thinking less of me because I threw over Lee because I was a sissy. I was no sissy. Lee may be scary, but not *that* scary. I could out-margin-of-error-acceptance any bitch that came along.

"I'm gonna get the brownies," I told Kitty Sue.

She patted my knee. I got up and went straight to Lee.

He was sitting in a lawn chair with his legs stretched out in front of him, Hank, Malcolm and Ally sitting with him. He watched me cross the lawn and didn't move a muscle.

"Can I talk to you?" I asked.

He didn't answer but got up. He followed me through the sliding glass door and into the kitchen. I slid the door shut behind us and turned to him.

"Are you mad at me?" I asked.

He crossed his arms on his chest. He didn't answer me, but I guessed that was a yes.

I tried to cute my way out of it and flashed him a tilty-head smile.

"What'll it take for you to get un-mad at me?"

He didn't answer.

Okay, that didn't work.

I sighed and threw up my hands. "It was never Hank. It would never be Hank. Hank is not even a possibility."

"For Christ's sake, stop talking about Hank!" he exploded, taking my hand and pulling me deeper into the house and out of eyesight and earshot of everyone in the backyard.

"What is it then?" I asked his back when he stopped in the living room.

"Think about it," he answered after he turned.

"I don't want to think about it. If I knew what it was, I'd already be explaining it or apologizing for it. You're gonna have to tell me."

"I'm not tellin' you."

"Oh for fuck's sake!" I yelled. "How can I make things better if I don't even know what I did wrong?"

"Forget about it. I'm not angry with you anymore."

"Yes you are," I countered.

"No," he said in his scary voice, "I'm not."

"Boy, are you moody. You're the most moody guy I've ever met."

"If you really want to make things better, you could start by not talkin' about all the men of your acquaintance. That would help."

I gasped.

"You make me sound like a slut!"

He walked up to me and I stood my ground. He was so close I could feel his heat.

"All right, Indy. First, I don't like thinkin' of you with other guys. There may not have been a lot, but even one puts my teeth on edge. Second, I don't like bein' compared to Hank or the idea that you think Tom would accept him easier than he would me."

The light dawned, and it dawned brightly on the fact that I was *such* a moron.

"Lee—"

"I'm goin' for a drive. I'll be back to take you home."

"Lee—"

He took off and I stood in the living room staring out the big picture window to the front yard. The Crossfire was long gone by the time the door to the bathroom opened, Dad came out and he looked at me.

"How much did you hear?" I asked.

"All of it. You were talking pretty loudly," Dad answered, coming up to me.

I put my head on his shoulder and he put his arm around my back.

"I'm a moron," I declared.

"Well, I don't know what you said, but it doesn't sound good."

"I'm a moron."

Dad kissed the hair at the side of my head.

Then he stated, "He'd be all kinds of fool if he didn't come back and accept your apology. Lee is a lot of things, but that boy is no fool. I'll take the brownies out."

Dad went into the kitchen and I heard the sliding glass door open and close.

I went to the bathroom, not because I needed to use it, but if Dad could hear, then the others could as well, and I needed to get my head together. Not a good start, the first family get-together and I said something stupid and pissed-off Lee to the point he had to take a drive to cool off.

I was contemplating how I'd make it up to him when I left the bathroom and the doorbell rang. I walked to the door, thinking maybe it got locked somehow. The only person it could be was Lee and he would normally just walk in or walk around the house to the backyard.

I opened the door and stared the shooters in the face, momentarily stunned that they were standing on the doorstep of my childhood home and ringing the bell.

I opened my mouth to scream. One of them leaned forward, arm extended, and then it was lights out.

Chapter 11
Story Time for Bad Little Girls

This kidnapping was entirely different from the last.

They didn't ask me if I was okay and they weren't cordial.

There was no cream damask sofa either.

They didn't even talk to me at all. This was good. It meant I didn't talk to them either, and thus didn't draw undue attention to myself nor have the opportunity to piss them off so much they shot at me or punched me in the face.

They cuffed my hands behind my back and tied me to a chair with nylon rope. I thought doing both was a bit overkill, but figured it wise not to share my opinion. Being cuffed and tied was not comfortable, to say the least. In fact, if I moved at all, it hurt. Either the rope gouged into my skin or my arms strained against all natural limits. I didn't have my limb coordination back from the second stun-gunning of my life so I didn't get a chance to struggle while they were tying me. It wouldn't have mattered. They both had guns. I'd quit self-defense classes before week three, and as far as I knew I was not bulletproof like Superman.

I was in a house. God knew where, just that obviously no one lived there and hadn't for a long time. We were in the filthy living room and there was an old, beat up, dusty couch and the chair I was sitting in. That was it, the extent of the décor, unless one counts dust mites the size of cocker spaniels.

The two guys who grabbed me were the shooters who shot at Rosie and me and started this disaster. One of the shooters spent a lot of time in another room and I could tell by the drone of his voice that he was on the phone. The other shooter stayed with me. These guys were not as panicked as Rosie and clearly had showers in the last couple of days. However, their eyes scared me. This was serious shit. These guys were professionals and they were not fucking around.

I probably would have been more scared if I didn't have to go to the bathroom.

I normally had a cast iron bladder. Everyone always commented on my bladder control. It usually took me twice as long to break the seal as it did others. I could drink freely from the keg before a gig and not miss a single note of a song during the concert. My bladder was almost as legendary as my encounter with Aerosmith's Joe Perry. But now, the Fat Tire beer had worked its way through my system in record time and I was dying for a wee.

I had no idea how much time I was there. I was concentrating on keeping my mouth shut and keeping from peeing my pants. I didn't want to ask them to let me go to the bathroom. I didn't have my shit together enough to think of an escape plan. I didn't wonder how long it would take for my family to realize I was gone, especially since the Lee Incident meant I would be in hiding for a while before showing my face in the backyard again. I didn't even consider thinking about the fact that this might not go well for me and the last thing I had done was fight with Lee.

I was staring out the window, thinking maybe I could get a lock on where I was if I had a good look, and if I focused on something I wouldn't focus on the fact that I had to pee or that my life might soon be over.

That's when I saw the top of a big, blond head and a pair of eyes, the wild mass of hair tamped down by night vision goggles.

Tex was peeking through the window.

Holy crap.

No sooner had I seen him than he was gone.

"What are you lookin' at?" the shooter asked me, turning to look out the window.

The other shooter came in. They were both big guys, kind of in the bent of Goon Gary and Terrible Teddy, wearing slacks and dress shirts with the sleeves rolled up. No ties.

One of them, the one who talked on the phone, was older, his brown hair peppered with gray. The other one who was left to watch me had sandy blond hair and may have been cute at one point, but now looked like he was careening headlong toward middle age.

"He agreed. He'll do the swap, the girl for the diamonds," Phone Guy Pepper Shooter told Watch Guy Sandy Shooter.

"She was lookin' at something outside. I'm checkin'," Sandy Shooter told Pepper Shooter.

Pepper Shooter looked at me while Sandy went outside.

"Your boyfriend out there?" Pepper asked me.

I shook my head and kept my mouth shut. I hoped Tex was long gone and calling 911. I feared that Tex was close and planning Armageddon.

Pepper went from window to window, standing at the side and looking out. He was beginning to look a little less professional and serious and a little more panicked and desperate.

"Fucking Nightingale!" he spat and turned to me, pulling his gun out of the waistband of his pants and pointing it at me. "Did you see him out there?" he yelled.

"No," I answered, not telling a lie since he was talking about Lee, and I didn't see Lee outside. Therefore, I'd die without at least that lie darkening my soul.

Pepper didn't hold a gun like Rosie. He held it steady and with practiced ease and he was scaring the shit out of me. So much so that I totally forgot I had to pee.

"What were you lookin' at?" he pushed.

God, I was such a moron. Why couldn't I be cool like in the movies? Whistle and pretend I didn't see anything, then calmly communicate an entire escape plan to my rescuer using only my widened eyes and a couple of jerks of my head while my kidnappers were turned the other way.

"I wasn't looking at anything," I lied. "There's nothing to look at so I was looking out the window."

He kept holding the gun pointed at me. He didn't have to say what the gun was saying pretty clearly: talk or lights out.

"Listen, I have to use the bathroom," I blurted. "Seriously, I had three Fat Tires before you guys stun-gunned me. I think all that electricity did something to my bladder. Usually, I can hold it, but I totally have to go."

He kept staring and pointing the gun and the other guy came in. Pepper didn't move an inch. He didn't even look at Sandy when he came in.

"No sign of anyone," Sandy said.

"You wouldn't find sign of Nightingale if he was out there, asswipe. He's smoke."

Sandy looked from Pepper to me.

"Why do you have a gun on her?" Sandy asked.

"You said she saw something," Pepper answered. "I think if I put a bullet in her kneecap, she might tell me what she saw."

Holy crap!

Sandy was just as shocked as me.

"Jesus, Rick. Have you lost your mind? We're supposed to turn her over for the diamonds and not with a bullet in her fucking kneecap. You think Nightingale's out there as smoke? You put a bullet into his woman and he's gonna hunt you down and skin you alive."

"She'll be breathin'. He'll have to make do. All the rest of her parts will be workin'. She doesn't need her kneecap to fuck," Pepper Rick replied.

That's when I quit breathing.

I guess he hadn't forgiven me for mouthing off a few days ago.

Then the front door flew open and both Pepper Rick and Sandy whirled toward it. Nothing was there, but something rolled across the floor.

Both men and I stared at it as it bounced across the floor, hit the couch, rolled back and then came to rest a couple of feet away from the couch.

It looked kind of like a grenade.

Of course, I'd never seen a grenade so it could have been something else.

No sooner had the first thing come to a rest then something else bounced across the floor. It also looked like a grenade but its sides were smooth and it was leaking white smoke.

"Is that what I think—?" Sandy started to say.

The first thing exploded.

I was right, grenade.

Smoke and dust were everywhere. I was choking on it, blinded by it and I couldn't move.

There was coughing, shouting, thuds of flesh against flesh. Someone came at me and then my chair was tilted and I was dragged across the room.

I looked behind me but my eyes were tearing from the dust and smoke. It was torture. I couldn't wipe them without the use of my hands.

Nevertheless, I swore I could see a blurry version of Tex behind me, wearing what appeared to be a World War II gas mask.

He pulled me out the backdoor and righted the chair. He did something behind my back that made the rope fall free, pulled the mask off his face and shouted, "Run!"

I wasted no time, jumped up and ran. This was not easy. I was stiff and sore from sitting tied in the chair. I had my hands cuffed behind my back. I was still coughing and choking and could barely see. And I was wearing flip-flops, not exactly the chosen footwear when running for your life.

You do what you have to do, especially when doing nothing might mean you'd never have the opportunity to see Lee's cabin in Grand Lake. I ran for all I was worth, keeping the blurry vision of Tex in my sights.

We got half a block when I heard gunfire. Tex whipped around and batted me with a beefy arm, sending me sprawling headfirst into some bushes. I heard the ratchet of a shotgun and then, "*Boom!*"

The bushes were tearing at my skin as I rolled out. There was more gunfire, then another "*Boom!*" I thought I saw Tex, both feet planted wide, presenting a huge target like the madman he was, looking oblivious to the flying bullets and calmly reloading the shotgun.

I had rolled onto my back and I was like a turtle, trying to push myself this way and that, entangled half in the bushes, my arms pinned behind my back. I heard the squeal of tires, shouting, gunfire and another "*Boom!*" More gunfire and I saw Tex do a scary jerk backward and then go down on a knee.

"Jesus Christ!" I heard Hank shout. "Lee, she's here!"

I think I focused on what could have been Hank looming over me, but I still couldn't see. Then I was hauled up and Lee was there. I could tell because I could smell faint traces of leather, spice and tobacco.

"Hold your arms back as far as you can, wrists wide and keep them steady," Lee ordered.

I did as I was told and felt a strong hand wrap around my forearm, and then a gunshot made me jump, but also made my arms fly out beside me.

Free at last.

Regardless of the pins and needles running up my arms, my hands went straight to my eyes and I swiped at the tears running freely from them.

"Don't rub," Lee instructed. "You need to rinse the gas off your face. You okay?"

I nodded but said, "Tex."

Lee's blurry head looked to Hank. "You got her?"

"Yeah," Hank answered.

Then Lee took off.

I staggered to where Tex was now sitting cross-legged in the grass, holding his shoulder. I still couldn't see very well, but I dropped to my knees beside him and wrapped my hands around his good upper arm and held on. I had no idea what I was doing but it would have taken a crowbar to pry me away.

There were sirens and the squad cars would slow, but Hank was signaling them to continue down the road and they sped off.

Mr. Kumar showed up out of nowhere, carrying paper towels and bottled water from his store. I let go of Tex long enough to pour water over my face and on my hands. When my vision cleared sufficiently, I could see that Tex was bleeding so I ripped open the paper towel and pressed a big wad of it against his shoulder.

I saw we were in Tex and Mr. Kumar's neighborhood. If we'd made it the last half a block, we would have been at Kumar's corner store. The shooters took me nearly right to Tex.

Was I lucky or what?

Was Tex unlucky or what?

I saw the flashing lights of a squad car that screeched to a diagonal halt in the road.

Brian Bond and Willie Moses angled out of the car and came jogging up to Tex and me.

"Holy shit, Indy. What the fuck?" Willie asked.

Willie was a friend, graduated high school the same year as Hank. Still in uniform, and he preferred it that way. He wanted action, not a desk. And anyway, the uniform looked good on him. *Real* good. He was tall, with perfect smooth-as-satin-black skin, a beautiful white smile and a body made of pure muscle. He was a full scholarship wide receiver for the University of Colorado. He was good but not good enough for the NFL. Just like Hank, he graduated college and went right to the Academy. He taught me how to play poker, badly on purpose, and beat me every time we played. I'd met Brian a couple of times, but he was barely out of rookie status.

"Call an ambulance," I said to Willie.

Brian answered, "It's two minutes behind us."

"Let's get you up," Willie grabbed my upper arm.

"No, no way. I'm not letting go until the ambulance gets here." I was trying hard not to cry and pressing the now soaked-through-with-blood towel against Tex's shoulder. The blood was coming fast and there was a lot of it. In normal circumstances this would make me gag, and possibly vomit, but I was fast acquiring new skills, including adrenalin-fueled nursemaid.

"Now you're bein' a girl," Tex said. "Soon you'll be slobberin' on me. It's just a shot to the shoulder. Shit, I've had worse than this."

148

I looked at Tex. He was pale, his eyes were in a permanent wince and his voice betrayed the pain. I decided to communicate in a way he'd understand.

"Well, excuse me!" I shouted. "I've never seen anyone shot in the shoulder. I've never seen anyone shot at all! News flash, Tex. I *am* a girl and I'm not fucking letting go until the fucking ambulance gets here. Do you fucking hear me?"

Willie let me go and took a step back.

"All right, no need to get all PMS about it," Tex relented, then his eyes focused beyond me and I looked over my shoulder.

Lee strolled toward us, one of his arms down, a gun held loosely in his hand. He was pushing Sandy forward with the other hand and Sandy's arms were cuffed behind his back. Lee shoved him into the yard we were all occupying and Sandy went down, hard, to his knees.

"This one of them?" he asked Tex, not looking at me.

"Yep," Tex answered.

"He shoot you?" Willie asked.

"Shot *at* me, and Indy. The other guy nailed me though."

Brian and Willie were no longer listening. They only heard "and Indy" and then half the night air was sucked into their lungs, and Brian and Willie's eyes narrowed on Sandy.

Almost worse than shooting a cop was shooting *at* a cop's daughter.

Sandy just bought a first class ticket up Shit Creek.

It was then the ambulance came.

⌐╦─╦⌐

I made the ambulance crew allow me to ride in the back with Tex. I did this by having the hissy fit to end all hissy fits. Until they wheeled him away in the Emergency Room, I stuck by his side. Tex allowed this, mainly because he'd witnessed the hissy fit and knew I was hanging on by a thread. There were times when you humored a woman, even if you were a crazy man unafraid of flying bullets, and this was one of those times.

Tex told me in the ambulance that Kumar lived a couple of houses away from the one I was taken to and saw them unload me. As was apparently practice in the 'hood, Kumar went straight to Tex and Tex gave him my card and told him to call Ally and ask for Lee. That was how Hank and Lee got there so quickly.

Detective Jimmy Marker, who had long ago caught me underage drinking, bought the case and questioned me in the hospital waiting room. Jimmy was somber and trying not to look as pissed-off as he actually was. When I was eight, Jimmy took me to a father-daughter day because Dad was on-duty. We did the three-legged race together. I suspected he would have preferred to be escorting Sandy, wearing cuffs and ankle shackles, down a very long, steep flight of stairs.

The questioning took a while because half of the Denver Police Department came through the waiting room to see if I was okay. I'd amassed a lot of buddies on the Force. Half of them had babysat me and the other half had partied with me.

Then, of course, there was Kitty Sue and Ally's hysterical arrival with Malcolm and Dad dogging their heels.

Kitty Sue wasn't crying and carrying on. She was shouting and carrying on. Gram told me often enough growing up that in times of emotional strain shouting was just as good a release as bawling. Both of them made you ugly, but only one of them ended in red, puffy eyes and a blotchy face. Kitty Sue was the wife of a cop. She'd long since learned that teary hysterics would get her nowhere, but yelling captured attention. Men as a whole didn't know what to do with tears, but they'd do anything to make a woman stop yelling.

Mr. Kumar had come to the hospital, too, and he didn't seem to know what to make of these goings-on, so he remained quiet and tried to be invisible. Jimmy questioned Mr. Kumar after he questioned me.

Once Jimmy left, I finally went to the bathroom, and I kid you not, the relief was so immense I nearly cried.

Then I told everyone I was waiting for Tex to get out of surgery. I did this in a way that no one said a word in protest. I still had the cuff bracelets on my wrists and a goodly amount of blood on my body from cuts from the bushes, and possibly also from Tex. I wasn't in a state, physically or mentally, to be trifled with.

I sat down next to Mr. Kumar, grabbed his hand and held on tight. Mr. Kumar didn't seem to mind this, but then again, he'd witnessed my hissy fit too.

Everyone else settled in for the long haul.

On Kitty Sue's command, Dad and Malcolm went in search of refreshments and hideous machine coffees were passed around. Kitty Sue and Ally hung close to Kumar and me. Lee and Hank had disappeared.

I'd lost track of them during my hissy fit, but waiting for news of Tex, moments of clarity came to me. Memories were jogged and pieces started floating together.

I was pretty pissed-off I'd been kidnapped again. I was also pretty certain I was about five seconds away from losing a kneecap. I'd never paid a lot of attention to my knees, but after inspecting them closely in the waiting room, I decided I liked them just the way they were.

I'd been afraid. Afraid for my life, afraid for my kneecap, and although I'd been nearly blinded by tear gas, I'd seen Tex take a bullet for me.

Being afraid made me mad. It made me mad that I'd been kidnapped on the doorstep of my home. It made me mad that Kitty Sue was hysterical. It made me mad that Malcolm stood, glancing at me every few seconds as if he wanted to say something but thought I was too fragile to hear it. And it made me mad that my Dad sat across the waiting room wearing his worried expression.

And as I ciphered the bits and pieces of the puzzle that had been floating around me for days... pieces of the puzzle I'd been too stupid to fit together, I became pretty fucking angry.

The thing was I was pretty certain that Lee had played me.

Lee and Hank walked into the waiting room and everyone looked at them. Lee's face was stony. Hank looked angrier than me and he shook his head in negative once to Malcolm and Malcolm's face became even tighter. At the silent communication, Dad cursed loudly.

I guessed (correctly) Pepper Rick got away.

Hank walked right up to me, pulled me out of the chair and gave me a tight hug that stole my breath.

Lee stopped at Dad. Malcolm joined them and they started to have a quiet discussion that I couldn't hear.

This made me mad, too.

Hank came to hug me, but Lee barely even looked at me.

Jerk.

I mean, he might still be mad at me for what I'd said at the barbeque, but I'd just been kidnapped, for God's sake. That deserved at least a pat on the shoulder.

Hank let me go because the doctors came in and said Tex was okay. The bullet entered at the shoulder, breaking the shoulder blade, and ricocheted out a second hole.

They said if we were quiet and didn't stay long, Mr. Kumar and I could go and visit Tex together.

Tex looked out of place, too peaceful and way too big for the bed. I didn't know what to make of him without his night vision goggles.

I barely knew this man at all and he'd saved my kneecap.

He came to, groggy, opened his eyes and they focused on me.

"You're a fun date. What're we gonna do tomorrow night?" he asked.

After he asked the question, he fell back to sleep hearing my stunned laughter.

⇥⇤

Mr. Kumar drove to the hospital and took himself home. Ally took Kitty Sue home, while Hank drove the rest of us. Malcolm sat in front with Hank, and I sat sandwiched between Lee and Dad in the back. It was clear they were my honor guard.

Dad held my hand, tight, and Lee had his arm along the backseat of Hank's 4Runner which meant it also ran along my shoulders. This was not a show of affection, but so we'd have more room.

No one said anything. There was nothing to say.

Hank stopped in front of Lee's condo building and Lee unbuckled and slid out. He then unbuckled me and grabbed my arm, pulling me out with him.

I was a little surprised. I thought he was still pissed about what happened at the barbeque. I was pretty certain I was going home that night, not to Lee's. Furthermore, I wanted to go home. Lee might be pissed about me and my stupid mouth, but I had more reason to be angry.

"Liam," Dad called, and Lee kept his hand on my arm but bent at the waist to look in the backseat.

"Yeah?"

"You take care of her," Dad said, his voice gruff, and the Guinness folks could have popped by to record the occasion, such was my world record pissed-offedness.

I mean, no one makes my Dad sound like that. Those fucking kidnapping losers.

"Yes sir," Lee replied.

I bent over, too, and blew Dad a kiss. He smiled at me. Lee closed the door and they idled at the curb while Lee propelled me into the building. I probably should have told him I wanted to go home, but I thought everyone had enough drama for one night.

Hank didn't take off until the door closed behind us and we were well into the foyer.

There was no chitchat between us. Lee took the bracelets off in his bedroom with a universal key.

Once he threw them on a dresser and turned to me, I crossed my arms on my chest, hitched a hip and asked, "You still mad at me?"

He ignored my belligerent stance, a stance that communicated an unequivocal, "stand back" to every other man I'd known. Not Lee. He walked right up to me and put his hands on my hips.

"No."

"Then what's your problem?"

He didn't even hesitate. He answered me. He actually answered me. And it sounded like the honest to goodness truth.

"I'm angry at myself for reacting the way I did to what you said when you meant no harm, and I'm angry with myself for leaving you unprotected."

I stared at him for a beat, hiding my surprise, and then said, "Good. Now that's settled, I'm taking a shower."

His hands tightened on my hips and his eyes narrowed on my face. It was his turn to stare at me for a beat then he said, "I take it I'm not invited to this shower."

I pulled away from him. "Nope."

I took my shower, washed my hair and surveyed my new cuts and newest bruises while I let the water run over me.

When I'd stepped out of the shower, I noticed that, unfortunately, when I went into the bathroom, I didn't take any clothes with me. I had to grab Lee's light blue cotton robe from the hook on the back of the door. I wrapped it tight around me and tied it secure.

I went into the bedroom and Lee was lying in bed, his chest bare and the sheet pulled up to his waist. He was reading. Believe it or not, casually lying in bed *reading*.

Grr.

If I'd had something, I would have thrown it at him. Instead, I went straight to my bag, rooting through it to find underwear. I found it, straightened and glanced at Lee. He'd put the book down and was lying on his side, his head in his hand, watching me.

"It'll be a wasted effort, puttin' those on."

I sent him my best Polar Freeze Glare, turned my back on him and pulled up the panties.

"Talk to me, Indy," he said on a sigh.

I turned and put my hands on my hips.

He wanted me to talk? Then I'd talk.

"I've had some time to think, what with being kidnapped, cuffed and tied to a chair for part of my evening, and then spending the rest of it sitting in a hospital waiting room." I was lying about thinking while I was kidnapped, but he didn't need to know that. Anyway, it made my introduction more dramatic. "This morning, you told Hank you had a client. I thought you meant me, but I was wrong, wasn't I?"

Lee continued to watch me.

I went on, "The thing is, when this all started, you were in DC and Ally said you weren't due back. Then all of a sudden you were back and you knew about the diamonds. You knew about everything."

He kept watching me.

I went into accusatory mode. "You came back to look for the diamonds. You have another client. You're working for someone else."

Lee came up on his elbow.

"Smart girl," he murmured then patted the bed in front of him. "Come here, let me explain."

Ha! Not even.

"You walked into your own condo and I practically delivered the diamonds to you by bringing Rosie here. Then you tried to extort sex from me in payment for a job you were already getting paid to do, with diamond man lying on the couch for all you knew!"

"Indy—"

I cut him off, "No explanation necessary, Lee. I'm sleeping on the couch and tomorrow I'm going home. We're through. The end."

On that I huffed out of the room, put on the lights in the living room and grabbed the remotes. It took me ten minutes to figure out how to use them, five more minutes to set the sleeper timer on the TV and ten minutes to find something to watch. I turned off the lights and settled in.

Throughout this time, the light came through the open bedroom door, but not a sound from Lee. This ticked me off more. Five minutes into my program, the light went off in the bedroom. My anger hit uncharted levels. Five minutes after that, I realized that was it. When I'd said "the end", Lee didn't have a problem with it.

Okay, great, wonderful, that was fine by me.

Luckily, I'd had a pretty traumatic day, what with being kidnapped and shot at. Twice.

Not to mention two emotional dramas with Lee.

Even though my mind was racing, my body was crashing from adrenalin withdrawal. Before the sleep setting turned off the TV, I was already in snooze land. When the TV switched itself off, it woke me up. This wasn't too annoying, seeing as I didn't fully wake me up. I was three-quarters asleep and one-quarter dozing.

The next thing I knew, I was being lifted in the air.

Lee was carrying me to the bedroom.

"What are you doing?" I asked, half sleepy, half angry.

"Takin' you to bed," he answered, fully awake.

"I'm sleeping on the couch," I told him as he dropped my legs and stood me at the side of the bed. His hands went to the belt of the robe and he didn't respond.

"What are you doing?" I asked again.

"Gettin' you ready for bed."

"Stop that!" I slapped at his hands and he ignored me, so I grabbed the lapels of the robe and held them shut. "I'm nearly naked under this."

The belt came loose and he leaned into me. I reared back, nearly toppling on the bed. He straightened and held in front of me what I had, until a few hours previously, considered my confiscated Night Stalkers tee.

Since the likelihood of me winning a physical tussle was in the negative percentile and I was tired down to the bone, I snatched the tee from him and whirled around to give him my back.

I could sleep with him, I told myself as I pushed my head through the neckline of the tee. I'd slept with him the last however many nights and I'd survived. One more night wouldn't kill me.

I slid the robe off my shoulders and let it drop to the ground, and as fast as I could, I pushed my arms through the holes of the tee.

I wasn't fast enough.

Lee's hands settled on the skin at my hips just above my panties as the t-shirt dropped into place. Its hem came to rest on his hands.

His chin rested on my shoulder.

"How long are you gonna be mad at me?"

His voice was deep and kind of husky, and I felt a quiver in my nether regions.

"Forever," I answered.

His hands slid from hips to belly and he pulled me into his body.

"I can't discuss clients with you, Indy. I offer confidentiality with my services. I won't be able to talk about my work. It's something you're gonna have to get used to."

That was hardly the point.

Okay, it was *a* point, just not *the* point.

It was my longstanding theory that men missed *the* point on purpose.

His chin moved to pull the hair away from my neck and his mouth went to my ear.

Then he got to *the* point.

"You'd been dodgin' me for a decade and then you presented me with an opportunity to get your attention. I'm not big on missin' an opportunity so I took it. It worked. I got your attention. I don't regret it and I'd do it again, even considerin' in the process I lost diamond man."

Hmm, it was annoying, but it was honest, and it was annoying because it was honest.

I pushed forward and broke free of his hands, putting a knee on the bed.

I could have pushed the sleeping on the couch business, but I feared a wrestling match and he'd already gotten a nether region quiver. I'd never survive a wrestling match.

I crawled across the bed and stationed myself at the far edge, pulling the sheet up over me.

I felt the bed move as Lee got in and the light went out.

Then I was hauled across the bed and positioned in the half spoon/half pin he was so good at carrying off.

I didn't struggle. I was doing pretty good at the silent treatment so I just stayed tense and used my body to communicate that all was not forgiven. The Silent Treatment/Cold Shoulder was a perfectly honed weapon in my arsenal and I was not afraid to use it.

Apropos of nothing, Lee told the back of my head, "The last time I remember feelin' fear was during survival training. I thought if the good guys could think up that shit for training, what were the bad guys gonna do?"

Um.

Yikes!

It was apparently story time for bad little girls.

"Then I realized I might not be able to control what they were doing, but I could control my reaction. Fear breaks your focus, makes you lose control, makes you weak. It gives the enemy the edge. That was the last time I felt fear and the last time I lost control."

I was still tense, but now for a different reason, waiting to hear what he was going to say next.

"Tonight Ally called and told me you'd been taken. I left you there and they came to Tom's fucking front door and grabbed you. When I heard that, I lost control."

Holy shit.

What did that mean?

What was he saying?

Was he scared?

About me and the idea of maybe losing me?

Oh... my... *God.*

I waited for him to say more, to explain, but he didn't.

So I waited some more.

Nothing.

"What does that mean, you lost control?" I whispered.

More nothing.

After a while, his fingers brushed my hair aside and his lips touched my nape.

I let it go at that and listened to his steady breathing. I knew he wasn't asleep, and I also knew our talk was over. No way was Liam Nightingale going to admit, out loud, to being scared. That was as good as I was going to get.

And it was all I needed.

I let the tension go out of my body and settled into him, wriggling my bottom into his groin.

There was a time to hold a grudge.

This wasn't that time.

Chapter 12

I Did My Duty to the Pot

I woke up when I felt the sheet go down my hip and a hand go up it.

I turned bleary eyes to Lee who was sitting, from what I could tell in the dawns early light, fully-clothed on the side of the bed.

"I need coffee," I mumbled.

"You don't have to get up. I'm just sayin' good-bye," he answered.

I blinked in the semi-darkness. "Where are you going?"

But I'd lost his attention. He was looking in the vicinity of my hips.

"Do you always wear underwear like this, or is it for me?"

I rolled to my back and pulled the sheet to my waist.

"It isn't for you. I've been wearing underwear like this since Gram gave me my first Frederick's of Hollywood box on my sixteenth birthday. Now I owe Victoria's Secret my firstborn child."

Before speaking again, Lee waited several seconds that can only be described as "loaded silence". While this silence was going on, he pulled the sheet back down.

"You're tellin' me that since you were sixteen you've been sittin' next to me every year at Christmas Dinner wearin' underwear like this?"

I was having trouble processing all that was happening, seeing as it was oh-dark-hundred, Lee was dressed and leaving, and we were talking about my underwear.

Had I sat beside him at Christmas Dinner every year?

I had. At first because I finagled it, the last ten years by a cruel twist of fate.

"I didn't sit by you," I kind of lied.

"No, *I* sat by *you*."

At that unbelievable announcement, I got up on my two elbows and winced. Another learning experience: rolling around in bushes with your arms cuffed behind your back made you ache.

I glanced at the clock. Five after five.

"It's five after five! Where are you going?"

He leaned forward and brushed my lips with his.

"Hunting."

The way he said it made me fear for all the furry little creatures in the woods. Then I realized that Lee didn't hunt, at least not furry little creatures.

Yikes.

I considered what to say and settled on, "Be careful."

An arm went around me and he pulled me to him. I was not a big fan of morning kisses before brushing your teeth, especially if tongue was involved.

His kiss was so fine, I made an exception and kissed him back.

He dragged me across his lap and deepened the kiss. If the kiss got any deeper, my lovely sage green satin undies with smoky gray lace were going to spontaneously combust.

When he lifted his head, he said, "Call Hank if you go anywhere. I need my men working. Hank's gonna watch you today."

Since I didn't want to get kidnapped again, and yesterday had beaten out the day I called the ticket line and found out Pearl Jam was sold out as the worst day of my life, I replied, "Okay."

He kissed me quickly, deposited me back in bed and then he was gone.

I slept more, got up, drank coffee, sucked down some ibuprofen and called Hank to come and get me. I didn't know what I intended to do that day, but I was too wired by recent events to sit around all day in Lee's condo.

I surveyed myself in Lee's bathroom mirror. The semi-shiner was fading, but still there.

I looked down at my body.

I had added bruises on my wrists, biceps and thighs, as well as some small scratches on my arms and legs.

Very attractive.

To make myself feel better about this situation, I turned to my MAC cosmetics. MAC never let me down. I put on some dewy blush, eye shadow that really had no color but was mostly sparkles, that white under-mascara basecoat that makes our eyelashes look a mile long, and a double coat of mascara. I donned my Lynyrd Skynryd t-shirt, jeans, black woven belt with the big, square, silver buckle stamped with tiny roses and black cowboy boots.

I'd just tugged on the second boot when my cell rang.

"We have a problem," Duke's gravely, Sam Elliott voice crunched in my ear.

"Duke! God, I'm glad to hear from you."

"I'm at the store—"

"I closed the store for the weekend," I informed him belatedly.

"I saw the note. I opened it. We have a near riot on our hands here. People are freakin' that Rosie's not here. It started out pretty peaceful, but now the mob wants blood."

"Are you there alone?" I asked.

I was aghast. Staffing Fortnum's in the morning alone in the years pre-espresso counter was doable. Post-coffee, impossible.

"Dolores is with me," Duke answered.

Uh-oh.

Dolores drank instant coffee. This was not a good thing.

"I'll be there as soon as I can."

I flipped my phone shut and the buzzer went off just as my cell rang again.

The phone was Ally. I flipped it open and told her to hang on while I hit the button on Lee's intercom. It was Hank so I told him I'd be down to meet him.

"You doin' okay?" Ally asked.

"Yeah, I ache, but other than that, fine," I answered.

"What're you up to today?"

"Duke opened Fortnum's and just phoned in a potential Rosie Riot. I'm heading over with Hank."

"I'll meet you there."

Hank was not thrilled about heading into a riot situation as the first order of business during his Indy Watch. I talked him into it by alluding to concerns about his masculinity.

I walked in the door at Fortnum's and wished I'd let Hank talk me out of riot control. There were at least fifteen, maybe twenty people and the air crackled with hostility. It was pretty clear that the regulars were okay with a few confused Rosie-free days, but now the natives were getting restless.

Annie spied me before the door shut behind Hank. Annie had been coming every weekday morning for years, eight fifteen, wearing a suit, her blonde hair molded into a style reminiscent of a football helmet. We'd chatted over the counter hundreds of times and she was always pleasant if sometimes in a hurry. It was Sunday, and I'd never seen her there on a weekend.

"What the fuck is going on here? Where's the little guy who makes the coffee?" she snapped.

I stared at her and my mouth dropped open.

"Yeah. Where's Rosie and why was the store closed yesterday? Ellen never closed the store. As in ever." That was Manuel. He'd been a regular since before the days of caffeine. He used to read Vonnegut and Updike for hours in the T-U-V section. I'd known him for as long as I could remember.

"I go out of my way, seventeen blocks, for the Coffee Guy's coffee. What am I gonna do now? Where am I gonna go?" another guy asked. I didn't know his name, but he'd come with Rosie after he left the chain coffee shop and usually popped by a couple of Sundays a month and sometimes actually bought a book.

They started to press in and Hank pushed in front of me going into body-guard mode.

Really, I was fed up. I understood the love of coffee but this was ridiculous. I'd had the worst few days of my entire life. I was Lee Nightingale's girlfriend and we hadn't *done it* yet. I was a woman on the edge.

I stood on a chair, put my thumb and finger in my mouth and gave the ear-splitting whistle Dad taught me when I was eleven.

"Listen up people!" I shouted.

All eyes turned to me as I noticed Mr. Kumar walk in with an Asian woman his age and another one much older, the second one possibly prehistoric.

I turned my attention back to the mob.

"The Coffee Guy, whose name is Rosie, by the way, has moved to El Salvador," I lied.

This was not met with happy noises.

I went on.

"He's turned his back on coffee and is in the wilds of Central America building houses for the poor. I think we should all take a moment away from our quest for coffee satisfaction and think about this noble decision. As you clamor for caffeine and curse the hard-working but innocent staff at my store, Rosie is sitting in the bed of a beat up pickup bumping across dirt roads to make one room homes out of mud for those who have nothing at all."

I was kind of laying it on thick and had no idea what I was talking about, but I was counting on American insularity. Since we hadn't been to war with El Salvador, what did anyone know about it?

Now people were staring at me as if I was a performer in the Jim Rose Circus Sideshow.

Still, I kept going.

"I'll understand if you make the decision to move back to a franchise coffee shop, but consider this. In a couple of years, little businesses like mine, and Mr. Kumar's over there," I pointed at Kumar and his neck descended three inches into his shoulders, "are going to be taken over and America will be wall-to-wall franchises. The franchise is killing off America's Mom and Pop shops. Ask yourself… is that what you want? Is that what you *really* want?"

No one said a word.

"I said, *is that what you want?*" I shouted.

There was some shuffling of feet and someone said a quiet, "No."

It wasn't exactly a ringing endorsement or a cry to freedom, but I was beginning to feel like an idiot. I mean, I was talking like Tex, for God's sake, not to mention standing on a chair.

"Good. Duke's taking coffee orders. We'll get you all sorted out in no time. Thank you for your attention." I stepped off the chair and Hank was grinning at me. I figured Lee would hear about this. It didn't matter, they were used to me doing crazy shit. I ignored Hank and smiled at Kumar.

"Hey, Mr. Kumar."

"India," he said. "This is my wife, Mrs. Kumar, and my wife's mother, Mrs. Salim."

I smiled at the women. Mrs. Kumar was clearly a beauty in her day and the bloom was not yet off the rose. She smiled back and it reached her eyes with a dazzle.

Mrs. Salim's entire face was wrinkled and motionless and I fought the urge to listen for her breathing.

"You buy food at my store," Mr. Kumar stated. "We are here to buy books at yours."

Something about this show of solidarity made me want to cry. Mr. Kumar must have sensed it because he bowed his head to me. I bowed mine back.

"Then we are going to go to see Tex in the hospital. Then we will go and open our store," he finished.

"I'm going to see Tex later, too," I informed him.

He nodded. "Now I can see that you need to make coffee."

I nodded back and Ally pushed through the door. She saw Kumar right away and smiled, pushing forward. "Hey Mr. Kumar. Is this the missus? Whoa!"

Ally rounded the Kumars, saw Mrs. Salim and couldn't hide her reaction.

I left her extracting her foot out of her mouth.

Dolores was taking orders, saying such things to the customers as, "Skinny lah-tay, uh, come again?" and Duke was making coffee.

Dolores worked at the Little Bear, which was a very cool and could-get-rowdy bar in Evergreen. She could take an order for eight margaritas, two without salt, three frozen, three Jack and cokes, a white Russian and a Shirley Temple, fill it without a mistake and carry it all to the table on one tray. With coffee, she was hopeless. She came in to help out at Fortnum's every once in a while and it was never pretty.

I shouldered in next to Duke and made Hank a cappuccino with a triple shot. Pepper Rick was still on the loose and I wanted Hank hyper-alert. Hank positioned himself at the end of the counter in full view of the front door and in reaching distance of me.

"I guess I picked the wrong time for a bender," Duke said to me.

"Yeah, but I'm getting used to getting stun-gunned, kidnapped and shot at. Finding the dead body was a serious bummer, and Tex got shot in the shoulder last night, but other than that, no worries."

Duke went still. Dolores looked up from the paper cup on which she was frantically misspelling instructions in hot pink marker and stared at me with huge eyes. The customer standing in front of the espresso machine gaped at me.

Er, I guess Lee didn't fill Duke in yesterday.

"You wanna run that by me again?" Duke suggested.

I eyed the customer and pulled at the machine. "Later."

We cleared the throng just as the happy sound of the cash register at the book counter rang. As per usual, everyone looked up and Ally yelled the ceremonial, "I sold a book!"

Sometimes when someone sold a book, we shouted it. It was cause for celebration.

I did my book sale happy dance, waving my arms and turning in a circle. When I finished my dance, I noticed it was The Kumars' purchase. They were standing in front of Ally and I gave them a big thumbs up.

In slow motion, old Mrs. Salim returned the gesture and I feared that her thumb would break off in a poof of dust like the zombie's arm in Michael Jackson's "Thriller" video. She snatched the bag from Ally with bony fingers and they walked out on a wave, Mrs. Salim shuffling behind, her bag rustling.

"Now that we have a second, let's go back over the kidnapping and dead body thing," Duke said to me, his fingers scratching his forehead under his trademark rolled red bandana.

My cell phone rang.

Saved by the cell.

I flipped it open.

"Hello?"

Silence, then a quiet voice said, "I need a Rock Chick rescue."

"Sorry?" I asked.

"A scary guy was at the door. He's gone, but I know he's gonna come back, I know it. He knows I've got them and he's gonna get me like he got Tim."

It was The Kevster. Who was at the door, only God knew, but it didn't sound good. And The Kevster had something, something I hoped was glittery and worth a million dollars.

"Kevin?" I asked.

"You gotta help me."

The phone went dead.

I looked to Ally.

"The Kevster's in trouble." I swung my eyes to Hank. "We gotta roll."

I took off from behind the counter, but was halted on a skid when Hank grabbed a handful of my tee.

"What's goin' on?"

I gave him the lowdown, trying to pull him along with me, he stood stock-still and shook his head.

"I'll call it in," Hank said.

"No! No cops," I replied. "He's a little… sensitive."

Hank stared at me and his mouth got tight.

"I'm a cop," he reminded me.

"Not today," I tried.

I failed.

"*Everyday*," he returned.

165

"Hank, seriously, for some reason he trusts me and Ally. We gotta go and you gotta be cool."

"Indy, seriously, you aren't going anywhere and I don't gotta be anything." Ally walked up to us. "I'll go."

"You aren't going either." Hank looked at the both of us. "Jesus. I'll go." Hank started walking to the door asking where Kevin lived.

I followed close behind.

He turned and I slammed into him.

"Stay," he said.

"I'm not a dog!"

"You aren't going."

"I'm not staying."

Hank glanced at Duke and I was pretty sure they were going to gang up on me, so I burst out, "They kidnapped me at the front door of my childhood home! They won't think twice about coming here. I'm not leaving you and you have to go save The Kevster so I'm going with you."

"I'm going too," Ally said.

Turning the tables, Ally and I ganged up on Hank. He looked about ready to commit murder, but he relented. He'd known Ally and me long enough to know we'd get our way come hell or high water.

"You have to do what I tell you," he demanded.

That was not gonna happen.

"Sure," I lied.

He stared at me. He knew I was lying. He blew out a sigh and we left.

Hank had barely rolled his 4Runner to a stop outside The Kevster's house when I was out the door.

"Indy, for fuck's sake!" Hank shouted.

I ran to Kevin's front door and pounded on it.

"Kevin, it's me. Indy Savage, Rock Chick," I called, sounding stupid, but I was also thinking that maybe Kevin had the diamonds and I wanted them. I wanted this all to be over. I didn't want to be tied to a chair ever again. I wanted that enough to sound stupid.

I felt Hank come up behind me just as the door was thrown open.

Kevin reached out, grabbed my arm and tugged me inside. Every sore, aching muscle in my body screamed out and Kevin swung the door shut behind me.

Not fast enough. Hank had time to twist his torso and slammed his shoulder into the door. It flew open, sending Kevin careening against the opposite wall.

In two strides Hank was on him, his hand at The Kevster's throat, holding him against the wall.

"Hank, it's okay, that's Kevin," I said.

Hank turned to me then looked beyond me and said, "Jesus fucking Christ."

Ally was also in and she was staring behind me, and then she tipped back her head and laughed.

I turned and saw that The Kevster's living room was filled with pot plants. Every surface was covered with plants, and that included the floor. There was a narrow path forged through the plants, but other than that it was wall-to-wall marijuana. It was a pot jungle.

"Holy crap," I said.

"Gulk," The Kevster said.

"Hank, let him go," Ally said.

Hank's hand loosened at Kevin's throat and his other hand went to the small of his back. He was wearing jeans, boots and a gray t-shirt that fit snug on the shoulders and chest but sat loose at his waist. He pulled up the back of his tee and exposed a gun tucked into his waistband next to a pair of cuffs. He pulled out the cuffs and slapped a bracelet on Kevin then he yanked him toward a door and slapped the other bracelet on the doorknob.

Kevin was coughing and explaining at the same time.

"Dude! I had to save the plants! They were dyin'. They didn't do anything wrong. They're innocent. Rosie left them to die. *Someone* had to save the plants."

Hank ignored Rosie and turned to me.

"I want to talk to you," he clipped.

He stalked through the pot path and I followed him into Kevin's kitchen, which was also filled with pot plants.

Hank glanced around and then turned on me.

"What in *the* fuck?" he asked.

"How'm I supposed to know what the fuck? I thought he was calling about Pepper Rick, the guy who kidnapped me. I didn't know anything about this."

Hank stared at me for a beat and then looked to the ceiling.

"What're you gonna do?" I asked.

"I'm callin' it in," he answered in a no-nonsense cop tone.

Uh-oh.

"Can we take the plants back to Rosie's first and call it in from there?" I suggested.

Hank stared at me incredulously as if I'd just asked for permission to run the world and make every Tuesday International Pink Champagne Day.

I guessed that was not going to happen.

"Okay then, can the police take the plants and leave Kevin?" I tried an alternate. "They aren't his plants. He's just looking after them as a concerned environmentalist."

Hank put his hands to his hips.

I sucked some air into my nostrils and then let it out. "How much trouble is he in?"

"Indy, do you have any idea how much this shit is worth?"

I looked around. I'd seen pot. I'd been around people smoking pot. I'd even shared a few joints myself in my wild past. But I had no idea.

"Uh, no," I answered.

"He's in a lot of trouble."

I was afraid of that.

We followed the pot path back to Ally and The Kevster. The Kevster looked freaked. Ally had clearly cottoned on to the seriousness of the matter.

"What are you gonna do?" she asked Hank.

He walked right by her and out the door, pulling out his cell.

"This isn't good," I said to Ally.

"Why'd you bring a cop here?" Kevin whined.

"He's my bodyguard. I keep getting shot at and kidnapped," I told him.

The Kevster stared at me. This news always brought the same amazed look to everyone. Then again, it was amazing.

Then Kevin said, "Tim's dead. I heard it on the news. Rosie fucked us all."

This was true. Quiet little Rosie, the Coffee Guy, had fucked us all.

"Why did you bring the plants here?" Ally asked the million dollar question.

"Dude, I'm a pothead. This is the best pot in Denver, in Colorado, maybe in the world. It would be a crime to let it die. I did my duty to the pot, I pay the price. I have no regrets," The Kevster was getting dramatic in the face of incarceration. I thought that was a good way to go.

"Tell me about this guy who came today. What'd he look like?" I asked.

The Kevster shrugged. Obviously, a future of using the toilet with an audience made scary guys seem less scary.

"He was one that came before, but without his partner. Dark hair with some gray, big guy. I saw him out the window. He looked angry."

I turned to Ally, she raised her brows and I nodded.

Pepper Rick.

"When was he here?" Ally asked.

"This morning. It wasn't even light yet," The Kevster answered. "Bangin' on the door, bangin' on the windows, shoutin'. Freaked me out. I didn't leave my bedroom and your card was on my fridge. I waited for, like, ever. Then I had to pee and I grabbed your card and the phone on my way to the bathroom. I called you after I peed."

That was a bit too much information.

Unfortunately, Pepper Rick was probably long gone. I had to call Lee anyway. He was hunting and this was information about his prey.

I walked outside and saw Hank talking to a couple of uniforms. One was Jorge Alvarez, who was soon supposed to sit the detective exam, and, according to Malcolm, would likely be Chief of Police one day.

His partner was Carl Farrell, who Ally had made out with after an F.O.P. hog roast. Carl had a bachelor's, majoring in biology and political science, and was now studying forensics. Carl was tall, big, blond-haired and blue-eyed. Carl's hair was always a bit of a mess. Carl had a killer, dry sense of humor and Carl had a way of looking at you like he knew what you looked like naked. In other words, Carl was very sexy. If I hadn't been so hung up on Lee, Ally'd have had competition for Carl.

I waved to Jorge and Carl as they walked inside. Jorge shook his finger at me mock angrily. Carl grinned then winked as he walked by.

Hank headed toward me.

I was about to call Lee when my cell rang.

I flipped it open.

"Hello?"

"Hello yourself, woman. You comin' to get me, or what?"

It was Tex.

"What do you mean?" I asked.

"They're lettin' me out and won't let me walk or take a taxi."

I thought about this. He was at Denver Health and it was at least five miles from his house. Crazy Tex, roaming the streets whacked out on pain killers, did not sound like a peaceful afternoon for Denver.

Two more cop cars angled in, followed by a Channel 9 News van.

Great.

The pot jungle was going to be big news.

"When are they releasing you?" I asked Tex.

"Ten minutes ago."

"I'll be there as soon as I can."

I flipped the phone shut and Hank stared at me. "What now?"

Ally came out of the house just ahead of Jorge, Carl and The Kevster.

Or, I should say, Ally sashayed out of the house with a knowing smile on her face and Carl followed, staring at her ass, a knowing smile on his face, too.

Another cop car angled in and Channel 7 News jockeyed for a parking spot. Jorge tossed Hank his cuffs as he passed us, escorting Kevin to the squad car.

"Come visit me, Rock Chicks," Kevin shouted, luckily not holding any grudges. "Bring brownies!"

"You take him brownies and I'll kill you," Hank threatened.

I ignored his threat. "Do you have to stay here?"

"No, I briefed Jorge," Hank told me. "They have it covered. We'll go into the station later to give our statements."

"Good, we have to go get Tex from the hospital," I replied. "They released him ten minutes ago and he needs a ride."

Hank was shaking his head again. "We're not goin' to Tex's house. There's strong physical evidence that suggests he has tear gas and grenades. I don't even want to think about what we'll find in *his* house. I'll have to call the ATF and those guys are nuts."

"Then don't come in," I suggested.

"Indy—"

I pulled out my trump card.

"He took a bullet for me."

That did it.

"Lee owes me big time for this," Hank muttered as he walked to his SUV.

My cell rang as we pulled away from the curb.

The display said, "Lee calling."

"Hey, I was just gonna call you," I said.

"The office phoned. You're all over the police band."

Oopsie.

"I kind of led Hank to a house full of pot plants and he went all cop on me."

Silence.

"Lee?"

"Why aren't you at the condo?"

"Duke called, he opened the store. There was a Mini-We-Want-Rosie Riot. We settled that, and then The Kevster called and told us someone was at his house, scaring him. I thought it was my kidnapper, Pepper Rick, and it was. That's why I was gonna call you, because he was at Kevin's early this morning banging on the door. I thought you'd want to know."

Silence again.

"Lee?"

"Where's Hank?"

"He's driving, we're on our way to get Tex and take him home. The hospital released him."

"Let me talk to him."

I looked at Hank. Hank looked unhappy.

"I don't think that's a good idea."

"Why?"

"I think he's kinda mad at you."

"Let me get this straight, he's supposed to be lookin' after you, and he takes you to a house where your kidnapper was, just hours ago, and *he's* mad at *me?*"

Yikes.

"I guess the feeling's mutual," I remarked.

More silence.

"I kinda talked him into it," I admitted.

"Yeah, I suspect you're good at that."

"If it makes you feel better, he's already threatened to kill me."

I heard the sigh before, "Be safe, for Christ's sake."

Then he hung up.

When Hank swung in the SUV, Tex was at the Emergency Room entrance, sitting in a wheelchair, his arm in a tight sling with a stocky guy in scrubs and clogs standing behind him.

Tex pushed himself out of the chair as we walked up to him and he shot a filthy look at the guy in scrubs.

"Fuckin' wheelchairs. Fuckin' orderlies," Tex groused.

"I'm not an orderly. I'm a nursing assistant," Clog Guy said, and from the look of him, there was no way I'd disagree. He could be anything he wanted.

"Whatever," Tex muttered and his eyes settled on me. "What'd I miss?"

I ran it down for him with a little more detail than what I did for Lee: the riot, Kumar's prehistoric mother-in-law, the Kevster call, kidnapper sighting, pot plants, police and two news vans.

"Fuckin' A, darlin'," he said to me.

"Fuckin' A," I replied. "Now what?"

Tex lumbered to the SUV. "Now we feed the cats."

Chapter 13
Pandemonium at the Gay Bar

We went to Tex's house, he changed clothes and we fed his gazillion cats and cleaned out five litter trays. It wasn't the most pleasant job I'd ever done in my life, but the kitties were appreciative. Tex made us stay long enough to give them cuddles, dangle feathers and jiggle laser lights, because according to Tex, it was important to keep their minds and bodies active.

Luckily, there were no stockpiles of firearms and explosives on display.

When we started to leave, Tex followed.

Hank stopped and turned.

"Where are you goin'?" he asked Tex.

"With you," Tex answered.

"I don't think so," Hank replied.

"You think *you* can protect Little Miss Calamity here all by yourself?" Tex scoffed, jerking a thumb at me.

Er, excuse me? Little Miss Calamity?

"You have your arm in a sling," Hank returned.

"Listen man, I been on this block for twenty years without leavin' except to go to the fuckin' dentist when I had a toothache in 1998. I got off it last night, and for the first time in years, I feel free."

Hank considered this.

Hank was a tough guy, but he'd always been somewhat of a soft touch. The only fights he ever got into were when people were teasing the unpopular kids at school or saying shit about girls that he knew wasn't true (these girls were usually Ally and me). When he was a kid, he used to bring home the lame dogs and damaged birds. I always thought that Hank got into the cop business far less to serve than to protect.

"Lee owes me big time for this," he repeated, giving in.

We walked down to Kumar's and stocked up on junk food and got the makings for a late lunch. Then we went to the station and gave our statements about the happenings at The Kevster's pot farm. Then we went to my house.

Stevie and Tod were in the front yard mowing, weeding and pruning. Kitty Sue was taking in the sun on my front porch in my old, weathered butterfly chair that once had a bright turquoise canvas seat that was now a bluish-gray. Marianne Meyer was sitting on my front step playing with a baby, and Andrea was chasing after a toddler who was streaking across my side of the lawn, while two more of her kids were rolling around in the grass looking like they were trying to kill each other.

Hank parked across the street from my duplex and we all walked up to the house. Everyone stared at Tex, for even without the night vision goggles, he was a sight to see.

Then Marianne's attention focused on me.

"Well?" Marianne asked.

"Well, what?" I retorted.

Marianne threw up her hands. "Does Lee have the bow off your panties?"

Grr.

Tod and Stevie came up, saving me from having to answer.

"Kitty Sue told us you were kidnapped last night," Stevie noted with concern.

"Again," Tod put in.

Before I could say anything, Kitty Sue called from her chair, "Why didn't you tell me Tod was performing tonight? You know I like to see Burgundy do her thang."

"What's this about panties?" Tex broke in.

"Do you think we could turn the hose on the kids? It's so hot and they'd love it," Andrea shouted from across the lawn, struggling to get a pair of shorts on the streaker.

"Oh, by the way," Kitty Sue said, getting up from the butterfly chair, "we've decided to go out for pizza before Tod's show, all of us. Won't that be fun?"

Everyone was staring at me and I was at a momentary loss. Okay, it wasn't as if I'd lived an uneventful life. My life was pretty active and kind of exciting, but all of it had been controlled. This was out of hand.

Ally, as she had many a time, saved my bacon.

"Marianne, it's none of your business, so quit asking and go get yourself laid, for God's sake. Hank, get the hose and turn it on those monsters before they tear up the yard. Tex, go upstairs and lay down for a while. Mom, help me make everyone a sandwich." Then she shoved forward, taking our shopping bags, opened my house with her key and went in.

"I love your sister," I said to Hank.

He threw his arm around my shoulders, pulled me into his body and gave me a sideways hug.

Tod and Stevie had gone back to yard work and I felt the guilt pull. Their side of the lawn was lush, green and manicured. The edges that butted our brick walkways were cut precisely. Colorful flowers grew healthy along the front, black wrought iron fence, down the wooden fence at the side and in the beds in front of their porch. They had a basket on the porch overhang that happily dripped fuchsias, and terracotta pots on each step of the stoop trailing ivy and bursting with flowers.

My side of the lawn was also mowed and had clean and cut borders, but only because Stevie did it. I'd planted flowers in my flower beds, but they were being choked by weeds, had not been watered in days and looked dry and close to death. The fuchsia basket that Tod bought me to balance the look of the duplex was bedraggled and only in slightly better shape than the flower beds because it didn't have weeds attacking it.

Their side looked like Martha Stewart. My side looked like Sanford and Son.

I needed to help with the yard work. It was my neighborly duty.

I went into the house and up to my bedroom. I was running out of clothes at Lee's place so I dumped the contents of my ever-ready, rarely-used workout bag and shoved items in just in case my stay there lasted longer. I took off my clothes, slathered myself with factor 8 and put on a pair of cutoff jeans shorts and a kelly green camisole with a shelf bra. I gathered my hair in a messy knot on top of my head, grabbed my phone and called Lee.

"Yeah?" he answered.

"How's it going?"

"Not good."

He didn't sound happy.

Yikes.

"If you get finished in time, we're going out for pizza before Tod's show tonight," I shared.

"Who's 'we'?" he asked.

"Your Mom says 'all of us' so I'm guessing that means Marianne Meyer, Andrea Moran and her kids, probably Ally and Hank, likely Dad and Malcolm, and select players from the Colorado Rockies," I paused, "oh, and Tex."

"Marianne Meyer and Andrea Moran?"

"They're on a Lee and Indy Sex Watch."

"Come again?"

"They want to know when we've *done it*."

Silence.

I went on, "If we don't do it soon, they might force us to at gunpoint."

"Christ."

"I know. No pressure though. I told them we're taking it slow."

"You have to report in?" he asked.

"I kind of feel obliged," I admitted.

"How's that?"

I didn't want to tell him I'd recruited them both for Lee Maneuvers in the past, so I said, "Never mind."

"If something doesn't happen soon, it's gonna be bad. I can't keep focused. All I can think of is what's on your Victoria's Secret credit statement."

"You need to keep focused," I told him. "Bad guys are after me."

"Tell me about it."

He hung up and I went into the other bedroom. Tex was lying on the couch, a sandwich on a plate and an open bag of chips both balanced on his sling. My remote was in his hand, the TV was on and a ballgame was blaring.

"You okay?" I asked.

"Peachy." He flipped through channels, acting for all the world as if he was a regular houseguest.

I got a sandwich from Ally and Kitty Sue, ate it standing up and then went outside. Hank was alternately hosing down Andrea's monsters and watering my fuchsia and lawn. I hunkered down to weed my front flower bed, got into it about three feet and decided to take a break.

I laid down on my back in the grass and fell into an impromptu Disco Nap. What could I say? Yard work did that to me.

Something soft trailed down my temple and across my cheek. I opened my eyes and saw Lee crouched beside me, blocking the sun.

"I don't like yard work," I told him.

"My condo doesn't have a yard," he replied.

Hmm.

I sat up. He grabbed my hand and helped me to my feet. Someone (probably Kitty Sue and Marianne) had weeded the side and front beds. The one I was working on was still only half done. The yard was quiet. I took in a happy breath at the sweet bliss of aloneness.

"Don't get too excited. We have an audience watching us from three different windows," Lee told me.

Lee was close, looking down into my face, forcing me to tilt my head to look up at him. He always looked handsome, but now I could see the tiredness around his eyes and mouth. It occurred to me he'd been at this for days, nonstop. I'd been lucky enough to squeeze in a couple of Disco Naps.

"How did hunting go today?" I asked.

"I'm used to better results."

"That doesn't sound good," I noted.

"It isn't," he agreed.

"What are you thinking?"

"I don't think he's gone to ground, one of my contacts would know something. That means he's either skipped town, which is unlikely, or he's dead."

I sucked in breath.

"Is dead an option?"

"He has some enemies, starting with Coxy," Lee answered.

"You wanna explain that to me?"

"Not now. It's nearly pizza time and I need to go home and shower."

"Do you want to shower here?" I tried to ignore the thrill the thought of a naked Lee in my shower gave me and pretend it didn't affect me.

"I want to shower with you. Are you comin' with me?"

Okay, I couldn't pretend he didn't affect me. He seriously affected me.

I looked back at the house and saw faces swiftly disappear from the windows. "I don't think I should. I have company."

He grabbed me and kissed me, hard and quick and also disappointingly fast.

"Wear sexy panties tonight," he said against my mouth.

"I don't have any other options except commando."

Lee's arm tightened spasmodically right before he murmured, "Christ."

Lee met us at the Beau Jo's.

Beau Jo's offered huge, thick-crusted "mountain pies" that were the best pizza I'd ever had outside the times Dad and I visited Aunt Sunny in Chicago. Mountain pie crust was so thick you saved the edges, smothered them with honey and ate them for dessert.

Our table seemed a mile long and it was mayhem. As if Andrea's children weren't enough to make us loud and obnoxious to all other customers, Duke and Dolores joined us, as did Dad and Malcolm. Duke, Tex, Dad and Malcolm seemed to be in a contest to out-booming-macho-male talk each other.

Lee slid into the seat beside me, his hair still wet from the shower and curling around his neck and ears. He was wearing a pair of beat up, faded, army green cargo pants and a light blue, loose-fitting collared shirt, untucked, the right-amount of buttons left undone and the sleeves rolled partially up his forearms.

He looked hot.

For no apparent reason, before Lee fully settled into his seat, Andrea's baby let out a high-pitched scream. I liked kids, of course. Other people's kids. In small doses. Very small doses.

Once Andrea had cooed it to semi-quietness, I turned to Lee.

"Do you want children?"

His eyes slid to me as he grabbed a menu.

He answered cautiously, "Yeah."

"How many?"

He turned to me and his arm went around the back of my chair.

"Three."

I thought about three children. They weren't pleasant thoughts.

"And you?" Lee asked, gently tugging my hair.

"Hmm?"

"Kids?"

"I can't even take care of my yard," I reminded him.

He smiled The Smile and I immediately decided I'd like three kids a whole lot.

"How are things?" Dad asked Lee.

Lee glanced at Dad, took his arm from my chair then studied the menu. "Depends. Some are great, some not so good."

Dad nodded, apparently happy with that answer or at least understanding it. I sat there thinking a lot more was said than what was actually said. Men had a mysterious way of communicating.

We ate. We chased after children who wanted to visit other diners' tables. We talked. We laughed. And after a while I began to relax. Life had been so weird lately I didn't even realize how tense it was making me. I didn't realize how much I needed a night like tonight.

I poured honey on my crust and watched Tex, who seemed not like a man who had barricaded himself on his block for two decades, but like someone relaxed and who fit in with my family and friends.

Then again, you bought yourself some serious loyalty by saving a daughter/sister/girlfriend from being held hostage and getting shot for your troubles.

I ate my honeyed crust and my eyes moved to Lee, who was listening to Dolores. His thigh was pressed against mine under the table, and twice he had handed me the honey without me having to ask for it. The Savages and the Nightingales had been to Beau Jo's dozens of times, either in Denver for whatever occasion, or Idaho Springs after a day of skiing.

Lee knew when I wanted the honey.

Yikes.

How did this happen?

There was no denying we were actually *together*, not test driving it. We'd blown right past the "getting to know you" phase of the relationship because we didn't need it. We were smack dab into the comfortable part of a relationship, the part that held shared intimacy because of history.

Even so, we still had the thrill of the newness about our situation. Discovering hidden things about each other, like him having a housekeeper, keeping good java in the kitchen, being incredibly moody, kissing really, really well and having a naked body that was a gift from the gods.

At these thoughts, inexplicably, panic overwhelmed me.

Sensing it because he was a freak of nature, Lee's head immediately turned to me.

"What's the matter?" he asked.

Self-preservation kicked in over the panic and I lied.

"Nothing."

He turned fully to me and his arm went around the back of my chair again, his other forearm resting on the table, fencing me in.

"What's the matter?" he repeated.

"Nothing!" I snapped.

He watched me for a couple of beats and then he said calmly, "We're gonna have to work at kickin' your lying habit."

"I'm not lying," I lied.

He leaned in. "What we have here is good, and if you'd get over your thoughts that it isn't gonna last, you'd realize how much better it's gonna get if you'd just relax."

See! He totally knew me. It was beginning to be scary.

Since lying wasn't going to work, I changed strategies and went for annoyance.

"Get out of my brain, it's pissing me off," I warned him.

Then I learned (or more to the point realized) something new about Lee. Something he'd been showing me for days.

Lee didn't play games and he didn't like me doing it either. Perhaps surviving life-threatening situations and living a life filled with danger made you more honest and less apt to waste precious time.

"What kind of underwear are you wearing?" he asked.

"What? Why?"

"Because if you describe it to me, I might decide you're worth the trouble."

It was best to cut my losses so I crossed my arms on my chest and glared at him.

He turned away, completely unperturbed.

I caught sight of Dad, who was sitting down the table from us. There was no way he could have heard what we were saying because Lee had his back to him and spoke low. Still, Dad was shaking his head.

"What?" I snapped at my father.

"Jesus, it's uncanny. You're just like your mother."

⋇

Everyone dispersed to get ready for Burgundy Rose's show, Ally taking responsibility for Tex, Lee taking me home in his Crossfire.

I'd showered before Beau Jo's, but hadn't prettied myself up because most of my makeup was at Lee's. We walked up to the bedroom so I could change and Lee saw the bag.

"What's this?"

I didn't want to admit what it was and what it meant that I packed it. Since Lee saw through most of my lies, or was cocky enough to zip it open and see for himself, I came clean.

"I was running out of stuff at your place so I packed more provisions."

His eyes crinkled their approval. His arm snaked out and pulled me to him. And his mouth went to the skin below my ear.

"You done pretending to be mad at me to hide bein' scared?" he murmured.

My whole body stiffened.

"Don't be a jerk."

His head lifted and he looked me in the eye.

"You're right. That was an asshole remark."

Holy shit.

What did you say to that?

"I'm tired, it's been a long day," he continued, his hand coming up to pinch his nose between his eyes.

"That's all right," I said. "And no, I'm not mad at you or pretending to be mad. But I need to put makeup on and all my good stuff is at your condo so I have to visit Chez Burgundy."

I had put my Lynyrd Skynyrd outfit back on for Beau Jo's. I changed my top to a thin, black, silky, partially-beaded, spaghetti-strapped affair that was in the Sushi Den section of my closet. This necessitated no bra, and since Lee seemed quite happy laying back on my bed with his arms crossed behind his head, watching me change (and I would have felt like a naïve fool locking myself in the bathroom), I had to pull a Jennifer Beals *Flashdance* move and take the bra off after I put the top on. I kept the jeans, but exchanged the belt for the one with rhinestones and the boots for high-heeled sandals with jet beads sewn across the front strap. I added about two dozen shiny black bangles on my wrist and some dangly earrings.

When I was done, I turned to the bed. I thought Lee was watching me, but he was asleep.

I sat next to his hip and the minute he felt my weight on the bed, his eyes opened.

"Why don't you rest?" I asked. "We'll come back after the show."

His hand came from behind his head and his finger traced the silky strap at my shoulder. "I'm not lettin' you out of my sight."

My breath had started coming faster when he touched me. "It'll be okay. Everyone'll be there."

His eyes locked on mine and I read that nothing more could be said. Lee had made up his mind.

His finger hooked in the strap and tugged it toward him. Either I could resist and risk the fragile strap breaking or I could acquiesce. I liked the top so I leaned into him.

His arms circled me and I rested my hands on his chest.

"How long is this gonna last tonight?" he asked.

I thought about it.

"It should be over around one or two. I'm on drag duty, so I have to stay until the bitter end."

His eyes had become melty-chocolate, but now they hardened with impatience.

"I'm never gonna do anything but sleep with you in my bed, am I?"

God, I hoped that wasn't true. That would suck. Now that I was kind of coming to terms with our togetherness, I was looking forward to certain things we hadn't gotten around to doing, like the exchange of bodily fluids.

I opened my mouth to speak, but the melty-chocolate had come back into his eyes.

"You don't have to answer. Your face said it all."

Great.

We went out the back and through the adjoining gate to Tod and Stevie's. I knocked at their backdoor and put my head in.

"Yoo hoo!" I called.

Stevie yelled from the bowels of the house for us to come in and we entered the kitchen. Chowleena came clicking through and she butted my legs with her head then she stepped back and barked twice at Lee, her front paws coming up with each exertion. When she was done with her warning, she butted his legs, too.

"She likes you," I told Lee. He bent over to scratch Chowleena's ears and I called, "I've got Lee with me."

Stevie appeared in the doorway and blatantly and thoroughly looked Lee over.

Then he smiled his approval at me.

"I'm Stevie," he said, his eyes moving back to Lee, and he came into the room.

"Lee."

They shook hands then Stevie gave me a kiss on the cheek.

Chowleena barked again and then clicked out of the room, her bottom swaying pertly, full of attitude.

We followed.

The living room-slash-dining room was closed up tight from any looky-loos. The Burgundy Rose transformation was firmly hidden behind drawn curtains and a closed front door. The dining area looked like the backstage of a New York fashion show had exploded in it. There was makeup scattered across the dining room table, two lighted mirrors and three foam heads with wigs on them. Formal dresses in every color and fabric were strewn across the backs of chairs. Sequins sparkled and feathers swayed slightly in the breeze of the ceiling fan. Shoes were lying around everywhere.

Tod was in semi-drag. He was sitting in a robe, panty-hose on and I could tell he had his girl figure already sorted under the robe. His hair was in a skull cap ready for a wig, his base makeup was heavy and his eyes were mostly done. He had the spidery shape of a false eyelash dangling from his fingers and a cigarette dangling from his lips.

He narrowed his eyes through the smoke at Lee.

"No one, and I mean *no one,* but Indy's Hunk of Burning Love would be allowed to see me this way. You talk, you die."

It was an empty threat and everyone knew it. Firstly, who was Lee going to tell? Secondly, Lee could kick anyone's ass.

"Anyone want a drink?" Stevie, ever the good host, said into the void.

"I need makeup. My stuff is at Lee's," I told Tod.

Tod extracted his smoke from his mouth and gestured to the dining room table.

"What's mine is yours."

It took nearly an hour to get Burgundy to BJ's Carousel. She was not only performing but MC-ing, so she had several dress changes. Stevie and I carefully slid the dresses that Tod indicated into garment bags. We schlepped them—three wigs, six boxes of shoes, a Louis Vuitton tote-bag of emergency provisions (extra hose in case of runs, packets of cigarettes, lighters, smaller bags filled with bracelets, earrings, necklaces and other accessories, fingernail polish remover, etc.) and Tod's enormous, steel-encased MAC tackle box filled with cosmetics—into the CR-V.

Lee and I followed Tod and Stevie to BJ's in the Crossfire. The bar was on Broadway, about a mile or so south of my store, just past the I-25 overpass. It was a small dive bar, but you couldn't tell because it was dark and the Diva Queens on the tiny stage could make it come alive.

We went in the back way, all of us loaded down with Burgundy's stuff, and entered the small area set aside as a dressing room. It was so smoky you could barely see and it was chockfull of drag queens, their partners, fag hags and other hangers on. The minute we walked in, everyone, man, woman or queen, turned and stared at Lee.

"Sweet Jesus," a Shania Twain look-alike standing three feet away breathed, her hungry eyes riveted on Lee.

Burgundy forged ahead announcing, "He's straight, he's taken and if he turns, I have first dibs."

Stevie dumped his load and Lee handed him the garment bag he was holding then turned to me and offered, "I'll get you a drink."

"Good idea. You don't leave, they'll jump and tear your clothes off."

Lee winced. "That's a pleasant thought."

"Don't think I'm kidding," I told him. "If you wouldn't mind getting me a…" I started to give him my drink order but he interrupted.

"I know what you drink, Indy."

Panic overwhelmed me again, fast and fierce.

Lee smiled. It was The Smile except magnified, warm and intimate. All air was sucked out of the room as surreptitious watching turned obvious when people saw The Smile. My reaction included both a quivering in the nether regions and a swelling of the breasts.

Lee's arm slid around me and his lips found mine for a quick kiss.

"Don't look so scared. I'm not gonna eat you," he murmured and then his hand slid down my ass and pressed my hips against his in a promise that belied his words.

Holy shit, shit, shit.

He left and half of our audience were fanning themselves, the other half adjusting their trousers.

Stevie and I got Burgundy sorted. By the time I made it into the bar, it was a crush. The Savage/Nightingale contingent found a table front and center. Everyone was crammed into it. Andrea had forked her children off on a babysitter and forced her husband to come, and he looked about as comfortable as a Republican at a Rainbow Gathering. For Tex, on the other hand, this was another day at the office. He sat relaxed, his feet on a chair that likely could be used to rest someone's ass, but no one would have had the balls to ask for it.

Two other seats were empty, one for Stevie, one for me, drinks in front of both.

Lee wasn't at the table. He and Hank both had their backs against the wall by the entrance, both holding a beer bottle by its neck, their arms crossed on their chest, effortlessly and unconsciously exuding aggressive heterosexuality. Even in the crammed bar they were given a wide berth.

The show started late and Burgundy came out giving some lip to someone who'd been imbibing too much, was getting impatient and yelled his thoughts about it.

Take my advice, never heckle a drag queen. They'll make mincemeat out of you.

The show was great, the drinks kept coming and I'd scoot out when Stevie and I got the high sign it was time for a costume change. Backstage, we'd struggle Burgundy and her foam rubber hips out of one heavy, sequined extravaganza and into another and we'd return to the table. Our group was generous with tips during the performances, handing the queen a dollar for an air kiss on the cheek and we quickly became a favorite and thus the focus of all the divas.

It was going well. I was relaxed, happy, enjoying myself, and I was remembering a life that was fun and exciting without bullets flying. I was well into my fifth spiced rum and diet when Burgundy took the stage and made a surprise announcement.

"Many of you know her and love her, and now we're gonna get her up here to show you what's she's got. Get your tips ready, ladies and tramps, we're

185

breaking tradition and bringing a real woman on the stage. Give it up for India Savage!"

Um, what?

Holy shit.

Holy shit, shit, shit.

That's when I heard it. The piano and strings starting Barbra Streisand and Donna Summer's "No More Tears." I'd sung it a gazillion times with Tod in Stevie and Tod's living room after over-imbibing chilled sparkling wine and a marathon of Yahtzee.

Never in front of an audience.

Never.

Ally pulled me out of my chair. Marianne, Dolores and Andrea pushed me to the stage, which was tragically too close, and Stevie shoved a dead microphone into my hand. Burgundy had already done her Barbra hum, I had no choice but to lip sync my Donna "oo".

Then I was on the stage, doing the slow introduction, singing about what lacked in Donna's romantic life and trying to play off Burgundy, trying to look her in the eyes like I felt the words deep into my very soul.

Problem was, I was stiff as a board and the disco bit was coming up.

Lee was watching. The last thing I wanted to do was dance around on stage in front of a hundred people, one of them Liam Nightingale, lip syncing badly to fucking disco.

I had to pull it together. This was for charity. I had no idea *what* charity, but what did it matter? I'd look more of a fool if I didn't loosen up and fast.

There was nothing for it.

We sang eye-to-eye while Barbra and Donna harmonized. Burgundy shot me a "for God's sake, pull yourself together" look and I shrugged my shy discomfort.

Burgundy gave it her all on Barbra's long note, closing her eyes with feeling and holding her hand to her throat. I stayed stiff on purpose, pretending to be uncomfortable and wanting to be anywhere but there.

When the disco hit, my "ahs" came on and I shuffled with discomfort, keeping up the sham.

Then the horns kicked in and I pulled out all the stops, strutting, shaking my hips and stomping across the tiny stage like a white, pissed-off Tina Turner, throwing attitude that would do Chowleena proud.

The crowd went wild and jumped to their feet. It helped that front and center were all my friends and family, not to mention it was well into the show and most everyone was shitfaced. They lifted their arms, fingers pointed towards us, wrists snapping and bodies bouncing to the beat.

I used Donna's lyrics to lecture the audience then Burgundy and I got nose-to-nose screaming at each other, shaking our hair in tandem with the angry words, and the crowd began chanting the chorus.

It was Barbra's song. Donna was only dessert, so I worked the crowd, leaning double at the waist, my hand at my hip, and got in the faces of the people who dared to approach me with dollar bills, snatching notes out of their hands like the tip was my God given right. I scrunched up my face with mock pissed-offedness and didn't give a single kiss. I even went so far as placing the sole of my sandal into a butch biker's chest and sending him careening backwards giggling himself silly.

The crowd ate it up, shouting, cheering and sending up deafening whistles and cat calls.

It was beautiful and the biggest fucking happy rush I'd had in my life.

It was when the disco slowed to the funky bit that was a wind up to when Barbra gets so pissed-off her voice goes husky that I saw Pepper Rick standing across the room, pointing a gun at me.

I froze.

Then, without my brain telling my body to do it, I whirled and threw myself in a body tackle, bringing Burgundy down. Both of our tip money and microphones flew out of our hands and Burgundy shouted a very male, "What the fuck?"

The crowd began to cheer, thinking it was part of the show, but the cheer turned to screams and shouts when gunfire rang out.

"Crawl," I hissed to Tod. "Stay low and crawl the fuck out of here."

We almost started to crawl as more gunfire rang through the bar, then I jumped back on Tod, covering him with my body. Once the sound of the guns cleared, I could hear Dad and Malcolm shouting orders to people trying to keep calm and stop a stampede.

We started crawling again. All I could see was Tod's sequined ass. I heard heavy footfalls on the stage, and all of a sudden I was lifted up. I let out a half-enraged, half-startled scream and tried to twist away, but I no sooner got a look at who had me when I was thrown, like a human discus, off the stage.

I flew through the air and hit Lee with a grunt, both his and mine, and his arms came around me as he staggered back a step to brace himself. Out of the corner of my eye, I caught sight of Tex, who had made it to the stage (and me) before Lee. Tex executed the stage dive to end all stage dives, his bulky weight toppling the unfortunate and unprepared people who'd been in his way.

I didn't get a chance to process this because Lee lifted me up by the waist and carried me to the door, moving anyone out of our way by either shoving them, punching them or just plain old body slamming them with his shoulder.

I saw Hank in front of us with Ally in a similar hold just as Malcolm pushed Kitty Sue out the door.

Lee dragged me to Ally's car, a newish, convertible Ford Mustang. Hank was shoving Ally in the driver's seat. Lee shoved me in the passenger side.

"Indy!" Dad shouted from somewhere.

"Here. Safe," Lee shouted back.

My eyes found Dad and I noticed he lifted his index finger and snapped it smartly at Lee in a "you the man" gesture. He got in with Malcolm and Kitty Sue as Lee started talking to me.

"Stay here, lock your doors, stay down and out of sight."

I turned to him. "Tod, Stevie, Tex. Ohmigod, Andrea's a mother!"

But he wasn't listening. He slammed the door and ran back to BJ's.

"And now you," I whispered, watching him go.

Ally's hand took mine.

"He'll be okay," she said. "You know, you wouldn't even want a man who wouldn't go back to save someone's mother and a drag queen."

This was true.

Her hand went from mine to my neck and forced me down and my torso explored the limits of the seatbelt Lee buckled on me.

"I'll tell you what's happening," she offered.

I bent forward as far as I could to hide myself. I heard the locks go on the doors and she started the car in preparation, just in case we needed a fast get-away. I listened as Ally counted off Duke and Dolores, who roared off on their hog. Marianne came out with Hank, who took her directly to her car. Andrea came out with Lee, trailed by Andrea's husband. Lee made sure they were in their mini-van before he went back in. Tex raged out on his own power, but this included from Ally an, "Uh-oh, I think he's bleeding again". I nearly shot up, but she kept me down with a hand at my neck.

The locks went. I was pressed further forward as the back of my seat was tilted. The seatbelt strained to its limits and cut into my chest, and Tex threw himself in back.

"Holy fuck, pandemonium at the gay bar!" he yelled.

I reached out and closed the door. The locks went again and I turned my head and looked back as best I could in the position I was in.

"You okay?" I asked Tex.

"Think I tore somethin' lose either throwin' you or doin' the dive, or maybe when I got in a fight with that guy in leather. Doesn't matter. I feel fuckin' great! It's bedlam in there. Fuckin' nuts!" He stopped, leaned forward and looked out the windshield. "Hey, that's the guy that shot me!"

My head popped up and sure enough, it was Pepper Rick.

He ran to a car with people in it, a little Mini. The people had left the bar and were trying to get away. I could hear sirens as I watched Rick yank the driver out, the passenger throwing himself out the other side. Rick got behind the wheel and burned rubber.

"Go! Go, go, go!" Tex shouted and Ally didn't hesitate, she laid rubber too.

I turned my head to her.

"What are you doing?" I shouted.

"He can't get away!" she shouted back.

With my head turned, I saw Terry Wilcox's boys, Goon Gary and The Moron as they exited BJ's.

Jeez, it was like an Indy Torture Squad convention.

Then I could notice no more as Ally jerked around a car trying to exit the parking lot and jumped the curb, screeching south onto Broadway, cutting off a car as we swerved across the two lanes going north, and pulling right out in front of a squad car coming south.

The cop car was about to execute a turn in to BJ's but jerked back out onto Broadway behind the Mustang.

"Pull over, let the cops have him," I said.

"No way! This guy shot me!" Tex yelled.

Ally wasn't listening anyway. She rocketed down Broadway, shifting gears quickly, ratcheting up the mph to levels so far beyond safe it wasn't funny.

"*Ally, pull over!*" I screamed.

"He's two cars in front of you. Pass! Pass!" Tex shouted.

We shot past two squad cars going north, their lights on and sirens blaring. One screeched to a halt and did a u-ie behind us.

"Stop now! There are more cops, he won't get away!" I yelled.

"Don't stop!" Tex shouted. "Never say die!"

I went to bars and clubs without my purse, usually carrying money, credit cards, driver's license and lip gloss in my front pocket and my cell in my back. It was now that I felt my cell phone vibrate against my ass as I heard it ring. I snatched it from my pocket and tore my eyes from the road long enough to read, "Lee calling".

I flipped it open as Tex crowed, "No cars in front of us, bump him! That's it!"

"Don't bump him!" I shrieked. "He's in someone else's car."

Ally didn't listen. We bumped Pepper Rick, did a nauseating, out-of-control jerk from side-to-side before Ally righted us and yelled, "Righteous!"

I was too scared even to scream.

"Indy." I heard Lee's voice in my ear and didn't realize I'd put the cell there.

"Yeah?" I replied, sounding calmer than I actually was.

"Bump him again, girl," Tex encouraged.

"Where the fuck are you?" Lee, on the other hand, didn't sound calm.

Another cop car going north screeched to a halt and swung a u-ie. I looked behind us and we had three squad cars trailing us now, their sirens blaring and lights rolling. It looked like other cars were back there, too, members of the chase. And one of them looked a whole lot like Lee's Crossfire.

I turned back forward and answered Lee. "We saw Pepper Rick so we're following him. Going south on Broadway."

A car shot past us, looking like it had Terry Wilcox's goons in it. It jerked in front of Pepper Rick and slammed on its brakes. Everyone behind it, including us, slammed on their brakes and went into evasive maneuvering. Ally's Mustang did a couple more sickening lurches and then we all accelerated, Pepper Rick and Coxy's boys jockeying for position in front of us like they were on a NASCAR track. Thankfully, everyone on Broadway was pulling well over because of the squad car posse behind us.

"Pull over," I heard Lee demand in my ear.

"She won't listen to me," I told Lee. "She and Tex are on a mission."

"Indy, tell Ally to pull... the fuck... over," Lee repeated.

"Ally," I said, "Lee wants you to pull over."

"I can't," Ally returned. "I can't do it. He's not gonna get away. He shot at you."

It was then I lost my mind, pulled the phone from my ear and screeched, *"Pull over, God damn it!"*

We were well into Englewood when a squad car came up beside us, Willie Moses at the wheel. I saw Brian Bond sitting in the passenger seat doing hand gestures at us, his face a mask of disbelieving fury. Ally turned her head to look at him and lost control of the Mustang.

We pitched right then left, nearly side-swiping Willie and Brian. Willie avoided us, shot forward and then we bounded across the median, cars coming the other way, swerving and blaring their horns.

With incredible luck, we careened into an old, unused lot, knocked down a chain link fence, driving over it and then coming to a smashing, bone-jarring halt when we slammed into a concrete slab.

Chapter 14
Was He Makin' A Call?

Upon impact, the airbags blew out.

I sat in a daze for a few seconds, my mind automatically doing a body inventory to assess any damage. When I realized that I was okay, I pulled back from the airbag and asked, "Everyone all right?"

Ally mumbled something. There was a grumble from the backseat and my door was wrenched open.

I saw a penknife puncture the bag, which deflated immediately. A hand was at my chest to hold me back against the seat so I didn't crumple forward with the loss of the airbag. Not that my seatbelt was going to let me go anywhere; it had contracted on impact and my chest was killing me. Lee was crouched in the door beside me.

"You okay?" he asked, though he was finding out for himself, his hands running along my limbs, his eyes doing a body scan, searching for blood or bones protruding through my skin. In the lights illuminating the vacant lot, I could see his face was pinched with anger and concern.

Hank was on the other side. Ally's bag was flat and he was doing the same thing.

"Yeah. I think so," I told Lee.

"We need to get them free of the car," Hank told Lee.

Lee reached across me and undid my buckle. He helped me out and walked me well away from the car toward the street. I used this time to pull my head together and take stock of the new aches and pains coming my way. I flipped my cell shut and slid it back in my pocket.

Ally and Tex were standing five feet away, Tex stomping his feet, for some reason looking like he was doing a war dance without moving his arms. There was a blood stain at the shoulder of his sling. Luckily, that was the only blood on any of us.

I decided in an instant I was going to kill them both.

"You're both nuts!" I shouted, charging forward, intent on murder, or at the very least maiming. "You could have killed us!"

I'd made it two strides before an arm snagged around my middle, hooking me and jerking me back. I slammed against Lee's body but still struggled forward, pumping my arms and stamping my feet.

"I can't believe, *cannot believe*, you just did that," I shrieked at Ally "You're crazy. Totally gonzo! What were you *thinking?*" I shouted.

"He was gonna get away!" Ally shouted back.

"*Who cares!*" I screamed.

"*I care!*" Ally screamed back.

"It wasn't very smart." Hank interjected his understatement in an angry voice. In fact, his voice, his face and his body screamed not only anger, but barely controlled fury.

Ally glared at me. Her head swung to Hank and then she blew out a breath of pure exasperation. "He shot at Indy! Twice! He kidnapped her. I'm not gonna let him get away. Give me a *fucking* break. I'm a Nightingale. If either of you..." she pointed to Hank then to Lee, "were sitting in a car and saw the opportunity, you'd take it without a thought. What? I can't because I'm a *girl?*"

Okay, she had a point there.

I stopped struggling to get at her.

"And you," she pointed to me, "someone did those things to me or your Dad or any of us, and you were behind the wheel of a car and had a chance to nab him, would you even hesitate?"

Hmm, another excellent point.

I bit my lip.

Being caught up in the events of the last several days, I had not stopped to consider how the people I loved, who loved me, felt about everything that was happening.

So I put my foot in the other shoe and the feeling it gave me was overpowering. Tears came up my throat and I swallowed them back.

"Ally, girl," I whispered.

Ally wasn't done. "I'm not a badass cop or a badass..." she stared at Lee, "whatever you are, but if I get the chance to do my bit, I'm gonna do it. I mean, that guy interrupted 'No More Tears'. Burgundy and Indy were kicking ass up there. Something had to be done!"

"I think you made your point," Lee said from behind me. His arm was still around me tight.

A car angled into the lot and Dad, Malcolm and Kitty Sue were there.

Malcolm charged out of the car, assessed that his loved ones were breathing and healthy and then roared at Ally, "Tell me you didn't just participate in a high speed chase!"

"We've covered this ground," Hank shared.

Lee let me go and turned me into Dad's arms. Dad held me and kissed my forehead.

"You okay?" Dad asked.

"Yeah," I answered.

A squad car angled in and Jorge and Carl were there. Carl shot out of the car, his face angry.

"Have you lost your mind?" he shouted at Ally.

It obviously wasn't going to be Ally's night.

Though I had to admit, I found it a tad interesting how upset Carl was. Hmm.

Jorge came out slower, his face set and showing little emotion. He approached Lee, Dad and me.

"I don't know what's goin' on, Nightingale, but you should consider putting Indy in a safe house until it's over," Jorge remarked.

Lee made no comment to this. Ally and Carl were shouting at each other and Dad was holding on tight. Lee and Hank started making phone calls, Jorge got out his notebook and we all made statements.

Lee put me in the Crossfire after a wrecker came in to tow Ally's Mustang. Carl sat in the car, the radio microphone in his hand, calling in a report. Tex was going with Carl and Jorge, who were taking him back to the hospital to get re-stitched up. Ally and Hank were catching a ride with Malcolm back to BJ's to pick up Hank's SUV.

I waved to everyone as Lee pulled away, heading north on Broadway.

"I don't want to go into a safe house," I told Lee.

"You're *in* a safe house. The condo's safe. You just keep leaving it."

I didn't like the way he said the last sentence.

"Are you thinking of cuffing me to the bed again?"

He didn't hesitate. "Yes."

Great.

"I wouldn't do that if I were you," I warned.

Kristen Ashley

"Thinkin' about it isn't the same as doin' it. You're a security challenge. I have to keep you safe while not lowering my chances of gettin' into your sexy underwear, or, more to the point, gettin' you out of them."

I thought it likely that Lee was up to that challenge. At least I hoped so.

"By the way, nice performance back there," Lee remarked. "I especially liked the part where you kicked the guy in the chest. Class."

Great.

At least his voice sounded a mixture of amused and admiring.

When we got to the condo, Lee let us in and I told him I had to do the round of calls to make sure everyone was all right.

I stood on the balcony with my phone and without me having to ask, Lee brought me three ibuprofens and a glass of water. He watched as I guzzled them, took the glass and then disappeared.

Holy shit.

He was *very* good at this togetherness stuff.

I called Tod and Stevie first.

They were home, safe and sound and maybe a little freaked out, but not mad at me. At least Tod wasn't. He was more interested in dissecting our act on stage.

"Girlie, we kicked *ass*. They were on their feet. They were chanting. We gotta go shopping. We gotta get you some mini-Burgundy outfits. We gotta take this *show* on the *road!*"

Andrea and Marianne were also safe, though Andrea's husband said she wasn't allowed to go out with me anymore, which caused a fight as no one ever told Andrea what she was allowed to do. No one. Richie Sambora, the great and glorious lead guitar of Bon Jovi and Andrea's dream man could have given her an order and she would have told him to go fuck himself.

Duke thought it was a hoot. Dolores was considering backing out of girl's night out on Wednesday.

I flipped my phone shut and walked into the bedroom. Lee was in the same position he'd been in last night: in bed, on his back, chest bare, sheet nearly to the waist. The light was on, but this time he didn't have a book and he was fast asleep.

I'd never really had the time to observe him while he was asleep, and he looked different. He looked kind of like the old, pre-Special Ops Lee, the hardness and scariness gone, just... Lee.

196

I wanted to kiss him, as in *really* wanted to kiss him. He looked good, lying there sleeping. Seriously good. Melt in your mouth good.

Instead I cleaned my face, brushed my teeth and pulled on the Night Stalker tee. I double checked the door was locked and the sliding doors to the balcony were secured. I tiptoed to Lee's side of the bed, switched off the light and then went to my side of the bed and slid in carefully, so as not to wake him.

I told myself over and over again that I was not going to kick or hit Lee in his sleep. This helped me force out thoughts of bullets flying and how totally out-of-control my life was.

⚜

I woke up to a hand in my panties, cupping my ass, and another one under my shirt, stroking the side of my breast. I was sprawled half-on, half-off Lee, my face tucked into his neck.

"You awake?" he asked.

I nodded, sleepily assessing my semi-aroused state.

His hand moved immediately to cup my breast, his thumb sliding across the nipple. An electric pulse shot through me and the "semi" part of my semi-aroused was a distant memory.

My head tilted to look at him and say something like, "coffee", "toothpaste" or "more" and his mouth came to mine.

He hauled me up so I was sprawled fully on him. His hand moved out of my underwear and both hands went up my sides. His mouth disengaged with mine and then, *whoosh*, the Night Stalker tee was gone.

I was skin-on-skin with Lee. I felt a moment of elation mingled with extreme panic, and before I could decide which one to give reign to I was flipped over on my back and Lee was on me.

At first he was kissing my mouth, his hands everywhere, skimming, gentle and arousing. Then his mouth left mine. It went to my neck, my throat, my breasts, my belly, following his hands and then…

Yikes!

My hips jerked in shock as he kissed me *there*, his mouth moving over my panties.

"You okay?" he mumbled against me.

I mumbled back, "Yes," but my mind said, *Yes, yes, a thousand times, YES!*

His fingertips went into the waistband of my underwear and I knew we were close, very, very close. Or at least I was close. Panic fled and elation and arousal took firm control and my hands moved, my fingers delving into his hair.

Then the door buzzer went, three quick shots, three longer ones, three quick ones.

Lee immediately stopped what he was doing and came up over me.

"Fuck!" he exploded. "God, I'm sorry. *Really* sorry."

He got up and stalked naked from the room.

I laid there, half naked and fully in shock.

Foiled again.

What kind of luck was that? Was this divine intervention?

I rolled. I felt my aching body cry out in belated protest, grabbed my discarded tee from floor and pulled it on. By the time I got it down, Lee was back in the room.

"One of my men has been shot," he told me.

All aches and pains fled and I jumped out of bed.

"Oh my God."

"Bobby and Matt are comin' up. I've gotta jump in the shower. Let them in, will you?" he asked and disappeared into the bathroom.

I ran to the kitchen, tore through the cupboards and set the coffee to running when there came a knock at the door.

I looked out the peephole and let Bobby and Matt in.

They looked grim.

"You guys okay?"

Nods, no words.

"Who is it? How is he?" I went on.

"He was wearin' a vest. Armor-piercing bullets." This was all Matt said. This was all Matt needed to say.

"Oh no." I scrambled through the kitchen. Lee had a collection of travel coffee mugs, definitely a man-on-the-go, not one that hangs around and sips his coffee. I yanked three down and asked, "Have you had breakfast? Do you want breakfast? I can make some quick toast."

"Not hungry," Bobby forced through stiff lips.

We all stood there staring at each other. I couldn't stand not doing anything, so I pulled the coffeepot out, wedged a travel mug under the spout and filled the other two mugs with coffee. I was screwing on the tops when Lee came in, hair wet and freshly shaved.

"Let's roll," he said and Matt and Bobby started moving.

I handed out coffee, yanking the last mug out from under the spout and tossing the pot back underneath, trailing behind Lee while I screwed on the top.

"This one isn't full," I told Lee at the door, feeling stupid and useless.

"That's okay." He grabbed it.

"Call me when you know something."

He bent to kiss me quickly and then he was gone.

While Stevie and I were packing up Burgundy the night before, Lee had gone over to my house and grabbed my bag. He'd brought it up to the condo last night. This was good. I had new clothes to wear, and as it was early I could get to Fortnum's and help open. The Monday coffee crush would take my mind off Lee's current activities and the fears that were encroaching that whoever this guy was got shot doing something to help me.

I'd take Lee's Crossfire. I was pretty sure he wouldn't mind.

I showered and sucked down coffee and ibuprofen. I decided to let my hair dry by itself, slapped on some happy makeup and tried not to look at the shiner, which was finally fading. I pulled on my yellow t-shirt that had a picture of Starsky and Hutch's car, the Striped Tomato, emblazoned across the chest. I yanked on faded jeans, my red belt and red cowboy boots and eased myself down to the garage.

I was sure the Crossfire was absolute heaven to drive, but my mind was filled with too much garbage to process it. I didn't know if the cops had caught Pepper Rick last night. I didn't like considering Lee, man of action, stuck in a hospital waiting room and what he might learn when the wait was over. I didn't want to think of what the day might bring.

It was ten past seven. We opened at seven thirty, and as I drove up I saw Jane standing outside the store, looking at the sidewalk. I parked the Crossfire right out front and got out, my eyes on Jane, who hadn't moved.

Then I looked to where she was staring and stopped dead.

Pepper Rick was lounging in the doorway to Fortnum's. It opened onto the corner at an angle and he was sprawled, butt and back to the sidewalk,

Kristen Ashley

shoulders and what was left of his head resting against our door. He was dead, dead, *dead*, just like Tim Shubert, except there weren't any splattered brains.

"Jane, honey, step away from there," I said quietly.

She was frozen still and I noticed she had her cell phone in her hand.

"Jane," I said a little more loudly, trying to get her attention.

She jumped. Her cell came out of her hand, flew end over end through the air and landed on Pepper Rick's chest, clattering down to rest by his hand.

We both watched the cell fly, land and settle.

"Oops," Jane said, and I think I saw her make the mental decision to get a new phone.

I dug my cell out of my purse, considered who to call and settled on Hank.

"Yeah?" he answered.

"Um, it's Indy. I hate to tell you this, but there's a dead guy lounging in the doorway to Fortnum's."

Silence.

Duke rounded the corner and Jane and my eyes turned to him. His face began to light with greeting, his eyes flicked down and he stopped short.

"Fuckin' hell!" he boomed.

"Duke just arrived," Hank said in my ear.

"Yep."

"I'll get someone on it. Do we know this dead guy?" Hank asked.

"Well, I don't have to worry about being kidnapped again," I said by way of answer.

Hank disconnected and Duke looked at me. "Was he makin' a call?"

I wanted to laugh, then before that thought fully formed, I decided I wanted to cry. Seeing as crying wasn't an option for me because I wasn't a sissy, I decided I wanted to scream.

In fifteen minutes, the place was surrounded by cops, including Hank, Dad and Malcolm, and the scene was taped. Gawkers and coffee customers were being directed away by uniforms.

I stood off to the side and scrolled down my phonebook to Lee and hit his number.

"Everything okay?" he said as a greeting.

"You've heard from your office," I replied, thinking the mysterious forces behind his commando cartel had already alerted him to my latest adventure.

"Heard what from my office?"

Oopsie.

"Well, I don't want to disturb you, but I thought I should tell you before your office hears it on police band. Pepper Rick's dead body was propped into the doorway of Fortnum's this morning."

Silence, then, "A present."

"What?"

"I'll be there soon."

"Lee, you don't have to—", but he'd disconnected.

Jimmy Marker walked up to me and after asking a few questions he wiped his eyes with his hand.

"Indy, tell me you aren't keepin' anything from me."

After Tex got shot, I told Jimmy everything at the hospital; about Rosie, the pot, the diamonds, Terry Wilcox, everything. Well, not everything. I left out my B and E, so *almost* everything. I had nothing left to tell, and if Jimmy was getting frustrated and impatient, he should step into my shoes.

"Jimmy, I may be crazy, but I'm not stupid and whatever you think, I know right from wrong. I told you all I know at the hospital."

Dad walked up to me and slung an arm around my shoulders.

"I just want to know why you're the focal point of all of this," Jimmy said.

"I'd like to know that too," Dad put in.

"Well, when you find out, tell me because this is beginning to *piss me off!*" As I talked, my voice rose and I was screaming by the end.

Jimmy took a step back and a bunch of heads swung in my direction.

I saw an SUV double park and Lee slid from behind the wheel. His eyes were on me, but Malcolm and Hank stopped him before he could make his way to me.

"I take it you know what's going on," I said to Dad, taking my eyes off Lee.

"What there is to know. Cops talk, you're my daughter. Jimmy's keeping me briefed," Dad replied.

"Why haven't you said anything?" I asked.

"I trust Liam to sort it out and I trust you to do the right thing," Dad told me.

Simple as that.

Dad was cool. Dad had always been cool. Somewhere in the last couple of days, Lee had been given Dad's blessing. Probably when I started to have certain incidents, incidents the like of which any father would want Liam Nightingale to be his daughter's boyfriend.

I walked to the Nightingale huddle. Malcolm had his back to me. Lee and Hank were at his sides, their backs mostly to me.

As I walked up, I heard Malcolm say, "Hank, I know you use Lee to do the shit that'd get your hands dirty, and Lee, I know you play the game pretty loose. I let you boys play it the way you feel you need to 'cause so far, whatever deal you got goin' works. But I don't like what I'm smellin' and..."

Lee's head turned and he looked at me out of the corners of his eyes.

"Indy," he muttered, and I think he said this more to Malcolm than to me.

All the Nightingale men turned to me and whatever was happening stopped.

Great. Whatever. Fine by me.

I walked up to Lee and stopped, though not close enough for his liking because his hand came out and curled around my neck, pulling me into his side. Hank, Dad and Malcolm moved off.

"How're you doin', gorgeous?" he asked me.

"I'm losing my patience. This is getting old," I told him. "How's your man?"

"No word, I have to get back to the hospital. I see you confiscated the Crossfire."

"Do you mind?"

"Nope."

I turned into him and put my hand on his stomach before asking hesitantly, "Your man, he wasn't doing... something... for me?"

Lee's hand around my neck twisted and he tugged softly at my hair. "A different assignment, nothin' to do with you or the diamonds."

I felt a tremendous relief. I already had Tex's injury, Ally's totaled car and everyone else's worry resting on my shoulders. I didn't need something else. Then I looked at Lee and realized all that, plus whatever this new thing was, still rested firmly on his.

"You need to go," I noted.

"Yeah."

I started to pull away, but his hand dropped. His arm curled around my shoulders and turned me into him, full-frontal.

"With Rick out of the way you should be safe, but you need to be careful. Coxy isn't a threat but he's a wildcard."

I nodded.

"I want to come home to you," he declared.

My breath disappeared. I didn't suck it in and I didn't let it out. It just vanished.

I did a mental shake and got myself together.

"Sorry?" I asked.

"Tonight. I'll phone you when I'm on my way. All you need to get you into the parking garage and condo is on the Crossfire's key ring. Even after Luke gets out of surgery, I've got things to do, but when I come home tonight, I want you to be there."

I only hesitated a second. "Okay."

He looked at me for a while. His eyes got soft and he said quietly, "I'm sorry about this morning."

"It couldn't be helped."

"We'll finish tonight."

Finally, something to look forward to.

◥◣◥◣

Duke made six big posters, taping them in all the big windows, announcing Fortnum's was closed. Hard to open with police tape stretched across your front door.

Thank God I didn't have a mortgage.

I had the day yawning ahead of me and no bodyguard following my every step. It felt weird.

I went to Tex's to give him an update and help him with the cats. He'd been re-stitched and let go last night. I wasn't sure what his reaction would be Pepper Rick's demise. I guessed jubilation, but was wrong.

"We live, we die," he remarked.

Philosophical.

Cats fed, litter boxes cleaned and laser lights jiggled on the walls, I headed to Kumar's to stock up on stuff for the condo and have a gossip. He wasn't there, but I had a chat with Mrs. Kumar, who was behind the counter with Mrs. Salim motionless on a stool behind her. I thought, but did not say, that they might do better business if it didn't look like a mummy was propped up behind the cash register. Then I worried if God would strike me with lightning for such a thought.

I got my bits and pieces from Mrs. Kumar and headed to Ally's.

She made me coffee and gave me more ibuprofen.

"I know about the dead guy. Dad called Mom, Mom called me. You okay?" she asked.

"I'm getting tired of this," I told her.

"I bet," she mumbled.

"What are you doing today?" I asked.

"Laying low. I got a shift tonight."

Ally now worked at My Brother's Bar down by Platte River. They'd been around long enough for the wooden tables and walls to look weathered and worn and they had the best bar food in Denver. Members of the symphony hung out there after performances, and they pulled an excellent pint of Guinness.

"I was beginning to think you'd quit," I noted.

"No, had a shift the night you got kidnapped, but apparently it's cool to call off when your best friend is being held hostage," she replied.

"Good to know," I muttered.

She offered a manicure and pedicure and I took her up on it. I returned the favor by washing and styling her hair. I would have gone to beauty school if I hadn't inherited Fortnum's. Since I'd hit teenage status, I always gave good hair. With Ally, it wasn't hard to give good hair. Her hair was soft and thick with just enough wave. It never looked bad.

"How're things with Lee?" she shouted over the hairdryer as I was roller brushing her hair.

"I'm totally freaking out," I shouted back.

"I sensed that." She was still shouting.

I turned off the hairdryer and looked at her. "He's good at this stuff."

"What stuff?"

"Relationship stuff. He's a natural. It's weird. We're new and we're old. I can't get my head around it."

"He's shit at relationship stuff. He's only good at it because it's you."

"Sorry?"

"You're shit at it too, but only because it was never him."

Uh-oh, Ally was on her you two were meant for each other kick.

I turned the hairdryer back on, subject closed.

After visiting Ally, I went home. I cleaned my house, went through my mail and watered my yard and flowers. Then I watered Tod and Stevie's. Then I went to their front door and knocked.

Stevie answered then looked beyond me in case he could see a sniper.

"I watered your flowers," I told him.

"That's nice."

"I'm sorry about last night," I went on.

"I'm not sure I forgive you. Though Tod says you threw yourself on top of him to protect him from bullets so I guess I'm not so mad. Tod thought it was a blast. Says it reminded him of home."

"The way Tod tells it, I don't think I want to go to Texas."

Stevie didn't say anything.

"Anyway, it's easy for Tod to say it was a blast. He was protected a foot deep by foam rubber."

We both knew bullets would tear through Tod's rubber.

I kept talking. I knew Stevie was mad and somehow couldn't help myself.

"The dead body of the guy who started it was set in the front door of Fortnum's this morning."

Stevie's eyes widened.

Okay, so now I was beginning to let the shock of it all wear through me. Not to mention Stevie was mad at me, and I didn't like people I cared about being mad at me. It wasn't my fault, even though it felt like it was. Tears sprang into my eyes.

"Talk to you later," I said.

"Girlie, you're a mess. Get in here."

He yanked me inside, gave me a drink and sat me on the sofa. I let it all hang out, including the fact that even though we'd get closer each time, Lee and I hadn't *done it* yet.

Stevie listened, hugged me occasionally, got me tissues when the tears threatened to spill and cast no judgment. Then he took me home, snapped through the hangers in my closets and opened and closed boxes of shoes until he found what he was looking for. All the while he communicated His Plan.

While Stevie walked me to the Crossfire, he told me that Tod was at Denver International Airport. He had a flight and wouldn't be back for a few days. Stevie was leaving late the next morning to do the same and asked me to look after Chowleena while he and Tod were gone.

"If I need to take her to Lee's, would that be a problem?" I asked.

"Just write us a note."

Then, like a fairy godfather (pun intended), he waved me off on my errands that would eventually end with Lee.

I went to Cherry Creek and popped into Linens 'n Things. I grabbed a few necessities and went over to Fresh and Wild, got the stuff I needed for the night and added a few things for the morning (and just in case my stay at the condo was even longer). I carted it all, plus the stuff from Kumar's store and the dress and the shoes, up to Lee's condo.

I dumped everything and started work. I made the chocolate cream pie first then prepared the au gratin potatoes and topped them with aluminum foil ready to put in the oven. I trimmed the green beans, ready to be blanched. I left the steak in the fridge. I could broil it in ten minutes and Lee told me he'd phone when he was coming.

I set the table and put out the placemats and cloth napkins circled with napkin rings that I bought at Linens 'n Things. I tried to buy the most macho placemats, napkins and rings I could find, as they would be adorning Lee's table, but they didn't really do macho in that kind of retail.

In the center of the table I placed the high, tapered candles in silver candleholders I also bought. I arranged the flowers I got at Fresh and Wild in the vase I purchased. I got out the deep bowled glasses I'd noticed in Lee's cupboards, and, as a finishing touch, I put the expensive bottle of red wine between them on the dining room table.

I didn't exactly need to plan a seduction, but a little romance never hurt, or at least that's what Stevie said. And anyway, Lee was running himself ragged. I knew he liked steak, au gratin potatoes and chocolate cream pie. Kitty Sue made it for him every birthday. He deserved a treat, and maybe after I gave him one, he'd give one to me.

I went into the bedroom with dress and shoes and stared at the chair. Both my bags were gone. I did a check in the closet and a couple of drawers. Not only were my clothes put away, but the dirty ones were cleaned, ironed and also hung in the closet or were folded in the drawers. I looked around the room and the bed was made with fresh sheets, the carpets freshly vacuumed.

Obviously Monday was a Judy the Housekeeper Day.

I did the whole girlie thing, going overboard with full, wild Tawny Kittaen hair, the front pulled loosely back in a clip and dark makeup on my eyes. I put on the dress Stevie chose: black satin, thin strapped, skimming my body in a clingy, but not obvious, way, decent cleavage but the kicker was a killer dip in the back. I put on Rock Chick sandals: high, death-defying, thin heel with so many straps you had to wrap some of them up your calves. Subtle perfume. No jewelry because, in the heat of the moment, who wanted to waste time taking off jewelry?

It was getting late so I slid the au gratin potatoes in to cook. Even if Lee was really late, I could warm them easily enough when I broiled the steaks.

I found a John Grisham and started reading. I took the potatoes out and went back to reading. Then later, I got up and went to the kitchen, got my cell and Lee's cordless and put them both on the coffee table so they were within easy reach and went back to reading. I settled on my side to get more comfortable and kept reading.

Then, being who I was and seeing as it was late, I fell asleep.

Chapter 15

You Didn't Say Anything about Pie

My hair slid off my shoulder and fell down my back.

I opened my eyes and Lee was sitting on the couch in the cushion exposed above by my curled legs.

"Hey," I said.

"Hey," he replied.

"You didn't call," I told him.

"It was late. I was worried I'd wake you."

I got up on my elbow. "What time is it?"

"Comin' on midnight."

I did a mini-stretch and came up a bit more. As I was doing this, his hands found my waist and twisted me around onto his lap. My book fell to the floor, but neither of us went for it. He settled into the sofa and I settled into him, putting my head on his shoulder and wrapping my arms around his middle. One of his arms was around my waist, the other hand resting above my knee.

"You planned dinner," he said. "Is it ruined?"

"I made stuff that would fit into an uncertain schedule. We can have it tomorrow or I can make it tonight. You hungry?" I asked.

"Not for food."

His hand slid up my thigh, taking the hem of my dress with it.

My stomach did a dip.

"Are you tired?" he asked.

"I was asleep," I stated the obvious.

"That wasn't what I asked."

"Aren't *you* tired?"

"I was. I'm not anymore."

"Oh."

Yikes.

His hand came up more and his head bent so he could touch his mouth to my neck.

"How's your man?" I asked.

"Alive," he answered the skin below my ear. "Critical, but he's a fighter." His tongue touched my skin and I shivered.

"That's good, I guess," I whispered.

"Do you wanna go to bed?"

"Yes," I told him.

He lifted his head and his hand slid around my thigh, going under the fabric of my dress. The tips of his fingers glided across the edge of my panties at my leg.

"Let me rephrase that. Do you wanna go to sleep?" he went on.

Was he high? Did I want to go to sleep? What kind of question was that? I tried to be cool. "Not really."

He smiled The Smile.

My stomach melted.

"Good," he murmured. Then he kissed me.

It was a fucking great kiss. Long, slow, deep and hot. When it was over, his mouth slid across my cheek, down my neck and across my collarbone. His hand at my waist went up my back and he tugged at my hair, making me expose my neck, and then his tongue dipped into the indentation at the base of my throat.

He let go of my hair, his hand cupped the back of my head and he kissed me again. A repeat of the first, but better, lots of tongue. One of his hands was holding my head. The other one went to slide across my breast over the fabric of my dress.

This was all well and good. In fact it was beautiful. The problem was Lee was acting like we had all the time in the world. He was acting like at any moment the door buzzer wasn't going to buzz out some secret code tearing him away, leaving me high and dry, or more to the point, panting and wet.

I pushed up, changed position and straddled his hips. I yanked his t-shirt free of his jeans and pulled it over his head, throwing it wherever. I slid my hands down his chest, scratching his abs just a touch with my nails, watching his muscles tighten reflexively, and I went straight for the button fly on his jeans.

I got the top button undone when his hands grabbed my wrists and stopped them.

My eyes went to his and I saw the crinkles deepened at the corners.

"In a hurry?" he asked.

"Uh…" I said in a "duh" tone, "yeah."

"There's no need to rush." He pulled my hands away, let them go and slid his up my sides.

"You were in a rush this morning," I told him as he watched his hands slide up then stop at the sides of my breasts. His right hand curled and he slid his knuckles along the side right to the nipple. It hardened and he watched that too.

I bit my lip at the shock that went from nipple to nether region then called impatiently, "Lee."

His eyes moved from my breasts to my face.

"This morning was different."

"Different how?"

"I'm a guy," he stated as if that explained it, and it kind of did. I'd never known a man who didn't wake up with one thing on his mind, usually ready for that thing before his eyes opened.

"Well, how it was for you this morning is how it is for me *now*," I told him, my hands going back to his fly.

His hands went again to my wrists and he pulled them behind my back.

"I thought you wanted to take this slow," he said.

I could swear I heard laughter in his voice.

Bastard.

"How about this? You do it your way, I'll do it mine," I suggested.

His eyes locked on mine.

"This should be interesting."

"Damn straight," I muttered.

I kissed him. I knew he liked the way I kissed. He'd told me so, and so far, he hadn't lied to me.

He responded immediately.

He let my wrists go and put his arms around me.

My hands went back to his fly, but instead of opening it I slid my palm against it, feeling the length of him. It felt nice, *real* nice.

His hands went to my waist. He flipped me on my back on the couch and covered me with his body. I grabbed at his shoulders to hold on and lost my previously won position.

He kissed me, topping it by his hand going to cup my breast, his thumb sliding across my nipple. His finger joined his thumb and he began a delicious roll using the satin of my dress to deepen the friction.

Wow.

As in *wow*.

I lifted a knee for leverage. His hips fell between my legs, I wrapped the other leg around him, held on to his shoulder with one hand, pushed my other elbow in the couch as I braced my weight with my foot, bucked and rolled.

We fell off the couch, him with a grunt landing on his back, me on top.

I lifted up before he could recover, straddling him again. I bent over, arcing my back, my mouth on his chest. Sliding my lips, scraping my teeth, across, down, my tongue tracing the definition in the muscles of his abs. He tasted good and his skin felt nice over hard muscle.

It was glorious.

My fingers pried another button loose at his fly and my mouth went lower, my fingers working the next button just below my waiting lips. I was looking forward to this.

All that time, his hands were under the dress, holding my ass. As I moved down his body, they slid out and up, forcing my back and torso straight. They went under my arms and yanked me up over him, then he flipped me.

Our legs and hips hit the coffee table. It flew to the side, teetered and toppled, remotes, magazines and phones flying everywhere.

His body on mine, he captured my wrists and pulled them over my head and he looked at me. "You really are in a hurry."

"I said I was, didn't I?"

His mouth brushed mine. "Relax."

"*You* relax! Can you guarantee that the buzzer isn't gonna go on the door?"

"No."

"Can you guarantee that your phone's not gonna ring? My phone's not gonna ring? The whole western part of the United States isn't gonna fall into the Pacific Ocean?"

I felt as well as heard him give a soft laugh.

"No."

"I'm sorry about your man, I really am. That sucks and I'm not blaming you, but *I* didn't get *my* buzzer rung while *you* had *my* mouth between your legs. Catch my drift?"

He nuzzled my neck, still not letting go of my hands.

"I'm beginning to see your point."

"Well?"

"We're still gonna take it slow."

I gave an impatient noise.

Then I asked, "Why?"

"Because I want to," he told me.

"What about what I want?"

His head came up and he looked at me again, his eyes warm.

"You'll get what you want."

I glared at him thinking, *you bet your sweet ass I will.*

He went back to nuzzling and I started squirming. I couldn't help it, his mouth on my neck felt good.

Don't get me wrong. I wasn't in a race for an orgasm because this was Lee Nightingale or because I hadn't had one for a while (which I hadn't, at least not one that wasn't self-induced), but because I was seriously aroused and had been nursing a slow burn for days.

Lee was good with his hands, with his mouth. His body was so warm it was hot, and it not only felt good because of the warmth, but because it was hard and heavy. He was strong, which made me feel safe. Something else was hard and pressing against my thigh, and I knew what that something looked like and I wanted it. First in my hand, then in *me,* and if there was time in between, there were other things I was considering doing with it.

His hands slid down my arms and his mouth went lower. He skimmed my breasts over the fabric with his lips then he came back up to kiss me.

My hand went to his ass, inside his jeans, grasping it. When his lips broke from mine, my lips went to his neck. Using the tip of my tongue I explored his throat and jaw.

My hand moved from his ass, around the side, to the front.

"Indy," he said, part warning, part growl, part laugh.

I didn't bother with the buttons. My hand dove in and while I kissed him, I found him. With what little room I had between his jeans and his package, I wrapped my fingers around him.

Finally.

"Yes," I whispered against his lips as I stroked downward.

"That's it," he declared.

Lee jackknifed up and I lost my hold. He bent over, grabbed my hand and pulled me up.

"What?" I asked.

He bent over again, put an arm behind my knees, one at my waist and lifted me.

"You want fast, we'll go fast."

"Yippee," I said.

He was carrying me to the bedroom. "Did you just say 'yippee'?"

Oopsie. I didn't realize I spoke aloud.

"It slipped out," I told him.

"Well, this is one thing I'm gonna allow you to cute your way into." He dropped my legs when he reached the side of the bed. He released me and sat down to take off his boots, but looked up at me. "Don't get used to it," he warned.

Whatever, I thought and bent to tug the bows on the straps on my shoes. The tight straps immediately came loose so I kicked the shoes off and straightened, pulled my dress over my head and threw it aside.

I put a knee to the bed, started to crawl in and two hands caught me, flipped me onto my back, and in a flash my panties were pulled off my legs. Just like that, *poof,* I was naked.

I hadn't been paying attention. Lee'd been watching me and I was guessing he liked what he saw. Lee also hadn't wasted any time getting himself naked. He came over me, his eyes so melty-chocolate they were glistening.

His hand went between my legs. I felt strong fingers and they were magic.

"We don't have to go *that* fast," I said, but pressed against him.

"Too late."

His fingers went away. His hands opened my legs and his mouth went to where his fingers were. The choir had already warmed up, and within minutes his talented mouth and tongue sent me straight to the high note of the aria.

God, it was amazing.

Before I'd finished singing, he was up and over me, sliding inside me, and it felt so unbelievably good that even though the first act was pretty spectacular, the second act followed close on its heels and it rocked my world.

"I think I'm hungry," I told him after.

"Again?" he asked. "By my count, you came twice."

Grr.

He *would* be counting.

I did come twice. Well, maybe three times, or the second was just really long.

We were all tangled up so I detangled, slid away from him and searched under the pillow. I found that Judy had not only cleaned but ironed the Night Stalker tee (who irons t-shirts?) and I tugged it on.

"For food." I turned and looked at him. "Do you want food?"

"What did you make?"

"I was going to make steaks, green beans and au gratin potatoes. I only finished the potatoes."

His eyes softened when he heard the menu and he said, quietly "I could eat."

I guess I scored a hit with the meal even if I hadn't been able to cook it for him.

I padded into the kitchen and went straight to the wine. I was struggling with the cork when he followed me in wearing only his jeans. He took the wine from me and effortlessly uncorked it. I grabbed the glasses, set them on the counter and he poured.

I slopped a mess of potatoes in a bowl and nuked them. To satisfy my own hunger, I decided I would skip the potatoes and go straight to the pie. I sipped my wine and watched the microwave, feeling weird. We'd taken another step towards togetherness. The best step by far, but it still freaked me out.

"How was your day?" I asked, trying to cover my discomfort.

Boy, that sounded lame.

"Progress is better on my other cases," he replied behind my back.

The dinger went. I pulled the potatoes out, set the hot bowl on a folded towel and handed it to him with a fork. He leaned a hip on the counter and ate standing up.

I sucked down more wine and headed to the fridge.

"I've decided to work the Rosie case again. I'm gonna recruit Tex. He has good skills," I shared.

By this, I meant he wasn't scared of anything, including breaking the law. Not to mention he thought I was a fun date.

215

I opened the fridge and slid out the pie.

Lee was watching me. "You didn't say anything about pie."

"Chocolate cream."

He stared at me, fork frozen halfway to his mouth. Something was working behind his eyes. Whatever it was, he processed it and I could tell it pleased him, but he didn't share it with me. I let it slide. He'd tell me if he wanted me to know, but it didn't take a brain surgeon to realize he liked the idea that I made his favorite pie.

"Why are you goin' after Rosie?" he asked.

"Because he got me into this and I'm sick of dead bodies and bullets flying. Everyone I love is scared for me and Rosie's the key. I'm gonna root him out, kick his ass and then things will get back to normal."

I walked to the other side of the kitchen, slid the pie on the counter and grabbed a fork.

"What you mean is, you're gonna get Tex to kick his ass," Lee said.

I considered cutting a piece, but decided against it. It was just Lee and me, no reason standing on ceremony. I dipped my finger into the cream and turned to Lee.

"I could take Rosie. No problem." Then I stuck my finger in my mouth.

His eyes dropped to my mouth as I sucked my finger. I cocked my head and grinned at him. He one-upped me by gifting me with The Smile. The problem was, The Smile was not only amped up with a good deal of warmth and intimacy, it was mega-watt with the knowledge of the great sex that had gone before and the promise of what was to come.

My legs got a little weak.

"Last time you saw Rosie, he was waving a gun at you," Lee pointed out.

"Tex has a gun."

"Tex has a *shotgun*. Civilians with guns are a little scary. Civilians with guns they don't know how to use are very scary. Toting around a shotgun is just nuts."

I shrugged, jumped up and planted my ass on the counter. I crossed my legs and took another sip of wine. Then I picked up the whole pie, took a moment to decide where to start and decided to start with the best part. I grabbed the fork and I dug straight into the middle.

After about four bites, I lifted my eyes to Lee. He was holding his wine and watching me, his bowl in the sink.

"What?" I asked.

"Are you upset about me bein' late? You went out of your way with dinner."

"Nope," I replied.

"You lie as easy as you breathe, be honest."

I stared at him.

"Why would I be upset? Do I seem upset? You said you'd call when you were on your way home. I know you're busy and you have a lot on your plate. I planned dinner accordingly. Nothing's going to spoil. Jeez, Lee. I may fib every once in a while, but only when it isn't important. It's just dinner, not missing a Led Zeppelin reunion."

He took a sip of wine and kept watching me.

I scooped out a huge wodge of pie and turned the fork toward him.

"Want some?"

His face changed and he set the wine aside.

"Yeah," he said, coming toward me.

Holy shit.

I was thinking he wasn't talking about pie.

I wasn't wrong.

He took the fork and tossed it into the pie. Then he took the pie and set it aside.

"I wasn't done with that," I said to him.

"You can go back to it later."

He pressed open my legs. I hadn't put any panties on and I felt immediately exposed. He came between them, sliding my ass across the counter and the feeling went away as I felt his warmth against me.

"What are you doing?" I asked, even though I knew exactly what he was doing.

"Dessert," he answered and he kissed me.

He tasted like wine. I was sure I tasted like pie.

I wasn't lying, I wanted more pie, but after he started kissing me I didn't miss it much.

One of his hands was steady at my hip, the other hand was working between us. He was undoing his fly.

"Brace your hands on the counter edge," he ordered.

"What?"

In answer, he jerked me forward, tipping my hips. I grabbed the edge of the counter quickly, and all of a sudden he slid inside me.

Now, I'm no prude and I'm no saint, but I can't say I'd had an adventurous sex life. At least I'd never had sex on a kitchen counter.

It was fantastic. Slightly naughty, slightly illicit and you knew in the back of your head you'd remember it when you were making coffee.

"Now who's going fast?" I asked, wrapping my legs around his hips.

He ground his hips into me and it felt so fucking good, I bit my lip.

"Have anything more to say?" he asked back.

I shook my head, then I said, "Wait a second, I do. Do that again." His body went still and his eyebrows went up.

I put my mouth against his and murmured, "Please."

Then I got another version of The Smile. The sexiest, the best and *the* most dangerous: the warm and intimate smile you get when Lee's moving inside you.

After, we had pie.

Then, we had a shower.

What with wet, soapy, naked bodies, especially with one of them being Lee's, things got out of hand and we tumbled out of the shower onto the bath mat.

After that, I said a silent thank you to the unknown Judy as the bathroom was sparkling clean and the bath mat smelled of fragrant dryer sheets.

Later, we were in bed and I was pressed up against his side, his arm around my waist, my arm curled around his abs. I'd thrown a leg over his thigh and I had my head on his shoulder.

I was comfy, warm and very sleepy.

I felt good, and if I allowed myself to think about it (which I did, but only a little), I was happy.

"About you lookin' for Rosie with Tex. I'm gonna have to ask you not to do it," Lee announced.

I didn't want to have this conversation now. I was tired, very relaxed, maybe even happy. I didn't want a conversation that might get heated.

So I ignored him.

He shook me a bit.

"Indy."

"Mm?" I mumbled into his shoulder.

"Did you hear me?"

"I heard you."

He sighed.

"You're thinking of cuffing me to the bed again, aren't you?" I asked.

"Yeah."

I tilted my head to look at him without moving my cheek from his shoulder. "Why don't you want me looking for Rosie?"

"How many reasons do you want?"

"Two." I was still relaxed, but beginning to feel snippy.

"You don't know what you're doin' and Tex is a fucking crazy man."

"Both good points."

Holy shit.

Did I say that out loud?

What was it with me? I was blurting out my honest thoughts willy-nilly.

He rolled into me. His thigh came between my legs, forcing one of mine to hook around his hip and his hand went to my ass and pressed me to him. His other hand tucked my head in his neck.

I realized he thought I agreed with him and this was my reward.

It was a good reward, being held by Lee like that. Really good.

He didn't have to know that even though I agreed with him, I was still going to do whatever the hell I wanted to do.

⋈

I woke up when the bed depressed with Lee's weight.

I opened my eyes and blinked at him.

"Coffee," he said, and I saw the steam rising from a mug he was holding.

I scooted up, arranged the pillows, pulled the sheet up over my chest and took the coffee.

I took a sip. It was strong.

"My hero," I breathed into the joe.

"What are your plans for the day?" he asked.

Automatically, I lied, "I'm not caffeinated enough to have plans."

He stared at me.

He knew I had plans.

He stood. He was wearing a pair of seriously faded, once navy-blue sweats that rode low on his hips, bringing the tops of his hip bones out in sexy relief. The sweats had been cut off and the ragged edge hit mid-thigh. His hair was messy, not only with sleep, but because I'd made it that way. With the sweats and the hair, I was beginning to feel mildly turned on.

He walked across the room and came back.

I took another sip and absently heard a clink of metal but was still not awake enough to process the noise.

The mug was swept away, my wrist was seized and halfway up to the headboard when I realized he had cuffs.

Too late, he slapped it on my wrist and I heard the ratchet of the bracelet. I twisted, but I heard the second ratchet and I was stuck.

I twisted back to him, pissed-off.

"You're kidding," I snapped.

He slid in bed alongside me, pulling the sheet down. "Nope."

His hands were on me and his mouth came to my neck.

"Un-unh. No way." I pushed at him with my free hand. "You aren't gonna cuff me to the bed and have your wicked way with me."

He grabbed my free hand by the wrist and twisted it behind me. "Wanna bet?"

His other hand pushed the sheet over my hip and I was fully exposed.

"Are you gonna leave me here all day?" I asked.

"After... yeah," he said into my ear.

Grr.

"Uncuff me!" I demanded.

"No," he replied.

"Lee, this is not funny," I told him. "And anyway, morning sex isn't working for us. You start this and someone is gonna buzz the door and tell you that The Alamo has been attacked and you're gonna take off."

His hand had wandered to my ass, his mouth came to mine. "You'll survive."

"No I won't!"

His mouth slid past mine to my ear. "You've done it before."

"That was before I knew what I was missing!"

His head came up and he grinned at me.

Fucking Lee.

"I'll uncuff you if you promise me you won't go off looking for Rosie with Tex." I opened my mouth, but before I could say anything he said, "Promise me and mean it."

I closed my mouth.

If I could have crossed my arms on my chest, I would have. Instead, I explained.

"Stevie's mad at me because Tod was in the line of fire. Ally's chasing down bad guys, totaling her Mustang. My life's completely out-of-control and taking others with it. I can't sit around and wait. I have to do something. I'm tired of being scared."

I was trying to twist away. He threw a thigh over mine and pinned me, let go of my wrist, got up on an elbow and traced the line of my jaw with his finger, looking in my eyes.

He was deciding something.

Then he decided.

"Then you work with me."

My body stilled. Was he serious? Work *with* the Mysterious Badass Liam Nightingale?

"What?" I asked.

"We'll look for Rosie together."

My mouth dropped open.

"Seriously?" I breathed.

He nodded.

I started to smile, but then he said, "There are conditions."

The smile went away and I narrowed my eyes at him. "What conditions?"

His eyes softened and crinkled at the corners.

"You're very cute," he muttered.

Excuse me? Cute?

"Conditions?" I snapped, deciding to deal with the "cute" comment later.

"You do what I say when I tell you to do it and you keep your mouth shut. If we get into something and I get a bad vibe and feel you shouldn't be there, you don't argue, you just go."

I thought about it and decided I could do that.

"Uncuff me," I said again.

"You agree?"

"I agree."

He uncuffed me. I started to roll away, but he hooked me and rolled me back.

"Where you goin'?" he asked.

"Just 'cause I agreed to work together with you doesn't mean I'm not angry with you for cuffing me. You want honesty, I'll give you honesty. You've pissed me off."

He nuzzled my neck, apparently unaffected by my announcement.

"I can help you work through that."

"You're way too cocky," I told him.

"I know, but you still love me."

I froze. "Excuse me?"

His arms came around me, holding me tight as if he knew I was about ready to bolt and he was preparing early. He lifted his head and looked at me. His eyes were dark and warm.

"You love me."

I stared at him and lied through my teeth (glad to know I could still do it), "I *do not* love you."

He pulled me even deeper into him.

"Liar," he whispered. "You've loved me since I held your hand at your mother's memorial service when you were five years old."

It was then my head exploded.

Chapter 16
Must... Stop... Brain

"What?" I shouted.

He was watching me closely.

I bucked, pushed and tried to get away, but he held on tight.

"Let me go," I demanded.

He didn't say anything, just effortlessly held me to him.

I stilled and looked at him.

There was no denying it. His intelligence about when my infatuation started was too detailed to lie about.

"How did you know about that? Was it Ally?" I asked.

"I read your diary."

Oh... my... God.

"What? When?"

"I don't know. When you were fifteen, sixteen. You were schemin' and throwin' yourself at me pretty steady, recruitin' your friends to help. Some of it was ingenious. I was lookin' for ways to..." he hesitated then found the words, "diffuse your eagerness."

Holy shit.

How embarrassing was that?

It was a long time ago and I didn't remember what I wrote in my diary. What I *did* remember was that it was nearly all about Lee and all of it was very personal.

I pressed my hands against his chest and tilted my chin down so I couldn't see him.

I was never going to live this down. It felt like my whole body was on fire with mortification. I had to get the fuck out of there before I exploded. I was the Embarrassment Bomb.

"Indy."

"You shouldn't have read my diary. That was low," I told his chest. "But it was a long time ago. Things change I've changed. I don't feel that way anymore."

"That's why you made chocolate cream pie last night."

I lifted my head and glared at him. "You'd had a hard couple of days. I was trying to be nice."

"Last night *was* nice, *very* nice."

"Go to hell."

I was too embarrassed for compliments or to be fair or rational. I just wanted to get away.

"Considering I've finally had you, had you in three different rooms, and feel pretty fuckin' pleased about that, I'll let that comment slide," he said, sounding like he was beginning to get annoyed.

"Nice of you," I hissed.

I bucked again to get away and he rolled on top of me.

"Settle down," he ordered.

"Get off me."

"Right," he clipped, (yep, definitely annoyed). "Shut up and listen to me."

My eyes rounded with anger, about to pop out of my head. Before I could say a word, he started talking.

"First of all, back then, you were underage. No way I could touch you legally. Not the way I wanted to, anyway. There aren't a lot of people whose opinions I care about, but your father's is one of them. He'd have lost his mind if we'd hooked up then because my reputation wasn't exactly unearned."

This was true.

I still glared at him.

He kept talking.

"It wasn't easy to keep sayin' no. You're fucking gorgeous and always were. I wanted you then, but you were a wild child. Everyone knew you were a handful. I wasn't gonna go near you until you calmed down. It might be entertaining to watch when you're removed, but if you'd been mine, you'd have driven me up the wall. I knew myself well enough to know that."

This might have been true, but I certainly didn't want to hear it.

Lee wasn't done. "Regardless of that, I intended to have you, one day, and that was always at the back of my mind. So I considered you mine even when you weren't. It was common knowledge our families were close. Half the assholes I knew came to me tellin' me they wanted a piece of you, the other half lyin' about havin' a piece. Why do you think I fought so goddamned much?"

Yikes.

That was news.

He went on, "I knew I had to get my shit together before I got us together. By the time that happened, you were avoiding me. We've discussed this part, without much of your honest participation. This brings us to now."

He stared at me.

I kept my mouth shut.

"You can jump in anytime you feel like it," he invited.

Hmm, sarcasm.

"You shouldn't have read my diary," I snapped.

"Get over it."

"I'm not gonna get over it. That's personal. How I feel about you should be for me to tell you."

He waited a beat then, "Point taken."

That's as far as he went. No apology and no remorse.

Jerk.

"I was a young girl with an infatuation," I informed him. "You shouldn't mistake who I was for who I am now."

Lee made no comment so I kept going.

"That said, I am what I am. I'm still a wild child. I still do stupid, crazy things. I listen to rock 'n' roll, loud. I lip sync with drag queens. I find it fun to try to out-attitude the Sushi Den hostesses, and sometimes Ally and me even joyride around Denver. I haven't changed and you can't control me. If you even want to, I'm gone."

"There's a difference between controlling and protecting," he remarked.

"Yeah, be careful not to cross that line. A line, I might add, you crossed this morning." I was on a roll. "And while we're talking about control, I may not have changed, but *you* have. The Lee I thought I loved when I was a teenager is not you."

That pissed him off and his eyes narrowed. "*I'm* not hiding anything."

"Do you mean to imply that I am?"

"Jesus, Indy, if you had the wall around you any more fortified, it'd be so deep you'd be in fucking Mexico."

"I've always let it all hang out!"

"Bullshit."

I made an angry noise that sounded like someone had punched me in the stomach.

"You got something to say?" I demanded.

225

His face changed. There was something there I'd never seen before. Something the looks of which scared the hell out of me.

When he spoke, his voice was softer, even gentle.

"You live every day like tomorrow isn't gonna come. Your mother died before she reached your age. You watched your father choose to live a lonely life rather than replace her. It doesn't take a psychologist to put those things together and figure out why you allow yourself to take care of all the Rosies and Texes of the world, but don't allow anyone to get very close to you."

That was when I felt like I *had* been punched in the stomach.

I turned my head away and bucked again. "Get off me."

"Un-unh." He curved his hand around my chin and jaw and forced me to look at him. "I'm not gettin' off, not goin' away, not playin' anymore games or wastin' anymore fuckin' time. I don't believe in fate or destiny or any of that bullshit. What I know is that, as far as I can tell, there isn't another woman I've met who fits my life. Who doesn't care if I get home late after she's made a special dinner. Who doesn't have a hemorrhage when I talk about one of my men gettin' shot, goin' off about how *she* feels about my work. You got up and made everyone coffee, for fuck's sake. You're a woman who tells me to be careful when I tell her I'm out hunting humans instead of bitchin' and wantin' to process how my career choice makes *her* feel. If an employee walked into their kitchen with a gun and shot at their neighbor, most people would lose their fucking minds. You spent the morning makin' brownies and the afternoon sleepin' in the sun. You live hard, play hard and don't seem to be scared of anything, but manage to keep a softness about you that's almost unreal. You wanted me to tell you why I'm sure about you, that's why I'm sure. You grew up and your only parent was a cop. You know the drill. I don't have any interest in trainin' someone to get it and I need someone strong enough to live with it. That's you."

I stared at him, eyes wide. I'd never heard him say so much all at one time in my life. And I'd known him my entire life.

"How often do your men get shot?" I asked.

"Shot at, too often. Shot, luckily, rarely."

I wanted to ask how often he got shot at or had been shot. I wanted to ask, but I didn't want to know the answer. So I didn't ask.

"Smart decision," he murmured. He was in my brain. Again.

"I do get scared," I whispered. "You scare me."

His eyes crinkled. "That's the best thing I've heard in a week."

I was stunned. "That you scare me?"

His mouth brushed mine.

"If I scare you then you care. I'm the same Lee, just older and smarter. You love me. Eventually your wall will come down and you'll admit it to yourself, and then you'll admit it to me."

Jeez, he was *so* cocky.

His hands started moving on me and he began to nuzzle my neck again.

Apparently our little drama was over.

"I don't think I'm done being pissed at you," I told him.

"That's okay," he said against my ear. "I can still make love to you when you're angry."

Unbelievably cocky.

"I don't think so," I said.

His hand went between my legs, his fingers executing a delicious little swirl that was just enough pressure to get my attention, but light enough to make me want more.

Bastard.

I opened my legs a bit, I couldn't help it.

He kissed me as reward.

"I promised to show you who I was, which mostly you know. Today you'll learn more," he said when he was nuzzling my neck again. I was kind of listening, but his fingers were exerting more pressure and doing some more swirl action so I was finding it hard. "And I promised to tell you what I wanted and give you time to decide."

Oh no, this wasn't fair.

I'd opened my legs further and the swirling was getting serious. I was running my hands up his back and had my face shoved in his neck. There was no way I could process important discussion.

"Can we..." I panted, "talk about this later?"

I thought he agreed. He slid between my legs and entered me.

Nice. Very, very nice.

He started to move. "I want you in my house, in my bed. I want you to move in by the weekend."

My eyes were closed, but they flew open and I saw he was looking at me. I still wanted to take our relationship slow. He was talking hyper-drive.

I could not deal with this, not now. He hadn't stopped moving and he felt good inside me.

I wrapped my arms and legs around him, sliding a hand in his hair.

"Lee..."

I didn't intend to say anything else, just shut him up so I could concentrate.

"Jesus," he buried his face in my neck, "there's nothin' better in the world than hearin' you say my name when I'm inside you." He slid in deep, filling me. "I've been waitin' years to be right here."

Holy crap.

His mouth was at my ear.

"I could be on assignment, in a desert as hot as an oven, in a jungle as close as fuck and sometimes I'd get through it dreamin' of you sayin' my name like that."

Holy crap, crap, crap.

"I'll move in by the weekend," I said.

He lifted his head and smiled.

Fucking Lee.

I was in the bathroom swiping on makeup.

The bruise on my cheek was nearly gone, and my mental body checkup declared only slight aches and pains after a day of no mishaps and a night and morning of great sex, which apparently was an effective muscle relaxant. I was thinking my luck was turning as yesterday, outside of finally *doing it* with Lee, my adventures only included one dead body, which fortunately wasn't mine. Therefore good and bad instead of all bad.

Then Lee walked into the bathroom wearing just the faded navy sweatshorts.

I glanced at him in the mirror and tried to tamp down my panic.

In the heat of the moment, I'd agreed to move in.

Okay, so it was more about what he said than the heat of the moment, but I'd still agreed to move in.

Further, I'd just noticed something I hadn't really taken in the night before. Judy had given me a makeup drawer in Lee's bathroom vanity.

It was all too much.

He slid a fresh mug o' java on the vanity counter and put my cell beside it.

"Your phone's beeping," he said.

I moved aside to make room as he prepared to shave. I took a sip of coffee and let my mind run wild.

Dear Lord in heaven, I was putting on makeup and Lee was shaving, at the same time, in the same room. After having sex. Lots of sex. Even sex in this very room!

I stood frozen to the spot and stared at him.

He lathered his cheeks with a thin gel and his eyes slid to the side. He checked me out from their corners.

"Something wrong?"

"I'm not really a bathroom sharer," I informed him.

He looked back in the mirror and continued doing exactly what he was doing. "Honey, it's good you're gorgeous or you'd be a pain in the ass."

Well, I'm *so* sure.

I grabbed my phone, looked at the display and saw seven missed calls.

Yikes.

How did that happen?

I called my voicemail while I leaned as best I could on my half of the vanity (I had to admit, it was a big vanity… maybe I was being a *bit* of a wuss) and swept mascara on my lashes.

Four voicemails.

First up, Willie Moses.

"Indy, Willie… call me."

Hmm.

Second, Marianne.

"I know Ally said it's none of my business, but give me a break. I live with my parents. I don't have a life. Yours is better and I want to know *everything*. Let's meet at The Hornet tonight if you can guarantee we won't get shot at."

Yikes.

Third, Stevie.

"Well? How'd it go? Don't forget Chowleena. I'll be leaving just before noon. Tod will be home tomorrow, early, so if you still have her for a sleepover, just leave a note. Kisses."

Fourth, Duke, who obviously was talking before being given the beep.

"... ass in here or I'm gonna kill him."

I poked myself in the eye with the mascara wand.

"Holy crap," I said.

"That looked like it hurt."

I was blinking fiercely. My eye was tearing up, making my other eye tear up, and I was trying to see my phone to replay Duke's message.

Lee tore off some toilet paper, handed it to me and took the phone.

"Listen!" I told him. "The last message."

I opened my mouth as far as it would go, which was a feminine mechanism that one had to use to open one's eyes as far as they would go. I dabbed at the tears and blotches of mascara, trying to avert a cosmetics disaster.

"Who does he want to kill?" Lee asked.

"I don't know. It's Duke. He has the patience of a gnat and a three centimeter fuse. Do you think it could be Rosie?"

"Where is he?"

"I don't know! It's Duke!" I cried, exasperated. "He refuses to buy a cell phone or answering machine. He's a fucking caveman."

Lee was scrolling down my phonebook and he punched a button.

"Dolores? It's Lee. Can I talk to Duke?"

Quick Thinker Lee decided to call Duke and Dolores's home phone. Simple. I hated it when I was an idiot. Thank God he was the private eye in the family.

Oh jeez, did I just think "in the family"?

Must... stop... brain.

I reapplied some shadow and fixed the mascara while Lee was talking, and then he said, "Yeah? Got it. Thanks."

I screwed on the cap to the mascara and threw it in the drawer while Lee flipped shut the cell and slid it on the counter. Then he calmly went back to shaving. I slid the drawer shut with my hip.

"Well?" I prompted.

"The police took the tape down at the store. Willie called you to let you know and when he couldn't get you, he called Duke. Apparently, there's a crazy Italian guy at Fortnum's saying he's your new coffee guy. Jane called Dolores because Duke was getting heated. Dolores called the cops. They're handling it."

"What crazy Italian guy?"

Lee tilted his head to see his jaw and slid his razor up his neck. "Don't know."

"I didn't even know we were open today!" I stated loudly then announced, "We have to get down there."

"Dolores didn't seem upset."

"Dolores lives with Duke and thinks he's cuddly. She works at The Little Bear where people throw around their underwear. Dolores isn't a good judge of when to get upset!"

Lee looked at me in the mirror. "I'm thinkin' at this point you aren't either."

I was dressed, khaki low-rider shorts (not Britney Spears low-rider, but they showed a hint of back), sky-blue fitted t-shirt with the word "Xanadu" across my chest in glittery lettering and a wide dark brown belt with a thick matte-silver buckle.

I walked out and went to the closet and grabbed a pair of flip-flops with ribbon straps with sky-blue funky shapes against khaki. I slid them on, snagged my purse and pulled it on my shoulder. I walked back to the bathroom, snatched up my phone and dropped it in my bag. Then I rested my hip on the edge of the counter and clicked my nails against the top, my other hand on my hip.

And I stared at Lee.

He grabbed a towel, wiped his face and threw it in the sink.

"Hey! You can't just throw your towel in the sink!" I declared heatedly. "Who's gonna fold that towel and put it back on the rail? I'll tell you who it won't be. Me!"

That's when he grabbed my hips, pulled me to him and grinned.

"You're tryin' to break the land speed record for gettin' an offer to move in rescinded, aren't you?"

"No. And it was hardly an offer as much as sexual blackmail."

His grin widened into a smile.

Fucking Lee!

"Hello!" I called. "Fortnum's? My bread and butter? The family business for the last..." Wow, I didn't even know how long it had been in the family. I'd have to wing it. "Umpteen years! Crazy Italian guy? Duke's homicide threat? Ring a bell?"

He drew me closer to him. "Have I told you you're cute?"

Grr.

We walked into Fortnum's and my crazy morning got crazier.

Terry Wilcox, Goon Gary and The Moron were all facing off against Duke.

"What's going on?" I asked when I walked in, my stomach lurching. You could feel the bad energy in the room.

No customers (thank God, kind of) and Jane was nowhere to be seen (thank God again).

"This idiot has brought the Italian guy *back* after the police took him *away*. Says he's a fucking *present*," Duke shared.

"India. You look well," Terry Wilcox said, his eyes sliding down the length of me.

Yuck.

I was getting that queasy feeling that my body seemed to save for my encounters with Terry Wilcox. I was hoping they would only number two, this one and the last.

Luckily, Lee's hand felt warm and strong where it settled at my hip.

"Coxy," Lee greeted.

"Lee," Wilcox replied.

"You know him?" Duke asked.

"Yeah," Lee said and that one syllable said he didn't like him much.

Duke moved toward us at the same time that Lee put pressure on me to move behind him. I planted my feet and stayed where I was.

Goon Gary and The Moron were shifting, getting ready for action.

Great. Just what I needed, a brawl in Fortnum's.

Wilcox decided to play peacemaker.

"There's no need to get excited, boys," he said. "India, you said you had a problem. You lost your coffee guy and were losing business. I've brought you a new one, from Italy, where they invented espresso. This is Antonio and he's very talented."

I looked at a man I hadn't noticed who was standing behind Goon Gary. He looked like an Italian version of Rosie, except better groomed. Slightly better.

The door opened as I was saying, "I don't need a coffee guy, thanks. We're covered."

Then from behind me came, "Uh-oh, major bad vibe. What's shakin' now, woman?"

I turned to the door and saw Tex.

Wonderful, it just kept getting better and better. Now Tex was in the mix.

"What're you doing here?" I asked Tex.

"Came for coffee."

Of course.

"How'd you get here?" I went on.

"Drove. I have a car but I usually let the neighbors use it."

I gaped at him. "You drove with your arm in a sling?"

"Fuck yeah, only got tricky when I had to shift."

I lifted both of my hands and put my palms to my forehead. It was a 'Calgon, take me away' moment.

"Coxy, she doesn't want your man. You can send him home," Lee said, his voice calm but scary.

"He's a present for India. It's hardly for you to say," Wilcox returned, also calm but combative.

"Lee says he goes, he fucking goes!" Duke roared, not at all calm.

"I make coffee!" the Italian guy shouted, looking a bit more at ease when someone was shouting.

I was having visions of Goon Gary flying through the front window of my store.

"Everyone makes coffee, twerp. I make coffee. Jeez-us. Why the big deal about coffee?" Tex declared and lumbered to the espresso machine as if the air wasn't thick enough with tension. He pushed himself behind the counter. "What'll it be? I'll make *everybody* coffee."

Oh... my.... God.

This was not happening.

I saw my life flashing before my eyes, or at least my bank balance.

I turned to Lee and whispered, "Lee, that espresso machine cost thousands of dollars..." I stopped speaking and winced when Tex banged something, loud, "If he breaks it, I'm totally screwed."

"Come on! What'll it be? Give me orders. Woman, what's your order?" Tex was pointing the portafilter at me.

"I am barista. I am the best barista in Milan. I make coffee!" Antonio shouted and dashed behind the counter. "*Signorina*, I make you espresso."

Lee was ignoring me so I yelled generally, "Someone stop them!"

"She drinks vanilla lattes," Duke called.

I grabbed Lee's arm. "Lee!"

Lee was watching Gary and The Moron. He didn't look at me when he said, "He breaks it, I'll buy you a new one."

I pressed up against him. "When I say 'thousands of dollars', I mean, like, *seven* of them!"

Lee's eyes moved to me. "Indy, honey, what did I say?"

Yikes.

Okay, Lee was concentrating, and obviously it was best to leave Lee alone when he was concentrating.

"Ha ha!" Antonio crowed watching Tex slam around. "You know nothing about espresso. I am barista. My father was barista. My grandfather—"

"Shut the fuck up and make coffee if you make coffee, turkey," Tex boomed.

Wilcox took two steps toward us. Lee moved in front of me and Duke closed ranks.

"That's close enough, Coxy," Lee warned.

Wilcox was looking at me, but he stopped at Lee's warning.

"You keep sending back my presents," Wilcox said to me.

I got a chill up my spine. His eyes were weird, intense and frightening. "Thank you. You're being very nice, but it would be rude for me to accept them."

"You accepted the one I gave you yesterday," he remarked.

Lee's body tensed and it seemed as if electricity sparkled in the air.

Then it came to me in a flash.

I was on the phone to Lee yesterday, telling him about Pepper Rick's body, and Lee had said, "A present."

I hadn't thought of it again, but that's what he meant. Wilcox had killed my kidnapper and brought him to me as a present.

Oh... my... God.

How totally gross was that?

I was standing mostly behind Lee and grabbed bunches of his t-shirt in my hands, but I didn't take my eyes off Wilcox.

"You didn't," I whispered.

"*I* can keep you safe, India. My present yesterday proved it," Wilcox said.

I felt bile climb up the back of my throat.

Then something else hit me. The store was bugged. Days ago, Lee had bugged the store. If I could get him talking, maybe it could get taped or someone at Lee's Command Headquarters was listening. Then Wilcox could be picked up for murder and I'd never have to worry about him again, or, at least, until they let him out.

"Lee keeps me protected," I told Wilcox. I didn't know what to say to draw him out.

He smiled his oily smile. "To do it properly, you have to eliminate the threat."

"Is that what you did? Eliminated the threat and put him at my front door?" I pushed.

His smile didn't waver and he didn't answer.

"I didn't know he was from you. How was I to know the dead guy was from you? You should have left, like, a note or something," I said.

"Antonio!" Wilcox shouted, the suddenness of it making me jump. "We're going. The lady said she doesn't need your services."

"But I make coffee," Antonio whined.

Wilcox just slid his eyes to Antonio, and without another word he rushed out from behind the counter.

Wilcox winked at me, nodded to Lee and Duke and then left with Antonio and the rest of his goons on his heels.

I was holding my breath. When the door closed behind them, I let the breath out in a whoosh, sagging against Lee's back.

"I'm surprised you didn't put your fist in his face," Duke said to Lee.

"I'd rather put a bullet in his brain," Lee replied in a voice that was oh-so-much more scary then the calm one he'd used earlier. Mainly because he sounded like he intended to do it.

He twisted, pulled me around to his front and kissed my forehead.

"You did all right," he told me.

"This has to end soon. I'm coming apart at the seams."

His arm wrapped around my shoulders and neck and held me close.

Jane wandered out from the bowels of the shelves, reading and walking at the same time, her face buried in an open book. Oblivious to the most recent drama, she seemed to sense the presence of others. She looked up in surprise as if she'd just encountered us all in her living room, not standing at the front of a huge, used bookstore. She stopped dead, staring at Tex.

"Hey Jane, honey. How're you doin' today?" I asked, worried that she'd have ill-effects after seeing a dead body yesterday.

Her eyes went from Tex to me then flickered to Lee and I could see her blush.

This didn't surprise me. Lee had that effect on women.

She didn't answer me, just nodded and wandered behind the book counter.

"She's hangin' in there," Duke mumbled, answering my unspoken question.

"Indy, are you gonna try my coffee or what?" Tex called.

I disengaged from Lee and walked on shaky legs to the counter. I took the cup from Tex and before I even took a drink, I stopped and lifted my eyes to look at the big, crazy man.

I could smell it and it smelled good.

I tasted it.

Divine.

"Tex," I whispered, "this is the nectar of the gods."

"I told you anyone could make coffee," Tex replied.

"You want a job?" I asked him.

Tex stared. "You shittin' me?"

"Nope."

"What about the cats?" he asked.

"Sometimes they need to play and sometimes they need to sleep. They can sleep while you're making coffee," I answered.

Chapter 17
Bitch Triple Threat

We left Tex to fill out employment forms and Lee drove into LoDo, turning into underground parking. There was a bank of spots with signs that said, "Nightingale Investigations" and Lee reversed the Crossfire into one. Most of them were empty. One held a soft-top Jeep, another the Mercedes Lee was driving when Tex and I did our breaking and entering. Another held a red Miata and one held a black Ducati Monster Testastretta next to a silver Harley Dyna Low Rider.

I'd seen Lee on the Ducati and it was sweet. I kinda hoped the Harley was his as well.

I couldn't concentrate on happy thoughts of maybe getting a ride on the Ducati, or the Harley, because I was too excited about the fact that I was about to visit Lee's LoDo offices.

We got off the elevator on the second floor and I saw a door with a small brass plaque that had Lee's company name on it. Lee opened the door for me and I walked in.

It was decorated in "Man" with wood paneled walls, a hulking reception desk, leather couches, thick carpet and dark wood. There were heavily framed cowboy prints on the walls with a bronze statue of a bucking bronco on a column in the corner.

The final touch was a glamorous blonde woman who looked like a supermodel sitting behind the reception desk.

She glanced up and the moment her eyes caught sight of Lee, they went from enquiring to inviting.

"Hey Lee," she said, or more like *breathed* in a "happy birthday, Mr. President" way.

"Dawn. This is Indy," Lee introduced, but Dawn was already looking at me and sizing me up.

She was wearing designer clothing. She had a fresh French manicure and her yearly budget for hair highlights probably was more than my new furniture.

She looked ready to step on a private jet. I looked ready to go to Six Flags Elitch Gardens.

She knew this, I knew this, and when her eyes flickered to Lee, I also knew Dawn wasn't working here because it was an exciting career opportunity.

I smiled sweetly and lied, "Dawn, nice to meet you."

She smiled sweetly back and it was fake, fake, fake.

"Indy," she greeted, and her eyes turned again to Lee. "Luke's out of critical. I thought you'd want to know. I've e-mailed your phone messages through. Two are priority but you're expecting them, and there's a new high-bond skip that needs your attention. The file's on your desk."

Lee nodded and propelled me with a hand at my back toward a hallway. "Can you get Indy outfitted with a belt, stun gun, Taser and spray?"

Yikes. What did I need all that for?

I decided not to ask.

"Sure thing," Dawn answered, clearly ever-helpful.

We walked down the hall and into Lee's office, which was more of the same but with a bigger desk. I was shocked when I entered. It was obsessively neat and tidy. A sleek coffee mug sat on a leather coaster on the desk, the mug shiny clean. A laptop also was on the desk, closed and positioned perfectly at an angle to the side. Fancy leather and wood desk accessories adorned the top as well, but they were empty except for a pencil holder filled with perfectly pointed pencils and one folder sitting in the in tray.

"This is scary. You're a neat freak," I remarked.

Lee walked behind the desk, opened the laptop and hit a button. "Dawn keeps it like this."

That was not surprising.

"I bet she does," I mumbled.

Lee's eyes came to mine. "I'm not exactly in the business that allows me to keep open files on my desk."

Hmm.

Locking away confidential files was one thing. Keeping your boss's designer coffee mug shiny clean was another. I gave myself one guess as to who bought Lee that mug and that guess was Dawn. I wondered if it was a "thanks for the great sex gift" or a "wish we were having great sex gift".

I didn't answer Lee. I made a show of studying the cowboy print on the wall and decided not to tell him that it was likely that Dawn would clean his Crossfire with her toothbrush if he asked.

Knowing Lee, he probably already knew.

"She's dating a Bronco linebacker," Lee told me, as ever, in my brain.

"Un-hunh," I told the wall.

There was a big difference between dating a guy who, on Sundays a couple seasons of the year, played at being a tough-guy-badass while wearing pads and a guy who simply was a tough-guy-badass. The linebacker may get big bucks, but he was not the real thing, and anyway, Lee wasn't hurting money-wise, that was certain.

When I looked back at Lee he was studying the file, but he had the eye crinkle going.

I was amusing him.

"What's funny?" I asked.

He didn't even look up. "You're jealous."

As if!

"I am not!"

He shook his head, but didn't answer and kept scanning the file.

"Lee, if you think she doesn't have the hots for you, you aren't as clever as I thought. And if you've already screwed her, you *really* aren't as clever as I thought."

He closed the file, dropped it on the desk and moved around it, toward me.

"Dawn's organized and cordial. She's always on time, willing to do over-time at a moment's notice and doesn't get flustered easily. I know she's attracted to me, but she's my employee and she's a good one. No way I'd touch her. You don't shit where you live."

He was backing me up across the office and doing his disarming straight talk thing. I had to admit I was a little pleased Lee hadn't sampled his reception-ist. Not only would it make things potentially difficult for me in future, it was tacky. Though thinking about it now with a clearer head, she wasn't his type.

"All righty then," I said when the backs of my legs hit a leather couch.

His hand went to my jaw. "You don't have anything to worry about."

Kristen Ashley

"I wasn't worried." This was almost not a lie. Dawn was pretty but she was super-thin. Lee liked a woman with curves, always had and (hopefully) always would.

"No?" Lee asked, his eyes warm, his face wearing what had become a familiar soft look. A look I'd only ever seen him give to me.

Still, he didn't believe me.

"You like booty, not bony. She's pretty and all, but not exactly your type," I told him.

As if to prove me right, his hands went to my ass.

I pressed my hands against his chest. "Are we gonna do some of that kick-ass PI stuff now?"

Lee was leaning into me. "In a minute."

I was having trouble staying upright. Lee was pressing into me, his hands on my behind, and he was looking at me with melty-chocolate eyes. His intentions were clear.

"Um, excuse me, but the door is unlocked. Anyone can walk in and we have a renegade coffee guy to catch. We don't have time for this. What are you thinking?"

"I'm thinking of fucking you on my couch."

Holy crap.

I did a full body tremble, starting at the toes and going up.

"Lee! We have things to do, places to go, butt to kick, and we're in your office with Dawn just down the hall, for goodness sakes. What if she walks in with my stun gun?"

He let me go, walked to the door, locked it and came back.

I scooted away, but he hooked my waist, pulled me back and gave me a bit of a shove so I fell to the couch. He followed me down.

"I can see why you haven't found Rosie or the diamonds yet. You're easily distracted," I noted.

He was nuzzling my neck.

"Yeah, you're distracting," he agreed readily. "Not to mention I rarely get into the office. I prefer being out in the field. I hate sitting in this office." He said this to the space below my ear and then moved his head to brush his lips against mine. "From now on, when I have to be in here I can look at this couch, remember having a piece of your sweet ass on it and the time will go a fuck of a lot faster."

Yikes.

I should have been horrified, maybe, or offended. Instead I liked the idea of him thinking of me in his office, even that way, or maybe especially that way. I liked the fact that he told me, matter-of-fact. It wasn't a roses and champagne compliment, but it worked all the same.

"Oh, all right," I gave in on a sigh, wrapping my arms around him.

He kissed me, but I could swear I felt his body shaking like he was laughing.

⋙⋘

After we broke in his couch, I used his private bathroom while Lee checked his e-mail messages and made some phone calls. Once I had all my clothes and hair back in order, we walked out of his office. He was going to give me a tour, and he took me down the hall in the opposite direction to reception.

There were several doors and he opened the one next to his office. It was large and held an exercise bike, a treadmill, a set of free weights, a flat screen TV and a big, comfy couch.

"This is a room for downtime, waiting or on call." This was all he said before he closed the door.

He turned across the hall and opened another door and I peered inside. It was a bathroom, two sinks under two mirrored medicine cabinets. There was a double-front, free-standing cabinet with glass doors showing one side stacked with towels, the other side holding male toiletries like shaving cream and deodorant (okay, that was all the male toiletries, but males didn't have a lot of toiletries, and from what I noticed, Lee, nor any of his men, were into primping and putting shitloads of product in their hair). It was mostly taken up with various medical supplies. This I found slightly alarming, but I set it aside. There was also a toilet in a stall and a big tiled space with two shower heads in open bays. All of this was pristinely clean and new-looking.

He closed the door while saying, "When you're in the office, you use my private bathroom. This is males only."

I felt a weird thrill that he gave this instruction using the word "when". Maybe the next visit would include me walking down the hall when someone opened the door to the bathroom with open shower bays. Maybe I should bring

Kristen Ashley

Marianne here; it might change her life. I was beginning to think Dawn was a very clever girl, even though I still didn't like her and definitely didn't trust her.

"What does Dawn use?" I asked.

He gave me a look. "Don't know. Don't ask."

We walked further down the hall. He opened the door to a small room that was lined with about a dozen lockers, a big, fireproof cabinet with an electronic lock and a kitchenette at the end. No explanation needed for this room and I was glad to know where I could find the coffee.

Then he turned, knocked twice on a door and slid a fob across a pad on the side. A green light went on and he opened the door.

Woo hoo!

Now we were talking.

The nerve center.

We walked into a room with a bank of, like, a gazillion television screens on one wall, each with a DVD recorder beneath it. Underneath that was a console full of buttons and knobs. There were several multi-line phones on the console. Another wall held radios stacked in inset shelves. I could hear the police band squawking quietly. Two guys were sitting in the room, but there were four chairs. Most of the television screens had visual, but a few were blank. Against the wall, opposite the screens, were a couple of desks that were a heck of a lot messier than Lee's with folders, papers, empty pop cans and dirty coffee mugs.

Huh.

I had my proof about Dawn.

Both men were sitting with their sides to the door. Both men turned when we walked in and both men grinned when they saw me. I had the weird, uncomfortable feeling they both knew what happened in Lee's office ten minutes ago.

"Indy, this is Monty and Vance. I think you boys know Indy."

Say what?

"Hey, Indy," Monty greeted. He had a blond military cut, a well-maintained body with a laidback posture, and I was guessing he was about ten years older than Lee. He was still grinning at me, and he lifted his hand and pointed a finger at a bank of four screens, all of which had visual on different angles of the inside of Fortnum's.

Ah-ha.

Now I knew how Lee would think they'd know me.

242

Then I stopped thinking and watched in horror as Tex banged the portafilter on top of the espresso machine. Monty hit a button and the police band was drowned out by Tex's voice shouting, "Fucking steam! Give me some more fucking steam, you monster!" Which was followed by Duke shouting, "It only gives as much steam as it gives, man!"

Wonderful.

Now I knew why they were both grinning at me.

I looked away from the current frightening goings-on at Fortnum's to check out Vance.

Vance was younger than Lee, but I was guessing not by much. He had shiny, straight black hair pulled into ponytail, a lean body, and the fabulous bone structure and coloring of a Native American.

Oh, and he was seriously hot.

Yep, I was definitely going to have to bring Marianne here. And probably Andrea, and more than likely, Tod.

It was like Chippendales, but better.

I found myself captured by Vance's good looks and watched as he and Monty exchanged glances over Tex and Duke's exchange.

Vance's lips were twitching. He thought Tex was funny.

Vance looked up to me and caught me staring. I gave him a tilty-head smile and he smiled back, all white teeth against dark skin.

"Hi," I said to him.

His smile widened.

Mm, yum.

Lee's hand curled into the waistband of my shorts.

Oopsie.

Monty and Vance turned back to the monitors and I looked at them, too. There was an angle of the foyer of Lee's condo building and his empty parking spot in the condo garage. There was also an angle of the reception area where Dawn was on the phone (likely tearing me apart to one of her girlfriends) and two screens showing the Nightingale Investigation parking spots. I was pretty much praying at that point that one of the blank screens didn't show a visual on Lee's office.

There were eight screens showing various things, mostly inside. Some had people in them, both at home and in offices.

Lee started talking. "We used to do security. Even though it paid well, it was boring as hell. Made employee retention difficult."

"Won't have a problem with retention if we keep monitoring your store. It's like watching a sitcom," Monty said, his voice heavy on the amusement.

Great.

Monty turned to me. "We asked Dawn to do a transcript of your speech about El Salvador, Mom and Pop shops and the American way, and we e-mailed it around. Hank isn't even on the payroll and he was awarded honorary 'employee of the week' for taking duty on you that day. I would have paid to see his face when he walked into that pot farm."

Double great.

Not only did Dawn do the transcript, I could be sure she made certain to e-mail it to Lee.

Not to mention the fact that I was break-in-the-day-entertainment to Lee's troops.

Lee let go of my shorts and said, "Fortnum's will be wired for a while, and we need to get a camera on the front door."

I looked back at him. His eyes were moving along the screens, and I got the impression he didn't miss a trick.

He briefly glanced at me then back to the screens. He was being professional, but I also got the feeling he was ticked about something and trying not to let it show in front of the guys.

He continued talking. "Currently, we do mostly investigations, mainly corporate, embezzlement, fraud, theft. We pick up some domestic investigation, only high-income, usually gathering evidence to substantiate adultery or other incontrovertible grounds to get large alimony and settlements."

"Usually poking the nanny," Monty put in. "That's fun to watch."

"Depending on the nanny," Vance spoke for the first time, his voice deep and rich. His eyes were off the screens and on my legs, saying he wouldn't mind watching me get poked if I was the nanny. I was also hoping he wasn't communicating he didn't mind just watching me get laid by Lee.

Yikes.

Though, you had to admit, he had balls checking me out in front of Lee.

Lee kept going. "Staff does rotation in here, depending on what assignment they're on. That way they don't have to sit in a windowless room very often and can keep sharp doing field work."

Lee started to move me to the door and I called, "Later, guys."

Both looked at me. Monty gave a small wave. Vance grinned. I wondered if I would see the guys later, like, say, if Lee had a company picnic.

"Do you have cameras in your office?" I asked Lee when he closed the door.

"Nope."

Thank God.

"Tell me about Monty," I went on.

"Monty's an ex-SEAL. Knee injury took him out. The only guy who takes five shifts in surveillance a week. He manages the room. He comes in if we have any field operations, most of which he plans because he's good at it. He's been married twenty years, has five kids and may look mellow, but even with a bum knee, he's a serious guy you do not want to mess with."

Yikes.

"Field operations?" I asked.

"Sometimes, end work on a corporate investigation. Mostly when we work with the PD or Feds."

"What do you do with the police and the government?"

Lee didn't answer.

I didn't push.

"And Vance?" I pressed on.

"Vance is the master of multitasking. He's off the rez. A recovering alcoholic and ex-con; grand theft auto. He has quick hands and quiet feet, can make himself invisible, is an excellent tracker and can do anything with cameras and electronics. He usually traces skips, but he also does a lot of our wire work. He wired Fortnum's. I would have given him the new skip, but he just bought himself a week in the surveillance room. As for you, if you look at him like that again, I'll cuff you to the bed and only let you go for bathroom breaks."

"Jeez, now who's jealous?"

I said it out loud but I meant to think it, and might I add that this was a habit that was becoming alarming.

My comment was a big mistake.

Without warning, Lee's hand closed on my upper arm, he opened the locker room door and pulled me inside. He slammed the door shut behind us, shoved me against the lockers and came up on me so there wasn't room to move.

I looked up at him, about to say something, but thought better of it because his face was Badass Angry.

"Something to learn about me, since you haven't already taken it in," he said in his scary, calm voice, "I realize I'll have to put up with you receiving attention. I've no problem with that. I've had a lot of practice. What I *don't* like is that you flirt as easily as you lie. It's second nature. You're gonna have to make an effort to stop because I don't like it. I especially don't like it when you do it with my men. They have to keep focused, and we've already established you're distracting. It's okay for me to think of fuckin' you on my couch. I don't want it shoved in my face that Vance'll be thinkin' of fuckin' you in the surveillance room or on his Harley, which he no doubt saw you starin' at like you'd do anything to be astride it."

"So that's Vance's Harley," I said. Yep. Aloud. Again.

Lee came even closer and his body pressed me back into the lockers.

"Lee, move back," I warned, beginning to get pissed-off.

He didn't move.

So I went into being full-fledged pissed-off, wedged my hands between us and shoved.

He still didn't move.

"It's harmless," I told him.

"Does it feel harmless to think of me workin' late nights with Dawn?"

I blinked at him, confused. After the mind-bogglingly good time we had on the couch, I was *way* over any upset about Dawn.

"Well, yeah," I said.

He stared at me, his face stony.

"For goodness sake, she's not your type," I explained. "Vance is cute, for certain, but he isn't my type."

"From a decade of keepin' close watch, I wouldn't say you had a type."

It was my turn to stare at him because that was just plain insulting.

Men were so stupid, and Lee was at the top of the list.

I mean, didn't he just admit this morning to reading my diary? Didn't he realize I only had one type and that type was him? Wasn't he the one who told me I was in love with him and I'd eventually admit it?

We were together. Finally. Liam and India together, even moving in for goodness sakes.

This was something I was going to have to get used to when I had time to wrap my mind around it. Truthfully, unlike nearly everything else in my life, it was coming naturally and it was one of those few things I didn't have to process at length with Ally, Andrea or Tod and Stevie.

Did he honestly think I was going to screw it up by engaging in some byplay with one of his men?

"You're an idiot," I told him.

His eyes narrowed and that scary muscle jumped in his cheek.

"What did you just say?"

"You... are... an... idiot," I repeated. "Think about it and when you're ready to apologize, I'll listen. But I'll accept an apology now for the insult you just dished out."

"How about you explain," he suggested in a way that was clear it wasn't a suggestion.

"No explanation, but I'll give you a hint. In all my vast experience of men, through what you consider was India's Decade of Slutdom, I've never, not once, even so much as had a toothbrush at another man's house."

He just stared at me. He didn't get it, or was too angry to process it. And he wasn't moving and still had me pinned to the lockers. I was forced to explain further and I got a little carried away.

"I had one at yours after the first night I stayed there. Okay, so it was in your stash, but it's a toothbrush, Lee! One use and it's *mine*. And we hadn't even *done it* yet! Not to mention undies in your drawer and wearing your t-shirts." I put my hands on my hips. "And sleeping at your house, like, all the time. None of that, never with another guy, never, never, *never*. Huh! Get it now?"

Something changed in his eyes, but whatever it was just intensified the feeling already there. It went from scary-but-under-control to totally-out-of-control.

My stomach did a clench because I wasn't sure what was going to happen next.

His hands went to my hips and pulled mine against his. Then his arms wrapped around me, one hand going into my hair. He tugged it, not gentle, but as if he couldn't control his strength.

My head went back and I let out a little cry, but it was cut off when his mouth came down on mine and he kissed me. It was not like any kiss he'd given me before. It was hard and wild.

Somehow he'd lost control, and I had to admit that I liked that I could make him lose it.

I liked it a lot.

When his head came up, he immediately dropped his forehead to mine, his eyes closed and he didn't say a word. We were both breathing heavily and my hands were at his waist, clutching the t-shirt there. He was having an internal battle, I could tell, and when his eyes opened I realized whatever battle he was waging, he'd won.

"Did I hurt you?" he asked when he lifted his head.

I shook mine.

"Fuck, Indy, you turn me inside out."

I stood there a beat and then said, very quietly, "Lee, I'm not doing anything to you. You're doing it to yourself. I'm beginning to think you don't know me either. There were guys, but…" I was going to stay "none of them was you" but I stopped myself just in time and said, "It was just fun. Half of them didn't even get to second base. I'm not the slut you think I am."

"I don't think you're a slut."

"That's not the way you make it sound."

"I've been watchin' men sittin' in what I considered my position for a long time and I didn't like it. I should have done something about this a long time ago. That's my problem. I'm taking it out on you."

I stared at him and realized that I'd spent years throwing myself at him and being rebuffed and watching him go off with every other girl who caught his eye. Each time it tore at my heart and each new time it hurt more.

What I didn't realize was that for years he'd been experiencing the same thing.

"My flirting is harmless. You don't have anything to worry about," I assured him.

"I'm still gonna ask you not to do it," Lee replied.

I looked into his eyes for several seconds and then sighed. "All right. I'll quit flirting."

His arms were still around me and they pulled me deeper into him.

"That's my girl," he murmured, and my heart stopped beating.

This was it. I was Lee's girl.

And it felt great.

Holy shit, shit, shit.

I pulled back a little to hide my reaction and said, "Can I bring Marianne here? Just to meet Vance and Matt... er, and maybe Bobby?" Lee stared at me and I continued, "Also, Tod wouldn't mind popping by."

"No," Lee answered, but he was grinning his 'Isn't-Indy-cute?' grin.

"I didn't think so," I muttered to myself. "Can we go find Rosie now?"

After I tamed the wild, broody Lee Beast in the locker room, Lee finished his tour.

There were three more doors to discover.

Room one was a blandly decorated room with a double bed, a reclining chair, a TV, DVD player and bookshelf full of books and DVDs. It had a private bath and was called the safe room. To get into it, you needed a fob for one pad, you had to put your thumb to another pad *and* you had to use an old-fashioned key.

Room two was a room with four work cubicles in it, all complete with chairs, desks, computers and filing cabinets underneath the desks. Brody, Ally's and my computer nerd friend, popped up from one of the cubicles.

"Indy!" he shouted.

"Holy shit, Brody, what're you doing here?" I asked, walking toward him and smiling. When I got to him, I gave him a hug. He was a total slob: black shirt, black jeans, black Doc Martens, wild dark hair and Buddy Holly glasses. His body had no shape, defined, as it was, by sitting in a chair in front of a computer all the time.

"Ally told me I needed to get out of my house so she got me a part-time job with Lee. What are you doing here?" He looked between me and Lee. "Oh yeah, I forgot. Ally told me you and Lee hooked up. Finally. Cool. Bet you're happy."

I glanced at Lee. The Lee Beast had disappeared and Cocky Lee had taken his place.

I ignored it and turned back to Brody. "You do programming?"

"Nope, hacking, usually tracing embezzlement stuff but sometimes—"

"Brody," Lee cut in and Brody stopped talking, his eyes got wide and he stared at Lee.

"Yeah, sorry, yeah, yeah, yeah," Brody muttered and looked at me. "Confidentiality," he whispered. "I keep forgetting."

I looked around the room, fascinated by what Lee had built in a short period of time. It was a huge-ass operation.

"The other cubbies are for searches and stuff." Brody started pointing. "That's Kim's cubbie. She's hilarious, you'd like her. Her husband is a paramedic so she likes to work when he's on shift, sometimes seven to three, sometimes three to eleven. Then there's Pablo, but he's part-time, like me. I do morning, he does afternoons. The other one is for the boys when they need to do computer work we can't see."

"Ah," I said.

Brody looked to Lee. "See, I told her the whole thing without talking about *the job* we're doing."

Lee stared at Brody, obviously reevaluating doing a favor for his sister.

"That's good, Brody," I said to him like he was a lovable dog, which, in a way, he was.

Lee put his hand at my back again, indication it was time to go.

"When we leave, lock the door and don't open it for fifteen minutes unless you get a knock. Three, two, two. Got that?" Lee said to Brody.

"Three, two, two. Got it." He turned to me. "Lots of codes around here. Three quicks then a long. Three short, three long, three short. Shit, what's this new code again?" he asked Lee.

Lee sighed. "Three, two, two."

"Yeah, okay. Three, two, two. Later, Indy. By the way, really dug the El Salvador e-mail. That was hilarious. Where do you come up with that shit?" Brody asked, but didn't expect an answer and then walked back to his desk chanting, "Three two two, three two two…"

Lee guided me out of the room and back to the reception area. Dawn was behind her desk and she schooled her features into a benign smile at our approach. Her immaculate desktop was marred by a gunbelt, which Lee picked up with the barest hint of a nod of thanks to Dawn.

He pulled out a flat black thing with two prongs at the top.

"Stun gun," he stated. "You have to be close to use this. Take down is half a second so it's quick. Don't touch the prongs or you'll get cranked with 625,000 volts."

Holy crap!

Is that what happened to me?

625,000 volts?

That seemed like a lot.

A lot, a lot.

Lee was still talking. "Batteries are new. Switch it on and touch the prongs to your target and he'll go down."

"*You* should know about those, considering," Dawn chimed in sweetly. "They're not pretty, but they work!"

Lee's eyes cut to her and she immediately turned her attention to the computer, and I just stopped myself from sticking my tongue out at her and giving her a "nanny nanny foo foo" head wag.

Lee shoved the stun gun back into the belt and pulled out something that looked somewhat like a real gun.

"Taser," he said. "You can use this from a distance. Point and shoot, same result as a stun gun. Prongs come out and juice him. Don't worry about clothes. These prongs will even go through a vest."

"That's a bulletproof vest," Dawn cut in again.

"Thanks," I snapped sharply on a saccharin smile with a bitch glare, a combination better known as the Bitch Triple Threat.

When I looked back to Lee, his eyes were crinkled and he was shoving the Taser back into the belt.

He thought we were the funny.

I decided not to go into bitch smackdown mode. I'd been giving Lee's employees enough entertainment for a week.

Lee pulled out a canister. "Pepper spray. Shake it to make it live, make sure you point it correctly. This one sprays at distance. You've got up to fifteen feet. Aim at his face. Don't do it in an enclosed area or you'll get it, too."

"Okey dokey," I said quickly before Dawn could give any helpful hints.

Lee turned to Dawn. "You're goin' to lunch."

Without a word, she grabbed her purse and walked that long-legged, one-foot-in-front-of-the-other, ass-swaying catwalk out the door.

Lee and I watched and I changed my mind again about Dawn.

I turned to Lee. "I'm just gonna say, she's a problem."

Lee put the belt on me, shook his head and caught my eye.

His eyes were serious and Dawn was a distant memory.

"The fun part of the day is over," he said in a no-nonsense voice, securing the belt at my waist.

Uh-oh.

"You're gonna see and hear shit that you might not like. This is my work and you have to remember, whatever it is, there's an explanation behind it or it's being controlled. Talk to me before you react and *listen* to me. Pay attention and be smart. If something gets too much, too intense, you just say, no matter where we are or what we're doin', I'll take you away. Yeah?"

That didn't sound good.

Lee watched me closely and waited for me to respond.

"Yeah," I agreed.

"We're goin' to the holding room. If we capture a skip and for some reason can't get him to the station, we use the holding room. You'll see now it has other purposes."

Yikes.

"Keep your mouth shut, your eyes open and know where your weapons are. Do not use the pepper spray. We've got someone in there and we're lettin' him go. I don't know how he'll react."

"Letting him go?" I asked. I didn't know who he was, but whoever he was he was in a holding room, and letting him go didn't sound like a good idea.

"He's part of a bigger picture. We've been workin' with him for a few days, tryin' to get him to talk. He hasn't felt up to it. Now it serves the higher purpose to let him loose."

I had questions to ask, but I had no time to ask them. Lee was already moving away and I had no choice but follow or run away.

Chapter 18
Naked Gratitude

For better or worse, I followed Lee down the hall.

He knocked twice on the surveillance room door, used his fob and went in.

"It's time," he announced.

Vance got up and walked to a desk. Monty leaned forward and flipped some switches and some monitors came on. On the monitors, I could now see Brody working, the empty hall, and a room with a bed, a toilet and a sink. A guy was lying on his side on the bed. I couldn't see much of the guy and then Vance was in my way. He had a gunbelt doubled up in one hand. He put it behind his back, opened it and strapped it on. It had the same stuff mine had, plus a real gun and cuffs.

He lifted his hand. His dark eyes locked on mine and flirty look was gone. He pointed to the door.

I walked out behind Lee. Vance followed me and closed the door.

Lee walked down to the end of the hall to the last door, the only door Lee hadn't opened to show me what was inside.

"You know where your weapons are?" Lee asked.

I felt around my belt and nodded. I felt like Super Idiot with the belt on, not Super Cool like Vance looked. Lee wore no gunbelt, just the killer dark brown leather one holding up his faded brown cargo pants.

Lee jerked his head at Vance. Vance used a fob and a light went green.

"Follow me in," Lee said to me. He opened the door and walked in.

I did as I was told, and once I was in the room, I saw Terrible Teddy, Coxy's goon who hit me what seemed like years ago. He turned in the bed and stood.

I sucked in air.

He had a bandage across his nose and a wicked black eye. Both nose and eye were grotesquely swollen to almost Rocky Balboa post-Apollo Creed fight size.

Teddy spared me only a glance then he turned cautious eyes to Lee.

Vance stood in the door, one hand resting on his Taser.

"You're free to go. Vance'll escort you from the building," Lee declared.

Teddy's glance swung to Vance. Vance had unholstered the Taser and was gesturing with it for Teddy to leave the room.

My mind was reeling. I was trying to count the days since I'd had my brief encounter with Teddy, remembering that Lee told his boys to pick him up. Had he been in this little room that long? And furthermore, how did his face get like that?

"Free to go?" Teddy asked.

"Yep," Lee answered.

"Just like that?" Teddy went on.

No one said anything. Teddy looked at me. I didn't say anything either. Lee told me to keep my mouth shut, but even if he hadn't, I was too shocked to speak.

"I don't get it," Teddy said.

"Rumor's spreading that you talked," Lee told him. "I don't know how that happened."

Lee looked at Vance. Vance shrugged.

They were playing with him.

Lee kept talking. "Coxy's at war with me and he's tryin' to impress Indy. You remember Rick?" Teddy nodded slowly. "Coxy put a bullet in Rick's brain. He fucked with Indy and hurt her. Yesterday, Coxy gave Indy Rick's body as a present, half his head blown off. You hit her and marked her. Now you're out. Good luck."

"Fuck," Teddy cursed, looking at me like I could help him out. He hit me and I was pretty sure he was a bad guy, but I had to say I felt sorry for him.

"Let's go," Vance put in.

Teddy turned to Lee.

"I talk, he kills me. I don't talk, he kills me," he said as if trying to explain.

"Life's a bitch," Lee replied.

He turned his back on Teddy, jerked his head to me and I walked out of the room, followed by Lee. Vance went into the room after we left it. I kept walking until I got to Lee's office. He stopped me, opened the door and pushed me in. He lifted his fingers and stared me in the eyes, giving me a three, two, two. I nodded and he closed the door.

I locked it.

Holy shit, shit, shit.

Not five minute later, the knock came. Three, two, two.

I opened it and Lee walked in. "He's gone. Time for lunch. Let's roll."

⌐☰☷⌐

I waited until we were rounding the Brown Palace when I asked, "How did Terrible Teddy's face get like that?"

"Me."

"You hit him?"

"He touched you, you said it hurt. I found him and beat the shit out of him."

Oh... my... God.

"Please tell me you didn't do it in that little room," I said quietly.

"It was before he was put in the holding room."

At least that was something.

I was silent while Lee drove. I'd taken off the gunbelt and put it in the trunk with the one Lee took from a drawer in his desk. His was stocked like Vance's.

Lee parallel parked the Crossfire in a choice spot in front of Las Delicias.

I loved Las Delicias. It was the best Mexican restaurant in Denver if you didn't count El Tejado. Though, I really didn't have to choose since El Tejado was officially in Englewood.

I was also silent while they sat us in a booth and Lee slid in beside me rather than across from me.

I turned to him, looked down at the seat then up at him.

"Let me guess, you aren't much of a booth sharer?" he remarked.

I shook my head.

"Me either, but I'm attempting to control the environment."

I looked beyond him. He was turned toward me, his back to the restaurant.

"Wild Bill Hickock got shot with his back to the door," I informed him.

"I'm not controlling the room. I'm going to attempt to control you."

Uh-oh.

The waitress came and slid a basket of chips and a bowl of salsa on our table.

Neither of us had opened our menus. We didn't need to.

Ally and I went to Las Delicias or El Tejado at least twice a month, some-times more. Dad joined us on occasion. Hank joined us most of the time. Even when he was on-duty, he'd come in for a dinner break. Every once in a while, and looking back it had been much more often in the last year or two, Lee came. He was with us so often I could order for him. He'd have three chicken bur-ritos, smothered with lettuce and cheese, and a beer if it was evening, iced tea during the day.

Lee looked up at the waitress and ordered a diet pop for me, an iced tea for him, his burritos and my bean tostada and burrito chicharrone smothered with lettuce and cheese.

I guess Lee could order for me, too.

He turned back to me. "We're here because it's good and it's fast. We have things to do."

I nodded. I was still dealing with being totally freaked out so I wasn't processing much. I was just hoping I could process my burrito and tostada or I'd be paying for a professional cleaning of the Crossfire.

Lee's arm came behind me on the booth and he twisted fully toward me. "First, Teddy. Bottom line is he's not a good guy. Hittin' you is the least of the shit he's done. There's all kinds of justice. Hank delivers justice his way. I do it my way."

Um… yikes!

Lee kept talking (unfortunately).

"I'm in a dangerous business and I have enemies. You're in my life now. I have to let it be known that if anyone fucks with you, there will be conse-quences."

"Simple as that?" I asked, trying not to let on that he was kind of scaring me.

"Not simple as that. I didn't like standin' in my kitchen listenin' to you tell me someone hurt you. It was a pleasure puttin' my fist in Teddy's face and feelin' his nose break. He's a big guy, he could have really hurt you. He'll think twice before hitting a woman again."

Holy crap.

"Do you have a problem with any of that?" Lee asked.

"Yes," I answered honestly.

"Can you deal with it?"

"Yes," I answered, again, honestly.

"Do you want to talk about it?"

"No."

That was no lie, either. I really didn't want to talk about it. In fact, I was going to deal with it by using denial so talking about it would automatically defeat my dealing with it strategy.

Lee watched me closely, as if he was reading his special Indy Lie Detector Test, and then he leaned forward and brushed his lips against mine.

Guess I passed the test.

The waitress came back with the drinks.

If there was any fairness in the world, everyone would be able to have salsa from Las Delicias. Crisp, fresh onion, just enough cilantro. After a few margaritas, Ally and I could even make a case for salsa from Las Delicias bringing peace to the Middle East.

I picked up a chip and scooped a healthy serving of salsa. "What's gonna happen to Teddy?"

"If he's smart, he'll skip town," Lee said, scooping his own chip.

"Is he smart?"

"Not really. Coxy had two smart guys, Rick and Pete. Though in the end, apparently not that smart. Rick's dead. Pete's in jail facing kidnapping, assault and possibly murder, two of those against a cop's daughter. They'll want to give him his shoelaces, but they'll do everything by the book and be thorough to make sure he gets nailed. Pete's fucked."

I grabbed another chip and broke it in half, the better to scoop the salsa. I didn't have a lot of time to spare Pete, who I suspected was the guy I called Sandy. Pete had tied me to a chair and shot at me, twice. I didn't know what Lee was talking about with regards to shoelaces, but I had no problem that he was fucked.

"Who do you think has the diamonds?" I asked Lee.

"I have the diamonds."

"*What?*"

Okay, I shouted it. The other diners turned to stare. But what the fuck?

"Keep your voice down," Lee warned.

"Did you just tell me you have the diamonds?"

Lee nodded, still turned toward me, eating his chips and salsa with his right hand, his left arm fencing me in on the back of the booth.

"You better explain before I start plotting your murder."

His eyes crinkled. "You'd never get away with it."

"At this point, I don't mind doing time."

Lee took a tug on his iced tea then said, "I found the diamonds at Duke's the morning after Rosie left my condo. I have you to thank for that. Duke knows I have them. My contacts in Sturgis told him when they found him."

"Your contacts?"

"I farmed out the job to other PIs and bounty hunters in places I thought Duke would go. They looked around, asked a few questions, picked up his trail and the boys in South Dakota tracked him down."

"If you cost five hundred dollars an hour, what did that cost?"

"Let's just say you're not a cheap date."

My eyes narrowed. "You're getting paid for this, remember?"

"I've got three jobs involved with this mess, and one of them was finding the diamonds. I found them the first day. Making sure Duke was alive and safely home in Evergreen was something I did for you."

Even though I was pissed-off, my chest fluttered. "I'll pay you back."

His hand went to my hair and he wrapped a lock around his finger. "You don't have to pay me back."

I didn't know what to say, so I said, "Thank you."

"You can thank me tonight when you're naked."

Jeez.

The waitress came and slid our plates on the table. I unwrapped my cutlery from the weird perma-glue tab and napkin.

"Before we talk about naked gratitude, let's talk about how you've been lying to me for days about the diamonds." I forked into my burrito.

"I haven't lied. I've given creative answers."

"Uh-hunh."

He let go of my hair and turned to his food. "My having the diamonds was need-to-know information. You didn't need to know."

With effort, I swallowed my mouthful of burrito. "Excuse me?"

Lee downed his own bite and turned again to me catching my Polar Freeze Glare.

"All right," he said. "There's not much I can say, but I'll tell you what I can."

"I'd appreciate that."

"Some explanation first," he began. "Crime is very organized at the top. Criminals have levels of management. They have training. They have territories. Most of the time, these operations are multifaceted: running guns, drugs, girls, extorting payment for protection, whatever. People know who does what and they deal their own shit in their own neighborhoods. They step over the line only when they have the power to back up a takeover."

I nodded while Lee took another bite and he continued.

"Coxy doesn't play that game. Coxy does what he wants, where he wants. He's messy, greedy and insane. He's also determined, tenacious and, I'll repeat, insane. He's been causin' problems with Denver crime for a long time. There's something to be said for organization, even in crime. Mess is just mess. In this case more drugs, more guns, but worst of all more dead bodies. Coxy used to be a nuisance, but that's escalated. The criminals want him taken out just as much as the cops."

"I don't understand. Why don't the criminals just... um, take him out?"

"Family ties." I stared at Lee and he kept talking. "His mother's Italian. She's from New York and her family is powerful. Coxy had backing. If something happened to Coxy there would be New York retribution. Or at least that was the word, and New York backed Coxy in a number of jobs and cleaned up a number of messes."

"Are we talking about the mob?" I whispered.

Lee finished his second burrito and just slid his eyes to me.

Holy shit.

Then he spoke again. "Problem is, Coxy's made so many messes, rumor has it New York is done. Who knows how much backing he ever really had. His mother married outside the family, outside New York, to a straight and narrow guy from Denver who was worth a fortune. Maybe the ties don't stretch that far and Coxy pulled them to the breaking point. He's not a made man. Hasn't been through the program, as far as anyone knows he's a pipsqueak cousin in Denver."

I picked up my tostada and munched in an effort at acting nonchalant when really I was thinking about Tony Soprano and getting a little flipped out.

"Is all of this new?" I asked.

"No, it's been goin' on for years. The rumor that New York is out is new but unsubstantiated. To restore order, a deal was struck. Coxy had to be taken out, but it couldn't look like he was *taken out*. That way, New York wouldn't feel the need to act and all would be well in the world of crime again."

"What does this have to do with you?"

"I have connections on both sides. Eddie and Hank used me as go-between with Marcus and Darius."

I sat there with my tostada held aloft and stared at him.

Eddie Chavez and Darius Tucker were Lee's two closest friends in high school.

Eddie Chavez was good-looking, smooth-talking and morally dubious, exactly like Lee and then some. Everyone was pretty certain Eddie was going to go over to the dark side and spend most of his time *doing* time. Instead, he became a cop. He was now vice, considered a definite maverick (according to Dad, with hints of admiration) and a loose cannon (according to Malcolm, with hints of disapproval).

Darius Tucker was much the same, but he was also absolutely hilarious, so funny you'd nearly wet your pants laughing. He had soulful eyes and a dry shoulder to cry on, especially for the girls. Everyone was certain he'd quickly get married and settle down and make some woman a good husband. Instead, his Dad was murdered when he was seventeen and he went off the rails *and* off the radar. I hadn't seen him in years and I missed him. He was a good guy. He'd made me laugh and he'd let me cry on his shoulder plenty of times. According to Malcolm *and* Dad, he was now bad news.

I didn't know anyone named Marcus.

"Darius?" I asked when I could say anything at all.

Lee pushed his plate away and turned to me again. "Yeah. The deal was we all work together to cause problems for Coxy; delayed shipments, missing deliveries, cops turnin' up at inopportune moments. I shared information and me and the boys caused some of the complications that Hank and Eddie couldn't cause. Coxy's network of buyers and suppliers started to alternately freak or get pissed-off and his men began to defect. Rick and Pete decided on early retirement, and to augment their pension they stole Marcus's diamonds."

"Marcus?"

"A leftover from when I did security. He keeps us on retainer for certain jobs. He's powerful and not someone who appreciates being stolen from. I was in DC and got an urgent call from him when his diamonds went missing."

"Why'd he call you?"

Lee shrugged. "I'm good at finding all different kinds of things."

Oh, dear Lord.

I had a feeling this was one of those cases where I didn't want to know.

I changed the subject. "How on earth does Rosie fit into all of this?"

"Rosie had a good operation going. Small but popular, and not quiet, which was not smart. Coxy heard about it and wanted a piece, so he coerced Rosie into giving him one. Then he coerced Rosie into doing other things for him. Things Rosie didn't want to do, but didn't know how to say no. Rick and Pete decided to play innocent about the diamonds until they had their shit together enough to move to Brazil, which was only supposed to be a day or two. They stashed the rocks with Rosie, thinkin' he was scared enough to do what he was told. Apparently, he was pissed-off enough to use the diamonds to blackmail Rick and Pete to get him out from under Coxy. Unfortunately, he was playin' out of his league. In the meantime, word went out the diamonds were gone and Coxy found out his boys had gone renegade. Even Coxy isn't crazy enough to out and out kick sand in Marcus's face, especially not with his systems breakin' down. So everyone was in a rush for the diamonds. Enter you."

"I'm a little confused."

"I would be too if I came in at the end of this shit. It's fucked up."

"Why are you doing this?"

"I'm gettin' paid."

"That's it?" I asked.

"No, it's not. I should say I'm gettin' paid a lot."

"Is it worth it?"

His arm slid behind me on the booth and he twisted toward me again. I'd abandoned my tostada half eaten and was turned toward him.

"I like what I do, but it's like football. Your career has a shelf life. I intend to be retired by forty-five with the cabin in Grand Lake and a condo in Florida, a damn good boat in both places and enough money to make life good until I die."

"So, what you're saying is, it's worth it."

He went back to wrapping a lock of my hair around his finger. His voice changed and so did his eyes, from all business to warm and soft.

"Yeah, it's worth it," he stated then asked, "Do you like Florida?"

My stomach did a clutch. "Would Florida come with a housekeeper that puts your towels on the rail after you throw them in the sink?"

His eyes got warm. "That's the 'make life good' part."

"Then I might like Florida." His finger tugged my hair playfully, but I ignored it and asked, "Who's paying you?"

He let go of my hair, leaned forward and took out his wallet.

"Story time's over. We have to get back to work."

"I guess question time is over, too."

His eyes slid to me again telling me question time was definitely over.

We were in the Crossfire when I told him we had to go to Tod and Stevie's to pick up Chowleena.

"Sorry?" he asked.

"I'm watching her for a couple of days."

"We'll go get her later."

"We can't go get her later. If we go get her later, that wouldn't be me watching her. That would be her alone at home with *no one* watching her."

"I'm not takin' a chow dog out to work with me," Lee stated.

"She'll be good. I swear. She's a great dog," I assured.

"No."

I had to pull out the big guns. "There'll be naked gratitude in it for you."

Lee hesitated, but just for a moment.

"Shit," he mumbled.

He steered the Crossfire toward Baker District.

Chapter 19
Eddie and Darius

We cruised up to Paris on the Platte with Chowleena in my lap, her face out the open window, eyes squinty in the wind, mouth panting and fluffy fur rippling. Steve Miller's "Jungle Love" was blaring from Lee's radio.

There were some songs that it was a crime against nature to listen to quietly, and "Jungle Love" was one of them, although Lee didn't agree.

I was finding the promise of naked gratitude went a long way.

As Lee parked, I looked to Paris on the Platte; part-bookstore, mostly funky coffeehouse. It had been around for ages. They made Rosie's coffee look amateur.

Sitting out front at one of the tables on the sidewalk was Eddie Chavez, legs stretched out in front of him crossed at the ankles, elbows on the arm rests, hands hanging loose.

Pure cool.

He had on a white thermal, short-sleeved tee, a pair of worn out Levi's, black cowboy boots and a black belt with a big buckle pressed against his flat abs. He had dark skin, black hair and he was wearing a pair of kickass mirrored shades. Shades I knew hid eyes so dark brown, they were black. He was flashing a grin at us, ultra-white against his skin.

He looked damn good.

I knew Eddie well growing up. He, Lee and Darius hung out together most of the time and I tried my best to be wherever Lee was, so I spent a good deal of time with the three of them.

Since then, I'd seen Eddie a lot. He stayed close with both Lee and Hank. He came to Kitty Sue and Malcolm's parties and he'd come over to Hank's when we all went over there and watched football. I wouldn't say we were great friends, but I liked him and I knew he liked me.

In fact, I think he *liked* me liked me. He could be hilariously suggestive in a flirty way, but that wasn't it. That was just banter.

If Eddie was attracted to you, he didn't make it obvious by flirting. Eddie wasn't the kind of guy who flirted a girl into bed. His tactics were more subtle and practiced. He liked to play a game. He liked a challenge. He was the stealth seducer. Eddie showed his appreciation in nonverbal ways, mostly using his eyes and being tactile in a way that kept you guessing but felt provocative. I expected that was because that's exactly what he meant it to feel like. There wasn't a lot that Eddie did that Eddie didn't mean to do.

I got out of the Crossfire and led Chowleena on her leash to Eddie. The minute Eddie saw Chowleena, his grin widened to a blinding white smile.

"Indy." His arm slid around my waist, he brought me up against his hard body and he kissed my neck (see, provocatively tactile!). He was four inches taller than me, one of those inches from the heels of his boots.

I sat, Lee sat and Chowleena clicked over to Lee and laid down on his booted feet. Eddie watched, the smile never leaving his face.

His mirrored shades turned to Lee. "A Chow?"

"I don't wanna hear it," Lee growled, his voice low and impatient.

Eddie chuckled and I realized that a Chow was not good for Lee's Badass reputation. Especially not one whose big, fluffy fur was shaved into a dog version of a lion wearing chaps.

Lee needed a German Shepherd or a Rottweiler, not a Chow wearing fur chaps.

"There's naked gratitude in it for him," I blurted in an attempt to save Lee's reputation.

The mirrored shades turned to me.

"I should hope so." Eddie leaned in close. "Just for your information, for me, gratitude for hangin' with a Chow wouldn't be naked. It would include black lace underwear, a matching garter belt, stockings and stilettos."

Wow.

I didn't know, but that seemed pretty brazenly flirty. What did I do with that? Especially from Lee's best friend, right in front of Lee. And here was me, just having promised not to flirt.

Shit.

I turned to Lee. He was also wearing sunglasses, but his were Top Gun flight glasses, smoky lenses and gold frames. His face was blank but his mouth was tight.

"I don't have black lace underwear and a matching garter belt," I told Lee.

Eddie leaned back and chuckled again. Lee's face didn't change.

"I have *red* lace underwear and a matching garter belt," I said.

This was true, I did.

Eddie quit chuckling.

"And black *satin* underwear and a garter belt. And then there's my purple teddy thing with attached garters." I paused. "I'll model them all and you can choose."

I looked at Eddie out of the corner of my eye and the smile was gone.

Then I sat back.

My work was done.

Lee granted me A Smile. It was small but it was meaningful.

"You've always been a lucky fuck," Eddie murmured to Lee.

The waiter came and took our orders. I got my usual, a Café Fantasia; hot chocolate at the bottom, espresso at the top separated by a slice of orange and topped with whipped cream that had teeny sugared-orange sprinkles. Lush.

I ordered a bowl of water for Chowleena.

"You have anything for me?" Lee asked Eddie when the waiter walked away.

"Yep, word is Rick was done by someone from out of town," Eddie answered.

Lee sat back and his mouth got tight again. "New York?"

"Yeah, but not in the family. An independent contractor. Coxy's havin' to hire his guns these days. Gary couldn't put a bullet in someone's brain if he had the barrel restin' against his forehead."

I thought this was good news. Goon Gary seemed less of a threat if this was true. I was taking my good news as it came these days, no matter how freakishly scary it was.

"There's talk that there's two names on his list. Rick was only one of them," Eddie went on.

"Teddy?" Lee asked.

"Nope. Coxy wrote Teddy off, or at least he did until Teddy hit the street an hour ago."

"Who's the name?" Lee asked.

"Coltrane," Eddie answered.

Oh no, Rosie.

All the breath went out of my body and I stared at Lee. I was wearing shades too. Mine were huge, shiny, rock 'n' roll black, kind of a hybrid between Jackie O and Bono. I thought the lenses would melt with the heat from my stare.

The waiter brought our coffees, Chowleena's water and left.

"We have to find him," I told Lee.

"We'll find him," Lee replied.

I wasn't entirely sure how we'd find him considering we were sitting in the sun enjoying coffees.

As far as I could tell, there wasn't much to this PI stuff. In fact, it was more dangerous facing down the Rosie Riot than doing Lee's job.

Lee seemed completely calm about this news. This news did not make me calm. There was a hired hit man after Rosie. I was pretty angry at Rosie, but I still liked him enough to want his brains to remain in his skull for the foreseeable future.

"You should know bookies are takin' bets. You against Coxy, who'll win Indy," Eddie told Lee then looked at me.

Oh… my… God.

"Really?" I asked.

"Who's got the odds?" Lee asked.

My mouth dropped open and I stared at Lee. Was he nuts? Who cared? People were betting on us!

Eddie turned back to Lee. "You."

"You're joking, right?" I put in.

Eddie shook his head.

I turned my attention toward my drink which was the only sane thing I could do.

If in doubt, coffee.

I loved whipped cream, but I wasn't a big fan of whipped cream melting into coffee. Café Fantasias were stacked in a plastic ice cream parfait glass. I picked up the plastic glass and opened my mouth over the cream and sucked it all in one slurp. Then I grabbed my spoon to mush down the orange and mix the cocoa with coffee. I felt a tingling at the back of my neck and looked up at Lee and Eddie, both of whom had shades trained on me.

Eddie turned to Lee and muttered, "You lucky fuck."

Lee's phone rang. He snapped it open, said, "Yeah." Pause. "Un-hunh." Pause. "Be there in ten."

He flipped the phone closed then said, "We've got Rosie."

We went in Eddie's cop car, Lee in the passenger seat, Chowleena and me in the back. Lee had his gunbelt up front and mine was on the floor next to Chowleena.

We stopped in a 'hood where there were one-story row houses, the front steps and a small porch close to the sidewalks, one window denoting the living room. It wasn't a good neighborhood, it wasn't a bad neighborhood. It was just forlorn, ill-kept and quiet.

Eddied barely come to a stop when the backdoor opposite me opened and Darius Tucker slid in.

Lee and Eddie had moved naturally from good-looking boys that caused girls to have sweetheart crushes to handsome men that caused women's vaginas to quiver at the sight of them.

I noted that Darius hadn't fared as well. He'd always been tall and lean, but now the lean had turned a shade skinny. He had more worry lines. His once close-cropped afro was now sticking out in funky twists which were admittedly cool, but instead of the soulful dark eyes I remembered, he looked angry and even mean.

"What the fuck is she doin' here and what's with the dog?" he asked.

Well, hello to you too.

Luckily, I thought it but didn't say it.

Lee and Eddie had both turned to look at Darius.

"Do we have time to explain?" Lee asked.

"Don't know. Had business take me away for a minute and couldn't watch the house," Darius replied. "I know I don't have all day to waste on this shit."

"Where is he?" Eddie asked.

"Third door up," Darius answered.

Lee was focused on something beyond me, out the back window.

"We gotta move. Someone got here before us." His voice had changed, sounding clipped and urgent. His eyes cut to me. "Stay down, out of sight. Jesus Christ, how'd I let you talk me into this shit?"

"I was cuffed to the bed," I reminded him. I was speaking automatically and not really processing what was going on; just realizing that the vibes had turned bad.

"Lucky fuck," Eddie muttered. He opened his door and then he was gone. I swear to God, he disappeared into thin air. One second, he was exiting the car, the next second he was nowhere in sight.

"Your Dad teach you how to handle a gun?" Darius was talking to me and I looked at him. His eyes were cold and it was so wrong in his face, a face I'd once known so well, that I felt it in my gut.

I nodded to him.

Lee was leaning forward, reaching under the driver's side seat. He came up with a gun and handed it to me.

"Show me," Lee demanded, his voice sharp.

Shit.

Under pressure.

It was a Glock. Dad had a Glock.

"Safety lever in the trigger," I murmured then dumped the magazine. I pulled the slide back and a bullet flew out of the top. I snatched the bullet up, clipped it back into the magazine and shoved the magazine back into the gun.

I looked back at them. I didn't know what else to do.

They didn't say a word. They both opened their doors and were gone.

Poof.

Vanished.

Just like Eddie.

I pushed Chowleena down on the seat. She didn't seem real concerned about the drama, She thought it was time for a nap. I could have kissed her.

I took one look at door number three, Rosie's door, before scooting down in my seat.

Then I shot back up and stared into door number three's window.

Ally was in there with Rosie.

I'd only seen a flash of her but I knew she was there.

Holy, shit, shit, shit.

What was she doing there?

Did Lee know?

I couldn't exactly call him.

Shit!

Then I saw him walking down the street looking like he didn't belong there. Mainly because he looked like nothing, nobody, everyman. Made to fit in with the scenery. He was Tom Hanks. Problem was, Tom Hanks didn't live in this neighborhood.

I felt a chill up my spine.

I grabbed my gunbelt, pulled out the pepper spray and rammed it in my front pocket. Then I pulled out the Taser and rammed it in the waistband of my shorts. Then I shoved the Glock in the back of my shorts, pulled my Xanadu t-shirt over the gun butts and before my mind could think of excuses, I got out of the car.

I had no idea what I was doing or why I was doing it. All I knew was three guys with guns were out there as smoke, as well as a potential bad guy, and Ally was between all of them and Rosie.

I hurried across the street and down the sidewalk.

He was nearly to door number three when he heard my flip-flops.

He turned.

Casually I lifted my chin and smiled as if I was a passerby saying hello and kept walking toward him.

His eyes dropped to the waistband of my shorts.

Unfortunately my t-shirt was fitted, not loose around the waist so the Taser butt showed in obvious relief.

He moved and I moved, yanking the Taser out and bringing my shirt up and out with it, giving him a flash of my lacy lemon-yellow bra. The shirt snapped back as I lifted my arm and pulled the trigger. The prongs went sailing forward and snagged him as he yanked the gun out of his shoulder holster, momentarily taken aback by my accidental flash of bra. I didn't care. He was down before he got his arm straight and I didn't have any holes in me seeping lifeblood.

No sooner had he hit pavement than strong hands snagged me around the waist and I was slammed against a parked car, a hand pressed against my stomach holding me there.

"Where do you think we are, the fucking OK Corral?" Eddie bit out, his face close to mine, and he was pissed. He yanked the Taser out of my hand and then he started talking in rapid-fire Spanish, none of which I could understand, but that might have been a good thing.

Lee materialized next to us. Lee wasn't pissed. He was furious. It rolled off him in waves.

"Ally's in there. I saw her through the window," I told Lee.

Both Lee and Eddie turned toward door number three. I felt the fury waves recede. They knew I'd put myself in front of a bus, a train or an assassin to save Ally.

The door opened and Ally stood in its frame behind a rickety screen.

"What's going on?" she asked, looking down at the stunned hit man and then up at us, brows raised and cool as a cucumber.

Gotta love Ally.

There were some muttered oaths. Eddie's hand came away from my stomach and he moved to the hit man, cuffs out. Lee moved to Ally and I ran back to the car and got Chowleena. By the time Chowleena and I made it in the open front door, Eddie was rolling the cuffed hit man over on his back. When I walked in, I saw Rosie on his stomach on the floor, grunting and moaning, Lee beside him in a half crouch, one foot on the floor, knee bent, the other knee in Rosie's back. Lee was cuffing him.

Lee hauled Rosie up to his feet while Eddie dragged the hit man into the living room and propped his still stunned body on the couch.

Darius walked in on cat's feet from somewhere in the back of the house. He looked around at everyone.

"I forgot to bring the dip," he remarked.

I nearly laughed. That was more like the Darius I knew.

"Darius," Ally said, finally showing some reaction. She was staring at Darius and her face was wearing a tentative welcoming smile.

"I see you and Indy haven't changed much," Darius told Ally.

Everyone looked at everyone else. No comments were made because it was more or less true.

"That was anti-climactic," Eddie noted after several beats.

I walked up to Rosie and slapped him upside the head.

"Ow!" Rosie shouted at the same time Chowleena barked.

I stared at him then slapped him upside the head again, and Chowleena barked again. She thought we were playing and wanted to be in on the fun.

"You idiot!" I yelled and then smacked him another one.

"Ow! Quit it! She's hitting me." He looked at Lee. "Do something, you're the police!"

Lee simply watched.

"He isn't the police," I told Rosie and hit him again.

"Ow!" Rosie looked with desperate eyes to Darius. "You?"

"Me? Police?" Darius actually started laughing. It took years off his face and made him handsome again. If I wasn't in such a tizzy, I might have stopped to appreciate it.

I smacked Rosie upside the head again and Chowleena barked again.

Rosie looked wildly around and yelled, "You all have handcuffs and guns! How do you have handcuffs and guns unless someone's the flipping police?"

Instead of hitting Rosie upside the head, I shoved his shoulder.

Eddie slowly raised his hand. "Indy, guess I'm gonna have to ask you to quit doin' that."

I got up close to Rosie and stared down on him. "If I wasn't so happy you're alive, I'd kill you."

Rosie seemed to deflate.

"Indy, I'm sorry," he whispered, looking miserable and smelling worse.

"Sorry? A week ago you had three friends. Now Tim's dead, The Kevster's behind bars for trying to save your pot plants and I don't have all afternoon to tell you all that's happened to me. Newest nightmare, bookies are taking bets on if I'll go off with icky, creepy Wilcox."

Rosie blanched and noted, "Euw. He looks like Grandpa Munster."

"That's what I'm sayin'!" I shouted at him.

"I wish I had all day to watch this show, but I got things to do," Darius put in. "You gonna call this in?" he asked Eddie.

"Yeah." Eddie's eyes moved to Lee. Eddie had taken off his shades and slid an arm in the collar of his tee so they were hanging at his throat. "We gotta talk. Do you think Betty and Veronica here can keep an eye on these two?"

"I get to be Veronica," Ally called it instantly.

I turned to her. "Why do you get to be Veronica?"

I didn't want to be Betty. Betty was a doormat. Veronica had attitude.

"I'm *so* Veronica," Ally said in answer.

"Unh," the hit man groaned.

"Jesus," Darius muttered.

Lee jerked Rosie around and sat him on the couch next to his would be killer.

He pointed at Rosie and ordered, "Sit. Stay."

While I was watching Lee, I felt a hand at my back and my shirt was lifted up. I twisted my head to see Eddie there, then felt his hand slide into my shorts and pull out the gun.

He could have pulled it out by its butt and barely touched me. He didn't do that. He slid the length of his index finger along the gun, the rest of his knuckles fisting around the butt, grazing the small of my back, making certain

271

I felt his warmth against my skin nearly to the top edge of my underwear. And, I had to admit, it felt nice.

Provocatively tactile.

When I turned back to Lee, he was watching and the muscle was going in his cheek.

"Outside," Lee growled to Eddie.

Eddie handed me the gun and instructed, "Point this at the bad guy and don't take your eyes off him. If he moves, shoot him. Got that?"

I nodded.

Lee, Darius and Eddie left the house.

I pointed the gun at the hit man, pulled the pepper spray out of my pocket and gave it to Ally saying, "How'd you find Rosie?"

"You know all those leads I told you about?" she asked in answer.

"Yeah."

"Well, I tracked them down. Gave out more cards, the leads led to more leads and here I am. Rosie."

I was impressed.

"You are the shit," I told her.

"Damn straight," she replied on a grin.

Then we heard voices through the front screen door.

"She was on a ride-along," Lee clipped.

"Yeah, a ride-along with a Chow," Darius commented.

"She got in a fuckin' quick draw with a hit man in broad daylight and she was armed with a goddamned Taser!" Eddie snapped.

"It's none of your business, Eddie, but she and I made a deal," Lee shared.

"Yeah, I heard. A deal struck while she was cuffed to your bed. Christ, I never thought I'd see the day when *you* were led around by your dick," Eddie returned.

Uh-oh.

Them's fightin' words.

I chanced a glance to Ally and even she'd gone pale.

"Boys," Darius said low.

"You know, I'm almost compelled to let you have her for a week and see if you can control her," Lee put in.

Um... say what?

"I'd take a crack at that," Eddie replied.

Oh... my... God.

"Er... I think there's something I forgot to tell you," Ally whispered at my side but I wasn't listening.

"Yeah, I noticed that," Lee said and his voice had gone scary. "A kiss on the neck. Your hand down her fuckin' pants. I'm warnin' you, Eddie, it's the three strike rule."

"Uh... Indy?" Ally said.

"Shh!" I shushed her.

"I told you a year ago to make your move or I would," Eddie returned to Lee. "Now you have, and I get to the station and I hear she's runnin' through a Highlands neighborhood, her hands cuffed behind her back, tear gas in her face, Coxy's assholes shootin' at her and some crazy ex-con takin' a bullet for her. What the fuck is that all about?"

"Eddie," Darius said, obviously trying to break the tension. "This is Indy we're talking about. That sounds like a normal Saturday night."

No one laughed.

There was silence and it was heavy.

Then Eddie said, "You fuck it up with her, I won't hesitate. Do you hear what I'm sayin'?"

Ally grabbed my arm and I jumped. The hit man was mostly conscious and staring at us.

"What the fuck?" he slurred.

"Shut up," I said to the hit man, jiggling the gun at him threateningly. I turned to Ally, jerking my head to the door. "Did you hear that?" I stage-whispered.

Ally didn't look happy. "I heard it."

"What *was* that?" I asked.

"Well." Ally went from looking not happy to looking uncomfortable. Ally rarely looked uncomfortable and I knew I wasn't going to like what was coming. "The thing is, see..."

"Spit it out!" I snapped.

"Okay, you know about a year ago when Eddie and Lee stopped talking to each other?"

"No, I don't know. I was avoiding Lee remember? I told you, like, a million times."

"Well, about a year ago, Eddie and Lee stopped talking to each other."

"Great, thanks," I said.

"Anyway," Ally went on. "Hank told me that Eddie's had a thing for you for a while, though he's kept his distance because everyone knew how you felt about Lee and everyone was waiting for Lee to do something about it. It's been kind of a sticky situation, seeing as they're best friends."

Dear Lord in Heaven.

Just what I needed, my life to be that much more fucked up.

"And?" I asked.

"Last year, Eddie lost patience and told Lee if he didn't take care of business, Eddie would move in."

Holy crap!

"No way," I breathed.

Ally nodded.

"Why didn't you tell me this?" I asked.

"You were avoiding Lee and Eddie's hot. I thought if I told you about Eddie you might give up on Lee and I'd never have a niece named after me."

I looked at the hit man, who was watching us closely, and told him, "Don't think in the crazy-ass soap opera that is my life that I've forgotten about you. Or you," I said to Rosie.

I stared them both down and they both settled in. Clearly I was looking like a woman who wanted to be given the excuse to shoot someone.

"How long has Eddie had this thing?" I asked Ally.

Ally shrugged. "According to Hank, it ran parallel with your thing for Lee."

Holy shit.

"How parallel?"

"Apparently, last year was not the first fight they had over you. Remember when Lee showed up to pick us up from that haunted house and he had blood on his shirt and we could tell his nose had been bleeding? We saw Eddie later at Andrea's party and he was shitfaced and his eye was swollen?"

I remembered, kind of. It was my senior year. I was seventeen. Lee had blood on his shirt a lot back then and Eddie was also a brawler. I thought they'd been in a fight against other people, which happened a lot. Not with each other.

"Me?" I asked.

"You. That wasn't the first, and obviously not the last," Ally answered.

I didn't know what to do with this information. I didn't even want to *know* this information.

"I think it's time to step into Denial Zone," I told Ally.

"That would be my advice," Ally replied.

I was thinking that being with Lee I was going to spend a lot of time in Denial Zone.

Lee and Eddie came back in. Body language was not good. Darius was gone.

Without a word to us, they both got on the phone.

Lee called the office for a ride. Eddie called the station.

When Eddie was done, he said to the couch at large, "You're under arrest."

The hit man's expression didn't change.

"Me? What'd I do?" Rosie cried, clearly forgetting he was a primo pot farmer, and unfortunately that was still an illegal substance.

Eddie stared at him, and if looks could burn, Rosie would be scalded. "I'll think of something."

Lee was off the phone and looking at Ally.

"Later, we're gonna talk," he said to her.

"You gonna offer me a job?" She smiled at him.

Lee was not in a joking mood. His eyes swung to me. "Rosie's found. Our arrangement is over."

I was beginning to allow the fact that I'd just seen Scary Darius, the fact that I'd not only Tasered but flashed a hit man, and the news that Eddie was attracted to me to penetrate my Denial Zone Fortress. Regardless of that, most of the day had been good; some of it real good. And to be honest, I kinda liked being out on the job with Lee. It was fascinating and the last part was a serious rush.

One look at him told me that I should probably not push it.

"Okay," I agreed. "I need to get to the store anyway, and Marianne wants to meet at The Hornet for drinks tonight."

Lee expected me to mouth off. At my words, his angry face cracked and a look came in his eyes that gave me the feeling that if we didn't have an audience, he'd be on me like a rash.

Chapter 20
Two Souls Separated in Heaven

"You don't have to model. I know I want the red," Lee declared.

We were back in the Crossfire, idling in front of Fortnum's, Chowleena panting on my lap.

Rosie and the hit man had both been arrested. Eddie had the hit man's gun, which probably had been used to fire a bullet into Pepper Rick's brain. I'd given my billionth statement to the police in a week. Hank had swung by and seemed to be spending a lot of energy trying not to murder me or Ally and wasn't talking to Lee, but seemed to be siding with Eddie in the whole Indy Ride-Along Debate. Eddie was exuding a pissed-off vibe that kept everyone at a distance. Finally, Lee's man Matt came to pick us up and took us to the Crossfire.

I wasn't following the current conversation so I turned questioningly to Lee.

"First," he finished his thought.

"What?" I asked.

His hand came out and hooked me around the neck bringing me to him.

"Underwear, garters, stockings," he murmured against my mouth.

Of course.

I wasn't surprised Lee chose the red. It wasn't only racy, red was a power color.

His mouth brushed mine and then he let me go.

"Give me your phone," he demanded.

I handed it to him. His hand curled around it and he pressed buttons with his thumb.

"Let me know where you are, everywhere you go. I want to know you get there safe. I've got things to do and I don't know where I'll be. If you can't get hold of me, I'm programming your phone with the number to the surveillance room. There's someone there 24/7 and they can always get word to me."

"Okay."

"If I'm finished in time, I'll meet you at The Hornet. If not, I'll meet you at your house."

"What if you're not finished on time, but finished in the middle of the night, like last night?"

His eyes caught mine. "I'll meet you at your house."

"What if I'm sleeping?"

"I'll use my key."

"What key?"

"The key I had copied from Ally's key."

"Does Ally know you copied my key?"

He didn't answer. This meant no.

"When did you do this?" I asked.

His eyes crinkled, but there was still no answer.

"Why did you do this?" I pressed on.

One of his forearms was on the steering wheel, the other one on the back of my seat. He grabbed a lock of hair and wrapped it around his finger.

"I figured I'd need one eventually. So when I had the opportunity to take care of that chore, I took it."

"You're very cocky, have I told you that?"

"I think you've mentioned it."

He pulled my hair toward him and I had no choice but to follow it. He kissed me, no brush on the lips this time. This one left me a little bothered.

Okay, a lot bothered.

He waited until the door to Fortnum's closed behind Chowleena and me, and he took off.

Duke was behind the book counter. Tex was behind the espresso counter. There were no customers and no sign of Jane.

"You need to go home. You were shot three days ago," I told Tex.

"I was waitin' for you to get here. I wanted to hear about your day," Tex answered.

I threw myself full-body on one of the couches. Chowleena jumped up, sat beside me and stared at Tex. Everyone, man, woman and dog stared at Tex.

I ran down an abbreviated version. "I had a tour of Lee's Command Headquarters, nearly got into a bitch-slapping fight with his receptionist, then I Tasered a hit man in the street just before he got the chance to shoot me. We found Rosie and he's been arrested, and now I'm here."

Duke put his elbow on the counter and his forehead in his hand.

Tex stared at me and he looked disappointed.

Then he shrugged. "The day's still young."

I closed my eyes.

Tex left and I stayed where I was.

"Do you know how old that guy is?" Duke asked.

"Old... ish?" I answered the question with a question.

Duke didn't reply but instead he said, "Do you know he's an ex-con?"

"Yes," I said.

"Do you know he hasn't had a job since he got back from 'Nam?"

I opened my eyes and looked at Duke. "No."

"Totally dropped out. So dropped out that he makes me look like a soccer mom. Even before he went to prison and definitely after."

Yikes.

"How do you know this?" I asked.

"Hank came by."

I nodded and closed my eyes again.

"He makes great coffee. Everyone's talkin' about it," Duke said.

Finally, a *real* piece of good news.

When Duke spoke again, his gravelly voice sounded from right above me and my eyes popped open again.

"You're doin' a good thing by him. No man can live his life surrounded by cats, never leavin' his block."

I nodded again and said, "Outside of the gunshot wound, he's fit as a fiddle. He threw me through a window and you saw what he did on stage at BJ's. He's in good shape, at least physically. Mentally is still up for debate."

"Yeah," Duke replied then looked out the window. "Ain't none of my concern, but I gotta tell you, it's good to see you and Lee aren't circlin' each other anymore. Your grandmother used to say that you were two souls separated in heaven. She mainly meant you were both trouble and deserved each other."

Great.

Duke went on, "She'd be fuckin' thrilled if she was still alive."

I felt my throat close up. When it reopened, I said quietly, "Thanks, Duke."

"When we close, I'm walkin' you home."

279

It wasn't a question. I did, of course, have Chowleena with me, but I didn't think bad guys would be scared off by a Chow with fur chaps and attitude.

"Okay," I agreed.

⇤⇥

When I got home, I called Marianne and set up a time to meet at The Hornet. Then I called Lee to tell him I was home. He was at the hospital checking on Luke. I was glad I didn't have a ride-along on that one or my Denial Zone would be obliterated.

I gave Chowleena some kibbles and water. She put her nose up at the kibbles so I gave her a doggie biscuit. Then she gave me her pathetic look so I gave her another one. Then she pranced into the living room, curly tail swaying in the air, jumped up on my new couch, circled about twenty times, flopped down and settled in.

I jumped into the shower and did my Indy 'Out for the Night Preparations', complete with leg shave. I didn't really feel up to it. I was tired and hadn't had a Disco Nap. However, there was a possibility Lee was going to meet us at The Hornet and his receptionist looked like she stepped out of the pages of a fashion magazine. I thought it best to put some effort into it.

I grabbed my dress that was just a thick band of stretchy black from which fell a swath of olive green gauzy material swirled through with cream and black. The band fit above my breasts, the gauze fell in a scarf-like hem to above the knee. I put on a droopy black belt with a big circular silver buckle and bloused the dress over it, making it mini. I fluffed out my hair, pawed through the dregs at the back of my makeup drawer and slapped on some makeup, put on a pair of big silver hoop earrings, a bunch of bangles on my wrist, a bunch of silver rings on my fingers and pulled on my black cowboy boots. I shoved some stuff into a black purse and headed out the door.

I walked to The Hornet, which was only four blocks away, and I didn't waste any time. Rosie was found. Pepper Rick and Sandy Pete were out of the picture and the hit man was behind bars. I was likely relatively safe, but I wasn't going to take any chances.

Marianne was there when I got there, sitting on a stool at the bar. I'd asked Ally to join us, but she had a shift at Brother's. I'd braved the pissed-off brute and asked Eddie if he wanted to come but he was going to be bogged down in paperwork.

"I wish I could wear a dress like that," Marianne told me when I slid on the booth next to her.

Marianne used to be a size four. Her hair changed color with her mood, so much so that I didn't remember what it was when it started out. Now it was brunette. She had big gray eyes. She was always pretty and regardless of the weight, she still was a looker. She'd been popular, being so dainty and cute. Boys flocked to her. Her divorce had taken its toll. It was ugly, she still wasn't over it and she was eating through the pain.

I had no response for her and ordered a spiced rum and diet and excused myself and called Lee again to tell him I was at The Hornet. Marianne didn't question this. She'd been an innocent bystander in one of my shootouts, and anyway, Lee was hot.

"Well?" Marianne asked when I flipped my phone shut.

I sighed.

"Lee doesn't take the bows from bras or panties, at least not anymore," I said.

Marianne's eyes lit up. "Is he good?"

The way she asked it wasn't gossipy or voyeuristic. It was a friend asking a friend about her sex life, which in my circle of friends was a natural thing. We weren't exactly *Sex in the City,* but we shared. It also meant our conversation wasn't going to be e-mailed to half of the greater Denver Metropolitan Area by midnight.

So I answered her, "He's good."

"How good?" she asked.

My eyes slid to her. "*Real* good."

Her face spread in a smile and I returned it.

"I'm so happy for you," she whispered.

I was beginning to be happy for me, too.

My drink came and I ordered a buffalo chicken salad with extra bleu cheese dressing. Marianne announced she was going on a diet and she ordered one too, without the bleu cheese dressing.

We ate at the bar. The plates were whisked away, I was on my third rum and diet and Marianne had gone to the bathroom when my hair was brushed to the side, a hand gliding across my bare shoulders. I looked around, then up, and saw Lee standing over me.

He'd showered and changed and he looked good. He was wearing jeans that were worn in but still newish, brown cowboy boots and forest green collared shirt.

I smiled at him.

He frowned at me.

"Where're the rest of your clothes?"

I looked down at my dress then back up at him.

"These *are* my clothes," I said. "You don't like it?"

"Yeah, I like it. If you're wearin' it in my kitchen while cookin' steaks. I don't like it when you're wearin' it sittin' on a barstool and thirty guys are imagining your legs wrapped around their backs."

Jeez.

"Lee, you're gonna have to get over this jealous-possessiveness thing."

"Indy, you're gonna have to get used to the fact that I'm the jealous-possessive type."

Great.

I decided to change the subject. I wasn't going to change how I dressed and he wasn't going to start to like it. We were at a stalemate.

"Have you had dinner?"

"I grabbed something at the condo."

His eyes moved to the bar and he lifted his chin and said to the bartender, "Fat Tire."

Marianne still hadn't materialized so I decided to broach a new subject.

"We need to talk about Eddie."

Lee slid into the area between me and Marianne's barstool. His hip pressing my knees to the side, he rested his forearm on the bar.

"Yeah, we do. From now on, you see Eddie only when I'm with you."

My teeth clenched. "Okay, first we need to talk about you bossing me around all the time and how I really don't like it."

His eyes crinkled and I knew he thought I was being cute.

"I'm being serious." I went on.

His beer came. He slid a bill across the counter, took a pull and leaned into me. "This is how it works. I tell you how I feel. I'm honest about it. You do the same. A lot of the time we won't agree, but we'll deal."

I blinked at him.

Did he really think that was going to work?

Lee kept talking. "Obviously you heard our conversation. I know where Eddie stands, Eddie knows where I stand. If things are good between you and me, Eddie won't be a threat. They start to go bad, Eddie's movin' in."

"I got that part," I said.

"I don't intend for things to go bad, but that doesn't mean that Eddie isn't gonna give you hints at what you might be missin'."

Holy crap.

Lee continued, "So I want to be there when you're with him because I'm the jealous-possessive type. That's just the way it is, and now you know how I feel. If you see him when I'm not there then it's down to you. Okay?"

"So, you aren't telling me what to do, you're telling me what you want."

"If I wanted a woman who did what she was told, I wouldn't be with you."

I didn't know any women who did what they were told, but I suspected they were out there. I just didn't hang with them because that definitely wasn't my scene.

"If it's just you sharing your feelings, perhaps you can voice it less like an order," I suggested.

"I'm used to giving orders, and if it sounds like one then there's always a chance you'll obey."

I gave him a look.

He gave me The Smile.

Marianne walked up and our conversation ended. While Marianne and I chatted and finished our drinks, Lee stood close behind me and nursed his Fat Tire. So close, I got comfy and rested my back against his front. Every once in a while Marianne would take us both in and sigh.

When we were done, Lee and I walked Marianne to her car. I hugged her good-bye on the sidewalk and Lee and I watched her drive away. We went back to the front of The Hornet where Lee was parked at the curb almost directly outside the front doors.

"How do you get these parking spots?" I asked when Lee opened the door for me.

"Luck," he answered.

Bullshit. Luck. It was one of Lee's "ways".

We were coming away from the curb when his cell rang. He answered it as he was cutting across the four lanes of Broadway so he could make the turn right to my house.

"What?" he said into the phone and then barked out a clipped, "Details."

Before he was done listening, he moved back into traffic. He flipped the phone shut and slid it in the console.

"I thought it'd be a quiet night. I need a quiet night," he muttered to the windshield, not talking to me.

"What are we doing?" I asked.

"*We* aren't doin' anything. I've got something to do. You're waitin' in the car."

"Lee, that sounded like an order."

"That *was* an order."

Hmm.

Lee explained, "Luke was scheduled on call tonight, but since he's in the hospital, we're a man down. I thought it'd be a quiet night. Only one skip, who can wait, and most of the boys have been doubling up, working cases and doing stuff for you. All of your shit is either dead, behind bars or been offered employment at Fortnum's. An informant called Ike, who's manning the surveillance room. The skip has turned up. Bobby and Vance are on call, but instead of at the office, I let them go home. Vance lives in a cabin outside Golden. I'm closest. Bobby's comin' as back up. He's five minutes behind."

"How do they know you're closest?"

"All company vehicles have a tracking device. The Crossfire and your VW have one too."

My VW? This was news.

"Really?" I asked.

"Really."

"These days, my car never moves," I told him like he didn't know, since he took me practically everywhere.

"I know," he said.

"Are you gonna take it off now that Rosie's found?"

"You're now covered by Nightingale Security."

Er… what?

"I thought you weren't doing security anymore."

"Only special circumstances. The boys monitor the condo and now they monitor you."

"I don't know if I'm comfortable with that."

"You will be when some nut job with a vendetta against me uses you to get to me, and my boys get to you in five minutes rather than after you've been raped and murdered."

Yikes.

I hit the mental control that set up Denial Zone around that subject and changed it to a new one.

"Who's Ike?"

"Another of my men."

"How many haven't I met?"

"Luke, Mace, Jack and Ike."

Mace? Who had a name like *Mace?* Where did these macho idiots come up with this shit?

"You got a guy named Mace?" I asked. I couldn't help myself.

"His name's Mason. Mason is a shit name. We call him Mace."

That made sense.

"Oh," I said.

We pulled up outside a bar off Colfax Avenue that I never knew existed, though I couldn't say I spent much time on Colfax.

The bar looked rough.

Lee yanked the parking brake, turned off the car and twisted toward me.

"You stay here, stay down and keep the doors locked. Bobby will be here soon."

I nodded.

He got out. I locked the doors and watched him go in. Then I leaned across the console, found the trunk release and grabbed the keys. I got out and went to the trunk. My belt was there. As far as I knew, Ally still had the pepper spray and Eddie had the Taser, which left me with the stun gun. I grabbed it, closed the trunk, bleeped the locks and walked toward the bar.

I did this for several reasons. Firstly, I felt more vulnerable and exposed in the car. Second, I'd never liked to be left out. Not to mention I was beginning to see why guys liked this shit. It was a rush. Last, I wanted to see Lee in action.

I walked into the bar and stood stock-still.

Even though it had been less than two minutes since Lee left me, a humongous black guy was laid out on the floor, long arms and legs sprawled. One of his wrists over his head and he was cuffed to the foot rail that ran the length of the bar.

Lee was in the middle of the room. Some guy who was either drunk or not very good at what he was doing was aiming punch after punch at Lee. Lee dodged each punch with a calm jerk of his head and upper body. Then out of nowhere, Lee's fist came up and jabbed the guy in the left eye. Surprise and the power behind the jab sent the guy back three steps.

Lee was advancing on him when someone jumped Lee from behind, and I could see another guy was approaching. Lee bent at the waist and flipped the guy over his shoulder. Mid-flip Lee's torso lifted up. Using his strength and the guy's momentum, Lee threw him, upside down, into the guy coming at them. The two guys went toppling backwards, slammed into a table and drinks flew everywhere.

This heralded the beginning of the brawl, including shouting, grunting, flying beer bottles and broken furniture. One second, Lee was the show. The next second, everyone was in on the act.

Two new guys came at Lee and he turned to one. Not a small guy, not even average, though he wasn't huge. Lee grasped him by the collar of his t-shirt and belt of his pants, picked him up and threw him four feet across the room.

Just... like... that.

The guy that Lee jabbed was recovering and going toward Lee so I felt it was time to wade into the action. I hit the switch on the stun gun. It started to crackle and I moved forward and touched the guy with the prongs. He went still and went down.

Holy shit!

That was cool.

Lee's eyes locked on mine, he gave a small shake of his head and then turned and dispatched another guy with a smooth uppercut. The guy went sailing.

"Hey, whitey! What the fuck you doin'?" I turned to see a black woman, hand on hip, head wobbling from side to side. "You can't just stun gun my man... you can't just... eek!"

I put the prongs to her. She went still then went down.

"Yo, bitch! Who you messin' with?" The girl's girlfriend was coming at me, all pissed-off attitude, definitely in bitch smackdown mode. So I leaned forward, put the prongs to her, too, and she went down as well.

Regardless of the bedlam, people were giving me—and my crackling stun gun—a wide berth. Then two hands settled on my waist. I was lifted up and my butt was planted on the bar. Lee bent, grabbed my ankles, swung my legs around to the back of the bar, then with a hand between my shoulders, he gave me a shove and I fell over to the other side.

Bobby came in and spotted Lee immediately. He fought his way to Lee. They both bent down and I couldn't see them over the bar. The place was pandemonium and twice I had to duck, once to dodge a flying beer bottle, the second time to duck and run from a flying chair.

Bobby and Lee came up with the humongous guy, cuffed now at the back.

Bobby pushed humongous guy forward, half walking him, half scooting him along. The big guy was either mostly knocked out or stunned. Bobby, who was even bigger (in fact he was bigger than anyone in the room), didn't have a problem handling humongous guy or wading through the crowd.

Lee jumped the bar, lifted me up and planted me on the bar again, reverse action. He went back over the bar, snagged me around the waist and hauled me out of there.

Sirens were blaring and a cop car had already rolled up. Willie and Brian were headed into the bar as we came out and I saw another squad car approach.

Brian's mouth dropped open when he saw me.

Willie's eyes turned to Lee. There was some nonverbal male communication going on that I couldn't decipher, except I had a feeling that Lee was not going to win the Cop's Daughter Boyfriend of the Year Award.

"I'm droppin' Indy. I'll meet you at the station," Lee informed Bobby, as Bobby shoved the humongous guy in the backseat of an SUV then pulled out some ankle shackles.

I was jazzed. I'd never been in a bar brawl before, if you didn't count what happened at BJ's Carousel. Personally, I was classifying that as a shootout rather than a bar brawl.

I discovered I loved stun guns. Stun guns were righteous when they weren't used on you.

And Lee could kick ass.

He was calm, cool and totally in control.

No one touched him. No one even got near him.

Lee drove down Colfax, going fast, weaving in and out of traffic and not saying anything.

"You're thinking of cuffing me to the bed again, aren't you?" I asked.

"No, I'm wondering if I should skip town before getting lynched."

Hmm.

"Can I keep the stun gun?" I asked.

Lee didn't answer.

He pulled up in front of my house and I turned to him. I couldn't contain my excitement any longer.

"Is it a bad thing that I'm, like, totally jazzed?"

Lee twisted toward me, his face in shadow. "No."

"Did you learn to fight like that in Special Operations School?"

"I learned to fight like that in bar fights."

"Aren't you jazzed?" I asked.

He seemed so calm.

"Yeah, I'm jazzed. And I'd like you to get out of the car so I can go to the station and deal with the paperwork and get home so I can work that feelin' out with you."

Holy crap.

"Okay!" I chirped, leaned forward, gave him a quick peck and hightailed it out of his car.

Lee took off when I was safely inside.

I let Chowleena out the front for a change of scenery.

I ran upstairs and yanked out my red lace undies and garter belt.

There was gratitude owed, not to mention I was allowing happiness to seep through those walls Lee said I had built around me.

And I had one seriously hot, badass, good-looking boyfriend.

I didn't have any stockings that weren't black, so black would have to do. I had a pair of black pumps with a dangerously pointed toe, a thin stiletto heel and a saucy ankle strap and I yanked them out of their box. I pulled off my clothes, put on the underwear, threw on a short robe and ran and called Chowleena in. Then I smoothed on the stockings and lit the room softly with a small lamp on my dressing table that gave just enough light to see, but not enough light *to see*.

Then I paced, waiting for Lee. It couldn't take that long, and he was jazzed. He'd want to get home.

I put the shoes by the side of the bed so I could put them on when I heard him come in.

I laid down on my bed to wait.

Immediately my adrenalin crashed and I fell asleep.

Chapter 21
We Aren't Practice for the Real Thing

I heard Lee mutter, "Fuck," and my wrist was circled by his fingers.

I opened my eyes and saw him lay back in the bed, his hand at his jaw.

"Hey," I said sleepily.

"You didn't wait long," he answered, letting my wrist go.

"I crashed."

He was settling against the pillows, shirt unbuttoned all the way down, belt gone from his jeans. He looked warm and comfy so I snuggled up to him, burrowing my face in his neck. One of his arms slid around my shoulders, the other hand was rubbing his jaw.

"Why are you rubbing your jaw?" I asked.

"I was gettin' into bed, you turned and clocked me."

Oopsie.

"Sorry. That happens sometimes. I'm an active sleeper."

"So you've said."

I snuggled deeper into him and wrapped my arm around his abs. I closed my eyes, my cheek against his shoulder.

"What are you doin'?" he asked.

"Going to bed. I'm sleepy."

"What happened to being jazzed?"

"No more jazzed," I murmured and settled in. "Sleepy."

He turned and one of his hands went to my hip and pushed it back. My body went with it and I opened my eyes.

His hand went from my hip to smooth over the material of the robe at my ass.

I looked at him. It was dark, but I could still tell his eyes were warm and intent.

Mm.

I took a not so wild shot in the dark. "You're still jazzed."

"Totally pumped," he answered, then his mouth connected with my jaw, ran the length of it and dipped down to my neck.

His hand went under the robe, encountered the garter and froze.

I'd forgotten.

"Um... I had a little surprise planned for you before I fell asleep," I told him.

His fingertip followed the garter down to where it attached to the stocking.

"Yeah, I can feel."

He turned away from me. The bedside light went on and all soft, romantic lighting was gone.

"Lee, the light—"

"Quiet," he ordered. "I wanna see."

He untied the robe and spread it wide. I kind of felt like an idiot. I mean, I actually bought this underwear to wear. I found stockings more comfortable than hose. The underwear had never been used for this purpose.

Lee looked down at me then up and his eyes locked with mine. There was a hint of what I saw in the locker room at his offices and I got a thrill at the sense that he was just barely hanging onto his control.

"It's like Christmas," he said.

He traced the lace over my breast with his fingertip. Then his hand went away and his tongue traced the lace.

I found instantly I wasn't sleepy anymore.

Lee's mouth came up my chest, over my chin to my mouth.

"Is there sentimental value to this underwear?" he asked.

My brow furrowed with confusion. I wanted to kiss him and he was talking about sentimental value to underwear. Was this a jealous-possessive thing? Did he think some guy bought me the underwear?

I twisted into him and wrapped a leg around his waist, my arms around his back and I pressed against him.

"No, I bought it for myself, entirely utilitarian," I answered.

"So if I rip it off, I can replace it and you won't have a tantrum?"

Oh... my... God.

I looked into his eyes. The control was slipping and Lee Beast was coming out.

I didn't trust myself to speak so I just nodded my head.

"Good," he muttered.

＊＊＊

When we were done, I was on top, straddling him, my knees tucked into his sides, my upper body pressed the length of his and my face in his neck.

When I got my breath back, I whispered, "Am I too heavy?"

"No."

His hands were idly running up and down my back and over my bottom. I was glad I wasn't too heavy because I was considering staying where I was for the rest of my life.

His hands came up, and with both of them he gathered my hair in a bunch and gave it a gentle tug.

I lifted my head and looked at him. His eyes moved over my face and then a slow grin spread on his.

"What?" I asked.

"I like the look on your face after I've finished with you. You look happy, relaxed..." he paused and the grin grew into a smile, "satisfied."

I gave my head a tug and he released my hair. It fell over both of us and, as I nuzzled my face in his neck again, he swept my hair away by running his fingers through it at the side of my head.

"Cocky," I mumbled into his neck.

I felt his body move with laughter as his arms came around me again.

"I like that," I said sleepily.

"What?"

"Feeling your laughter. You used to laugh all the time. You don't do it so much anymore."

"You were avoiding me. I wasn't around you that much."

"So, you're saying you laugh all the time, I just don't see it?" I asked.

"No. I'm sayin' I used to laugh all the time because I was with you. You're crazy, you're funny. It's one of the things I love about you."

My entire body froze.

"What did you just say?" I asked.

"You're funny."

"No, the last part." He didn't answer so I lifted my head and looked at him. "One of the things you love about me?"

We locked eyes.

"Yeah," he said.

"What else do you love about me?"

He had that soft look. His eyes were melty and he had his own satisfied expression that was supremely sexy, but I had the feeling that he was very alert.

"I love your ass, your hair and your legs," he answered.

"That's it?"

"No, I also love your eyes."

The eyes he loved narrowed. "That's it?"

"Maybe I should say I especially love your ass."

I pulled up, but he rolled me over and pinned me under his body.

"I just wanna make sure I know what's happenin' here," he began. "Is this sleepy after sex talk and you're gonna drift away to dreamland any second, or are we havin' a serious conversation?"

We were having a serious conversation all right. I wasn't sleepy anymore. I was freaking out and my heart was hammering in my chest.

"We're having a serious conversation," I told him.

"Okay. Then now I wanna know if you've had the opportunity to throw up the defenses, or are we gonna have an honest conversation, one you're gonna participate in?"

Hmm, that was a *much* more difficult question to answer.

He looked at me.

"I didn't think so," he muttered.

Shit.

Shit, shit, shit.

"For what it's worth, I'll share my intentions," he went on. "You and me, we aren't practice for the real thing. It isn't that too much is at stake with family and friends. It's because I love you. You're funny, beautiful and you care about people. I like the way you look at me, especially when you think I don't notice it. I like that we have history and our kids will have a big family and share that history because there was never a time when their Mom and Dad weren't together. If you were a terrible lay, I might have second thoughts, but you and I are dynamite together. I intend to marry you and spend the rest of my life with you. If that freaks you out, tough, because now that we've started this, there's no goin' back."

After a couple of beats, I realized I wasn't breathing so I made a conscious effort to start again.

Lee was watching me. "Do you have anything you want to say?"

I had a lot of things I wanted to say, but none of them I was ready to say.

I asked, "When did you know you loved me?"

He sighed and slid off me onto his side. He brought me with him so we were face-to-face.

"I knew that last time you tried to seduce me before you started avoiding me. When I was home on leave and you tackled me in your Dad's living room and I told you that I thought of you like a sister."

My heart lurched at the thought. That had been the most hated, humiliating, horrifying memory of my life.

"I didn't tackle you," I said.

"It was close to a tackle."

Jeez.

Moving on.

"Why then?" I asked.

"Because what I wanted to do was get in your pants. It almost hurt physically to set you away from me. It *did* hurt when you got that look on your face after I told you that you were like a sister. It hurt to hurt you. That's when I knew."

"That was a long time ago," I said to him.

His hand was resting at my waist but it moved around my back and pulled me to him.

"Yeah, we've wasted a lot of time. We've got a lot to make up for."

He was nuzzling my neck, but I wasn't quite finished talking.

"You want to marry me?" I asked.

"No. I'm gonna marry you." He lifted his head from my neck. "You're movin' in this weekend. We'll get settled, get used to each other, spend some time up in the cabin, maybe go away somewhere with a beach. In a few months I'll get you a ring then we'll get married."

I didn't believe what I was hearing.

"You have it all planned out," I said.

"Well... yeah."

"That's it?" I asked.

"That's it. Isn't that how it normally happens?"

I guessed it was, but still.

I felt his body move against mine and knew he was laughing.

"Fucking hell, India Savage wants hearts and flowers."

I went up on my forearm. Hearts and flowers! As if! I was a Rock Chick!

"I do not!" I snapped.

He was grinning at me. "Yes you do."

"No I do *not*," I retorted.

He rolled me on my back and onto me again. His hands went into the hair at either side of my face and he looked me in the eyes.

"I don't do hearts and flowers, but I promise you won't be disappointed."

"You are so cocky."

"Honey, I don't give a fuck if you don't believe it's gonna be good between us. I know we'll both enjoy me proving it to you."

Wow.

My breath escaped me and I stared.

He ignored my stare, rolled off me again, twisted me around and fit my back to his front and held me tight against him.

I expected my mind to whirl. Instead, I gave into my exhaustion, his warmth, and the sweet feeling in the pit of my belly that I was exactly where I was supposed to be.

⚎

I woke up, my body snuggled against Lee's back, my cheek pressed against his shoulder blade.

I peered beyond him to the clock. It was five after six.

Unfortunately, as warm and comfy as I was, I was awake. And when I was awake, I needed to get up.

Since Lee was still sleeping, I carefully pulled away and started to roll to the other side of the bed.

He turned, snagged me by the waist and tucked me into him.

I waited for something to happen and then realized he was still asleep.

"Lee."

"Mm?" he mumbled, all sexy-sleepy.

"Honey, I need to go to the bathroom."

His arm loosened and I slid away.

I picked up the red lace underwear which Lee didn't rip off me (though it was close). I put it on and slipped on Lee's shirt, buttoning it up the front.

I went to the bathroom, brushed, flossed and washed my face. I grabbed an elastic hair band and tied my hair in a messy knot on top of my head and dug through the cabinets until I found my new toothbrush stash. I had three, not because I needed them for overnight guests, but because I was freakish about dental hygiene. I set one on the counter by the sink with the toothpaste in case Lee got up.

I walked downstairs, started the coffee going and let Chowleena out. I opened the gate between mine and Tod and Stevie's backyard so Chowleena had plenty of room to move.

I was on my second cup of coffee and sifting through mail, sitting at my dining room table with both of my heels on the seat in front of me and my knees to my chest when Lee rounded the bottom of the stairs.

His hair was sexy messy and he had a day's worth of stubble. He'd put on his jeans, but had only buttoned enough buttons to keep them on his hips while he moved. His eyes were still slightly sleepy as if he'd just that instant woken up and they were on me as he stalked toward me.

"Hey," I said.

He arrived at my side, wrapped his fist in my hair, tugged my head back and kissed me, hard and deep with lots of tongue.

When he lifted his head he said, "I don't like wakin' up and you're not beside me."

My heart stuttered to a halt and I blinked.

"Sorry," I whispered.

He let go of my hair and stalked into the kitchen.

Jeez.

Guess Lee needed his morning coffee too.

The doorbell rang and I got up, went to the window and looked to see who it was at that ungodly hour. Likely, the world was coming to an end and Lee needed to save the day.

It was Eddie.

Shit.

I went to the door, grabbed the key off the hook beside it, unlocked and opened it then unlocked the security door.

Eddie was dressed exactly like yesterday. Except his jeans were even more worn, which meant they fit him all the better, and the white thermal tee had been exchanged for a black one.

I pushed open the security door and greeted, "Hey Eddie.

He walked in, pulling off his mirrored shades.

"Indy," he replied. "I'm lookin' for Lee." His eyes dropped down to my body and he took in Lee's shirt. "I guess I found him."

"Eddie," Lee said, and both Eddie and I looked into the house.

Lee was standing in the doorway to the kitchen holding a coffee mug, jeans buttoned, eyes cold, face blank.

Yikes.

This was weird.

Nobody moved. Nobody said anything.

I decided to forge into the breach.

"Eddie, you want coffee?" I asked, sidling around him and into the living room.

"Sure, three sugars and cream. Thanks."

I tilted my head and noted, "You like it sweet."

Damn!

Shit, shit, shit.

I'd flirted. I didn't mean to, it just came out.

Eddie looked at me, an amused twinkle in his eye. "Yeah, I like it sweet."

Shit.

"All righty then," I muttered and hurried across the room.

Lee was still standing in the doorway to the kitchen, and as I walked toward him he didn't move.

Moments before I'd have to stop, he stepped to the side but just barely. I had to squeeze by him and I felt the heat from his glare as I did so.

He moved out of the doorway and into the dining room when I went into the kitchen.

"Eddie," I heard him say, "what're you doin' here?"

"Lookin' for you," Eddie replied.

"You found me." This was not said in a welcoming tone and the bad vibes were snapping in the air.

"I heard about you and Indy being in a brawl on Colfax last night," Eddie said.

Uh-oh.

Not a good way to start.

I pulled out a coffee mug.

"We weren't in a brawl. I was pickin' up a skip and Indy was supposed to sit in the car. She got a hankerin' to test out her new stun gun so she followed me in, dropped anyone who came near her. My back up came and we got out." Lee waited a beat and finished, "She's got a new found fondness for stun guns."

There was silence and then Eddie replied, "Yeah, I heard that too. Willie saw her with it, said the floor was littered with her victims."

More silence.

I held my breath as I spooned sugar in Eddie's coffee.

Then I heard low chuckling.

I let out my breath.

Okay, they were bonding over my crazy antics, which was somewhat embarrassing, but at least they were bonding.

I walked into the dining room and handed Eddie his coffee.

"I'm going to go get dressed," I told them both.

Lee's eyes moved over me and I couldn't guess what he was thinking.

"Bring my shirt back down when you're done with it, would you?" he asked.

I nodded, wondering at his mood, guessing it was not good after the flirty incident, and I scooted up the stairs.

I put on the red bra, a pair of red track bottoms that had a wide white stripe that ran from the side of the ankle, up the leg, across my upper ass and down the other leg. To this, I added a thin, white, tank top that showed a bit of cleavage. I spritzed on some perfume, rolled on some deodorant, rubbed in some moisturizer and slapped on some powder, blush and mascara, not feeling like the full treatment. I slid on some red flip-flops and headed back downstairs.

By the time I got there, Lee and Eddie were both sitting, or more to the point, lounging in king-of-the-castle fashion at my dining room table.

Jeez.

That didn't take long.

I walked up to the table.

"It's Tex's first day with the morning crowd, I need to get to work," I informed them, walking to the table.

Lee's eyes had moved over me again as I approached, and Eddie's gaze came around then dropped straight to my chest.

I ignored Eddie, stopped and handed Lee his shirt. He took it and shrugged into it.

"See you all later," I said.

I started to go but Lee caught my wrist.

I turned back to him.

"You're forgetting two things," Lee said.

"What're those?" I asked.

His eyes moved to my tank top. "First, you need to change into real clothes."

Um… excuse me?

"Sorry?" I asked. Just in case he hadn't just been totally out of line, I'd give him an out.

"You aren't wearin' that out of this house," Lee replied.

I hadn't missed it. He had been totally out of line.

I wasn't sure if it was the room or just my head that started rumbling, like in the movies before the earthquake that swallows cars and whole buildings.

"Um, *sorry?*" I repeated, this time chockfull of attitude.

Eddie lifted up his hand and started inspecting his fingernails. I could mostly see just his profile, but I knew he was grinning because I could see his fucking dimple.

"Maybe we should have this conversation upstairs," Lee suggested when he saw my attention turn to Eddie.

"Maybe we should have this conversation in an alternate universe where Alternate Indy gives a shit what Alternate Lee wants her to wear."

No way to miss the attitude in *that.*

Eddie stood. "I'll just top up my coffee."

"I'm sorry, Eddie," I said to him as he walked into the kitchen.

"Don't mind me," Eddie returned, making a beeline to the coffee.

Once Eddie disappeared, I hissed at Lee, "Tell me you just didn't tell me what to wear in front of Eddie."

"I'll tell you that when the image of you flirting with him isn't freshly burned into my brain," Lee replied.

Yep, I was right. Lee was not in a good mood about my flirting with Eddie.

I ripped my wrist out of Lee's hand.

"It's okay Eddie," I called. "You can come back. I'm leaving."

"You try to leave, I'll carry you upstairs and change you myself," Lee threatened.

Eddie leaned his shoulder in the doorway of the kitchen. "I'm thinkin' you aren't quite finished." Then Eddie decided to throw down. "For what it's worth, I'm with Lee. If you were my woman, there's no fuckin' way I'd let you out of the house wearin' that."

I glared at him. "Did someone ask you?"

"Nope. Just tryin' to be helpful," Eddie answered, grinned and walked into the room.

I opened my mouth to, I don't know, scream, shriek, talk in tongues, when a sound came from the backdoor.

"Yoo hoo!"

Tod came in wearing his flight attendant uniform. "I saw Chowleena healthy and happy out there and your door open. I knew you'd have coffee. You always have coffee and I need coffee. The Beemer's in the shop so we only have one car. I have to stay awake and go back to DIA and get Stevie later this morning and I'm dead on my feet. Your coffee's so strong, you could melt nails in it and..."

Tod had been talking while he entered the kitchen through the backdoor and grabbed himself a mug o' joe. He stopped dead in the kitchen doorway and his mouth dropped open. He stared between Lee and Eddie. Back and forth. Back again and forth.

Then his eyes swung to me.

"What're you doing? Collecting the straight, super-macho Village People?"

Eddie burst out laughing and Lee looked down and to the side, but I caught the fact that his eyes crinkled.

I clenched my teeth.

Once Eddie quit laughing I said, "Tod, Eddie, Eddie, Tod."

They nodded to each other.

Then I didn't hesitate. I was being ganged up on, I needed back up.

So I asked Tod, "What do you think of my outfit?"

Tod looked around again, but this time only between me and Lee.

"Uh-oh, is there trouble in paradise?"

"Just answer the question," I snapped.

"Okay, girlie, keep your pants on." Tod went into assessment mode, looking me up and down. "Very cute pants. You *know* I'm not fond of flip-flops but they work. Pretty bra but I only say that because I can see every inch of it. Normally, my motto is, if you got it, flaunt it, but with your bazungas, you *really* got it. You in that top and bra might cause traffic collisions. Are you prepared to live with that on your conscience?"

Great.

I avoided looking at Lee and turned in a huff and headed to the stairs. "Fine. I'll change. I wouldn't want to cause bodily harm."

I went back upstairs, changed the track bottoms for jeans, put on a fitted, plaid, cuffed-short-sleeved, western Style shirt with pearl snap buttons up the front and on the two breast pockets and switched out the red flip-flops for brown leather ones and stomped back down the stairs and into the kitchen.

Tod was now sitting with the boys at the table enjoying his coffee, Chowleena lying beside him on the floor. Chowleena followed me into the kitchen and I threw her a biscuit for her show of camaraderie.

"We girls have to stick together," I told her as I rifled through my junk drawer, looking for my crazy, thick gold Elvis-framed sunglasses that would be kickass with my shirt.

I found them as Lee walked into the kitchen. I threw him a glance that would pulverize rock and slid my glasses into the mess of hair on my head.

"Later," I said, intending to walk right by him.

He stepped in front of me, advanced, and backed me into the corner next to the fridge by the coffeepot, a corner that you couldn't see from the dining room.

"We haven't talked about the second thing you forgot," he said to me, his hands settling on the counter on either side of me.

Ignoring his fencing me in, I planted my hands on my hips. "And what's that?"

His arms wrapped around me and kissed me.

After he finished, trying to recover from the kiss and not let it show, I demanded, "Move back."

"You're pissed," he stated the obvious.

"Damn straight," I confirmed.

"We'll talk about it tonight."

"No we won't. Tonight is girl's night out. I'm busy."

"I'll come and get you for lunch."

"No lunch, no dinner, no tonight. Today, you and me, we're on a break. No talking, no seeing, no nothing. Maybe, if I've cooled down, I'll see you tomorrow."

"Indy, you can have space today, but you're in my bed tonight."

"I don't think so."

"I'll be here tonight when you get home."

"I'm not coming home."

His eyes got kind of scary and he leaned into me a bit. Considering he was pretty damn close to me, leaning in was seriously invasive.

"Honey, you forget, part of my job is findin' people. Do you think you can hide from me?"

No, I didn't think I could hide from him, but I was going to try.

"I'll see you tomorrow," I repeated.

I shoved through his arms, huffed through the living room giving a wave and a farewell to Eddie and Tod, who both wisely kept quiet, and soared on my anger all the way down the block towards Fortnum's.

Chapter 22
Friendly Neighborhood Serial Killer

I almost made it to the door of Fortnum's when I noticed, out of the corner of my eye, that stapled to every telephone and light pole down Broadway, for as far as the eye could see, was an acid green piece of paper with what looked like a photo with some writing underneath.

I thought someone really, really wanted to find their missing cat so I stomped up to check it out and stopped dead at what I saw.

It was a picture of Tex. No night vision goggles (thankfully), but with wild hair and a crazy-ass smile on his face, looking like your friendly neighborhood serial killer. The picture was obviously color, copied in black and white, which made it blobby and grainy and even more frightening.

Underneath his picture it said, "Tex" and underneath that it said, "New Coffee Guy" and underneath that it said, "Fortnum's".

Holy crap.

I snatched the flier off the telephone pole and prowled into Fortnum's.

There were five customers, three standing in line, two waiting at the other end of the counter for their coffee. Tex and Jane were behind the counter.

I shouted, "What the hell is this?" Then I waved the acid green poster around.

Tex looked up at me, then looked out the window, then looked back at me and pointed the portafilter at me. Unfortunately, he hadn't pounded out the used coffee grounds so they went flying in an arc in front of him and the customers stepped wide on either side to avoid them.

"What're you doin', woman? That was prime advertisin' space, right outside the store. Why'd you pull it down?"

I didn't know what to say. I didn't want to tell him he looked like a serial killer.

But, for God's sake, he looked like a serial killer.

"Tex, you look like a serial killer in this picture!" I shouted.

"Yeah, so?" Tex answered.

I stared.

"You think people wouldn't pay good money to have a serial killer make them coffee?" he boomed.

He had a point. This was America. People would stand in line to touch the swastika on Charles Manson's forehead.

I stomped to the back to get the mop to clean up the grounds. After I did that, I spelled Jane behind the counter. Tex cursed, banged, slammed and crashed through every cup of coffee he made, as if each creation had to be wrenched by force out of the seven thousand dollar machine. I tried to put this down to the fact that he was making coffee one-handed due to the sling, but it took all my willpower not to put my hands to the sides of my head and scream bloody murder.

"What'd you…" *Bang!* "get up to last night?" *Clank!* Tex asked.

"Bar brawl…" *Smash!* "stunned-gunned a few people…" *Kablam!* "Lee caught some guy who jumped bond then we came home." *Crash!* I answered then asked, "You?"

"After doin' the posters, the cats and me had a quiet night." *Bam!*

The morning passed relatively normally, not counting Jane and I jumping every time Tex bashed the espresso machine or cursed (which was a lot). I spent the morning trying to decide where I should go to avoid Lee for the night because, let's face it, telling your girlfriend what to wear was bad enough. Doing it in front of someone else was a serious transgression.

If he was anyone else, he'd have his walking orders. Since he was Lee, and he loved me, and he wanted (or more to the point, was *going*) to marry me, I was willing to be pretty fucking angry for a while and then carry a mean grudge.

I couldn't stay with anyone I knew because Lee knew everyone I knew. This meant hotel, which was easy pickin's. He'd probably get Brody to write some program to hack into the computer register of every hotel in Denver and find me in half an hour.

No, I needed to be clever. Unfortunately, I wasn't that clever.

Around eleven thirty, Duke staggered in, looking hungover because he was. Duke being hungover and Tex banging on the espresso machine was not a good combination, so fifteen minutes later, Duke took off for some hair of the dog.

The coffee crowd was long gone and Tex snatched up the poster I'd pulled down. I watched him stalk outside with a staple gun to put it back on the pole. It was then I got a brilliant idea and followed him out.

"Hey Tex," I said.

"What?" He stapled the semi-mutilated poster so many times it was going to have to wear off the pole.

"Would you mind if I crashed at your place tonight?" I asked.

"Don't you have a place?"

"I can't go to my place," I told him.

"Doesn't your boyfriend have a place?"

"His place isn't an option."

Tex stopped stapling and turned to me. He watched me for a couple of seconds, ciphering something in his head, came to a decision and then shrugged.

"You can share the couch with Tiddles, Winky and Flossy."

"Thanks."

I had to admit, I really liked sleeping with Lee. His body was comfy warm but strong and solid, so I felt cozy and protected all at the same time. I didn't think Tiddles, Winky and Flossy were going to have the same effect, but it was just one night. I'd cope.

⌁

It was three o'clock and Duke hadn't come back. Jane was off doing whatever Jane did when she wasn't at Fortnum's (I imagined her tapping away at an old electric typewriter like Angela Lansbury). I was sitting behind the book counter reading through a magazine someone had left behind, and Tex was sitting in the middle of one of the couches, looking wild-eyed and frightening.

"This is boring," Tex said.

I looked up from the extraordinary tale of the courage of a young man faced with a rare form of cancer and then looked back down without answering.

What could I say? It *was* boring.

"Do something," Tex demanded.

I looked up again. "What do you want me to do?"

"I don't know, something. Isn't it on someone's schedule today to kidnap you and hold you hostage?"

Oh, dear Lord.

"All the bad guys are either dead or behind bars," I told him.

"Bummer."

Great.

The door opened and Mr. Kumar came in. Behind him shuffled in scary, living-dead Mrs. Salim.

"We came to sell you back your book," Mr. Kumar announced.

Double great. That triumph was short-lived.

"That's cool, Mr. Kumar, but I don't buy them for as much as I sell them," I told him.

Mr. Kumar nodded. "It's like a rental."

I looked at him.

I could live with that.

Mrs. Salim shuffled into the bowels of the bookstore.

"She wants another one," Mr. Kumar told me.

My day brightened.

"That's cool too," I told him.

"Hey, Kumar. You want coffee?" Tex called.

"Hello Tex! No, no coffee. I'll take some tea, though," Mr. replied.

"No tea," Tex stated.

I turned my head and looked at the gazillion boxes of Celestial Seasonings lined up on shelves on the wall.

"We have tea," I told Tex.

"Okay, then, *I* don't make tea."

I sighed and went behind the counter and made Mr. Kumar some tea.

I was handing him a cup when the door opened and Ally and Kitty Sue walked in.

"What's shakin'?" Ally asked, then spied Tex and Mr. Kumar. "Hey Tex. Mr. Kumar."

"Do you want coffee?" Tex barked.

Both Ally and Kitty Sue took a step back.

"He's replaced Rosie. He's a java savant," I told them.

"Yeah, I'll take a coffee," Ally said (which was smart).

Tex lumbered behind the counter and started banging away.

"Girl's Night Out still on for tonight?" Kitty Sue asked me.

"Yep," I replied.

"I'll take some of that action," Tex put in.

We all looked at him.

"It's *Girl's* Night Out, Tex," I explained.

"So? What? Are there rules?" Tex asked.

"Yes. The rule is it's a night out *for girls,*" I answered.

"Woman, you think I'm missin' another bar fight or quick draw, you're crazy. I'm comin' out with you tonight."

Kitty Sue's face got pale.

I figured it was best to give in before Tex gave Kitty Sue a heart attack.

"I'll ask Tod and Stevie, too. Even out the numbers," I mumbled.

The door opened and a short, slight, dark-haired man walked in with fashionably mussed hair and a well-tailored suit. He was carrying a bright greeny-blue Tiffany's bag.

"Is there an India Savage here?" he asked.

My heart stopped.

It had to be a gift from Lee. He said he didn't do hearts and flowers, but that was before he told me to change my clothes in front of Eddie. This must be an apology gift and any apology gift in a Tiffany's bag was The Apology Gift to Beat All Apology Gifts.

I didn't know what I was all bothered about. It wasn't like Lee hadn't given me gifts before. Last Christmas he bought Kitty Sue, Ally and I a day at the Tall Grass Spa in Evergreen. He'd also bought me a black belt with matte silver rivets and big square buckle last year, a special gift for my thirtieth birthday. Usually, he got me select pieces of silver jewelry from Cry Baby Ranch or gift certificates from Wax Trax.

Tiffany's didn't seem his style, but I wasn't going to complain.

Before I could get to the Tiffany Guy, Tex was there, snatching the bag out of his hand. Tiffany Guy stayed rooted to the spot, staring at Tex in horror.

"What is it? Is it ticking?" Tex boomed.

"Tex, give that to me," I said, rushing over.

Tex shoved the bag under his sling and pulled the tiny blue box out of the bag. He defiled all that was Tiffany, and, using his teeth, he tore open the little white satin bow and shook out the case, snapping it open.

I skidded to a halt beside him and stared at a pair of diamond stud earrings. *Huge* diamond stud earrings.

Wow, Lee must be really sorry.

"There's a card," Tiffany Guy said, gingerly taking the bag from under Tex's sling, pulling out a little white card and handing it to me.

I slid it open, pulled out the card and saw one word scrawled on it.

It said, *Terry*.

I felt my stomach roll.

"Put them back," I said to Tex.

"What?" Tex was dazzled by the diamonds.

"Put them back." Tex didn't move, so I shouted, "Back, back, *back!* Put them back!"

"Cripes, woman, don't get your panties in a bunch. I'll put 'em back," Tex replied.

"I want you to take them back," I told Tiffany Guy.

"I can't take them back. I have express orders *not* to take them back," Tiffany Guy returned.

"You have to take them back!" I shouted.

"I can't," Tiffany Guy said back.

I snatched the box out of Tex's hand and pushed it toward Tiffany Guy. He put his hands up and took a step back.

"Take them!" I yelled, jerking my arm toward him.

"No, I can't. We were told not to accept a refusal."

"*Take them!*" I shrieked.

"For God sake, take 'em, man, she's gonna blow," Tex boomed.

He didn't take them so I threw the box at him. It bounced off his chest and landed on the floor. We were all staring at it when I heard the tone from my cell.

I felt something on my arm and looked down at Zombie Mrs. Salim. She was holding onto my arm and looking into my eyes. Her fingers squeezed my arm with surprising strength, and I felt a weird sense of well-being steal over me.

It was then I realized I was totally freaking out and I took a deep breath. I nodded to Mrs. Salim and picked up the box. I snatched the bag out of Tiffany Guy's hand and put them back in the bag and set them on the book counter.

Whatever.

I'd give them to charity or something.

"Indy, it's Lee," Ally was standing by me now and she was holding out my phone.

Chapter 23
Say It Ain't So, Tex

Tex and I were on our way to Twin Dragon for Girl's Night Out Does Chinese.

I'd spent the afternoon at Flat Iron Crossing Mall.

The next best thing after rock 'n' roll to calm a girl's soul was retail and Auntie Anne's pretzels, both of which I exercised in therapeutic proportions.

Since it wasn't safe to go home (because by now, Vance likely had the whole place wired direct to Command Headquarters), I bought myself a new outfit for Girl's Night Out, including underwear and makeup.

I called Tod and Stevie and invited them, and Tex called me to tell me Kitty Sue gave him a ride home.

I took a shower at Tex's with a cat lying on the toilet seat watching the whole show. I put on my new red, satin drawstring pants, a bronze silky camisole with sequins stitched across the neckline and strappy bronze sandals. I figured red and bronze were the way to go when going to Twin Dragons as I'd fit in with the décor.

Tex was driving. I was shifting.

"What's with the earrings?" Tex asked.

"The earrings are bad news," I told him.

"Not a lot of women would think that about a pair of diamond earrings."

"I'm not a lot of women," I replied.

"You can say that again."

We stopped at a light. I downshifted and explained.

"There's a war going on. You know that creepy guy who looks like Grandpa Munster who came in yesterday morning? Him against Lee. Who will win me. Bookies are taking bets on it."

"So creepy guy is tryin' to buy you with diamonds," Tex deduced.

"Yep, and a seventeen hundred dollar dress from Saks."

"What's Lee giving you?"

I counted and then told him, "Six of the best orgasms I've ever had in my life."

"Too much information," Tex returned.

We shot forward from the light and I shifted to second.

"And I've been in love with him since I was five," I went on.

Tex nodded as I shifted up to third. "No contest, then."

I sighed.

"No contest."

We parked and went in. The table was round and full of Marianne, Dolores, Tod, Stevie, Kitty Sue and Ally. Two seats were open between Ally and Dolores. Tex took the one by Dolores, leaving me to sit by Ally.

I turned to her.

"Are you over it?" I asked.

"Whatever you're mad at Lee about… are *you* over it?" she returned.

Okay, guess we knew where we stood.

I turned to Tex.

"Are you driving home or am I?"

"Feel like gettin' smashed?" he asked.

"Yeah," I answered.

"Go for it."

I ordered a spiced rum and diet and told the waitress to keep 'em coming. I didn't think she understood, seeing as the only English she spoke was what was on the menu, but she nodded and smiled which was encouraging.

We ordered our drinks, we ordered our pu-pu platters. We ate our pu-pu platters then we ordered more drinks.

The pu-pu platters were whisked away and the soup was being served when Tex inquired, "What next?"

"What next what?" I returned.

"What next tonight?" Tex explained.

"You mean after we eat?" I asked then answered, "We go home."

Tex stared at me.

"Tex, it's Girls Night Out. We talk about needing to lose weight while we drink and eat a lot. We talk about how all men are scum and lazy and useless, mostly Marianne's ex-husband, who *is* scum and lazy and useless, and a rat bastard to boot. Last, we gossip about people, pretending we're trying to be thoughtful and caring as we rip their lives to shreds. Then we hug and go home. That's it. Girl's Night Out."

Tex kept staring at me and my soup was put in front of me.

"Shit, if it isn't Indy Savage."

At the voice, the hairs went up on the backs of my arms and all the air was sucked out of the room by the gasps going around the table.

I turned, looked up and could not believe my eyes or my fucking, shitty, rotten luck.

Cherry Blackwell was standing behind me.

She was a tall, cool blonde. She had ice blue eyes, masses of white-blonde hair and the best body in Denver, all tits and ass. She was Barbie in human form.

She had been two years ahead of me at school and the most popular girl, bar none. Her Dad was rich. They went to Hawaii and the Caribbean on Spring Break and to exotic places like the south of France and villas in Italy during the summer.

She'd dated Lee for six months during his senior year and they were the most miserable six months of my life. He'd even taken her to prom. He'd broken up with her before graduation and I celebrated by drinking approximately half a keg at a party. I passed out in the back of Lee's Mustang and he carried me to bed (this last Ally told me; I'd been unconscious at the time, more's the pity).

Cherry and Lee had hooked up again four years ago. They were together for three months, and the last two days of their short relationship were marred by a pregnancy scare. Two more of the most miserable days of my life.

The pregnancy scare turned out to be an attempt at entrapment. During those two days, Lee was in such a foul mood I wasn't the only one avoiding him. After he found out she was lying, it was over and he never went back. That was the last we heard from her until a year ago.

Rumors flew that Cherry had a fling with Marianne's husband. These rumors were spread by Cherry, which meant they were probably true. It was the straw that broke the camel's back of Marianne's marriage.

One more thing that was important to know about Cherry was that she was a first class, grade A prime, bitch.

"I heard you hooked up with Lee," Cherry said to me.

"Yeah," I told her, hoping this would be short and not too painful.

She didn't work into the slam, she delivered it straight out.

"I'll give it a week."

I went stock-still. I could feel practically everyone at the table shifting into bitch smackdown mode.

"It's already been a week," Ally butted in.

Cherry looked at Ally, then at me, and I noticed two of her Barbie-esque girlfriends behind her, Brunette Barbie and African-American Barbie.

"Wow. Congratulations." This was said by Cherry with extreme, catty surprise.

"Cherry, we're trying to have a nice dinner." I was going for diplomatic. I really did not want to have an incident. I needed a good night with friends to relax, get drunk, pass out and face tomorrow's horrors hungover. I'd only had one rum and diet. I needed at least six to face down Cherry.

Cherry scanned the table and locked on Marianne, whose face was bright red.

"Marianne, lookin' good," she purred cattily.

I couldn't help it. I slid my chair back threateningly.

"Cherry..." I began.

Cherry's attention returned to me and her eyes were glittering cold.

"Just a little pointer, Indy, girl to girl. If you want that week with Lee to last into two. He likes it when you go down on him in the morning. He's a fucking animal in bed, but give him a morning BJ, he'll return the favor and *rock your world*."

Every muscle in my body froze solid.

"What did she just say?" Stevie asked.

"She *did not* just say that in front of me," Kitty Sue said.

"Holy crap," Dolores said.

"Oh... my... *gawd*," Tod said.

"You fucking bitch," Ally said.

"This is more like it," Tex said.

I started to come out of my chair, intent on ripping Cherry's face off, when the lady at the table behind us spoke.

"Excuse *me*, we're trying to *eat*," she told Cherry.

I looked at the lady. She was Kitty Sue's age, hair died a stern brunette, petite and soft in the middle.

"Pipe down, you old bag. I'm having a conversation," Cherry said to her.

Like I said, first class bitch.

The woman looked to her husband who was sitting across the table from her. "Did she just call me an old bag?"

He looked scared. Menopausal Martha had obviously been unleashed.

She looked back to Cherry. "You can't call me an old bag. I'm only fifty-two. Fifty is the new forty," she told Cherry.

"Old's old, and you're old," Cherry told her and then turned to me. She opened her mouth to speak again when a pea flew through the air and settled in Cherry's Farrah Fawcett locks.

Uh-oh.

This was not good.

Cherry felt it and started batting at her hair like she was being swarmed by killer bees.

Once the pea flew out, she turned to the older woman. "Did you just throw a pea at me?"

In answer, the woman picked another pea out of her fried rice and threw it at Cherry. It bounced off Cherry's chin and landed on the floor.

"Food fight!" Tex boomed, and I turned and shushed him.

"What going on here?" We all looked at Dragon Lady who was front of the house at Twin Dragons. She was absolutely cool, cool, cool. Gorgeous, slim, her black hair always pinned back in an elegant bun, and she was a top notch artist with eyeliner.

"Nothing," I said, trying to be peacemaker and salvage the night so I could have more drinks and get to my sesame chicken.

"She called me an old bag," the other lady said, foiling my plan.

Dragon Lady turned to Cherry. "Did you call her old bag?"

"She *is* an old bag. Jeesh, what's the big fuckin' deal?"

"That not nice," Dragon Lady proclaimed.

"And! This table was minding their own business and she just walked up and started talking about..." the lady's voice dropped to a whisper, "*blow jobs.*"

Dragon Lady's turned to Cherry and her eyes narrowed frighteningly.

"You harass my customer with dirty talk? What you problem?" she asked.

Then, out of nowhere a bowl of egg drop soup came flying through the air. The bowl collided with Cherry's head, the soup dripping down her hair and shoulder.

We all turned to see Marianne standing and panting, her hands fists at her side.

"*You slept with my husband!*" Marianne screeched.

Oh Lord.

At this announcement, the lady Cherry insulted threw the whole plate of fried rice at Cherry and it scattered in little tiny bits everywhere. Cherry screeched at the top of her lungs, then several more bowls of soup were hurled at Cherry, all of them by Tod and Stevie, who were pretty good aims.

Then Marianne ran around the table and tackled Cherry and they went down, rolling, grunting and pulling hair. Ally and I tried to separate them, while the lady who Cherry insulted jumped on top of all of us, and we were wrapped up in the mayhem. Cherry's two friends got caught in it, mainly because we rolled into them and they toppled over like bowling pins.

I don't really remember much after that, except Dragon Lady screaming, "Help! Police!" and running away.

Cherry and I somehow ended the scuffle together, rolling around in soup and fried rice, kicking, biting and pulling hair, when I was hauled up with two hands under my armpits.

I turned to see Tony Petrino, a uniform cop I knew, but not well. We'd seen each other at a couple of parties and once spent hours drunk in lawn chairs trying to decipher the hidden meaning to the words to Don McLean's "American Pie".

He dragged me straight out the front door and to the side of the restaurant where the parking lot was. Then he turned and unclipped the strap to his weapon.

"Back away, big guy," he said to Tex.

"I'm with her. Bodyguard," Tex replied.

Tony looked at me, eyebrows raised.

"It's true, kinda," I said, because it was. "Are you gonna arrest me?" I asked him.

He shook his head, "No fucking way. Your Dad and Malcolm would have a cow, and I'm not arresting Lee Nightingale's girlfriend. He'd have my balls. I like my balls where they are. Get in your car and get out of here."

Tex and I didn't wait around. This, as pertains to my current life, was a gift from the gods.

I thanked Tony, we got in the El Camino and took off. Tex turned into the Sonic a few blocks down and we parked at a menu speaker.

I looked around. I loved Sonic. They were the only fast food restaurant I knew that served tater tots.

But Sonic was a franchise.

"Tex—"

"I know, I know. But I saw it on a commercial. I'm hungry and they bring food to your car. No one's gonna let us in with you wearin' wonton soup and fried rice."

This, unfortunately, was true.

"I'm sorry about the El Camino, it's gonna smell like hot and sour. I'll pay to have it cleaned."

Tex shrugged. "Better 'n' normal, I say."

Then he asked me what I wanted, he barked our order into the speaker and I did my round of calls to the girls and boys of my circle, making sure they were okay, uninjured and unarrested. When I knew all was well in the world and I'd eaten tater tots smothered in frightening orange cheese chased by a chocolate malt, Tex fired up the Camino and we headed to Cat Land.

I took my second shower with the cat (named Rocky) watching me from the toilet seat. In my buying frenzy I'd forgotten sleepwear, so Tex gave me a clean flannel shirt and sweatpants, neither of which fit nor even came close, but something was better than nothing. I shoved my Chinese Food clothes in a plastic bag and tied the handles tight.

Tex gave good sleepovers. After my shower, he got out his hooch, which burned when it went down but seriously took the edge off. He also got out a bag of corn chips and one of those huge-ass bars of chocolate with almonds. We snacked and camped out in front of the television and watched whatever was on, including commercials, which in the Age of the Remote was unheard of. Tex's big console TV appeared to be purchased during America's Bicentennial and didn't have a remote, and neither of us felt like getting up to change the channel every ten minutes.

Finally, Tex gave me a sheet, a pillow and a blanket and introduced me to Tiddles (a fluffy gray who settled on my belly), Winky (a sleek tiger-kitty with white feet who settled between my ankles) and Flossy (a tuxedo who settled in the crook of my arm). Tex put lights out and, as was per usual, I fell asleep.

I had a weird dream that started with the dial of a rotary phone, something I hadn't heard in years.

Then, in my dream, I heard Tex say quietly (yes, quietly, this was how I knew it was a dream), "This Nightingale Investigations?" Pause. "Yeah, this is Tex MacMillan. Tell your boss I got somethin' of his."

Then the phone was replaced in its cradle.

I knew this was a dream. It had to be a dream because Tex would never give me up.

Never.

⧡

The next thing I knew, I was being lifted in the air and cats were flying everywhere.

I opened my eyes and saw Lee. He was adjusting me in his arms but looking over me at something.

I turned my head to see Tex coming towards us with my plastic bag, purse and shopping bags.

"Say it ain't so, Tex," I whispered.

"Don't let the sun go down on your anger," Tex returned.

I looked out the window then back at Tex. "The sun's been down for hours."

In the quiet voice of my not-so-dream, Tex replied, "You know what I mean, darlin'."

I made an annoyed noise because really, what did you say to that? I hated not having a comeback.

Lee was quiet through this exchange and started walking to the door.

Tex followed.

"I can walk, you know," I told Lee.

"You can also run," Lee replied.

"Not in these sweats, I can't. They're seven sizes too big."

Lee didn't answer. He also didn't put me down until we got to the passenger door. He pressed me inside, slammed the door and he and Tex put my stuff in the trunk.

Tex waved as we drove away.

Traitor.

I said nothing all the way to the condo. Once Lee pulled up the parking brake in the garage, I got out and shuffled on bare feet to the elevator, clutching the sweats at the waistband.

Lee grabbed the plastic bag filled with my Chinese food clothes, my purse and my shopping bags from the trunk and followed me.

We remained silent all the way up the elevator and Lee let me in the condo. I went straight to the bedroom to the drawer where Judy the Housekeeper put my undies. I dropped the sweats, put on some panties, left the flannel shirt on and slid into bed, on my side, with my arm wrapped around the edge and my hand tucked between the mattress and box springs. I was holding on for dear life. There was going to be no cuddling tonight.

I heard laundry noises. Obviously Lee was taking no chances with my Chinese food clothes and was relegating them to the washing machine without delay.

I refused to be embarrassed by this.

Lee entered the room and I ignored him. I heard the rustling of clothes. I felt him get into bed and he settled. He didn't touch me or pull me to him like he normally did. I stayed tense and waited, five minutes, ten. Then, when I was *this close* to falling asleep, his arm wrapped around my waist and he pulled me across the bed and half pinned, half spooned me.

I went rigid.

I felt him bury his face in the back of my hair and then he said, "I'm an ass. I shouldn't have said that in front of Eddie. I'm sorry."

Shit.

Shit, shit, shit.

Not only could you not be mad at someone who apologizes, straight out, you couldn't hold a grudge either. It was a double whammy.

I kept silent. Not being a bitch. I just didn't know what to say.

"I really don't like your flirting," Lee continued.

"I'm getting that."

His hand came up and brushed the hair away from my shoulder and neck. Then it slid down my arm until it encountered my hand and his fingers laced with mine.

"We aren't doin' very well at this, are we?" he asked.

"Not really," I answered.

He sighed.

"I saw Cherry Blackwell tonight," I told him.

Silence for a beat and then, "I heard."

"She was in fine form."

More silence.

"She said, right in front of your mother, that you like blow jobs in the morning."

Another beat of silence.

"She's wrong," Lee finally said. "I like 'em anytime."

This time I was silent for a beat, not certain I liked this answer.

Then, mainly because I couldn't help myself and had residual anger (and Lee was the only one around), I said, "Is she better in bed than me?"

Another sigh and his fingers tightened on my hand. "Indy, don't ask questions like that."

Oh… my… God.

She was!

Cherry Blackwell was better in bed than me.

If she wasn't, he would just say. He was a straight-talker. He *never* lied, just avoided the truth on occasion.

"Right," I returned, all pissed-off.

I flipped around and pushed at his shoulders until he was on his back. My mouth was at his chest and moving down when he hauled me back up.

"What are you doing?" he asked.

"I'm going to give you something to compare. You can score us, me against Cherry, like the ice skaters in the Olympics."

"The Head Olympics?" Lee asked, his voice amused.

"Something like that," I replied, totally angry now because he thought I was funny. I broke free of his hold and started down again.

He hauled me back up.

"Your mouth isn't gettin' anywhere near me when you're pissed-off," he decreed.

I tried to carry on and he kept hauling me back. This became somewhat of a wrestling match, which, with even a small amount of effort, Lee could have won. I could tell he was being gentle and trying not to hurt me, which put him at a disadvantage.

We tussled, tangled in the sheets. We rolled, tussled more and ended up falling on the floor, me on the bottom. Luckily, Lee's arm was around my waist, and it tightened and he threw his other one out to break our fall, doing kind of a one arm push up with me in the middle. Still, my ass slammed against the floor and Lee's hips mashed into mine.

This nearly knocked the wind out of me, but I continued, rolling him over then he rolled me over.

Then somehow arms, legs and rolling were joined by lips, tongues and groping and the wrestling match got interesting.

We were both breathing heavily. I was seriously hot and bothered, when all of a sudden the flannel shirt was whisked over my head, my panties were gone and Lee slid inside me.

I instantly stopped wrestling, wrapped my legs around his thighs and my arms around his back.

He was moving inside me and I was moving with him, our lips touching but not kissing, our breath coming fast. I lifted my head to kiss him, but he pulled away and kept moving inside me. Then his lips came back to mine and I tried to kiss him again, but he pulled away again.

"Lee…" I whispered. I was going to tell him I wanted to kiss him and he should stop messing around.

He drove in deep and said against my mouth, "There it is."

Then *he* kissed *me*.

⚜

After, my legs were still wrapped around his thighs. One of my hands was in his hair, the other one on his ass. Lee's face was tucked into my neck and he was still inside me.

"Cherry's a four. You're off the scales," he said to my neck.

I might have thought this was bullshit, but one thing Lee wasn't was a bullshit artist.

"I shouldn't have asked," I said.

"No, you shouldn't."

He pulled away, carted us both into the bed and he settled me against him, full-frontal.

"I didn't mean to flirt with Eddie," I told his throat. "It was a reflex action."

One of his arms tightened around me, the other hand started fiddling with my hair.

"I'll try to do better… with the flirting," I said.

"I'd appreciate that."

"You need to do better… with the jealousy thing. Not every guy wants to get in my pants."

"You're wrong. Every guy does want to get in your pants," Lee replied.

"Tex doesn't."

"Tex isn't every guy. Tex is a crazy guy and he's old enough to be your father."

"Duke doesn't," I tried.

"Dolores would chop Duke's dick off if he so much as looked at another woman, and he's old enough to be your father."

"Hank doesn't," I persevered.

"Hank doesn't count. He thinks of you as his little sister."

"Darius doesn't." I was a dog with a bone.

"Darius doesn't fuck white women."

Jeez.

I tried a different tact.

In a quiet voice, a *very* quiet voice (because I kinda hoped he wouldn't hear me), I whispered, "You know it's only ever been you."

He heard me.

His body went still. Then his hand fisted in my hair and he tugged my head back. He kissed me, long and sweet, and when he was done, he tucked my face back into his neck.

I took in a deep breath and then let it out.

"That wasn't so hard, was it?" he asked softly.

It was harder than hell. It was scary and it made me feel vulnerable.

Since I felt I'd done my sharing for the night, I stayed quiet.

Lee let me have my emotional space.

"Ally tried to take the earrings back to Tiffany's. They refused the return. I'm not approaching Coxy, for various reasons. You're stuck with them."

"That's okay," I said. "I've decided to give them to charity."

"Good plan," he replied and then, "I was in the surveillance room and saw them come in. You thought they were from me."

"Yeah."

"You want anything, just say and we'll get it. You can pick out what you want."

I held my breath.

"Seriously?" I said when I let it out.

"I'm not gonna try to read your mind when there's something you want. Just tell me and I'll get it for you."

Well, hell. That made things easy for him.

He didn't have to ask clever questions, do any detective work, put any effort into it at all if I just told him what I wanted.

I decided to change the subject because that one very well might tick me off.

"What was Eddie so hot to see you about this morning?" I asked.

Lee rolled onto his back and I snuggled into his side, my cheek on his shoulder.

"Darius has some trouble."

"What kind of trouble?"

"The kind Eddie can't get involved with. He's got some pressure from the Department about Darius. They don't like the relationship and they want Darius out of commission."

"Eddie won't do it?"

"Eddie's a Mexican-American, family is all important. He thinks of Darius and me as brothers. It's one of the reasons why he and I survived both of us being in love with you. Eddie would never take Darius down."

I wrapped my arm around his waist.

"What happened to Darius?" I asked.

"After his father was killed, the life insurance covered funeral expenses and some bills. Not enough money comin' in, standard of living crashed. All of a sudden, Darius and his Mom were responsible for a house and Darius's three younger sisters. It was hard, he was young. Darius was offered an easier path and he took it. No one would have guessed he'd make that choice, but after what happened to his father, Darius was one seriously pissed-off black man. He was lookin' for trouble and found it."

"Can he get out?"

"Easier to get in than out, but yeah. Anyone can do anything if they want it bad enough."

"Does he need help?"

Lee's fingers had been drawing randomly on my back, but they stopped. His arm came around me and his other hand tilted my chin to look at him.

"Do not try to save Darius," he ordered, his voice firm.

I made a huffy sound then told him, "That sounded like an order."

"The brothers are not fond of women messin' in their affairs. Especially white women. This includes Darius. The guy you knew in high school is gone." His voice got kind of scary.

"All right," I gave in. "You don't have to get all freaky about it."

He let go of my chin and I snuggled into him again.

"I'm beginnin' to feel my mother's pain. I just have you to worry about and it's doin' my head in. She had all four of us," Lee said.

"You're a big, tough, badass dude. You'll survive," I told him.

He rolled into me and ran his mouth down my jaw to my ear. "Your job is to make it worthwhile."

I had a feeling I could do that.

Chapter 24

A Metallica Moment

We were sitting in Lee's teak chairs on the balcony. It was post morning sex. I was wearing one of Lee's tees and a pair of hot pink lace hipsters, drinking my coffee, my feet up in Lee's lap, zoned out with my gaze settled on the Front Range. Lee was also drinking coffee, but he wasn't zoned out. He was reading the paper, which was spread out on the table. He was absently stroking one of my feet and was wearing a pair of gray sweatpants and nothing else.

Even though it had been an active morning, I was still only on coffee number one and my mental processes hadn't yet kicked in. Regardless of this, I realized the feeling I had was contentment, and yes, even happiness. Maybe even *real* happiness. Maybe even off the charts happiness.

Lee put the paper down and sat back. He stretched his legs out in front of him, crossed his and took a drink of his coffee. His gaze leveled on me and although I wasn't looking at him, I could feel it.

He put his coffee down and started to massage my foot, this time with both hands. It felt super nice. He had strong hands and he knew how to use them.

"I've asked Dawn to get some guys to come in, pack up your stuff and move it and your furniture to storage. Today, you need to pack anything you want to bring over, and I'll come around tonight and we'll move you in."

Happiness fled instantly and panic seized every cell in my body. My eyes moved from the Front Range to Lee and I stared, unable to speak.

Lee kept talking. "I know a property management service. I called them yesterday. They'll rent your place, make sure it's a good tenant and maintain it for a fee. We'll get it advertised next week."

I finally found my voice. "I know I promised to move in by this weekend, but... isn't this going a bit fast?"

Lee's hands moved to my other foot.

"Yep," he answered.

"Don't you think we should slow down?" I asked.

"Nope."

Kristen Ashley

"Why?"

Okay, you could hear the panic edging my one word question, but still.

Instead of answering, he dropped my feet, bent double to get up and kissed my forehead as he did so. Then he walked into the condo.

I stared at him moving away from me.

He walked well; confident, close to a swagger but not quite. His sweats were drawstring and rode low. His back was beautifully muscled. I kept staring into the living room even after he was gone, zoned out again, the image of his back pleasantly burned on my eyeballs like after you accidentally looked directly at the sun.

Then I saw him come back.

He sat down, lifted my legs at the calves, put my feet back in his lap and threw a little pink case at me across the table.

I stared at it in horror.

My birth control pills,

I'd forgotten them, totally and completely.

Holy crap.

I grabbed it and looked. The last one I took was Monday. I was all over the place these days, I wasn't in my normal day-to-day schedule. I was two pills behind, too late to catch up, and I'd been having sex. A lot of sex. Apparently a lot of unprotected sex.

I slapped the pills back down on the table.

"I didn't do it on purpose, I swear," I told him.

"I know you didn't," he said, his hands back to massaging my foot.

"We have to stop having sex, like, immediately."

His hands stopped massaging, "That's not gonna happen."

"Lee! What if I'm pregnant?"

He grinned. "Then we'll make a beautiful baby."

I yanked my feet out of his lap, stood up and started to jump up and down.

"Ohmigod, ohmigod," I chanted.

Lee stood and pulled me to him.

"Calm down," he said, but I could tell he was kind of laughing.

"This isn't funny!" I yelled. "We can't get through a week without having a break. This is too new, too fast, too weird, too much. Ohmigod, ohmigod," I began chanting again.

This was a serious, life changing moment and I needed Van Halen.

No, no Van Halen wasn't going to do. This was a Metallica Moment.

I could tell by the feel of his body against mine that he was not kind of laughing anymore, he was flat out laughing.

"Why are you laughing?" I shouted.

"Because you're cute," he said, looking at me. "And you're funny and you're overreacting. This isn't the end of the world. You don't even know if you're pregnant, and you're moving in, for fuck's sake."

"Why'd you show me the pills?"

"Because if you're pregnant, we shouldn't waste time movin' in together. If you're not, we should take different precautions and we shouldn't waste time movin' in together."

"Why do I have to move into your place? Why don't you move into mine?"

"I could do that."

I stopped freaking out and stared. "What do you mean?"

"We'll put my shit in storage and I'll move to your place. Doesn't matter to me."

I was beyond staring and went straight to gawking.

"What about your view?" I asked.

He shrugged.

"I only have one bathroom," I said.

"We could make that work."

"I have a yard. You'd have to mow the grass. I don't think Stevie will keep mowing my side if you live there."

"Your yard's the size of a postage stamp. I think I can manage mowing the grass."

"It isn't secure. There isn't even an alarm system."

"Vance will put one in."

"What about the Command Center? I don't have a room where you can put your top secret PI stuff."

He started laughing again. "Do you want to move or do you want me to move? Make up your mind."

"I don't know," I said, and I didn't.

"Well you have to figure it out now because one or the other of us is moving in tonight. No more fucking around."

"I can't figure it out now. I'm too stressed. I may be pregnant. I think I need to go out and buy vitamins or something."

He pulled me deeper into him and I could feel his body shaking with his hilarity. I didn't think it was hilarious. I thought it was scary as shit.

When he pulled himself together he said, "We'll move to your place. It's close to Fortnum's and you have good neighbors. And I like your bedroom. I'll rent this place out."

Somehow, that made the panic ease but not totally subside.

He looked down at me.

"Happy with that?" he asked.

I nodded.

He got that soft look on his face and the melty look in his eyes. My knees started to buckle and I leaned into him.

Then the door buzzer went.

"Fucking hell," he muttered.

He let me go and went to the door.

When he came back, he said, "Darius is coming up."

I'd already met Eddie in Lee's shirt. I wasn't going to gallivant around in front of Darius in Lee's tee. I mean, I was possibly pregnant. Pregnant women didn't run around in front of just everyone wearing nothing but panties and t-shirt.

I grabbed my coffee, topped up and ran to the bedroom.

I slapped on some happy makeup: lots of glittery eye shadow, thick mascara and dewy-blush. I topped some jeans and the black belt with rivets that Lee gave me with a white t-shirt that said, "I shot J.R." in black, and slid on my black flip-flops.

I flip-flopped my way back to the coffeepot, poured some in a travel mug and headed to the balcony where Darius and Lee were lounging.

I stood in the French doors. "Hey Darius."

He'd watched me while I approached, and he nodded and gave a bit of a smile but didn't say anything.

I turned my gaze to Lee. "I gotta get to the store."

"Take the Crossfire. I'll take the Duc in this morning," Lee said.

"The Ducati's here?" I asked.

"Yeah."

Wicked.

I kinda wanted him to take me to work on the Ducati, but I wasn't going to ask.

"I'll take you out on the bike tonight," Lee offered, the crinkles showing beside his eyes.

"Get out of my brain," I returned, putting my hand on my hip.

That made him give me an out and out smile.

"Walk me to the door?" I requested.

I watched him get up and I started to turn toward the front door, then came around and looked at Darius again.

"We're having a family barbeque on Saturday, Ally's place. I'm sure everyone would like to see you," I told him.

Lee dropped his chin and gave a couple of shakes of his head in that "I don't believe she's such an idiot" way.

"Thanks Indy. I got things to do," Darius replied.

"Okay, come after you're done," I said to him.

Darius shook his head.

"Then come before, bring your Mom and your sisters. I haven't seen them in ages." I kept going.

Lee's hand wrapped around my upper arm and he turned me and marched me toward the door. I twisted around and I could see Darius grinning.

"See you later!" I called, already around the couch and in the kitchen.

As we passed, Lee snatched the Crossfire's keys off the kitchen counter and at the front door he pulled me to a stop.

"What'd I say about trying to save Darius?" he asked.

"What? I just asked him to the barbeque."

"You're a nut," he said.

I put a hand on a hip. "Excuse me?"

Lee shook his head. "Nope, not gonna happen. I'm not biting. We are *not* fighting today. No matter how far you push it."

I was *so* sure. Like *I* wanted to fight.

I got up on my toes and kissed him, giving him a quick peck and then grabbed the keys out of his hand.

"What was that?" he asked.

"A kiss good-bye," I told him.

He took two steps forward and I took two steps back, slamming into a wall. His hands went to my ass and pulled me against him and he kissed me breathless.

"*That* was a kiss good-bye," he said when he was done.

I took in a shaky breath.

It sure was.

⚚

Ally and Tex were behind the coffee counter at Fortnum's when I got there. There were six people waiting in line and three people who'd already ordered and were waiting for their coffee. Every chair and couch had someone's ass in it, all of them drinking coffee.

Mötley Crüe was blaring "Girls Girls Girls" from the CD player.

I looked at my watch. It was ten to eight. We'd only been open for twenty minutes.

Apparently people *would* pay to have a guy who looked like a serial killer serve them coffee.

"Holy shit," I said.

"Get your butt behind this counter, woman! Does it look like there's nothin' to do and you have time to stand around gawkin'?" Tex boomed.

I walked around the counter and saw Annie, the blonde, helmet-head lady who yelled at me during the Rosie riot. She was staring at her cup with a reverence normally only befitting the unveiling of front row tickets. She looked up at me.

"Where do you find these guys?" she breathed.

"Luck," I said and got to work

We were so busy, for hours I thought of nothing but coffee, milk, syrup and all the money that was being shoved into my cash register. We'd never been this busy, even with Rosie. We had good crowds, but this was crazy.

By ten thirty, the crowd had died down. Duke came in and manned the book counter, which was also seeing business. We had a goodly number of folks sitting, reading and enjoying their coffee.

"Are we still ticked at each other?" Ally finally had the chance to ask me.

"Well, since you being pissed at me went hand in hand with me being pissed at Lee... and since Lee and I are no longer on a break... then no, we aren't ticked at each other."

Ally grinned. "Good."

That's the way it was with best friends. You got mad, you got over it.

I turned to Tex. "But you're a traitor and I'm not talking to you ever again," I told him.

"You get number seven last night?" he asked.

I stared at him, not knowing what in *the* hell he was talking about.

Then it dawned on me.

Orgasm number seven.

Yikes.

Maybe I *did* share too much information with Tex last night.

Since I got number seven last night and number eight that morning, I didn't answer.

It must have shown on my face because Tex let out a booming laugh then said, "You have no reason to be mad and I don't wanna hear about it."

"What's he talking about?" Ally asked.

I turned to her. "Orgasms." Her eyes got round. "Never mind. Do you know when you can take a pregnancy test?"

Now her eyes were about to pop out of her head. "No way."

"I don't know. I fucked up. I forgot to take my pills for a couple of days."

"No *way!*" Ally shouted and a couple customers looked up.

"I didn't do it on purpose," I said.

"This is great," she returned. "I'm calling Mom."

"No!" I cried. "Don't call Kitty Sue! Don't call *anyone*. This is not great. I don't want a baby. Well, maybe I want a baby… maybe I want Lee's baby… but not now. He hasn't even seen all my underwear!"

"You aren't getting any younger," Ally noted.

Dear Lord.

"Just answer my question," I demanded.

"What question?"

"Pregnancy test."

"I think you have to miss a period. I'll run down to Walgreens and look at one."

Then off she went. Luckily, Walgreens was only a few blocks away.

"Tex, can you make me a skinny vanilla latte, please?" I asked.

"So you're talkin' to me again?" he asked back.

"Just make me one!" I snapped.

"Who're you? The Man?"

"No, I'm The Woman who wants a vanilla latte!"

"Fine. Jeez. I'll make you a latte. I'll make it decaf so you'll calm down."

"If you make it decaf, you're fired," I informed him.

"Caffeine may not be good for the baby," Tex replied.

That's when I screamed, full-on *Nightmare on Elm Street* scream your lungs out.

The customers jumped and stared.

The bells over the door went. I stopped screaming and saw Eddie coming into the store.

He didn't look happy.

In fact, he looked scary unhappy.

His mirrored shades were off and his dark eyes were intense.

My frustration at my crazy, fucked up life went out the window and I walked up to him.

"You okay?" he asked.

I felt my stomach pitch. He wasn't talking about me screaming.

By the look of him, I was assuming something happened to someone I loved. Seeing as I was a cop's daughter, this moment was always in the back of my mind. For me, especially coming from Eddie, it could be anyone; Lee, Dad, Malcolm, Hank or dozens of other guys who were friends of mine or Dad's.

I opened my mouth to answer and I heard then saw the Ducati. It stopped in front of the store. Lee pushed down the stand and swung his leg off. He came inside.

His mouth was tight, his eyes were blank, his expression was grim.

He looked at me then at Eddie then back to me.

"You okay?" he asked.

"What the fuck is going on!" I shouted.

"She needs caffeine," Tex shared, handing me my latte.

Lee came closer to me. Both he and Eddie were less than a foot away, crowding me in. Tex was still beside me and Duke had wandered over, feeling the vibe, and was standing close behind me.

Bad news was coming.

"Cherry Blackwell's car exploded this morning," Lee said.

I stared at him.

What the fuck?

"Jeez-us. She the loopy-loo you scrapped with last night?" Tex asked me.

I ignored Tex and said, "Please tell me she wasn't in it."

"She wasn't in it," Lee replied.

I let out a breath and then took a sip of latte. Even in that tense situation, I noticed that the latte was divine.

"What happened?" I asked.

Eddie answered, "We don't know. Car's still too hot to get near it. They're guessin' she was four, five feet away when it went. She got hit with flying debris and she was burned by the fireball. She's at Swedish Medical Center."

"Is she okay?" I asked.

"No update yet," Eddie said.

Jeez, I didn't like Cherry. In fact I hated her, but I also didn't like the idea of her getting hit with flying debris from a car explosion. The only person I'd want that to happen to was Osama bin Laden but I would prefer for him to be *in* the car.

I looked at Lee and he was still looking grim. I realized that they may have parted badly, but she had still been his girlfriend. Twice. I slipped my hand in his.

"Are *you* okay?" I asked.

"Yeah," he said, looking at me funny.

"She doesn't understand," Eddie muttered.

"Understand what?" I asked.

Then it hit me. Last night, I was rolling around in fried rice with Cherry, today she'd almost been blown up.

I looked at Eddie. "I have an alibi. Actually, I have two! And I don't know anything about explosives."

This wasn't exactly true. Ally and I had famously set off a couple dozen bottle rockets in Nina Evans's front yard after Nina had started a nasty rumor that Ally had herpes.

Still, bottle rockets and car bombs didn't exactly compare.

"Yeah, she spent most of the night with me and the cats, eatin' chips and drinkin' moonshine. She wasn't out of my sight until you came and got her," Tex threw in, looking at Lee.

Eddie stared at Tex, some of the intensity going out of his eyes at the thought of me, Tex and the cats eating chips and drinking hooch.

"Darius told me that one of his guys was at a strip club last night and heard Coxy's boy Gary talkin' about your cat fight with Cherry," Lee said.

Kristen Ashley

This wasn't interesting news. I figured I'd been a prime topic of conversation on police band for at least a week. I probably had my own code by now, Indy-666 or something.

Anyone could listen to police band.

"And?" I asked.

"And Coxy's already gone out of his way to eliminate what he might consider your problems."

I dropped Lee's hand and took a step back. "You think Wilcox tried to kill Cherry... *for me?*"

Eddie answered again, "Too early to know. Cherry didn't have a lot of friends, but crisping her seems harsh retribution for bein' a bitch."

"This isn't happening," I mumbled.

I was reeling. I didn't know what to do, what to think.

"You guys want coffee?" Tex asked Lee and Eddie.

"Sure, triple shot cappuccino," Eddie replied.

"Yeah, Americano, black," Lee put in his order.

Tex ambled off to the espresso counter while I continued my silent meltdown, searching the depths of my fried brain for Denial Zone.

Then Duke asked, his Sam Elliott voice low and serious, "Could we not talk about fuckin' coffee and maybe talk about how you two badass motherfuckers are gonna protect Indy from this crazy fuck?"

I turned to look at him and noticed immediately that he was pissed.

Duke looked at Lee. "Isn't it about fuckin' time you quit fuckin' around and took care of this fuckin' guy?"

Uh-oh.

Duke wasn't afraid to use the f-word, but he only dosed his vocabulary liberally with it when he was close to losing it.

Lee looked at him. "I'm workin' on it."

Duke took a step forward. "Work harder."

This was not good.

I knew, because I had seen, that Lee could kick ass. Duke was no slouch. He might be an old guy, but he also knew how to handle himself through a fuckload of practice.

I wasn't sure how Lee would take an accusation of "fuckin' around" and I didn't want two people I loved to go head-to-head in my bookstore.

"Duke—" I began.

336

Duke looked at me and the look in his eye made me move closer to Lee.

"We don't know when this fuckin' lunatic is gonna lose his patience and turn on you. Bullets are flyin', cars explodin', dead bodies everywhere. This has got to fuckin' stop. Now," Duke said to me.

"He's right," Eddie agreed. "Indy needs to be protected. You got a safe house for her?"

"Yeah," Lee answered.

Yikes!

"No! No, no, no," I cried, beginning to panic. "I can't go to a safe house. I can't. I'd feel like a sitting duck."

Lee's arm came around me. "It won't be for long."

I pulled away from him. "No! I can't do it. I'll climb the walls. I swear, Lee, you lock me up and the minute I get out, I'm moving to Argentina."

Either he didn't believe me or he knew he could track me through the wilds of Argentina because he didn't look like he was gonna cave.

So I kept pushing. "Lee, give me back the stun gun. I'll carry it every-where. Put a man on me. Anything, just don't lock me up."

"I'd put a man on you, but if we're gonna take Coxy down I gotta keep my boys on target."

This wasn't good. This was like being grounded, but without the tree out your window to climb down when your Dad was asleep. I hadn't been grounded in twelve years. I forgot how much I hated it, hated being penned in, hated my freedom restricted. I couldn't stand it.

Surprisingly, Eddie caved first.

"We'll take turns playin' bodyguard," Eddie offered, staring into my deer caught in headlights eyes. "I'll talk to Hank, Willie, Carl. I'm off-duty. I'll take the first shift."

Shit.

Out of the frying pan, into the fire.

This did not sound good.

Lee slowly turned to Eddie. "I'm not sure I like that idea."

Eddie looked at Lee. "Get over it."

They stared at each other and moments passed while testosterone perme-ated the air.

"Oh for fuck's sake. She might be pregnant with your baby, Lee. She's hardly gonna wander," Duke said.

My mouth dropped open.

Eddie looked at me. His eyes moved down to my belly then back up to my face. Then he turned to Lee.

"That didn't take long," he remarked.

"I'm not pregnant," I said, perhaps wishful thinking.

Tex came up with the coffees and handed them around.

"All right, boys, get to work," he ordered.

Eddie walked to the couch and sat down, putting one cowboy-booted ankle on the other knee, spreading an arm along the back of the couch and taking a sip of cappuccino. He was looking at me and grinning in a sexy way.

Great.

Lee snagged my neck and pulled me to him.

"You're gonna be okay," he said.

I nodded even though I didn't believe him.

He kissed me and walked out.

Ally waved at Lee, who was getting on his bike as she walked in, and announced, "You have to miss a period, but I bought a couple pregnancy tests anyway, just in case." And she waved around the boxes.

I looked at Eddie.

Eddie smiled.

Chapter 25
Long-Lasting Reliability

I filled Ally in on the Cherry explosion and the reason for my new body-guard.

Ally said, "There are a lot of things I imagined happening to her after she tried to trap Lee, but that wasn't one of them."

Then she put some Black Crowes in the CD player and turned up the volume.

Ally wasn't one to reflect. She preferred rock 'n' roll.

More customers came in, and luckily we were busy enough to keep our minds off the latest disaster.

I was sitting behind the book counter, finishing an emergency order for coffee, because if we continued at this rate we'd run out by the end of the week, when my cell rang.

It was Dad.

"Hey Daddy-o," I said.

"Hey, sweetie pie."

His voice was soft and mushy. My Dad wasn't a soft and mushy type of guy.

"Are you okay?" I asked.

"Kitty Sue called. If it's a boy, you gotta name him after your Grandpa Herbert. I promised him if your mother and I had a boy, we'd do it and we never got 'round to it, so it's up to you."

I was sitting frozen to the spot, like a statue.

"Indy?"

I stayed silent.

"Okay, you can use Herbert as a middle name."

"I'm not pregnant!" I shouted and everyone looked at me.

"Then why'd Kitty Sue call me asking me to your baby shower? Though, I'm not into this co-ed baby shower shit. I'll send a gift."

"I'm not pregnant!" I repeated.

"You're not?" Dad asked.

Kristen Ashley

Man, this was embarrassing.

"I'll call you later," I told him.

I flipped the phone shut and glared at Ally. "You called Kitty Sue."

"No I didn't," she replied.

Duke was edging to the door.

"Duke!" I yelled.

"Gotta go see a man about a——" he started.

"Stop right there! Did you call Kitty Sue?"

He turned to me. "Nope."

I narrowed my eyes at him. "Did you say anything to Dolores?"

He scratched under his bandanna. "I might have mentioned it."

I flopped my head down on my crossed arms on the book counter.

My life was shit.

I looked up and in the general direction of where one of Lee's hidden cameras had to be and talked direct to Command Headquarters.

"Lee! Your mother is planning a baby shower. Call her!"

I grabbed my purse and threw my phone in it. I stormed around the counter and pointed at Eddie. "You! Macho man! Come with me," and out the door I went.

I was flipping and flopping down the block, double time. Eddie caught up to me and grabbed a handful of my belt and the waistband of my jeans, forcing me to a stop.

"Hang on there, *chica*."

He threw his arm tight around my neck and my front was pinned against his side. I started up again, walking like a crab for a few paces then his arm loosened and I could walk normally. Even so, I walked normally with his arm wrapped around my neck, his hand dangling down and my shoulder and part of my body tucked into him.

He had his mirrored shades on but I could tell he was scanning. I realized he was being watchful and the way we were walking made him the easier target. This made me feel warm in my belly. He also smelled good, which helped that warmth to spread.

By the time we got to Walgreens and went inside I was in a little Eddie Daze.

See what I mean? Eddie didn't need to sweet talk you or toss you a line, Eddie was just… Eddie. That in itself was potent stuff.

340

He dropped his arm and took off his shades when we went inside the drugstore, and I shook off the daze.

I roamed the aisles, trying to remain focused on my task and thus ignore the cosmetics and candy aisles.

Then I found what I wanted and I came to a halt.

I turned to Eddie. "Okay, I've never done this. This is the guy's department. What do I do? We need to get Lee's size and we need industrial strength. Show me which ones to buy."

Eddie looked at the display and looked at me. "You're askin' me to help you buy condoms for Lee?"

"*Industrial strength* condoms," I reminded him.

Eddie stared at me like he was rethinking his crush on me.

"Okay," I started, trying to be helpful. "We'll break it down. We'll start with the size."

He shook his head. "First, I'm a little worried you're lookin' to me to tell you Lee's size. Lee *es mi hermano* but we aren't that close. Second, they don't come in sizes."

I couldn't believe it. That couldn't be true.

"You mean it's one size fits all?" I asked.

He didn't bother to answer.

"That's impossible," I said, and it was. It wasn't like I'd seen millions of them, but I knew they weren't all one size.

He remained silent, but his eyes got kinda scary.

Yikes.

"All righty then," I persevered. "Let's go on to the next category. Strength, durability, that kind of thing."

Eddie walked away.

My cell rang. I grabbed it and saw it was Lee.

"Where are you? The guys said you freaked out about a baby shower and took off with Eddie behind you," Lee said by way of greeting.

"Your mother is planning a baby shower."

"Where are you?"

"You have to call her," I told him.

"Where are you?"

"Lee!"

"I'll call her. Where the fuck are you?"

"I'm at Walgreens with Eddie. I'm actually glad you called because Eddie is refusing to help. What kind of condoms do you use? And please, nothing colored or flavored or any of that crap. I want the ones that are known for long-lasting reliability."

Silence.

"Lee?"

I could swear that the mouthpiece was being covered on his phone.

"Lee!" I shouted.

"Let me get this straight," he said, and I could tell he was laughing. "You dragged Eddie to Walgreens to help pick out condoms for me?"

"Well, I didn't know! I'm not the kind of girl who keeps condoms around. That's the guy's job and you said we were gonna have to use different precautions."

"Did you tell Eddie the part about long-lasting reliability?"

Oh Lord.

"Forget it," I mumbled.

"Indy?" he called.

"What?" I snapped, kinda pissy.

"I love you." He still had laughter in his voice, and there was something very cool about him laughing and saying I love you at the same time.

He hung up before I could say anything.

I grabbed a smorgasbord of condoms. Lee could have a selection.

Eddie caught up with me while I was lost in the lip gloss section and pulled me away. I managed to snag a bottle of multi-vitamins (just in case) and several bars of watermelon taffy before Eddie marched me up to the counter.

I bought my seven boxes of condoms, six taffy sticks and my vitamins, and then our little shopping expedition was over.

<hr />

After we closed Fortnum's, Eddie drove me and the Crossfire the one block to my house and parked it in the second space I owned behind the house, a space relegated to visitors.

I was pretty certain I was going to start hyperventilating at the idea of the visitor's parking spot being the permanent residence of Lee's Crossfire, but I managed to tamp down the panic.

We walked through my backyard. Eddie took my keys and opened the door.

The minute I walked in, I knew something was wrong.

"Someone's here," I whispered to Eddie and put my Walgreens bag on the kitchen counter.

Eddie turned and looked at me. "No shit, there's a television on."

Okay, so maybe I wasn't a natural born detective with a keen sense of danger.

"Stay here, I'll check it out," he ordered, pulling a gun out of his waistband and walking into the dining room.

I followed him.

He turned to me. "Which part of 'stay here' didn't you understand?"

"You're not leaving me behind. I don't like to get left behind. Sure, I get kidnapped and find dead bodies when I don't stay where I'm supposed to be, but I'm pretty certain it'd be worse if I stayed behind."

Eddie gave me a look that said I was quickly curing him of his unrequited passion.

We walked through the living room, up the stairs and the TV was on in the second bedroom. The minute I hit the landing and looked into the TV room, I came to an abrupt halt.

Eddie walked into the room and asked, "What's up, *hombre?*"

I could see through the open door that Lee's huge-ass flat screen TV was in the place where my old-ass tired TV used to be. I could also see some frames stacked against each other on the floor and leaning against the wall.

I turned my head the other direction and saw two big suitcases on the floor in my bedroom, one of them open, and it appeared to have exploded. Men's clothes, or more to the point, *Lee's* clothes, were all over the floor.

I looked into the bathroom and there was an open dopp kit on the counter of the bathroom vanity.

Lee had moved in.

I wandered into the TV room. My desk no longer had all my cute stationery, fun girlie boxes, knickknacks and brightly colored journals that I collected but never wrote in carefully lined up on the attached shelves with my laptop closed. Everything was shoved around. There was a huge flat screen monitor, wireless keyboard and mouse and a bunch of other crap littering the surface and floor, and all sorts of cords *everywhere*.

There was also an enormous safe next to the TV stand.

Lee was flat on his back on my big, red, poofy, deep-seated, comfortable couch. All my fancy toss pillows, which were normally arranged artfully, were shoved up behind his head and shoulders. He had a beer dangling from his fingers and a baseball game on.

He and Eddie were chatting, but when I came in Lee looked at me.

"Hey," he greeted.

I didn't answer. It was a physical impossibility.

I wandered out of the room and into my bedroom.

I was vaguely aware of Eddie leaving and was staring at the exploded clothes when Lee walked into the room.

"Cherry's gonna be all right," Lee told me.

I didn't answer. Not that I wasn't glad, as any good human would be, that Cherry was going to live to see another day where she could make other mortals feel inferior, just that I was freaking out.

I walked forward and opened my closet doors. I put both my hands at the very end of the hangers on one side, and with all my might I shoved them to the other side. It was a superhuman effort. Hangers clacked together and all my clothes scrunched up and I managed to free about a foot and a half of space. I stepped back and looked at Lee's exploded clothes on the floor.

It was then I began hyperventilating.

Lee's arms came around me from behind and he rested his chin on my shoulder.

"Breathe deep," he advised.

I did as I was told. In. Out. In. Out.

"Feel better now?" he asked.

"No," I answered.

He walked over to my CD player and sorted through some CDs. Then I heard Stereophonics "Dakota". It was a really good song. I was beginning to feel better.

I looked at Lee and took a deep breath. "Give me a minute, I can do this."

He left me to it.

Half an hour later, I was losing it. I had freed another foot in the closet and there was a small pile of stuff that I should have thrown out years ago lying in the landing.

It wasn't going to be enough.

"It's not gonna be enough!" I shouted hysterically.

Lee walked back in.

"You could help, you know," I told him, hand on hip.

He walked to the closet, slapped through a couple of hangers and brought out my butterfly-winged shirt liberally threaded with silver that I wore when I wanted to pretend I was Olivia Newton-John. It wasn't my best look, but I'd seen some good times in it. It was a memory shirt.

"Don't even think about it," I warned.

His eyes crinkled and he put it back, slapped through a couple more hangers and pulled out an embroidered camisole that had a big rip in it. It used to be gorgeous, but could never be repaired. It had also seen good times.

"Are you nuts? I went to the Red Hot Chili Peppers concert in that!" I cried.

He put it back, walked out of the room and down the stairs. He came back with two open bottles of Fat Tire, gave me one and then walked out again. It wasn't a lot of help, but it wasn't a bad effort.

Forty-five minutes later, I'd scaled the mountain. There was a huge pile of my discarded clothes in the landing, along with some shoes, bags and other junk. Lee's suitcases were unpacked, zipped up and out on the landing too. He had two and a half drawers all to himself and about a third of the closet.

I was face down on the bed, listening to Kelly Jones doing a fucking great job at singing Rod Stewart's "Handbags and Gladrags", which I thought was apropos.

I felt the bed depress with Lee's weight and a hand at the small of my back.

"I ordered a pizza. I'm walking to Famous to get it. You wanna come?"

I shook my head and Lee left.

I finished the song, replayed "Have a Nice Day" then turned off the CD player. I stumbled in the TV room and threw myself onto the couch. A couple minutes later, Lee walked in with a pizza box with two opened Fat Tire bottles balanced on top.

"Please tell me that's pepperoni mushroom," I begged.

He smiled. "And black olives."

Thank God.

We ate. We watched baseball. When we were done, Lee took the box and empties downstairs and came back with full bottles.

This wasn't so bad.

Lee pulled me off the couch. He lay down on his back and pulled me on top of him, shifting me to the side then tucking me in. I was snuggled up, cheek on his chest, watching the Rockies night game.

Okay, so, this wasn't bad at all.

After I made that momentous decision, I fell asleep.

><

Lee woke me up by shaking me and saying, "Time for bed, gorgeous."

I rolled over him and got up from the couch.

I disrobed between couch and bedroom, crawling between the sheets wearing nothing but my hot pink hipsters, too tired even to brush my teeth.

It took several seconds for me to notice that Lee was moving around the room but the noises he was making were not bedtime noises.

"What're you doing?" I mumbled.

"I have work."

I knew better than to ask, and furthermore, I didn't want to know.

He turned off the light, leaned over me and kissed my temple.

"Be careful," I told him.

"Always," he whispered.

Then he was gone.

><

Lee woke me up getting into bed.

I rolled into him and he tucked me against his side.

"Everything okay?" I muttered, though I couldn't imagine he heard me because my mouth was mostly mushed up against his chest.

"Yeah. Go back to sleep," he replied.

I laid there a second, close to dreamland, then I asked softly, because I had to know, "Is this gonna be my life?"

His body was tense when I rolled into him, but had relaxed after he tucked me in. It got tense again at my question.

"Yeah," he answered, ever the straight-talker.

I took a deep breath into my nostrils and let it out my mouth. "Just promise me one thing."

"What?"

"I want you to wake me when you get home."

His body stayed tense for a beat then relaxed. "I can do that."

"Thanks," I said.

Then I fell asleep.

Early the next morning, I was standing outside in the middle of my yard wearing a pair of cutoffs and Lee's olive drab shirt that said "Army" across the chest. I had a coffee cup in one hand and the hose in the other hand, the spray gun locked down, and I was watering my flowers.

I heard a door open and then Stevie called, "Do ours too, will you?"

Still in my morning stupor, I lifted my coffee cup in a half-assed "gotcha", not even bothering to turn around, and I heard the door close again.

I noticed Lee run across the sidewalk at the front of the house. He stopped, opened the front gate and walked into the yard to stand a couple feet away from me.

I looked up at him. He was wearing another pair of sweats cut at the thigh, these black and faded. The shorts were topped with the white Night Stalkers tee that I considered mine, the shirt plastered to him with perspiration. His running shoes were shoes that had been run in, not fancy-ass, look-at-me shoes.

Even with all that sweat, he was somehow not breathing heavily, and if I wasn't in a haze I would have jumped him, I didn't care how sweaty he was.

"Hey," I said.

He looked at me then looked in the direction of the spray. His eyes crinkled and he looked at me again.

"Hey," he said.

"I'm watering the flowers," I told him.

He shook his head. "Honey, I hate to tell you this but you're watering the fence."

I looked toward the spray and saw that I was aiming a little high. The force of the flow was hitting the fence and running down, *not* hitting the flowers.

Oopsie.

"I haven't had enough coffee," I explained.

He walked up and took the hose out of my hand.

"Perhaps you shouldn't operate complicated machinery in the morning," Lee suggested.

A hose spray nozzle wasn't exactly complicated machinery, but I wasn't going to argue.

"Do Tod and Stevie's too, would you?" I asked, and then I walked into the house and sat on my new couch and put my feet up on the ottoman, staring off into space until I'd emptied the cup.

I topped it up and walked up the stairs where I put my mug on the bathroom counter, took off my clothes and got in the shower. I had a head full of shampoo and was rinsing when the shower door slid open and I heard Lee join me. Lee's hands started on my hips and began gliding around, which made it kind of difficult to concentrate on the task at hand, but I persevered.

Once the soap was rinsed from my hair, Lee moved me out of the spray and took my place. I grabbed my conditioner and started to massage it into my hair.

"So, how exactly do you work all night, wake up before six in the morning and go for a run?" I asked.

"Practice," he answered.

Soap was running down his body. At the sight, I kind of lost interest in the conversation. I abandoned my conditioner and started to glide my hands around Lee's body, the soap making him nice and slippery. I began to explore in earnest, the water falling over both of us. Then I decided to make it a multisensory exploration, using hands and mouth, which Lee allowed for a while then he pulled me up and pressed me against the wall.

I looked into his eyes and noticed that I had unleashed Lee Beast.

One of his hands went down my ass and thigh. He lifted my leg and wrapped it around his waist.

"Did you bring the condoms up from downstairs?" I said against his mouth.

"I'll pull out," he replied.

"No! That never works. Ask Andrea."

"Don't worry about it. I want you pregnant."

Holy crap.

"*What?*" I screeched, coming out of my zone. "Like… now?"

"Not now, but if it happens, I won't be disappointed."

My mind boggled for a moment and then I put my hands to his face, which was looking down at my body, and made him look me in the eyes.

"I gave in on the together thing and the moving in thing, going a lot faster than made me comfortable. You gotta give me time with this baby thing, Lee. It's only been a week."

He kissed me and I slid back into my zone. When he lifted his head away from mine I found I was totally okay with the baby thing, but he said, "I'll go get the condoms."

He got out, wrapped a towel around his waist and went downstairs.

Yep, this wasn't so bad after all.

⚔

We were lying on my bed, me face up, Lee face down with his arm wrapped around my waist.

We got kind of carried away, what with seven boxes of condoms within easy reach, and after christening the shower, I discovered (to my great fortune) that Cherry was right. Use your mouth on Lee in the morning, he'll return the favor.

"I have an idea," I said.

Lee got up on his forearms and looked at me. "The last idea you shared with me got us caught in a cemetery in the middle of the night. You and Ally fell into a freshly dug grave and made such a ruckus the neighbors called the cops."

I smiled. That was a good night, a night just before I started to avoid Lee. Eddie, Lee, Ally and I were sitting around drinking and I dared them to go to a graveyard at midnight. It was fun. Though, I could have done without the falling into the grave part.

"This is a better idea," I told him.

He rolled to his side, the eye-crinkle thing going. "Let's hear it."

"I think I should pretend to let Wilcox win. I can go out to dinner with him and—"

I petered out when the eye-crinkle faded and Lee's face got hard and scary. "That's not gonna happen."

"Listen, Lee, I can wear a wire, maybe get him drunk, get him talking—"

"It's not gonna happen."

"It's a good plan!" I said, kind of loudly.

"It's a screwball plan."

I'm *so* sure!

I sat up and stomped to the dresser, pulled out a pair of cream panties with little orange squares on and pulled them up. I grabbed a matching bra and struggled into it, the whole time I was saying, "At least we can try. I can carry a stun gun in my purse. You can have someone follow us... oof!"

All of a sudden, his arm came around my middle, knocking the wind out of me as he pulled me forcibly backwards. I landed on the bed and bounced a couple of times before his body settled on mine.

"Do you love me?" he asked.

I stared at him, getting my breath back.

"Do you love me?" he asked again, this time impatiently, and the muscle was going in his cheek. Something else was happening here. Something that didn't have to do with Wilcox or the current fucked-upedness of my life.

Shit!

Shit, shit, shit.

"Lee—"

"Answer me, Indy."

Shit!

When I hesitated too long, he said (or more like exploded), "Christ!" and then he knifed away from me.

He went to the dresser and opened and slammed the drawers until he found his and pulled out a pair of those sexy, white brief shorts.

"Lee—"

"I feel like I've wanted you for a lifetime. Now I've got you, you want to put yourself even more in the line of sight of a crazy man. He's already so dangerous you can't make a move without protection and you want to bait him *and* use yourself as bait."

"Lee—"

He pulled on the briefs and a pair of Levi's.

I sat up on the bed.

"Problem is, you're so fucking determined to take life by the throat the only way I can be certain you won't do it on your own is to force you into a safe house, which'll mean I could lose you." He pulled on a white tee and kept talking. "What decision do I make? Keep you alive and piss you off so much you'll take off, or let you risk your life, which, crossing Coxy is a possibility."

"Lee, if you'd quit ranting and listen to me—"

He turned to me and the look on his face was frightening.

"I'm not ranting," he said coldly. "I'm very serious."

I was getting that.

He looked away and started to slam through the drawers again, and I stood up on the bed and shouted, "Liam Nightingale, listen to me!"

He turned and looked at my middle, not expecting me to be standing, then his eyes traveled up.

"You don't want me to use myself as bait, I won't," I yelled.

"How do I trust that?" he yelled back.

Now I knew how the little boy who cried wolf felt.

"I promise," I shouted.

"How do I trust *that?*" he shouted back.

"You just do!" I was back to yelling.

"Do you love me?" He followed suit with the yelling.

"Yes! Of course I love you, you big dope! *I've loved you since I was five!*" I decided to shake it up and this time I screamed.

He took one stride to the bed and leaned a shoulder into my thighs in a body tackle. My upper body fell over his back, lifting my feet from the bed. He pulled my legs around his side and tossed me back on the bed. He grabbed my ankle, yanked me across the bed and then, *whoosh*, away went the panties I'd just put on. He came down on top of me, his mouth finding mine, his hand between us, working the buttons at his fly.

When he stopped kissing me, his hand had moved and was working between my legs.

"You're wrong. It isn't me turnin' myself inside out. It's you. You drive me nuts," he told me.

"Thanks." It should have been snappy, but it was breathy because, as I think I may have mentioned earlier, Lee was good with his hands.

"Don't go after Coxy," he ordered then kissed me again.

"Okay," I said after he finished kissing me.

He reached and grabbed a condom, tearing it open with his teeth because his other hand was busy.

"Lee—"

He was multitasking, so he muttered, "Yeah?"

"I won't leave you even if you act like an asshole."

His head came up and he looked at me, and his eyes, which until that moment still held a bit of ticked off, went melty-chocolate.

"Christ, Indy."

I kissed him while I reached between us and guided him inside me. He started moving immediately.

In his ear, really quietly, I whispered, "I'm not going anywhere. I'm right where I've always wanted to be."

His mouth moved to mine and he replied, "It's about fucking time."

Chapter 26

Splat

Ally, Willie and I were sitting outside Liks Ice Cream Parlour. It was approximately three hundred degrees in the shade, but we were still sitting out on the patio because what else did you do when you're at Liks? Even in December you at least considered the patio when you went to Liks.

After Lee's and my love-in, Willie had come over because he'd pulled Indy Watch for the day.

Lee went to work, Willie and I went to Fortnum's, and in the afternoon, Ally and I took Willie to the mall.

We were treating him to a waffle cone because he'd managed to survive an 'Indy and Ally Do Cherry Creek Shopping Center Experience', complete with full-on explorations of Levi's, Lucky and Diesel, and fly-bys through Guess and Urban Outfitters.

After I'd asked Willie how he felt about the tenth pair of Lucky jeans I tried on, he told me he was going to hunt down and murder Terry Wilcox his own damned self.

Hmm.

I didn't buy the jeans.

I was feeling weird because I wasn't feeling weird about admitting to Lee that I loved him and I thought I *should* be feeling weird.

Question: what did you do when you got exactly what you always wanted?

Answer: you went shopping with your best friend then got ice cream.

I was barely keeping up with my melting double dip of dark chocolate with dark chocolate chunks when I heard, "Cool! It's the Rock Chicks."

I looked up and stared in total shock at The Kevster and Rosie, who were heading our way, both carrying their own double dip waffle cones (you didn't do a single dip at Liks, it was the law) and looking like they didn't have a care in the world.

At their approach, Willie stood, handing his cone to Ally.

The Kevster reared back at Willie's defensive posture and put up a hand, index and middle finger extended.

"Dude. We come in peace."

"It's okay, we know them," I told Willie.

Willie relaxed, slightly.

"I thought you two were in jail," I said to The Kevster and Rosie, coming to my feet.

"Made bond," Rosie replied, an "O" of ice cream coating his lips (if I had to guess, by the looks of it, rocky road).

"Who paid your bond?" Ally asked, also on her feet.

"Our fairy godmother?" The Kevster responded, and it was a question.

I looked at Ally then back at The Kevster. "You don't know who paid your bond?"

"Should we?" The Kevster looked confused, or, more confused than usual.

I wasn't getting a good feeling about this.

"Is that even possible?" Ally was talking to Willie.

"Did you read the papers?" Willie didn't respond to Ally. He was looking at the two grunge muffins and their ice cream cones, and he didn't seem happy.

"Papers?" This was clearly more than The Kevster could process.

Before we could continue this useless conversation, a black BMW with shaded windows came to a screeching halt on 13th Avenue. It didn't park. It stopped in one of the three through lanes.

"Oh shit," Ally said, eyes on the BMW.

"Get to the car," Willie ordered, all relaxation gone.

Before we could make a move, Goon Gary and The Moron were headed our way.

"Get to the car," Willie repeated.

For some reason, everyone stood stock-still.

"Dudes," The Kevster greeted Goon Gary and The Moron as they approached, obviously not knowing who they were, and also not feeling the tense vibe electrifying the air.

Rosie had gone pale and his ice cream cone was melting down his hand.

Goon Gary and The Moron ignored us, their eyes on Willie.

Willie pushed me behind him.

"You know who I am?" Willie asked Gary and The Moron.

The Moron nodded slowly. Gary didn't respond.

"Then you'll walk away," Willie continued.

"Mr. Wilcox wants to talk to you," Gary said. He was still looking at Willie but talking to Rosie. Not me. Rosie. Gary was on a mission; a mission important enough to ignore a police officer's order.

Not good.

"Hey, I know you! You came looking for..." The Kevster's four working brain cells finally fired and he recognized the boys. Then he shouted, "Fuck!"

He threw his ice cream cone at Goon Gary. It splatted in his face and The Kevster took off running.

"What the—" Gary started to say, stunned immobile. What looked like Liks famous strawberry cheesecake ice cream was dripping off his cheek and chin.

Splat!

Rosie threw his ice cream cone, too. It hit Gary on the side of the head then he took off after The Kevster.

Splat!

Ally threw one of her cones at The Moron and it hit him in the chest. At this, Willie grabbed me and started to pull me away.

Splat!

Ally threw Willie's cone. It hit Goon Gary in the shoulder.

Not to be outdone (even though it was a sacrifice—dark chocolate with dark chocolate chunks was the best), on the trot and being pulled by Willie, I aimed my cone at The Moron, and as he'd turned and started after us it nailed him in the belly.

We all jumped into Willie's Nissan Pathfinder. Goon Gary and The Moron gave up on us and headed to the BMW. Willie started up before we had our belts on. He took off and we rocketed from the curb. Ally hadn't yet seated herself and she was tumbling around the backseat in a crinkle of bags that were our take from the Lucky and Levi's stores.

I saw Rosie and The Kevster on foot, flying down the sidewalk.

"Stop!" I shouted to Willie. "Pick them up."

"Fuck no," Willie responded.

"Stop!" I screeched, my voice shrill, looking back at the BMW on our tail. "We can't let Wilcox have them!"

About a quarter of a block past the running grunge gods, Willie stood on the brakes and we all flew forward. The BMW swerved to avoid us and shot by.

Proof positive that men would do anything to stop a woman from yelling.

Ally threw open her door, leaned out and shouted, "Get in!"

Rosie and The Kevster jumped into the SUV. There was more crinkling of shopping bags, then Willie took off.

Everyone was silent. All you could hear was Rosie and The Kevster's heavy breathing.

Willie broke the silence.

"Lee owes me big time for this."

I didn't know if he was talking about the mall or the grunge invasion of his Pathfinder.

Likely both.

If I had known I was going to go to Lee's offices that day, I would have chosen my outfit more carefully.

Dawn was again wearing designer.

I was wearing my cutoff jeans shorts, an Air Force blue t-shirt with "USAFA" in white on the front (even though the man I loved was honorably discharged from the Army, I was an equal opportunity military supporter) and blue flip-flops. After three orgasms and a fight with Lee that ended up with me admitting I loved him, I was spent. Creating an Indy Outfit was beyond my capabilities. I hadn't even bothered with a belt.

Willie, Ally, Rosie, The Kevster and I invaded Dawn's pristine reception space and she looked at us in horror. Rosie still had the ice cream "O" around his mouth and remnants of the drip on his hand, too rocked by recent events to attend the basics. At the best of times, Rosie and The Kevster weren't overly bothered with personal hygiene, and these were far from the best of times.

"What now?" Dawn asked.

At Dawn's greeting, I wondered briefly if Lee knew what the word "cordial" meant.

"We need to talk to Lee," Willie said to Dawn.

She looked at Willie and her face changed. Willie was hot and Dawn was in heat, so she tucked away the attitude and gave him a brilliant smile.

"I'm sorry. He's in a meeting."

"Tell him we're here," Willie went on.

"I'm sorry, but when he's in a meeting, Lee says—"

"Tell him... we're... *here,*" Willie repeated in a tone that made Dawn's eyes go wide. She put her hands to the arms of her chair (manicured fingers pointed straight out, the better to be on display) and pushed herself up. She rounded the desk and disappeared behind the door to the Inner Sanctuary.

"I've never been here," Ally whispered to me.

"Really?" I whispered back, not knowing why we were whispering.

"This place is the shit," Ally said.

She was right, it was. I felt a strange sense of pride even though it had nothing to do with me.

I smiled at Ally. She smiled back.

"Are we, like, in trouble?" The Kevster asked, breaking into our moment.

Ally trained her eyes on Kevin. "You're, like, morons."

"Dudette!" The Kevster was aghast at Ally's insult.

"You better clue in before someone helps you check out," Ally told him. "People are getting shot at, stun-gunned, kidnapped and cars are exploding. Wake the fuck up."

Well, there it was. Couldn't get any more honest than that.

Rosie and The Kevster stared at Ally. Whether what she said penetrated was anyone's guess.

While all this was going on Willie was making a call, and after Ally's announcement he flipped his phone shut.

"Got someone checking," Willie said. "Odds are Wilcox bonded these two idiots."

"Why would he do that?" Rosie asked.

"I don't know. Maybe because it's easier to blow your brains out when you aren't under twenty-four hour police surveillance," Ally replied.

Okay, so maybe you *could* get more honest.

The door opened and Dawn and Lee came out. Dawn scooted behind the desk looking chastened.

Hee hee.

Someone got in *trouble.*

Lee did a room scan. His eyes fell on me then he did a body scan. After he ascertained I was all in one piece with no holes, blood leaking or body parts blown off, he looked at Willie.

"What happened?" he asked.

Willie ran it down for Lee.

Lee's face got hard.

"Get Mace," Lee told Dawn, and without delay she picked up the phone. "They weren't after Indy?" Lee asked Willie.

"Didn't even look at her," Willie replied.

"Except when she threw her ice cream cone at them," Ally put in.

Lee looked at me and I could tell he didn't know whether to laugh or yell. Instead, he muttered, "Christ."

I was pleased he found a happy medium.

"I'll take it from here," Lee told Willie.

Willie looked relieved. I knew he cared about me, but he had ice cream smears on his backseat upholstery and he spent three hours in the mall, not even with his girlfriend, racking up brownie points. He'd gone way beyond the call of duty.

"Thanks Willie," I said to him.

"Stay safe," he replied then he took off.

Lee was looking at Dawn and issuing orders.

"Take the boys to the safe room and start a DVD. Get Hank on the phone, and when Mace makes contact I want to know immediately." His eyes cut to Ally and me. "You two come with me."

I wasn't real fond of being bossed around by Lee, but I felt it best not to kick up a fuss in front of Dawn.

Ally and I walked behind Lee to the door to the Inner Sanctuary. I wish I could say I was the kind of woman who didn't do what I did, but I wasn't. I twiddled my fingers at Dawn in a "nanny, nanny, foo, foo, Lee's all mine" multi-finger wave. She totally got my meaning and her eyes became scary hard.

I was considering sticking my tongue out at her when I ran smack into Lee, who'd stopped to open the door. He looked down at me, and I knew he caught the whole thing and was in my brain, again.

He shook his head and let us in.

Okay, so maybe I could be jealous-possessive too.

Lee led us to his office.

Sitting in one of the chairs opposite Lee's desk tapping away at his Black-Berry was a handsome man with dark hair, blue eyes, and he was wearing a seriously cool dark suit.

He looked up when we entered.

"Marcus, this is India Savage and Ally Nightingale," Lee said then turned to me. "This is Marcus Sloan."

So this was Marcus.

He stood and shook our hands. I knew by the way he greeted us that he knew who we both were before the introductions.

He wasn't creepy like Wilcox. He didn't look Ally or me over. He was all business, by the look of his expensive suit, big business. Maybe a little dirty business, but he was professional, and you could tell, totally sane. He was still kind of scary. I didn't know why I thought that, he just was.

Lee ran down what happened outside Liks for Marcus. It was embarrassing, sounding like schoolyard antics being discussed by the teachers. Lee and Marcus were not the type of men who messed around with ice cream cones.

Marcus listened to Lee without reaction.

"You're being patient," Marcus commented when Lee was done.

"My patience just ran out," Lee replied.

A chill ran down my spine the way Lee said that. Something was happening here, something not about Rosie and The Kevster and ice cream cones.

"They didn't even look at me," I cut in. I probably shouldn't have, but what happened this afternoon was not about me, it was about Rosie.

Marcus ignored me.

"Your next move?" he asked Lee.

"Do a sweep. Come tonight, Coxy's out of commission."

Holy crap.

That didn't sound good.

Marcus nodded then his eyes came to Ally and me.

"Nice to meet you," he said politely, and without another word, he left.

I turned to Lee. "What just happened?"

Lee sat on the edge of his desk, leaned forward and grabbed my hand, pulling me to his side. I leaned a hip against the desk and looked at him. Ally moved in closer.

"Rosie and Kevin are going to a safe house. Hank set it up for them. I'm sendin' Mace out to pick up Coxy's boys, all of them. I want Coxy vulnerable before the show."

"What show?" I asked.

Lee didn't answer.

Uh-oh.

"Lee—" I started.

"I'm done fuckin' around. Tonight, it ends," Lee declared.

"What about the mob?" I asked.

"The mob?" Ally cut in.

"Don't worry about it," Lee said.

I put my hands on my hips. "I'm hardly not gonna worry about the possibility of you getting in trouble with the mob."

"In trouble with the mob?" Ally cut in again.

"I said don't worry about it," Lee ignored Ally and responded to me.

"Do I have to cuff *you* to the bed?" I asked.

Lee grinned, as, of course, he would.

This did not make me happy.

"Cuffed to the bed?" Ally persevered.

I ignored Ally this time. "Seriously, Lee. Maybe we should just go to the cabin in Grand Lake for a little while, let this blow over."

I was thinking maybe a year or two would do it.

"It's over. Tonight. If there are consequences, I'll deal," Lee replied. I opened my mouth to say something, but Lee beat me to it. "We aren't discussing this."

My eyes narrowed and my hands went from my hips so I could cross them on my chest in my 'We'll Just See about That, Mister' pose.

"Hello! I haven't ceased to exist. I'm still in the room. Is anyone gonna talk to me?" Ally was sounding a bit pissed-off.

Before either Lee or I could answer, there was a quick knock on the door. Then it opened and a man was there. Hand still on the knob, he barely entered the room.

He was not just any man. With one look at him, I knew he was one of Lee's men.

Tall, taller even than Lee, black hair, fantastic body, jade eyes. He looked like he had a hint of Asian in him. He was beautiful. Beyond beautiful. Artists and sculptors would likely beat each other to death for the opportunity to use him as a model.

Not that this guy would ever model.

It took all my effort, but I tamped down the instinct to flirt and I just smiled at him without the tilty-head-flirty bit. Lee was in a bad enough mood as it was.

The man's eyes swept over me, over Ally, face blank, then they settled on Lee.

When he'd looked at me I'd caught something in his eyes, something not happy. Something that tugged at my reflexive flirt instinct just to get a rise out of him; a smile, a grin, some reaction.

He was the Ultimate Girl Flirt Challenge.

"Oh my," Ally breathed.

Obviously, Ally felt the same.

"Mace, this is Indy and my sister Ally," Lee introduced us.

At this point, I was regretting my thought that any guy named Mace was a macho idiot. If anyone could pull off a name like Mace, this guy could.

Mace's eyes did another slice through Ally and me then they went back to Lee.

"Get Coxy's boys. Bring them to the holding room. All of them. I don't care how you do it and I don't care who you have to pull from their cases to help you do it. Just do it," Lee said.

Finally, Mace grinned.

Oh Lord.

Maybe I was wrong about that macho idiot thing.

Without a word, Mace backed out and closed the door behind him.

Lee looked at me. "You're hanging with the boys until I can take you home."

"Can I hang with the boys?" Ally asked.

Lee nodded.

Ally's face got happy.

"What boys are we talking about?" I asked. Lee had one guy in the hospital and the rest were probably going to be out rounding up bad guys.

"You have your choice, surveillance room with Monty or computer room with Brody."

Hmm.

Tough choice.

Not.

"Surveillance room," Ally spoke my thoughts immediately.

I thought it was prudent to inform her about Monty, just in case she got any ideas. "Monty's married and has five kids."

She looked at me.

"Surveillance room," she repeated.

I nodded.

Surveillance room definitely sounded better than computer room with Brody.

"We'll take surveillance room," I told Lee.

I felt a hand lightly touch my shoulder and I woke with a start to see Vance standing over me.

I blinked at him and stared.

I was in the surveillance room and had fallen asleep in my chair.

Ally and I had made the wrong decision. The *way* wrong decision.

The surveillance room might seem cool, but spend more than fifteen minutes in it and it was boring as hell. I wasn't into that kind of thing, but after thirty minutes of staring at pretty much nothing happening on the monitors I was praying for some poke-the-nanny action just for a little excitement.

"Let's go," Vance said.

I looked around. I had no idea what time it was, but I figured it was late. Monty was gone and Ally and I were alone in the room. Ally was staring at Vance. Even in all my years of knowing her, I noticed she was staring at Vance with a new look, one I'd never seen before. It was an oh-my-God-that-guy-is-hot mixed with an oh-my-God-what-the-fuck-is-going-on look.

My eyes turned to Vance and he was not in a flirting, grinning, hot guy mood. He was in a serious, badass, hot guy mood.

"Where's Lee?" I asked.

"Out," Vance replied and that was all I was going to get, and the way he said it made me decide not to go for more.

I stood, and as I did Vance got tense. His body turned so he was facing the closed door as well as standing in front of me, and his hand went to a gun holstered at his belt.

We heard a violent thud on the wall outside the door and a muted exclamation of pain.

My mouth dropped open and I stared at the door.

Ally came up beside me and she stared at the door.

Vance listened (also staring at the door).

After a while, there was silence. Vance relaxed and nodded to us.

He left the room.

We followed.

The place was darkened but not dark. The light on Dawn's desk was burning and the overhead lights were on but muted. The office seemed somehow sinister. There was not a good vibe in the air.

We ran into Brody in the parking garage.

"Hey!" he yelled, trotting up to us, all excited and happy and definitely not feeling the sinister vibe. "Guess what? Monty called and he's letting me do the surveillance room." Brody lifted a plastic bag filled with cheese puffs and energy drinks. "All night. I'm, like, one of the guys!"

"Righteous, Brody," Ally said quietly, definitely attuned to the sinister vibe.

"You guys want to do the shift with me? It'll be cool. We'll order pizza."

"No," Vance said, and Brody's eyes swung to him.

"No?" Brody asked.

"No. No pizza and no visitors. The office is no longer safe," Vance replied.

Brody got pale.

Ally took in breath.

I forgot to breathe.

What on earth did that mean?

Vance kept speaking. "You lock down the surveillance room once you enter it. Watch the screens, field the calls and that's it. You don't open the door unless you get the code."

Brody was beginning to look a little panicked, but he hung in there. "Oh shit, another code. What's this one again?"

"Same as always," Vance said.

Brody looked blank.

Vance looked unhappy. "Three two two."

"Got it. Yeah. Right. Okay." Brody didn't say good-bye and walked away, whispering to himself.

I allowed myself a moment to hope Brody was going to be all right before we all climbed into a black Ford Explorer.

Vance took Ally home first, asking her address. She got out, quiet and looking worried, and she promised to call me.

Vance waited until the door closed behind her and her inside lights went on. Then he took me home and didn't ask my address. He walked me to the door, took my key from my hand, opened it and made me stand just inside the closed door while he checked the house. He came back downstairs, went out to the Explorer, came back carrying a small duffel and walked immediately to my dining room table.

He opened the duffel and started to put stuff on my dining room table, announcing each one as he set it down. "Gun, Glock, loaded. Extra clip. Taser. Stun gun."

I stared at the weapons on my table and then back to Vance.

"Lee says you know how to use them," he said.

I realized his statement was a question and I nodded.

"Lock all doors and windows after I leave. You don't open the door to anyone unless it's Lee, Mace or me. Even if you know them. Got me?" Vance asked.

I nodded then he nodded.

"Where's Lee? What's happening?" I asked.

"This will all be over soon," he said instead of answering. He went to the door, stopped and turned to me. "Close your blinds."

"Hang on a second." I went after him and grabbed his arm so he wouldn't go. "What the fuck is happening?"

He looked at me a beat, likely trying to guess my reaction to whatever dire news he was about to impart.

Then he decided that he could share.

"Lee's escalated hostilities. Wilcox has done the same."

"What does that mean?" I asked.

Again, he looked at me a beat.

Then a slow, arrogant, unbelievably handsome, shit-eating grin spread across his face.

"That means tonight we're gonna have fun."

With that, he left.

I stood staring at the door, thinking it didn't sound fun at all.

Chapter 27
Where the Hell Was Lee?

After I'd locked my doors and windows, closed my blinds and stopped myself from hyperventilating, my phone rang.

I ran to it hoping it was Lee, falling on the phone like a crazed woman who'd been on the Atkins Diet one day too long and just entered a bakery.

It was Ally.

"Do you know what's going on?" she asked.

"Escalated hostilities, on both sides," I answered. I wanted to talk to Lee, see Lee, hear from someone that Lee was okay, even if it was a disembodied communication from a higher deity.

"What does that mean?" Ally went on.

"Hell if I know."

And I didn't want to know. I was deep in my Denial Fortress. Way deep.

"Do you want me to come over?" Ally asked.

"I'm not allowed to open the door to anyone but Lee, Mace or Vance," I told her.

"Says who?"

"Says Vance."

"Since when do you do what you're told?"

"Since the words 'escalated' and 'hostilities' entered my vocabulary, and I finally told your brother I love him, and he's living with me and I might be pregnant with his child, and I haven't seen his cabin in Grand Lake yet and his office is not safe anymore and—"

"All right, all right, I get it," Ally cut me off. "Call me when you know something."

"Gotcha."

I hung up, stood in my living room and stared at the weapons on my dining room table.

Shit.

Shit, shit, shit.

This was all my fault.

Well, maybe not *all* my fault. It was mostly Rosie's fault, but if something went wrong I'd feel responsible. This wasn't the kind of something that could go wrong like jumping in a car with ten dollars in your pocket and a half a tank of gas, and driving to Colorado Springs in hopes of going to a bar, not getting carded and meeting hot soon-to-be fighter pilot cadets from the Air Force Academy, an endeavor doomed to fail (and I would know as I was the voice of experience on that kind of thing; how do you think I got my t-shirt?). This kind of something meant guns and bullets and Brody in the surveillance room where, outside the door, grunts of pain could be heard.

I wasn't really good at doing nothing. I was kind of an action girl and sitting around waiting was not my style.

Nevertheless, I pulled my cop's daughter shroud around me. It wasn't impenetrable, but it would do the trick in a pinch. I sat on my couch, pulled my heels up on the seat, rested my cheek on my knees and waited.

⊰⊱

Looking back, it was kind of an idiotic thing to do.

Not that I should blame myself too much. It wasn't like cars exploded in front of my house every day. Not to mention I was a little wired, what with the love of my life, who I'd finally hooked up with, done the deed with and started living with, out there escalating hostilities.

In my defense, Vance didn't say anything about not going outside if there was an explosion that shook your house, made your windows buckle and was so loud it made you think your ears were bleeding.

I wasn't totally stupid. I did look outside first. There was a car on fire in the middle of the street, burning debris everywhere. The car didn't explode. It *exploded,* and bits of it were all over the road, the sidewalk. Even in my front yard, wrecking Stevie's beautifully tended legacy. There were people shouting and running around. And anyway, what kind of neighbor would I be if I hid in the house if someone was out there, hurt, burned, whatever?

Not to mention that someone could be Lee.

I thought, with all those people, I'd be safe.

I was wrong.

I nabbed the stun gun (my premier choice in weaponry), unlocked the door and the security door, did a scanning sweep of my porch and stepped outside.

I got to the edge of my porch, which was where they took me down.

⌦⌫

This kidnapping was entirely different from the one before, *and* the one before that.

I came to in the backseat of a car, legs bound at the ankles, wrists bound behind my back with the added dimension this time of being gagged.

With hindsight, and a lot of time to lie in the back of the car thinking, the explosion was not a very ingenious tactic of getting me to expose myself. In fact, it was kind of crude.

I'd fallen for it, though, so what did that say about me?

We drove for a long time. I couldn't see much and I didn't try. Cherry had been nearly exploded the day before, so the minute a call came into dispatch about a car going up in flames in front of my house, the Denver Police Department, and Lee and his boys, would be all over it like flies on doo doo.

I couldn't imagine someone hadn't seen me being carted away, seemingly unconscious.

I couldn't imagine they'd be far behind.

I couldn't imagine they wouldn't rescue me.

You live, you learn. Unfortunately, all my life, I'd always learned the hard way.

⌦⌫

It seemed like we were driving forever. Maybe it was half an hour, maybe longer, when we finally started to do some turns, obviously coming off the highway. The car slowed. There were streetlights, then there were none. Then we hit a gravel road, drove for a few minutes and we stopped.

I was yanked out of the backseat by my ankles and thrown over a shoulder in a fireman's hold. I didn't see much. It was late, dark, and we were well out of the city so dark meant *dark*. I could tell we were in the mountains though.

Shit.

I was carted into a cabin and thrown on the couch, then arranged in a seated position.

When the new goon moved away, I could see Terry Wilcox was sitting opposite me in an armchair.

It was a nice cabin. Very swish, the kind of rental for upper-upper middle class Texans to rent when they felt like a change of scenery. Two guys were with us, both steroid-fuelled, like Goon Gary, Terrible Teddy and The Moron, but I had never seen these guys.

"Take off her gag," Wilcox ordered.

Both of the guys were dark-headed, one darker than the other, and taller, and maybe hitting the pharmaceutical websites a little too hard. He came forward and took off the gag. The minute he did, I realized how tight it was because my cheeks hurt. I opened and closed my mouth to exercise my cheek muscles.

Then I glared at Wilcox. "That hurt."

"I'm sorry, India. Precautions. We can't be too careful, can we?"

Was that a dig at my idiot act of walking out of my house and into the clutches of the villain?

My eyes narrowed.

I knew I was an idiot. I didn't need this guy rubbing it in.

"Excuse me?" I asked.

He ignored me. "Don't worry. We don't have to wait too long. The plane will be ready soon and we'll be leaving."

Uh-oh.

Did he say "plane"?

"What are you talking about?" I asked.

"You and I are going to disappear. We're taking a long vacation."

I stared at him.

I wasn't getting a good feeling about this.

"I don't want to go on vacation with you," I informed him, I thought, unnecessarily.

"You'll enjoy yourself."

My eyes got wide. "Enjoy myself?"

"Shopping, eating in the finest restaurants. I'll get you anything you want. We'll go wherever you want. I'll show you the world."

Wow, Lee wasn't wrong. This guy was nuts.

"Maybe you didn't hear me. I said I don't want to go on vacation with you."

"We'll spend time together. You get to know me, you'll like me."

Yep, totally nuts.

"You kill people," I told him.

"I do what I have to do to get what I want."

Holy crap.

"I don't like people who kill people," I shared. "They're creepy. *You're* creepy."

Perhaps I should have been more careful with what I said, but it was like he had selective hearing and he chose not to hear that part.

"We'll have to stay out of sight for a while. I have a friend who's letting us use his lovely house on the beach in Costa Rica."

Oh my God.

This guy was talking about lovely beach houses to a woman he kidnapped.

Totally a nut.

"You're creepy *and* icky," I broke in, hoping to get through to him. "I don't want to go to a beach house in Costa Rica with a creepy, icky guy who looks like Grandpa Munster."

He continued to ignore me and my insults. "You can sunbathe every day. I'll buy you two dozen bikinis. I think six months, maybe more. Then, perhaps, we'll go to Paris."

"I'm not going on vacation with you. I'm staying here," I announced.

At this, he smiled his oily smile.

Serious euw.

Time to get down to it.

"Listen," I started, changing tactics and leaning forward to show my sincerity, "I'm really, um…" I was losing it. I couldn't think of a suitable lie. I couldn't remember the last time I couldn't think of a suitable lie. I just went with the first word that popped in my head, no matter how hard it was to say it. "…honored that you like me and everything, but I'm in love with Lee. I've been in love with Lee since I was five. We're living together. We're going to get married, eventually, when he asks me. He has it all planned out."

"I'll help you forget Nightingale," Wilcox told me.

Okay, seriously, this guy was nuts. Even if he wasn't a weird, creepy, icky, scary bad guy who killed people, there wasn't a woman alive who would forget Liam Nightingale. Especially if she'd seen him naked.

And what was taking Lee so long? He should have stormed in here and saved the day by now, surely. I was somewhat experienced with being kidnapped and now was about the time for a grenade or tear gas, or Lee to saunter in looking badass and pissed-off and scaring everyone into doing what he wanted.

"Perhaps you should be asleep for the first part of our journey," Wilcox broke into my somewhat fevered thoughts.

I realized my mistake at once. I'd been spending so much time talking to Wilcox, I hadn't paid attention to the Steroid Sidekicks. One was walking toward me, carrying a loaded syringe.

I stared at him coming toward me and I felt the chill of fear.

This was just like in those movies where they tranquilized the heroine and she woke up lying on silk pillows, wearing an *I Dream of Jeannie* outfit and finding herself a member of a harem where all the other girls hated her.

I didn't want to be a member of Terry Wilcox's harem, even if I was the only one.

My mind filled with colliding thoughts and I realized I had two choices, let him drug me and sleep through my (hopeful) rescue, or, well, I didn't know what my second choice was, considering my extremities were tied together.

I was fond of naps, but only those I took myself or fell into naturally, not those induced by overdeveloped henchmen.

I watched him come at me and did the only thing I could do, because I sure as hell wasn't going to go down without a fight.

I rolled to the floor, rolled into him and took him off his feet. He fell over and hit the deck with a grunt and an oath.

I kept rolling to get away from him and struggling to get out of my bounds.

This surprisingly worked (almost). My hands must not have been tied very well because they started to come lose.

Once I dropped Bad Guy Number One, Bad Guy Number Two came at me. I rolled to my back, lifted my legs, and as Tex and The Kevster suggested, I aimed right between his.

I missed, but nailed him in the thigh with a good deal of force and some seriously pissed-off attitude. He staggered back and went down on a knee.

I kept struggling to get my hands free, reared up with a crunch of the abs that would do any personal trainer proud and found my feet. With my momentum and weight, feet and arms still bound, I toppled over and hit him, head to the chest and we both went down, rolling and struggling, him trying to get a hold of me and me squirming like crazy.

I was beginning to get ticked.

Where.

The hell.

Was Lee?

Finally, I freed one hand from the bounds, shook the other one free of the rope and started fighting in earnest.

This didn't last long. Even though I had the use of my hands, he was stronger and he subdued me humiliatingly quickly. He yanked me, still squirming, to my feet and whipped me around so my back was to his front and his hands held my wrists behind me.

"Give her the shot. Now," Wilcox ordered.

He hadn't even bothered coming out of his chair, the jerk. He was totally calm, eerily calm. Like he knew he was going to get away with this.

Bad Guy Number One came at me again with the syringe.

I felt a moment of total fear, no chill this time. This was so much fear, I was certain I'd pee my pants.

Instead, I screamed.

It was loud, it was shrill, and even though I was the one screaming, it even freaked me out.

When I quit screaming, I started struggling, harder this time, desperate.

But it was no use.

Holy crap.

I was going on vacation with Creepy Grandpa Munster.

How did this happen?

I hadn't even had a whole, complete day being out about my love for Lee and being able to enjoy that in all the shapes and forms that would take.

I had a sweet new t-shirt from Lucky Brand Jeans in a bag in the backseat of Willie's Pathfinder that I'd never get to wear.

This meant I might never see Lee's cabin in Grand Lake.

This also meant I might never have his children and tell them bedtime stories about how there was never a time when their Mom and Dad hadn't been together.

This... could not... happen.

As a last resort, I screamed, *"No!"*

But no one heard me scream.

This was because, at the same time, there was a gunshot.

Bad Guy Number One with the syringe shouted out a cry of pain. The syringe went flying, he buckled and went down.

When he did, I saw Eddie standing behind him, his gun in his hand and it was smoking.

Thank... you... God.

It might seem terrible that I was thanking the good Lord that someone got shot, but if divine retribution came in the form of Eddie Chavez and his service revolver, I was not going to quibble.

Before I could react or look around to see where Lee was, I heard from behind me in a voice I knew.

"Let her go."

It wasn't Lee.

It was Darius.

My wrists were let go. I turned my head and saw Darius standing behind and partially beside Bad Guy Number Two, a gun to his temple.

Wow.

"Step back," Darius said and Bad Guy Number Two and Darius moved back several steps.

Eddie came forward, gun pointed at the man on the floor who was rolling around, hands holding his thigh, blood seeping between his fingers.

I stared in horror. I wasn't really good with blood and there seemed to be a lot of it.

"Move away, Indy," Eddie ordered, and without the ability to walk, I hopped several feet then sat on the floor to untie the rope from around my ankles, eyes up and watching.

Eddie moved his gun to Wilcox, who finally had stood, and he snapped, "Sit."

Wilcox's gaze locked on Eddie the whole time, slowly, he sat. He still looked strangely calm, as if he had a secret. I didn't like the idea of Wilcox having secrets. I also didn't like the fact that Lee wasn't there.

I got to my feet and Eddie unsnapped the cuffs on his belt and held them out to me.

"Cuff Wilcox," Eddie said.

I didn't want to go anywhere near Terry Wilcox, but I figured now was not the time to argue. I was still recovering from my freak out when I thought I wasn't going to be saved. I didn't have it in me to give Eddie any lip.

I took the cuffs and walked behind Wilcox's chair.

"Lean forward," I said and I could hear my voice was shaking.

In fact, *I* was shaking, full body shakes, head-to-toe. I didn't want to admit it, India Savage, Rock Chick and Scaredy Cat, but there it was.

Wilcox leaned forward obediently. I cuffed him and then took two (big) steps back.

Darius had Bad Guy Number Two on his knees on the floor, Darius standing over him pointing his gun to his head.

Everyone stood around watching Bad Guy Number One moaning on the floor and bleeding.

"What do we do now?" I asked no one in particular. I figured that Bad Guy Number One was, of course, a bad guy, but I didn't figure it was all right to let him bleed to death on the rather nice rug.

"We need to call an ambulance," Eddie said, eyes still on the writhing sidekick.

"No ambulance," Darius put in.

Eddie's gaze cut to Darius and his mouth got tight. "Darius."

"No ambulance, Ed. Got the word from Mace. Gino's clean up."

That's when the air in the room changed.

Somehow, throughout my struggle and rescue, everything seemed to be normal. Well, at least kidnapping-and-rescue normal, so far as I knew it. Someone got shot (again), but the good news was this time it was a bad guy, and this time there was no tear gas. I hadn't worn any makeup that day so I wasn't in fear of mascara smears, but still, tear gas sucked.

Now, the atmosphere of the room was anything but normal.

"Gino?" Wilcox whispered.

The way he said it made me slide to the side to have a look at him, and I saw he was looking at Darius.

Darius didn't answer.

Instead, Darius grinned.

Somewhere along the line the tables had turned. Now it was Darius who had a secret.

Wilcox surged to his feet, wrists behind his back, body tense.

"*What do you mean, Gino's clean up?*" Wilcox screamed, and I jumped back. His voice was hoarse and so terrified I almost felt sorry for him. Bad Guy Number One had quit writhing and was lying motionless and staring at Darius. Bad Guy Number Two had dropped his head, eyes to the floor, looking defeated.

Yikes.

What on earth was going on?

Who was Gino?

And where the fuck was Lee?

Eddie raised his gun and pointed it at Wilcox. "Sit down."

Wilcox hesitated and Eddie's body moved imperceptibly. Eddie had been relaxed, cool, in control. In a blink of an eye, he was tense, hostile and his eyes were glittering.

"Sit... the fuck... down," Eddie commanded slowly and seriously pissed-off, and I got the impression that it was not only Wilcox who was pissing him off, but also something else.

Even crazy Wilcox sat at the tone of Eddie's voice. Wilcox wasn't calm anymore. He was scared out of what was left of his ever-lovin' mind.

"For God's sake, will someone tell me, where in *the* hell is Lee?" I finally asked.

"Here."

My eyes swung to a door behind Darius.

Lee was standing there.

He stood tall and straight. No blood, no bruises, nothing to indicate he'd seen any escalation of hostilities. In fact, he looked great in a white long-sleeved, torso-hugging tee, jeans, black belt and his motorcycle boots, like he'd just jumped off the Ducati after taking a joy ride.

I wanted to run to him, throw my arms around him, do a lot of girlie, oh-my-god-I'm-glad-you're-all-right and oh-my-god-I'm-glad-I'm-all-right stuff, but his body language was not inviting that. This was badass Lee, and hugs and cuddles were obviously not acceptable at this juncture. Therefore I kept my distance.

He looked at me and did his second body scan of the day, this time, a muscle leaping in his jaw.

"What happened?" he asked, eyes on Eddie.

Eddie walked to Lee and handed him his gun. Lee took it and shoved it in the waistband of his jeans while I stared. That wasn't Eddie's service pistol. It was a loaner. Eddie wasn't here in any official capacity. Any bullet that Eddie put in another human being wasn't going to be traced back to a weapon the police department had given him.

Holy shit.

"Brody tell you the story?" Eddie asked, and Lee shook his head.

"He told me where to find you," Lee answered.

Darius and Eddie looked at each other.

Then Eddie explained, "Darius heard something was goin' down and headed over to watch Indy's house. He'd barely got there when they dropped her outside after she left the house when the car exploded. Darius followed. Knowin' you were busy, he called me to do back up. I went to your office, got a gun, talked to Brody and told him to get a message to you. Darius waited until I got here and we came in."

I felt a weird warmth come over me.

Man, I owed these guys *big time.*

"She okay?" Lee asked, still not addressing me, even though I was maybe six feet away.

Hmm.

The sudden warm gooey feeling of having good, badass friends looking out for me faded. I didn't know what to make of Lee not addressing me, except I didn't like it.

I figured it'd be best to talk about it later, say, after 'Yay, It's Finally Over' sex.

"Bound. Gagged. Tossed around. She's okay. Where's Gino?" Darius answered Lee's question as if I was bound and gagged every day, which, in the past two weeks wasn't far from the truth (except the gagged part).

"Five minutes behind," Lee said. Then it was clear he was done with this particular conversation and his eyes locked on me. "Get in the car."

I didn't like that either. It was bossy. Way too bossy.

"What's going on?" I asked.

Wilcox moved. Lee's eyes sliced to him and he didn't answer me.

"If you're waitin' for the cavalry to arrive then you should know your boys outside are neutralized," Lee said and I felt my breath catch.

So *that* was Wilcox's secret.

And *that* was where Lee had been.

I wondered what neutralized meant, for, like, a second. Then I decided I didn't want to know.

"Relax Coxy," Lee went on. "Gino will be here soon. He's had an earful from Marcus. But I'm sure, since you're blood, he'll give you the chance to explain."

Uh-oh.

Gino was Wilcox's blood. And Gino's name was "Gino", which was a mob boss name if I ever heard one.

That meant the mafia was descending to do "clean up".

Okay, time for me to leave.

"I'll just wait in the car," I said

Lee looked back to me. "Good idea."

I started walking to the door at a loss for what to say. I felt a parting line was called for, but I didn't have one.

I stopped at the door and looked at Darius.

"See you later?" I asked.

He stared at me a beat, maybe attempting to determine my sanity. Then he grinned while shaking his head, but he didn't answer.

"Get to the car, Indy," Lee ordered.

I ignored Lee and turned to Eddie.

"Later, Eddie," I said.

Eddie was smiling flat out, but also shaking his head.

"Later, *chica*."

"Indy, get to the fucking car," Lee repeated.

"All right, jeez. I'm going," I muttered and turned to the door then mumbled under my breath, "So damn bossy."

⚔

Lee drove us home in his Crossfire.

He was silent.

I was silent.

I was feeling a good deal of relief. There was the distinct possibility that my life was going to go back to normal. I'd never been a fan of normal. In fact, I avoided it at all costs, but now it sounded really good to me.

I kind of wanted to ask Lee if it was truly all over, but I could tell Lee didn't feel in the mood to talk. I could tell this because there were scary "not now" vibes bouncing around inside the car so I figured later would be better.

He parked behind my, now *our,* duplex, and I didn't see any flashing lights or hear anyone running around or shouting so I figured the whole exploding car thing had been cleaned up and life was back to normal on Bayaud Avenue.

We walked in, Lee locking the door behind us, me flipping on the kitchen light.

I turned to him.

"You want a beer?" I asked.

He tossed his car keys on the kitchen counter and looked at me.

"What did you just say?" he asked quietly, face a little scary.

Um.

Uh-oh.

"Um... I asked if you wanted a beer."

"That's what I thought you said."

I decided maybe it was time to go back to silence.

He watched me for a while.

Then he said, "You left the house, where you were safe, and got yourself kidnapped. Again."

I gave a little wince. "Yeah... well—"

He interrupted me. "My boys were busy. You're fucking lucky Darius came to watch the house or who knows what the fuck would have happened."

"I realize it was kind of an idiotic thing to do," I admitted.

"Kind of?"

Jeez.

"Okay, it was a really idiotic thing to do," I gave in. "But—"

"Indy, for Christ's sake!" Lee exploded, body tight, face beyond a little scary, straight to semi-demented.

I did the only thing I could do.

I ran to him. One step, two, three, then I threw myself at him bodily. Jumping up, my arms went around his neck and my legs went around his hips. I bent my head, put my mouth to his and I kissed him.

I took him off-guard, which was good. He went back on a foot and his hands went to my ass, holding me to him. He resisted for, like, a second then he kissed me back; hot, deep, lots of tongue, full of relief and something else.

Something that felt like promise.

It was the best kiss I'd ever had.

Chapter 28
So Damned Cocky

Two mornings after my third (and hopefully last) kidnapping, I slid back into bed, pulled the covers up to my chin and stared at the ceiling.

After a couple of minutes, Lee walked in carrying two cups of coffee. He put one on the nightstand and then stood beside the bed looking down at me, sipping from his cup.

I ignored the coffee.

This heralded a momentous occasion. It was the first time I'd ever ignored a cup of coffee first thing in the morning.

"Well, the baby scare is over," I told the ceiling, not sure if I was happy or sad my monthly visitor had showed up. Then I was not sure whether I should be happy or sad about the fact that I didn't know if I was happy or sad. This was too confusing so I stopped thinking altogether.

The bed moved when Lee sat next to me. He leaned down. His handsome face filled my vision, his warm eyes melty-chocolate and his lips brushed against mine.

His head moved away an inch. "We have time."

I stared at him a beat.

He was right.

We did.

I smiled.

⌐⌐

To sum up:

First, Stevie was apoplectic about the state of the yard after bits of burning debris fell on it. He didn't talk to me for a week. He was flying a lot during that time so maybe he wasn't holding that much of a grudge and just didn't have time to forgive me (I was going with that thought).

Second, Tex was a coffee hit. We were so busy, I had to do a quick hire. Her name was Jet, which I thought was a kickass rock 'n' roll name, but she

Kristen Ashley

wasn't exactly kickass and rock 'n' roll. She was quiet. She was sweet. She was pretty. She made a mean latte, and the best part about her was, I could tell—hell, everyone could tell—she had a secret.

Third, Hank told me The Kevster was going to be okay. It was his first offense so he was likely to get community service. Rosie wouldn't fare so well. He'd probably get a jail sentence. Rosie announced he was seriously moving to San Salvador after he got out. It wasn't a joke or a drama. He was done with coffee, done with pot and wanted to be far, far away from Denver. I didn't blame him. Denver had not been good to him, even if it was all his fault, but I would miss him.

Fourth, Terry Wilcox and his goons disappeared.

Poof.

Gone.

Lee explained some of this to me.

See, Marcus had a meet with the mob in New York City with the goal of explaining his, shall we say, frustration at Wilcox's antics. Not only with the diamonds, but also with cutting into Marcus's action. Wilcox's Uncle Gino was already fed up with his nephew. Fed up with the constant clean up and fed up with the headache. It didn't take much for Marcus to talk Gino into intervening. It helped when Lee gave Gino a call and told him that Wilcox was not only pestering his girlfriend, but also that girlfriend was a cop's daughter. Gino had enough headaches. He didn't need the Denver Police Department getting interested. Gino decided to take care of Wilcox once and for all. This might have meant that Wilcox took that long vacation he planned. It also might have meant he was fish food.

I tried not to think about it. I really didn't like Terry Wilcox, but I didn't want him dead.

Incarcerated. Yes.

Out of my life. Absolutely.

Dead seemed kind of harsh, even for scary, creepy, icky Wilcox.

As for Wilcox's goons, Gary, Teddy, The Moron and the Steroid Sidekicks, Lee told me they would no longer be a problem. I got the impression that this had to do with Lee and his badass army "having fun" as Vance put it, but I tried not to think about that either.

Last, no one ever found out that Eddie shot someone on my behalf such was the clean sweep of Uncle Gino.

Eddie and Lee had issues about this. Lee had told Darius that he and Marcus were working together to take care of Wilcox once and for all. Eddie was kept out of this deal. Eddie might be a maverick cop, but he still liked to work within the bounds of the law (when it suited him). Stepping aside for a mob clean up was something he frowned on. With a bit of naked gratitude as incentive, Lee told me that Eddie and Lee had a chat with Darius playing intermediary. They worked it out, but I could tell it took a bit of effort.

That was it.

All that drama and then, in one day, it was over.

It was a few weeks after the final showdown and life had gone back to normal. Normal, that was, with Lee coming home to sleep in my bed every night, which was a new, happy normal that I really, really liked.

Lee was a good roommate. He brought me coffee in the morning, he wasn't in my hair all the time and he called to tell me when he was going to be late.

There were drawbacks, of course.

He threw the towel in the sink when he was done with it and thought that the words "floor" and "closet" where synonymous, but I was quietly working through these issues.

A girl could get through these things knowing that sometime during the night (or late morning, depending) the boy she'd loved since she was five was going to slide in bed beside her.

That, and there was also the fact that Judy, the housekeeper, also came with Lee moving in.

Ally and I were lying out in the sun on my balcony with melting spiced rum and diets, the phone and an egg timer, when we heard, "Yoo hoo!"

I lifted my torso up, looked through the balcony railing and down and saw Tod standing on the decking at the end of their yard.

"Hey," I called.

"Drag Duty, Saturday night. You up for it?" Tod called back, shielding his eyes with his hand, Chowleena sitting by his feet.

"Sure."

"Stevie's on a flight that night, Ally. You doin' back up?" Tod yelled.

"Um-hum," Ally mumbled loudly. She was lying on her stomach and her face was smushed into the lounge chair.

"What time?" I asked.

Tod paused then said, "Girlie, aren't you forgetting something?"

"What?"

Tod shook his head. "You're living with Hunk-A-Licous now. You might want to ask him if he has plans for Saturday night."

Ally's eyes opened and trained on me.

Shit.

I was really not good at this relationship stuff.

"Call Lee," Tod advised. "Then come over and let me know."

"Gotcha," I shouted and settled in, reaching for the phone and hearing Chowleena's nails tapping on the bricks as she and Tod walked back into the house.

I started to punch in Lee's cell number.

"I'm still pissed you're not pregnant," Ally said into the lounge chair.

"For goodness sake, why?" I asked.

"I'm never gonna get a niece named after me."

I hesitated before hitting the call button. "Ally, I hate to break this to you, but it's likely genetically impossible for me to have a girl. I don't think Lee's boys will allow the female chromosome to dominate."

"You can name a boy Ally," she tried.

"I'm not naming a boy Ally. He'll get the shit knocked out of him in school."

"Muhammad Ali didn't get the shit knocked out of him. He knocked the shit out of everyone else," she pointed out.

"Muhammad Ali was born with the name Cassius Clay. Cassius Clay is a kickass name. No one would fuck with a Cassius Clay."

"No one would fuck with Muhammad Ali either."

I couldn't debate that point.

I gave up and hit the call button.

Lee answered after the first ring. "Yeah?"

I got a thrill down my spine at Lee's voice saying that one word. I wondered when that would stop happening, and I hoped the answer was "never".

"Hey. Do we have plans Saturday night?" I asked.

"I thought I'd take you to Barolo Grill."

"Yippee!" I cried.

Shit.

Did I say that out loud?

I snapped my mouth shut.

Silence on the phone.

"Lee?"

"Gorgeous, I know you don't like it when I say this, but you're incredibly cute."

That gave me a thrill down my spine too.

I'd never in a million years admit that to Lee.

"Whatever," I said instead. "Anyway, Tod's asked me to do Drag Duty."

Lee, who *was* good at this relationship stuff, said immediately, "I'll tell Dawn to make it an early reservation."

Hee hee.

Lee was going to get Dawn to make our dinner reservations.

At the beautiful, fabulous, romantic Barolo Grill.

I *loved* that and I didn't even care, not one bit, what that said about me.

"That sounds good," I said, and I couldn't help it, I sounded happy. This was maybe because I *was* happy.

"Is that it?" Lee asked.

"Yes, no, yes," I answered, because I didn't want it to be.

Shit.

"Which is it?"

I lost my courage. "It's no. Later."

"Later."

Before I heard the disconnect, I quickly pulled myself together and told myself that even Rock Chicks could fall in love.

Then I said, "Love you."

Silence for a beat then, quietly, "Love you too."

That didn't only cause a thrill; it gave me a warm feeling in the pit of my stomach.

I hit the off button and Ally said, "You guys are kinda making me sick with all this gushy stuff."

I stared at her. "I just said 'love you'. That's hardly gushy."

"It's gushy for you."

This was true.

"Did Lee say it back?" she asked, squinting at me.

"Yeah."

"It's gushy for him, too. Off the charts gushy."

She wasn't wrong.

"Girls!" We heard Kitty Sue call from inside the house, luckily saving me from the gushy conversation.

"We're out here!" I yelled.

Kitty Sue opened the door and stuck her head out. "Come inside. I only have a minute and I have to do this now."

Then she was gone.

Ally and I looked at each other. Kitty Sue was using her Mom No-Backtalk Voice, and with years of experience, we both knew better than to argue.

Kitty Sue's arrival was a surprise.

"Do you know what this is about?" I asked Ally.

She shook her head.

We got up and wrapped sarongs around our waists. We grabbed the phone, our drinks and the egg timer and went into the house.

Kitty Sue was standing in the living room.

"What are you drinking?" she asked Ally when Ally had rounded the stairs.

"Rum and diet," Ally answered.

Kitty Sue yanked the glass out of her hand and downed it in two gulps.

Ally and I stared at her while she did this then turned our heads to look at each other.

"What's wrong?" I asked Kitty Sue because I knew something was wrong. Kitty Sue was no teetotaler, but she wasn't one to chug, especially not rum. I'd only seen her chug once, during an out-of-control, marathon game of Scattergories one Christmas Eve, and she'd not been able to think of an "s" word for the food category. That was so lame, we made her chug a beer as penance.

Good times.

"I'm not good at this," Kitty Sue answered me, breaking into my trip down memory lane.

"At what?" Ally asked.

"Being... doing... I don't know. Girls, sit down."

Ally and I exchanged another glance, then we sat.

That's when I noticed a small wooden chest. It had hearts and flowers painted on it, and some fading glitter stuck to it as well as some old stickers. It was sitting on the ottoman between my couch and armchairs.

"What's that?" I asked, putting my drink and the phone on the floor beside me.

Kitty Sue plonked down on my couch opposite us and put her empty glass on the ottoman beside the chest. "It's a Best Friend Box."

My breath left my lungs.

"What?" Ally asked quietly.

"It's Katie and my Best Friend Box. We put all our most precious stuff in there."

I stared at the box.

That was my Mom's box.

Oh my God.

I felt tears hit the backs of my eyes and I started deep breathing.

Kitty Sue looked like she was deep breathing too.

I heard Ally deep breathing beside me.

Kitty Sue leaned forward and opened the box.

"Let me see..." she began, and started pulling stuff out of the box; trinkets, costume jewelry, what looked like ticket stubs to concerts and movies. I watched these treasures emerge in fascinated silence.

Then she pulled out an old, yellowed envelope.

"Here it is," she said, and without hesitation, she opened it, pulled out a piece of paper, unfolded it and started reading. "*I, Katherine Maria Basore and I, Kathryn Susannah Milligan do solemnly swear to stay best friends forever. No matter what. Even if Curt Zacharus asks Kitty Sue to go with him even though Katie is in love with him and wants to kiss him with tongues. This is the strength of our Bestest Best Friendom. We will get married in a double ceremony and live in houses with white picket fences that are right next door to each other. When we have children, they will play together, and one day they will get married so we can be related for real. The End.*"

I was back to not breathing and I could feel Ally was not breathing beside me.

Kitty Sue stopped reading and turned the paper around to show me the flowery, young girl script on the front. She pointed to some brown stains at the bottom.

"Katie wrote this and we signed it in blood, kind of," Kitty Sue explained. "We poked our fingers with pins and then stuck them together in a blood pact, then mushed them on the paper."

My head slowly turned to Ally.

She was breathing again and she was smiling.

"Well!" Kitty Sue said sharply and jumped up. "That's done, then." She was rushing through putting the paper back in the envelope and she laid it on the ottoman. "Gotta go. Things to do. I'll leave the box."

"Kitty Sue—" I said, standing up.

"Mom—" Ally stood too.

Kitty Sue was headed to the door. "Don't forget, barbeque at Hank's on Saturday."

Damn.

Lee and I were never going to go to Barolo Grill.

I shook off thoughts of delicious truffle risotto and followed Kitty Sue. "Kitty Sue, wait."

She stopped at the door and turned. Tears were shimmering in her eyes, and the sight of them made me freeze. I didn't recall ever seeing Kitty Sue cry.

Ever.

Ally halted beside me.

Everyone was silent.

"Sometimes," Kitty Sue broke the silence, "I forget and pick up the phone to call her. Still. After all these years... it seems like just yesterday."

I swallowed and Kitty Sue began to get fuzzy as I looked at her, but I could tell she was looking at me too.

"She'd be so happy," fuzzy Kitty Sue whispered.

Before anyone could say anything, she opened the door and was gone.

Ally and I watched her through the window as she got in her car and took off.

"Do you think she'll be okay driving?" I asked, and my voice sounded funny so I cleared my throat.

"We'll call her in a bit, check on her." Ally's voice sounded funny, too.

"Good idea."

We stood there, silent, staring out the window.

Ally broke the quiet, the first to tamp down her emotion and get on with it.

As always.

"I need a drink. Mom downed mine."

"My ice is all melted," I said.

"I'll get you another one."

"I need to call Lee. I forgot about the barbeque. Barolo Grill is off."

"Bummer."

Ally picked up my glass and walked to the kitchen.

I stared at the box and decided to go through it later. When I was alone and no one would be able to call me a sissy or see my ugly, blotchy, red face when I was done.

⋈

I was lying in my darkened bedroom attempting a Disco Nap.

I heard Lee (or what I hoped was Lee) come in. The house was so silent, even at the distance of the kitchen to the bedroom I heard his keys hit the counter.

I decided we were going to have to have another talk about the keys on the counter business. I had a cute kitty-tails-as-hooks key holder on the wall by the backdoor. Keys went on one of the kitty tails. I'd already told him once, but did he listen? No. He just smiled at me like he thought I was cute.

I heard his footsteps on the stairs and put my arm over my face.

I'd gone through Kitty Sue and Mom's box and sifted through the memories. I'd read and reread the letter until I'd memorized my Mom's girlish handwriting. I had held the treasures in my hands, touched them, turned them, even smelled some of them.

Because of this, I had been crying and no way in hell did I want Lee to see me post-crying orgy.

"Indy?" Lee called my name quietly, and I knew he was standing by the bed.

I feigned sleep.

The bed moved when he sat on it and moved more when he took his boots off. I heard them hit the floor, one then the other. Then the bed moved again when he settled into it, turned to me and pulled my back to his front, arm around my waist.

"Stop pretending to sleep," he ordered.

"Go away. I'm taking a Disco Nap," I told him, my voice muffled as it was coming from under my arm.

"You've been crying."

What?

How on earth could he know that? He hadn't seen my face.

"Have not," I lied.

He sighed. "Mom told Dad about the box. Dad told me."

Shit.

This was going to be my life. I knew it. With Malcolm and Dad best friends, and Ally and me best friends, and Hank and Lee super close, and Kitty Sue and Malcolm married, nothing was ever going to be a secret.

I decided to keep quiet.

Lee decided he didn't like that.

He moved me so I was facing him.

I struggled for a bit, then, realizing I wouldn't win, I ducked my head and pressed it into his chest.

"Look at me, Indy."

"No," I said into his chest.

"Look at me."

"I said no."

"Why?"

"My face is splotchy."

His body started shaking with laughter.

"I don't fucking care if your face is splotchy." Amusement was heavy in his voice.

I was *so* sure.

Like it mattered that he didn't care. *I* cared.

"Well, I do," I snapped.

"Look at me."

"I'm not crying about the box. I'm just pissed we're not going to get to go to Barolo Grill, and especially pissed that Dawn doesn't have to make reservations for us," I lied again. Though I *was* kinda pissed about that, but, as Lee said, we had time.

"You're lying."

"Am not."

His arms went around me and he pulled me into him, tight.

I waited.

Nothing happened.

I waited some more.

Still nothing happened.

Then I realized Lee was giving in.

That made me feel warm and happy and, yes, gushy again, and I relaxed into him.

"Marianne called," I told him for no reason, face still pressed into his chest. "She put an offer on a house and it was accepted. She's moving out of her parents' house in a few months."

Lee's fingers started drifting up and down my spine but he didn't answer.

I went on, "Andrea called and she wants us to come over for dinner next Tuesday."

"Her kids going to be there?"

"Probably."

"Jesus," he muttered, and I didn't blame him. I'd actually had dinner at Andrea's house with her kids in attendance. I went home with Jell-o in my hair (the Jell-o fight wasn't my fault; Andrea's oldest started it, I just participated out of self-defense).

"Should I say yes or no?" I asked.

"Yes, but I might have to work. Do you mind if last minute you have to go alone?"

I tipped my head back and glared at him. "I do not *think* so. You aren't going to bail at the last minute because of some fake work thing."

He looked down at me. "It might not be fake."

"It'll be fake."

"It might not."

"It'll *so* be fake."

His eyes crinkled at the corners, his head lowered and he kissed me.

I forgot about my splotchy, blotchy, sissy-girl, crying face and kissed him back.

Then I forgot about Andrea's dinner party with kids from hell and Lee's fake work thing when his mouth opened over mine and his tongue slid inside.

Then I forgot about my Disco Nap when his hands went inside my t-shirt.

Then, sometime later, I forgot about absolutely everything in the entire universe when we were naked and Lee slid inside me and started moving.

Kristen Ashley

"Lee," I whispered.

His head came up. He looked down at me with melty-chocolate eyes and he smiled his Killer Liam Nightingale Smile.

Then his mouth came to mine and I could still feel his smile against my lips.

"You love me," he said there.

My hips tilted, he slid in deeper and it felt nice.

"So," I breathed (or, kind of panted), "damned cocky."

The Rock Chick ride continues
with **Rock Chick Rescue**
the story of Eddie and Jet